Being an author has a[...] dream. But it was only [...] during her final year at university that she realised how soon she wanted that dream to become a reality. So she got serious about her writing, and now writes the kind of books she wants to see in the world, featuring people who look like her, for a living. When she's not writing she's spending time with her husband and dogs in Cape Town, South Africa. She admits that this is a perfect life, and is grateful for it.

Having written over eighty-five novels, **Tara Taylor Quinn** is a *USA TODAY* bestselling author with more than seven million copies sold. She is known for delivering intense, emotional fiction. Tara is a past president of Romance Writers of America and is a seven-time RWA RITA® Award finalist. She has also appeared on TV across the country, including *CBS Sunday Morning*. She supports the National Domestic Violence Hotline. If you need help, please contact 1-800-799-7233.

Also by Therese Beharrie

Tempted by the Billionaire Next Door
Surprise Baby, Second Chance
Her Festive Flirtation

Conveniently Wed, Royally Bound miniseries
United by Their Royal Baby
Falling for His Convenient Queen

Billionaires for Heiresses miniseries
Second Chance with Her Billionaire

Also by Tara Taylor Quinn

Her Lost and Found Baby
An Unexpected Christmas Baby
Fortune's Christmas Baby
A Family for Christmas
Falling for the Brother
For Love or Money
Her Soldier's Baby
The Cowboy's Twins

Discover more at millsandboon.co.uk

SECOND CHANCE WITH HER BILLIONAIRE

THERESE BEHARRIE

THE BABY ARRANGEMENT

TARA TAYLOR QUINN

MILLS & BOON

First Published in Great Britain 2019
by Mills & Boon, an imprint of HarperCollinsPublishers,
1 London Bridge Street, London, SE1 9GF

Second Chance With Her Billionaire © 2019 Therese Beharrie
The Baby Arrangement © 2019 TTQ Books LLC

ISBN: 978-0-263-27221-5

0319

MIX
Paper from
responsible sources
FSC™ C007454

This book is produced from independently certified FSC™
paper to ensure responsible forest management.

For more information visit: www.harpercollins.co.uk/green

Printed and bound in Spain
by CPI, Barcelona

SECOND CHANCE WITH HER BILLIONAIRE

THERESE BEHARRIE

Grant.
Thank you for helping me believe in myself.

And to my wonderful readers.
Your support pushes me into giving you the best stories
I possibly can.
I appreciate you all so much.

CHAPTER ONE

WHEN WYATT MONTGOMERY walked through the door, Summer Bishop took three steps forward and stopped next to the first single man she saw. The man looked over at her, smiled, and she resisted the smile that courted her own lips. He was perfect. About her height, a pleasing enough face, and he wasn't standing next to anyone else.

He turned then, offering her a glass of champagne from his tray. All desire to smile vanished. The man was a *waiter*.

Heat crawled up her neck, but she refused the embarrassment. It simply wouldn't do. Embarrassment wouldn't get her through this weekend. Though she was sure it would make an appearance, she didn't have to pay attention to it.

Not when she spoke with her ex-husband. Certainly not when she pretended a man she didn't know was her date so she could avoid said ex-husband.

Fortunately, Wyatt didn't know she'd been trying to avoid looking like a lonely loser. Yet when she felt his gaze on her, she could have sworn he did. She took a glass of champagne from the waiter's tray—why the hell not?—and downed it in one gulp. Then she returned the empty glass to the tray with a quick nod of thanks, before trying to focus on what her parents were saying.

But she couldn't.

It was as if Wyatt had issued a wordless bet the instant he walked into her parents' party. Her skin was hot, prickly, as if he knew she was desperately avoiding his gaze and was taunting her from across the room. *Look at me,* he seemed to be saying to her, *stop pretending I'm not here.* His voice was annoyingly smooth, even in her thoughts. It reminded her of all the times he'd whispered things in her ear that had—

Don't you dare, Summer Bishop.

Adhering to the voice in her head that was kindly warning her against drooling over her ex-husband's seductive prowess, she tried, again, to focus on her parents. They exchanged adoring looks. Told the family and friends who were there to celebrate their vow renewal on their thirtieth wedding anniversary about their love for one another. Their loyalty to one another.

She took a deep breath. Tried to control how the champagne now felt as if it were burning a hole in her stomach.

When that didn't work, she slipped back, behind the waiter, and then past two more people, then four, until finally she was at the glass sliding doors that led to the patio. Grass stretched out from the end of the patio to the edge of the cliff the lodge had been built on.

Whatever she felt about being forced to attend the weekend celebration for her parents' anniversary, she couldn't deny they'd picked an amazing place to have it at. Granted, it was in the small town of Wilderness, six hours away from her home of Cape Town. But the cliff overlooked the most gorgeous beach, with a path a few metres away from her leading down. It was almost worth it.

Summer walked until she could see the white-brown beach sand. It called out to her, the crash of the waves on the shore chiming in. She wished she could answer. Wished she could strip off the dress she'd chosen to wear to the celebration she wanted nothing to do with and walk into the ocean.

She settled for dragging in a full breath of the salty air.

'Daydreaming of running away?' a voice came from behind her.

The goosebumps were because of the sea breeze, Summer told herself, before straightening her shoulders and turning.

'Wyatt,' she said steadily, as if her insides didn't feel as though they were disintegrating at the sight of him. 'How pleasant to see you again.'

Those sensual lips curved into a smile that seemed decidedly feline.

'Pleasant?' he repeated, cocking his head.

She tried not to notice how the wind was mussing his hair. Or that the top button of his shirt was open, revealing tantalising brown skin that sent an irrational image of her licking it flashing through her mind.

'Not quite the word I would use,' he continued. She stared at him for a second before remembering she needed to have a sassy response.

'Okay,' she said, trying to recover when she thought there might have been a saltiness on her tongue from the skin she'd licked in her imagination, 'how about it's a surprise to see you again?'

'But it's not a surprise,' he replied quite logically, slipping his hands into the pockets of his trousers. 'We knew this was coming.'

'Unfortunately,' she muttered.

He quirked a brow, then chuckled softly to himself. 'You couldn't get out of it.'

'I—' She broke off before she could give herself away. 'I didn't try,' she lied.

Again that not quite genuine smile returned to his lips. 'I'm disappointed. I thought an occasion that would force you to see your ex-husband for the first time in two years would at least warrant an escape attempt.'

'It's my parents' thirtieth anniversary,' she said, repeating what her twin sister, Autumn, had told Summer when she'd complained about having to attend.

'It's been eight years,' Autumn had said. *'We've moved on.'*

Autumn's voice had softened, which had been the worst part for Summer. Not that she couldn't skip the weekend celebration. Not because of the reasons she wanted to escape it. It was the *sympathy*. With Autumn, when they dared speak about their family dynamics at all, it was always the sympathy.

But Summer's feelings about her family, her parents, didn't warrant sympathy. They were valid. Autumn just didn't know the entire truth of it. Eight years later, Summer still couldn't share that truth. Not with her sister, and not with the man she'd once loved.

A familiar resentment bubbled inside her.

Summer released a shaky breath and met Wyatt's eyes. She did a quick intake of air at the intensity as their gazes clashed. It felt as if that air had stumbled on its way to her lungs. Tension crackled around them; she was almost positive she felt the ground shift beneath her.

No. This wasn't a natural disaster. Rather, it was a natural effect of seeing the man she'd walked away from two years before. An after-effect, she corrected, of the passion that had resulted in a hunger that had never quite been sated between them. It didn't matter how hard they'd tried. Or how often.

'Did you try?' she asked, desperate to distract herself. 'To get out of this?'

'No,' he said simply.

Automatically, her insides twisted and turned. Reminded her of how she'd felt all throughout their short marriage.

She knew what that simple 'no' meant. It spoke of Wyatt's loyalty to Summer's father. Trevor Bishop had chosen Wyatt to be his protégé while Wyatt had still been in university. Without any reason to, Wyatt had claimed when he'd told her the story, and despite his less than stellar academic record. But Trevor had seen something in Wyatt. He'd trained that something until it had become the discipline Wyatt was now known for. Once Wyatt and Summer had started dating, Trevor had begun to nurture it.

Summer had listened to Wyatt's recollection of it when they'd started dating. Had smiled and asked questions even though it had left a bitter taste in her mouth. She should have known right then and there that there could be no future for them. Wyatt clearly idealised Trevor. But it had been too late when Summer realised Wyatt didn't only idealise him; he wanted to be like him. Wyatt wanted to be like Trevor and follow in his footsteps.

She couldn't tell Wyatt why that was a problem. Oh, she'd planned to. But she'd been caught up in the whirl-wind of falling in love, and, honestly, was it so wrong that she didn't want her father to ruin that, too?

She should have let him though. Then she might not have found herself on her honeymoon, listening to Wyatt recount his experiences with his own parents, realising once again she'd have to lie for her father.

She might have still been married, too.

Wyatt didn't believe in fate. At least he hadn't, until he'd met Trevor Bishop.

The foundation for that belief had been laid when he'd actually attended the university class Trevor had been guest lecturing at. At that point, Wyatt's attendance re-cord had been similar to his academic record: he'd done the bare minimum to pass.

Wyatt thought about that version of himself in a very distant way. He knew it was him, but he couldn't relate to that boy any more. The boy who'd been full of hurt and anger at parents who'd abandoned him. The boy who'd had no purpose. Perhaps that was why meeting Trevor Bishop that day had been so significant. If he hadn't, that boy would have become a hurt and angry man.

That was not the man Wyatt was today.

Or so he'd thought until now, seeing his ex-wife for the first time since they'd signed their divorce papers.

Her arms were at her sides, her hands curled into fists,

her expression painfully tight. All signs she didn't want to be there. Proof she'd been lying when she said she hadn't tried to get out of this event, too. She hated being there. The only reason he could think of as to why was him.

Hurt curled in his belly; anger simmered in his veins.

It made no sense then that his eyes had immediately been drawn to her when he'd arrived minutes earlier. Or that he'd followed her outside, away from the crowd of people who would have protected him from the pain, the anger.

Yet there he was, desperately pretending seeing her again didn't stir up emotions he'd rather not feel.

'Why would I try to get out of this?' he asked, his voice deliberately pleasant. She'd started it, hadn't she? 'It's an all-expenses-paid vacation to a beautiful lodge along the beach of one of South Africa's most beautiful places.'

'Oh, yes,' she replied dryly. 'I'd forgotten about your meagre wealth.' Her eyebrow lifted. 'I'd forgotten how poorly travelled you are.'

He resisted the smile, though he accepted the jibe. She was right. He didn't need anyone to pay for anything for him these days. It was a stark contrast to his childhood. To the days after his father had left and his mother had drunk herself into oblivion. When he'd had to steal his school-mates' lunches for food or wear his father's clothes when his had grown too small.

That kid could never have imagined having the money Wyatt had today. Nor would he have imagined the trips Wyatt now took as the right-hand man of the CEO of Bishop Enterprises. He flew all over the world to secure deals for the import/export company.

His life had changed dramatically. All because fate had urged him to attend class on the day Trevor Bishop had been there.

Then again, fate had brought him Summer, too. Look how that had turned out.

'Let's put it down to the respect I have for my ex-father-in-law, then, shall we?'

'Yes,' she said after a moment. 'Let's.'

Her eyes met his, and he thought he saw a flash of vulnerability there. It quickly slipped behind a cool expression, which he was grateful for. A long time ago he'd cared about what was behind that cool expression. Hell, he'd thought he'd seen exactly what was behind that cool expression.

Because it was almost identical to the expressions he'd worn. The ones that said, *I'm pretending, but you'll never know why.* Or, *I'm hiding something, and you'll never know what.*

Back then he'd thought he knew why Summer was pretending. What she was hiding. She was the strong and powerful heiress of the Bishop empire; she had to act that way. She was hiding that she didn't want to.

Except now he wasn't so sure he'd known anything about her after all. Or was he just sour that she knew enough about him to think he wasn't worth the woman behind the mask any more?

Whatever it was, when she deemed him worthy to see the real her, it made him lose his ability to reason. He'd proposed spontaneously; married her within weeks of that proposal.

He should have signed the divorce papers at the same time and saved himself some trouble.

'Where is Autumn?' he asked, trying to get his mind off the memories. 'I thought she'd be here.'

Not that he noticed anyone after he saw Summer.

'She will be.' Summer clenched her jaw, then relaxed it. Forcibly, he thought. 'She's putting the final touches on a cake for a wedding tomorrow. Then she'll have to get it to the actual wedding, so she'll only be here on Sunday. Conveniently,' she added, distinctly softer than her other words.

For some reason, it amused him.

'Pity.'

'It is.' She narrowed her eyes.

'What?'

'You're using that dry tone that tells me you're making fun of me.'

'I'd *never* make fun of you.'

'You did it again.'

'Summer, I'm not responsible for the way you interpret my tone.'

He smiled easily at her, mostly because he knew she'd find it irritating. He really missed irritating her.

'As obstinate as ever, I see.'

'As sensitive as ever, *I* see.'

'I am not—' Summer broke off when his smile widened. 'I should have tried harder to get out of this.'

'Yes,' he agreed, not acknowledging her confirmation that she had tried to skip the event. 'It would have saved you a lot of trouble.'

Her expression went blank, her eyes shifting to the doors of the dining hall they'd come out of before resting on him again.

'Did you come out here specifically to annoy me, Wyatt?'

Since he couldn't tell her the real reasons he'd followed her—he didn't fully know what they were—Wyatt said, 'I did. I'm happy to see I'm succeeding.'

She shook her head and looked up, and for the first time he noticed her hair wasn't loose. Usually, she wore her curls wild and free; today, her hair was tied back into a stern bun. Sleek, sure, but tamed to within an inch of its life. It bothered him.

Or maybe what bothered him was the hunger that was restless in his body. As if his cells had been starved and were now being offered a feast. Which was, he supposed, not untrue. For two years, his eyes had been starved of the beauty of her face. He couldn't blame them for wanting to sate their hunger, despite the anger; despite the hurt.

So he allowed them to sweep over the oval slope of her brown eyes; the curve of her cheekbones; the dusting of freckles on the skin of her cheeks. He let them check whether the slight scar at her temple was still there, and if her lips were still pink and full and perfect for kissing.

He stopped himself then, because thinking about kissing and Summer at the same time was taking it too far. The prickling of his body told him so, as did the way those pink, full lips of hers parted. Which made him realise his eyes had dropped to her lips and had stayed there. That he was now showing her his hunger; revealing to her his feasting.

Though he warned himself not to, his eyes lifted to hers, and their gazes locked. A stampede could have passed them, the animals hurling themselves off the edge of the cliff, and he wouldn't have noticed. He would have just kept looking into Summer's eyes. He would have kept trying to see if his tainted past had been worth sacrificing that pull between them, especially when it still seemed to be alive and kicking.

He stepped back at the unexpected thought. When he realised it took him closer to the cliff, he took a step to the side. In his current state, being close to anything that might put him at risk of falling wasn't a good idea.

So run away from Summer, then, a voice in his head told him.

He swallowed.

CHAPTER TWO

SUMMER'S LEGS HAD gone unsteady under her. She desperately wanted to walk away from Wyatt; she couldn't. Because she was worried her legs wouldn't carry her away, yes, but also because it was more than just her legs that were unsteady.

It was her mind. It was offering her memories of that short period when they'd been happy together. When his snark had attracted her almost as much as it had annoyed her. When she'd been able to enjoy the breadth of his shoulders, the short curls of his hair, his unreasonably handsome face.

Her heart was unsteady, too. It was complaining about being put under this much pressure, torn between being happy to see him and aching at what seeing him reminded her of.

Heartache. Loss. Failure.

Loneliness.

She resented the feelings almost as much as she resented Wyatt's admiration for her father. She still didn't know how he could admire the man who'd broken his family with his infidelity. Who'd broken her heart by telling her to keep it a secret from her sister and mother...

Because Wyatt doesn't know.

Oh, yes. That was how.

'I should get back,' he said.

She nodded. 'Me, too.'

They both turned, and their shoulders touched. Her head turned so sharply for her to glare at the offending part of her body she was afraid she'd damaged her neck. But she didn't spend much time thinking about it. She was too busy looking at her traitorous shoulder.

How had they got so close they could touch like this anyway?

Not liking that she hadn't noticed it, she took a deliberate step to the side at the same time he did. Her head lifted from her shoulder to his face; she narrowed her eyes. It was fine that she didn't want to touch him, but how dared he not want to touch her? It didn't matter what his reasons were—and she refused to think about her own—it was offensive.

'You can't kill me with a glare,' he told her calmly, as if he were completely unaware of what had happened.

'Doesn't mean I can't try,' she replied sweetly, walking ahead of him before he could respond.

Except that the move wasn't quite as impactful as she'd hoped it would be. Her heels sank into the grass. Because she'd been storming off—quite appropriately—she hadn't been prepared to get stuck. Momentum pushed her forward and for the longest seconds of her life, Summer thought she was going to fall on her face. In front of her ex-husband. And a bunch of her parents' wealthy friends she didn't think much of.

Which didn't mean she wanted them to see her fall.

Instead of falling, though, she was pulled back up against a hard body. Her mind needed a moment to recover, so it took longer than she would have liked to realise the body was behind her, not in front. It took even longer to realise that she recognised the feel of that body against her.

No, no, no, no, no.

Wyatt had *not* saved her from falling. He was *not* standing behind her, his hard, delicious body pressed against hers, his arm around her.

She was not remembering how many times he'd seduced her from this very position. Sliding an arm around her waist, pulling her against him, dipping his head to the nape of her neck, brushing his lips over the sensitive spot he knew was there.

She was not thinking about how she would lean her head back to give him better access. Or how she'd let out a sound that had been somewhere between a purr and a moan when he obliged her. When he'd started seducing her more earnestly, his hand would move from her waist over her breast, linger there while teasing the sensitive spot in her neck. She'd push back onto his—

Two seconds later she'd stepped out of her shoes and was facing him.

'Thank you,' she said, her face burning. She couldn't command the embarrassment back now, though a part of her tried. She hoped he'd think it was because of her almost-fall rather than her overactive imagination.

He studied her for a moment, his expression unreadable, before bending down and removing her shoes from the ground. He placed them in front of her, looking up at her expectantly. She blinked. Then realised he wanted her to step back into them and felt the faint call of hysteria.

That was what this intense desire to laugh was, wasn't it? And did he really think she wanted to touch him again after what her mind had put her through minutes before?

Oh, wait, she thought. He didn't know what she was thinking. She also couldn't keep acting like a lovestruck teenager. She was feeling attraction. She was attracted to him. Had been the moment she'd seen him at her father's Christmas party three years before; would still be now, two years after their divorce. Attraction didn't simply go away because they were no longer together. In fact, it had probably grown because she knew what it was like to be with him.

Yes, that was the perfectly logical explanation for why she was so overwhelmed by how sexy he was. Simple, biological attraction.

She took a breath and slid one foot into her shoe. When she was unable to think of a way to avoid it, she rested her hand on his shoulder and stepped into her other shoe. He waited to see if she was steady, then rose. Slowly, languidly, as if giving her a chance to grow accustomed to his new position.

He was still much taller than her; his shoulders broad, his torso and hips narrow, held up by powerful legs.

And suddenly simple biological attraction didn't seem like the truth.

He lowered his head, meeting her eyes lazily.

'Put your weight on the balls of your feet,' he told her, before walking away.

She didn't walk after him. Instead, she took a moment to regroup. She had known this would be hard. She had known seeing him would be hard.

Seeing him at a celebration for an occasion she didn't quite believe in? Hard. Seeing him around her father? Hard.

But she hadn't expected this. This attraction that awoke every part of her body. Or the sharp quips or any discussion, really. She'd thought she'd avoid him. Avoidance was the perfect solution to any problem, she found.

Up until the moment when she was forced to face what she was avoiding.

Like how steady her parents were even though her father had had an affair; and how unsteady she still felt because of it. She was still an outsider to her family. To their unit: her mother, her father, Autumn. She'd been outside that unit for years. But she hadn't put herself there.

She couldn't tell her mother or Autumn that. Not when they'd moved on and their family had recovered from her father's affair. She couldn't tell Wyatt either. He looked at their family with the kind of awe that came from not having a supportive one as a child. He looked to her father as the gold standard. Of being a businessman, a husband, a father. Unfortunately, he didn't know that Trevor had put the first before the last two.

Or that he had done the same, and she'd ended up feeling like an outsider to their marriage, too.

She took a breath. Thought happy thoughts. Strangely,

those thoughts were still of the times when she didn't have to pretend to be a part of her family. They'd spent summers travelling the world; had almost daily family dinners. Her father's phone had been glued to his hand the entire time, but at least he'd been there.

He'd been more involved when she'd expressed interest in the company though. She'd spent weeks following her father around the Bishop Enterprises building when she was younger. She'd looked at how Trevor had turned the business her grandfather had started into an empire, and she'd been proud. So proud she'd wanted to be a part of it.

Until she'd found out he'd cheated on her mother and it had all felt like a lie.

She shifted gears, but what was left in her bank of happy memories was of her and Wyatt. Of the dates where she'd fallen in love with his kindness, his wit. Where he'd listened to her, really listened, and she'd felt understood for the first time since...since her father had told her she couldn't speak honestly to the two people she loved most.

As she thought it, it felt as if tar had been smeared all over her happy memories. They felt icky now. Messy. Shameful. No one could blame her for avoiding things when thinking about them turned out like this.

Not that she'd care if they did. Her plan was to stay on the outskirts of her parents' celebrations as far as she could anyway. She'd wait until Autumn arrived and use her sister as a shield. Against Wyatt, too, she thought, reminding herself to stay away from him.

She turned then, putting her weight on the balls of her feet as instructed, and walked towards the patio. As soon as she got there, her parents' guests started walking through the doors. She quickly stepped aside, keeping out of the way as she took in the scene.

The guests had blankets and picnic baskets, and were walking onto the grass in groups. Some of them nodded a head at her in greeting; she offered them one back. They spread out their blankets and began to relax on the grass, clearly preparing to watch the sun set.

She couldn't fault the actual activity. Watching the sunset on a cliff overlooking an ocean was pretty great. Romantic, too, which she supposed her parents had intended. The weather was warm in that careless way summer had. The waiters were moving around taking drink orders so the warmth would soon be combatted by icy cocktails and cold beers.

'The blankets and baskets are inside,' Lynette Bishop told her, stopping in front of Summer.

'Okay,' Summer replied slowly, looking past her mother to where her father stood in the doorway with Wyatt. Both their stances were casual; they were obviously comfortable with each other. Resentment pushed up in her throat, and she told herself to shake it off. Deliberately, she looked back at her mother.

'I think I'm going to go back to the cabin, Mom,' she said with forced calm. 'It's been a difficult week and—'

'I'm sure it has been,' Lynette interrupted. 'Running your own business must be so exhausting,' she continued, as if she hadn't spent her entire life running the Bishop social empire, which was pretty much its own business, 'which means you have to find time to relax.'

'I know.' She smiled. 'Like going to bed early so I can get some sleep.'

'Or taking a blanket and watching the sun set with your parents, whom you love.'

Lynette's smile was equal parts sweet, equal parts threatening. As if she were not only daring Summer to go back to the cabin, but daring Summer to contradict her statement, too.

But Summer had no desire to give in to her mother's dares. The first had been her taking a chance anyway; the second wouldn't be true. She *did* love her parents, which was why all of what they'd gone through—and what she, alone, was still going through—was so hard. Besides, she was there, after all.

She sighed. 'If I stay, I'm not sitting with you and Dad. I'd prefer not to embarrass myself like that.'

Lynette gave a light laugh. 'You will stay, but that's perfectly acceptable.' Her face changed slightly. 'Would you prefer sitting with Wyatt?'

'Mother.'

'You're not looking forward to the reconciliation?'

'I didn't look forward to it, no. Since we already had it, I can say that I was right not to.'

Her mother didn't say anything for a moment. Summer wondered whether it was because Lynette wanted to encourage her to sit with Wyatt. Her parents had always liked him. Which made sense, considering Wyatt so badly wanted them to like him.

It wasn't that Wyatt pretended around them, but rather that he wasn't entirely the man she'd fallen for when they were all together. She'd tried to avoid spending time with her parents during her marriage because of it. It hadn't helped. Wyatt had turned into that man anyway.

'Fine, dear,' her mother told her with a pat on the shoulder. 'You can sit by yourself. I just want you here with us.'

Summer nodded, swallowing her sigh. This added to her problem. Her mother was the same person she'd been before the affair. It hadn't changed her, finding out. Not for the first time, Summer wondered if that would stay the same if her mother found out Summer had known before Lynette had.

Not wanting to think about it, Summer walked past Lynette to get a blanket and basket, hesitating when she reached her father and Wyatt.

What was the protocol with this? Did she ignore them, or did she join in the conversation?

Because neither appealed to her, she offered them both a smile—small, polite, like the one she would have given to two strangers—and passed them. A hand closed around her arm before she could let out the breath she was holding.

'Are you looking for a blanket?' Wyatt asked her.

Her head lifted, though she wanted to stare at the hand that was sending uncomfortable shots of electricity through her body. Staring might make him stop touching her. She resisted, looking from her father, who was watching them with interest, back to Wyatt instead.

'Yes. I was told they're in here.'

'They were.' He lifted a hand, which held a blanket. 'This is the last one.'

There was a beat when she wondered what he expected her to say. *Okay? Thank you for telling me? Can we share?*

When all of them rang true, Summer let out a little breath.

'Okay. Thank you for telling me. Can we share?'

There was another beat, but this time it was long and awkward, making her stomach turn.

'Of course we can share, Summer,' Wyatt said slowly, *politely,* and she gave him a bland stare.

When she looked at her father now, he seemed almost amused. Which annoyed her, though she wouldn't show it.

Avoid, avoid, avoid.

'I'll leave you two to it, then,' Trevor said, giving them both a nod before walking out to join Lynette. Summer stared after him while the ball of tension in her stomach that was always there when she was around her father unravelled. She took a deep breath.

'That was weird,' Wyatt commented before she could say anything.

'What?'

'You were being weird just now.'

'I'm sorry, this is the first time I've had to interact with an ex-husband,' she said flatly.

His expression tightened, but he continued. 'I'm not talking about that. I'm talking about you and your father.'

Her heart immediately thudded in her chest, but she tried for an easy smile. 'Not sure what you mean, Montgomery.'

He blinked. She didn't need that to tell her she'd taken him by surprise though. She'd only ever called him by his surname when things had been good between them. When things had been easy. It hadn't been her intention, but she hoped it would be enough to distract him.

'I'll get us a basket,' she said, and headed to where the wait staff were standing.

She smiled at the waiter who handed her the wicker basket, then did a mental shoulder roll before heading back to Wyatt. She couldn't let him suspect anything was wrong. She'd hidden the turmoil between her and her father for the entire year she and Wyatt had been together. She hadn't let him see how his desire to be like her father had affected her either.

She wouldn't reveal it now. Which would be an effort, considering the anniversary—the vow renewal—was challenging for her.

But she would play the part. She wouldn't let Wyatt suspect she was keeping secrets. She wouldn't let her mother and Autumn suspect it either. She'd just let them all think she was being her usual surly self. And everyone could go on pretending everything was fine.

She swallowed down the wave of nausea.

When Wyatt reached out for the basket, she handed it to him, then took the blanket instead. In silence, they made their way to the grass. There was only one spot free, a little to the side of the cliff, where they wouldn't have a perfect view of the sunset. But the spot offered them a different view. Of the large green trees on the hills a short distance away; the houses amongst the trees; the ocean crashing against the rocky bases of the hills. Not seeing the sunset didn't seem so bad, considering.

She spread out the blanket in front of them, looked down. Realised she wasn't entirely sure how to sit. All her options seem to involve inelegance or flashing some poor unexpected guest.

'Need help?'

Her body tensed at the prospect of his touch, but she managed to arrange her expression into a careful smile.

'Yes, please.'

Wyatt held her hand as she settled onto the blanket, legs to the side, one angled over the other. Before he sat down, a waiter approached him with two glasses of what she thought was lemonade. She couldn't be sure since the ice filled the glass just as much as the liquid did. He handed her one of the glasses, then lowered his body onto the blanket.

'What is this?'

'Lemonade,' he confirmed. 'I ordered it when you went to fetch the basket.'

'Quick work,' she commented. 'Thanks.'

It was all either of them said for the longest time.

'How badly do you wish someone else had got the last blanket?'

'On a scale from one to ten?' she asked thinly. 'An eleven.'

'Ten being how badly you wanted it to be me then?'

She glanced over at him. His mouth curved. She let out a breath.

'You're being a lot less prickly than earlier.'

'I don't know what you're talking about.'

She didn't even blink. 'Sure you don't.'

Something flickered in his eyes. 'I thought it might be easier if I were nicer to you.'

'No, you don't,' she replied. 'You don't believe in being nice for the sake of easy.'

The edges of his mouth turned down. 'True,' he said softly. The tone of it brushed over her skin. 'Fine, then. Your father asked me to be.'

CHAPTER THREE

HE HADN'T MEANT to tell her that, and, somehow, he'd made it sound worse than it had been.

Which he knew based on the way the air around them was now standing to attention.

'Is that what you two were talking about just now?' she asked stiffly.

'Yes.'

'He asked you to be nice to me.'

It wasn't a question, and it sounded as if she was speaking to herself more than she was to him.

'Well,' Wyatt said, 'he said that he knew this was tough on the both of us. And he…suggested that it might make things easier if I cut you some slack.'

She made an impatient sound deep in her throat. 'Is that why you were being so polite earlier?'

'Yes.'

'Just because my father asked?' Her voice sounded strangled.

He shrugged. 'It made sense.'

'Because I'm the big bad wolf,' she muttered.

The anger he thought he'd set aside—much as he had the attraction—stirred. 'I think the person who asks for a divorce is generally the big bad wolf in the tale.'

'Not the person who signs the divorce papers without a fight?' she retorted, but quickly shook her head before be could reply. 'I'm sorry. I didn't mean that.'

He didn't believe her.

'I wasn't talking about you anyway,' she continued. Closed her eyes. Opened them. 'And you're right. It does make sense.' There was a pause. 'How about this view?'

He didn't reply. Was afraid if he did, they'd find themselves doing a post-mortem of their marriage. He'd decided—one desperate, torturous night two years ago—that the best thing he could do for himself was to forget that Summer Bishop existed. It had been hard to do considering the building he worked in bore her name, but he'd been determined.

For the most part, he'd succeeded. He'd buried himself in his work. Deeper, he qualified, since he hadn't stopped digging since Trevor had given him his first job opportunity. Trevor had shown him work was the kind of investment Wyatt could make without regret.

It had been the first of many lessons Trevor had taught him. Wyatt had paid attention to all of them. Who could blame him? Trevor had a life Wyatt hadn't dared to dream of when he'd been a child. Stability, security. Love, happiness. When Wyatt had realised it was possible, he'd been determined to do whatever it took to try and get it. The professional and financial success he'd managed; the personal success, not so much.

He wasn't sure why he'd thought things would be different with Summer. He'd had a string of short-lived relationships before her. A long-term relationship was bound not to work. Especially not with her.

It hadn't mattered that he'd thought she was a perfect match for him. Or that their life together had had the potential to inspire others—just as Trevor and Lynette's had inspired him. He and Summer weren't...suited. She'd made that clear when she'd asked for the divorce. When she'd said she wanted to focus on her business; that she didn't have time for their marriage.

A lie, he'd known immediately. What she hadn't had time for was him.

What else was new?

He shook the sinister question out of his head. He'd learnt his lesson. He wouldn't rise to her bait about how he hadn't fought for their marriage. She'd decided he wasn't good enough to be her husband. How was he supposed to fight that?

He did linger on her comment about her father though. It spoke to that thing he'd picked up between Summer and Trevor earlier. That…vibe. He wasn't sure how they were connected; he only knew they were.

'When people say silly things about Africa, I wish I could show them this,' she said suddenly, and he looked over. Her face had lost some of its earlier tension, making it seem softer.

Soft Summer made him think of Vulnerable Summer. Behind-the-Mask Summer. The effect of that was immediate. Potent.

He cleared his throat. 'You mean, you'd rather show them this than the picture of your pet lion?'

Her lips curved. 'Exactly. I'd prefer not to exploit Nala like that.'

Wyatt chuckled, and wondered if he should be allowing himself to enjoy her. She'd hurt him. This was the first time since he'd truly come to terms with the fact that she had—since signing the divorce papers—that he was seeing her. He shouldn't even be wondering about enjoying her. He should be tempering the anger; taming the hurt.

And yet he still found himself enjoying her.

'I'm sure Nala appreciates it.'

'I don't do it for the fame, Montgomery. It's the right thing to do.'

She lifted her glass and took a slow sip of her lemonade. His lips twitched. Heaven only knew why. He shouldn't be attracted to her sense of humour. He shouldn't be watching her tongue slip between her lips as it checked for leftover lemonade. That moment earlier should have been enough warning about his attraction to her. When he'd felt her body against his after he'd caught her, her butt pressing into an area that had immediately awakened, as if it had been in a deep slumber since her.

He'd told himself the fact that he'd had no sexual interest in anyone since his divorce was normal. He'd never been through a divorce before to know for sure, but it seemed logical. *Of course* not wanting to risk his heart in another relationship seemed logical.

Until he'd realised he'd never risked his heart in any of his relationships before Summer. He'd had a distinct sexual interest in the women he'd dated before her though.

Then he'd seen Summer again and his body had responded to her as if she were the prince in a fairy tale; he, the princess put under a spell that only she could break.

He was immediately disgusted with himself for the fanciful notion. The anger he'd been struggling to keep a grip on was suddenly firm in his hands, too. *She* was making him feel this way. Even though she'd left him as everyone else in his life had, he was allowing her to make him feel this way. Which made him just as angry at himself as he was at her.

He was angry that she made his body betray him. That for the second time that day, she'd called him by his surname. He was angry that he missed that. And that even though he'd missed it, he still didn't want her to use it.

It was something intimate. Something people who were close to one another did. He and Summer weren't close any more; they no longer shared intimacies. She had no right to use it in the same way she had when they'd still been married.

His anger had nothing to do with the fact that no one else in his life called him that now. It had nothing to do with the hurt he felt at that fact; or the longing; or the inevitable resentment. He still had Trevor. So what if their relationship wasn't a surname-calling one? Relationships didn't only look one way. Being close to someone didn't only look one way.

This was the worst part about seeing Summer again, he thought. Contemplations on things he'd gleefully ignored most of his life. *She* did this to him. She made him think about his feelings. Sure, feelings were natural—but they were feelings, and he had no patience for them. Not when he knew he shouldn't entertain them.

Not entertaining them had got him through a father who'd left when he was ten. It had helped him survive a mother who'd almost died from alcohol poisoning when he was fourteen. It had kept him sane when he'd been bounced between his mother's house and foster care until he was eighteen. It had kept him from hitting rock bottom when he'd returned from his first term at university to find out his mother was selling the family house and was nowhere to be found.

'I can hear you stewing,' she commented into the silence that had grown tense as he'd been thinking.

'I'm not stewing.'

'You don't have to stay here, you know,' she replied, ignoring his denial. 'I do, because my mother asked me to, and, obligation.'

'You don't think your father was asking the same of me when he told me to cut you some slack?'

'No,' she said simply. 'Though if he was, you've fulfilled that obligation. You've been perfectly cordial to me.' There was a brief pause. 'I'll be sure to tell him that if you like.'

'Why does this sound like a bribe?' he asked, feeling more sullen than angry. 'I leave, you get to spend time alone and you tell your father I've been nice.'

She snorted. 'No one said anything about *nice*.' She tilted her head towards him, though her eyes were still on the view ahead of them. 'Cordial. Or polite, though they mean the same thing. That's my final offer.'

He didn't reply, but he didn't move either. He supposed that gave her an answer.

She sighed. 'So, you're going to be stubborn.'

'I'm not going to leave the first event at your parents' anniversary celebration because you asked me to.'

'Especially not if you think my father would disapprove.'

'What does that have to do with anything?'

Her eyes slid over to his, and there was a sadness there he'd seen come and go during their short relationship. His last memory of it had been outside the lawyer's office after they'd signed the divorce papers.

'Everything,' she answered softly. 'It has everything to do with it.' There was a pause. 'But if you feel like you have to stay for his sake, I won't stop you.'

'Thanks,' he answered dryly, though he was still thinking about what her answer meant.

'We don't have to talk though.' She looked out into the distance again. 'In fact, I'd prefer it if we don't. We can just pretend that we did.'

'You were the one who heard my stewing,' he muttered.

'Pretend I didn't interrupt you.'

And he did. For all of a minute.

'What did you mean by that?' he asked. '"It has everything to do with it",' he repeated, when he saw she didn't understand.

'It doesn't matter.'

'Then tell me.'

'That would cause unnecessary drama.'

'So it *does* matter.'

'Let me rephrase this,' she said, turning towards him now. He didn't think she realised it, but in that movement, she'd cut off the world around them. 'It's too late to matter.'

He frowned. 'This cryptic thing doesn't work for you, Summer.'

'I don't particularly enjoy it either.'

She shifted again, her body seemingly relaxed as she set one hand on the ground behind her. The other still held her half-full lemonade. He'd forgotten about his. He took a sip, barely tasting it.

'We're being watched,' she said, a pleasant expression on her face. 'So I'm going to drink the rest of my lemonade, order another, and check the picnic basket so it doesn't look like we're arguing.'

'We aren't,' he said, for his benefit and hers. She gave him a look, but proceeded to finish her drink.

It made sense that they were being watched. And it explained why Summer had taken on a relaxed stance when he knew she felt anything but relaxed. He followed her lead, not wanting to give anyone something to talk about. Though he knew that their presence there together would already be cause for discussion.

Summer had stopped attending Bishop events after their divorce. It had been gossiped about endlessly for months after. There was a period when Wyatt couldn't join a group of people without them falling silent; the universal sign that he'd been the topic of conversation.

It had bothered him. He knew she struggled with maintaining her Summer Bishop persona. Cool, infallible heiress. It had been the first thing that had bonded them. He'd found her crying on the steps of her parents' Christmas party; when she'd joined the party though, there'd been no sign of it.

He knew what it was like to have to pretend everything was fine when it wasn't. His mother had made sure of it when she'd told him to keep her alcoholism a secret.

If Summer wasn't attending Bishop events, it must have meant that she could no longer continue with the façade. He wouldn't have been concerned about it had he not known she'd created the façade for the sake of her family, too. To support the idea of the Bishop unit, which was part of what made them so powerful.

He hated to think he'd somehow damaged that. Her ability to pretend or her relationship with her family. When he'd summoned the courage to ask Trevor about it, Trevor had gone quiet. Then he'd said it wasn't Wyatt's fault.

Wyatt didn't quite believe that. But if it was his fault, maybe he could do something about it now...

'You know,' he started easily. He didn't want to scare her off or alert her to how much what he was about to say smarted. 'Part of the reason I'm surprised you're here is because you haven't attended a single event since the divorce.'

Her eyes flickered up to his. There was something there before her expression became unreadable. She calmly opened the basket and pulled out the bottle of champagne that had been carefully laid over clear boxes of cheeses, breads, and fresh fruits.

She popped it open, seemingly forgetting that she'd told him she would be ordering another lemonade. She poured herself a generous glass. Then she leaned back, lifting the liquid to her lips as if his question hadn't affected her in the least.

Well. He supposed he hadn't damaged the mask then.

'I didn't realise you'd noticed.'

'It wasn't subtle.'

Cool it, he warned himself when his voice took on a hard edge.

'I was tired of being subtle.'

'The mystery still doesn't suit you.'

'Luckily what suits me is none of your business.'

Their gazes locked. All the muscles in his body tightened.

The anger was there now. He didn't have to long for it, or wonder where it had gone to. But it didn't cool down the attraction that had flared the moment they looked at each other.

Oh, who was he kidding? The attraction was *always* there. Through dating and through marriage and even through divorce. And now. Now when she made him think and feel when he would rather not.

His eyes slipped from hers almost of their own accord, lifting to the severity of the hairstyle that had once been a wild, lazy afro halo around her face when they'd been together. Being tied so tightly at the nape of her neck accentuated her already prominent cheekbones. It gave her a more drastic beauty rather than the easy beauty of her other hairstyle.

His gaze lowered to her dress. It was lace, with sleeves that went just past her elbows and a skirt that ended just past her knees. Perfectly appropriate for the occasion, which he knew would be why she chose it.

It wasn't for the reason that occurred to him now: so he could enjoy the way its material skimmed the curve of her breasts, the slope of her waist, the rounding of her hips.

He could still feel the softness of her body under his fingers; could still see her brown skin stretched over it. He remembered how he would run his fingers over the arches of her body. Remembered how he would trace the stretch marks, the indents at her hips, her stomach, her butt. How he'd follow his fingers' path with his lips, how they'd—

He took a deep breath, rearranging his body so that he sat up straight, as if somehow the stern position would help him regain control of his mind. His body. His emotions. And then his eyes met hers, and he saw an answering heat there.

'Sure, Bishop,' he murmured softly. 'Let's keep telling ourselves we're none of the other's business, shall we?'

CHAPTER FOUR

SUMMER PULLED THE jersey she'd thrown on tighter around her as a light breeze floated in the air. Not because the breeze was cold. The summer's day had appropriately ended in a warm evening. But the feel of the wind against her skin felt a lot like Wyatt's gaze on her during the picnic. And the sound of it was almost exactly the tone of Wyatt's voice when he'd told her they weren't each other's business.

She was annoyed that her mind would go there, but she was also beginning to realise she'd have to accept *annoyed* as her permanent state of mind this weekend.

And *achy* as the permanent state of her body.

It was the reason she was wandering around the lodge's property in her nightshirt at ten in the evening. She'd walked around the communal pool, and had been tempted, for a second, to dip her achy body in its coolness before she'd thought about the energy that would require. She'd walked along the edge of the cliff overlooking the ocean. Now she was at the wooden bridge that connected the side of the lodge where her parents and a select few friends stayed with the other side, where the rest of the guests had their cabins.

Trees lined the entire length of the bridge on either side. One thick branch extended from the left to the right, high enough so as not to obstruct anyone's way. It gave the lodge a woodsy feel; a stark difference from the beachside atmosphere she got when she took a few steps in the direction of her cabin and saw the ocean.

'You couldn't sleep either?'

Summer didn't need to turn to recognise the voice.

The gooseflesh that had once been her skin confirmed it to her. She wished now that the wind were the only thing her skin had to contend with.

She stayed where she was, but she said, 'It usually takes me a while to unwind after a long week.'

'I know.'

She felt him move closer, somewhere over her shoulder, but she refused to turn.

'No, I don't think you do,' she said. 'My days have got a lot longer since our divorce.'

'How is that possible?'

'Is that a criticism?' she forced herself to ask lightly. 'Because you know I was only taking my cue from you. Working hard. Focusing on building a name for myself.'

'You didn't have to.'

She turned around. 'I didn't have to what? Work hard? Or build a name for myself?'

'You didn't have to start your own business, Summer,' he said, his expression smooth as stone. 'You didn't have to work as hard as I did. You already had a place at Bishop Enterprises. I had to earn mine.'

She clenched her jaw. Her father had been busy since her and Wyatt's divorce. Though telling Wyatt she'd once had plans to work in the family business was tricky. It was Trevor's affair that had changed those plans, after all.

'That right there is why I couldn't,' she said, taking the safe route. 'I wanted to have something I'd earned myself.' She paused. 'Why are you saying this?'

His expression didn't change. 'I just didn't know Bishop Enterprises had been an option for you.'

'And you're romanticising the idea of it,' she said as she realised it.

'No,' he denied, frowning. There was a pause. 'But if you worked for your father,' he said quietly, 'you might not have asked for the divorce to focus on your business.'

Her brain took his words, processed them, coached her

on how to respond. But the message never reached her mouth. Her throat felt as if her voice box had been crushed. Her tongue felt thick. Her lips felt frozen.

She took a deep breath through her mouth, hoping the air would revive all the parts of her insides that had been affected by his admission.

Then, calmly—she hoped—she said, 'I probably would have worked harder if it was for my father.' She swept her tongue over her teeth. 'It's a tad hypocritical for you to stand there and tell me work wouldn't have been an issue in our marriage. You weren't home a lot. And you have the success to show for it,' she said hurriedly, not wanting to get stuck on that remark. 'You went from being an intern at my father's company to his number two in nine years. That's amazing, particularly considering the size of Bishop Enterprises.'

It had always been part of what she'd admired in him. His drive. His focus. She hadn't admired how much of that drive, that focus, he'd neglected to channel into their marriage. She'd focused so completely on her own job because Wyatt had been so focused on his. He wasn't going to turn her into the wife who waited at home for her husband. Summer refused to be the wife whose husband couldn't figure out what was more important to him: his marriage or his work.

She'd seen that happen with her mother. The end result had been her father having an affair. Summer couldn't bear for that to be her path, too. So she'd worked just as hard as Wyatt did. She'd turned her tiny brokerage into one of the most successful in the city. She might have done so at the expense of her marriage, but then, Wyatt had done that with his work, too.

At least this way, Summer had had a choice. She'd chosen to focus on work. She hadn't been coerced into the part of the sidelined wife. The outsider because of someone else's decisions.

'I had to work hard, Summer,' he said after a while. 'I had to thank your father for taking a chance on me.'

What about me? she wanted to ask. She didn't. It was selfish to worry about herself when she understood why Wyatt felt indebted. She hadn't before they'd got married. She'd thought his loyalty to her father had been gratitude. She'd only realised the extent of it when he'd told her the truth about his childhood...

The day after their wedding.

They'd eloped with only Autumn and her then boyfriend Hunter as their witnesses, telling her parents when they were already on their way to their honeymoon. She hadn't needed either of her parents' approval—why, when they didn't care about hers?—though they'd both wholeheartedly approved.

Which had annoyed her *just* a little.

When she and Wyatt had arrived in Mauritius, at the beachfront dinner the resort had arranged for them, Wyatt had told her about his parents. She'd always known they weren't in the picture, but she'd never known the details of it until that night. Since they'd only been dating six months before their quickie marriage, she'd known there had been things both of them had kept from the other. She hadn't paid too much heed to the fact that she hadn't known all the details.

She wished she had.

'I know.' She folded her arms. She wasn't sure if it was for comfort or to keep him from noticing she wasn't wearing a bra. 'I know you feel like you owe a lot to my father.'

There was a pause.

'You make that sound like a criticism.'

Since there was no good option for her to go with, she didn't reply.

His eyes narrowed. 'Something happened between the two of you, didn't it?'

She bit her lip. Lifted a shoulder.

'I hope it isn't because of me.'

'No.'

He let out a breath. 'Good. I can't imagine if after all he's done for me...' He trailed off. 'What? Why are you looking at me like that?'

'You're not worried that my relationship with my father is strained because you're worried about me,' she said, unable to stop herself. 'You're worried because of *him*. Of what he might think of you.'

It made her want to fall to her knees and weep.

'No,' he said, taking a step towards her. She shook her head. He stopped moving. 'No, I meant—'

'It doesn't matter, Wyatt,' she interrupted desperately.

She didn't want to go there, but all the little talks she'd given herself about staying away from the past seemed to be taunting her. In the form of her own words. In the form of her memories.

Just like that, she was back in Beijing again, the maître d' querying about her mother.

'My mother?' Summer asked, confused.

'Petite, short curly brown hair?' the maître d' clarified. 'She was with your father when they stayed here about a year ago? I'm sorry,' she added, 'of course you can't remember. The only reason I do is because it was the day before my maternity leave and she was so lovely to me. And so affectionate with your father! I remember hoping my husband and I still felt that way about each other when we're their age.'

Her confusion had had nothing to do with the time between that night and now. It had been because her mother was neither petite, nor did she have short, curly brown hair. Her world had slowed down and time had frozen as she'd realised her mother wasn't the woman the maître d' had been talking about.

That assumption had been made based on whoever that woman had been and her father's *affection* for one another. And, she only imagined, on the fact that her father had still been wearing his wedding ring. Presumably, the petite brown-haired woman had been wearing hers, too.

But it couldn't have been what she thought, she'd told herself. When her father had joined her at their table, she'd been too shocked to play coy. She'd asked him about it.

And everything had fallen apart.

Perhaps she could have accepted it if it hadn't extended beyond that. Sadly, it had. So much else in her life had fallen apart because of that night. How she felt in her family. Her career plans, though she'd somehow managed to salvage that. Her life with the man she'd loved though…

And here he was, standing in front of her, trying not only to please the man who'd put her through this, but to *imitate* him. He'd succeeded, too. Far better than he could ever know. Trevor had forced her to isolate herself from her family; Wyatt had forced her to isolate herself from him.

'Summer? What's wrong?'

She only then realised a sound had come out of her mouth. She wasn't sure what it had been, but since she'd been in pain—since she still felt it throbbing in her body—she understood the worry in Wyatt's voice.

And why, seconds later, he was in front of her, his hands gripping her arms.

'Oh.' She swallowed, blinked, turned to face him. 'I'm okay.'

'You're not okay.'

Her mouth opened to deny it, but, despite everything, all she wanted to do was lean forward so she could rest her head against his chest.

For once she didn't bother fighting what she wanted.

As soon as her head made contact, she felt his body stiffen. Knew why. She was touching him. Not only that; she was asking him for *comfort*. There was no point in denying it. Or the fact that she still found comfort in his arms, even though he was part of the reason why she needed it.

But for one short moment, Summer wanted to be comforted. She didn't want to think about how tired she was of being the only one who knew the whole truth. Or how she was the only one suffering for it.

She wanted to go back to the time when she didn't feel so alone. The last time that had happened was with Wyatt. Before he'd told her about his broken family. And how grateful he was to be a part of hers. She'd gone right back to feeling lonely then; the Wyatt who'd understood her had disappeared before her eyes.

She wouldn't get him back. She couldn't risk trying. Trying would involve telling him her family was broken, too. It would rob him of the life he'd always wanted.

The life she knew was a lie.

Summer pressed her face deeper into Wyatt's chest.

This was…disturbing.

Which was frightening, since *disturbing* wasn't a description Wyatt had thought he'd ever use for Summer. Unless he was describing her beauty. Or her ability to make him forget why relationships never worked out, resulting in impromptu proposals and weddings.

But a show of emotion from the Queen of Control herself? That *was* disturbing. And explained why his arms were folding around her soft body instead of pushing her away.

He should have. He should have acted like a complete jerk and pushed her away. *Run* away, for his self-preservation. Instead, he was diving head-first into the vulnerability that had made him fall for her in the first place.

He remembered it all too well, that day at the Bishops' annual Christmas party. It had been the first time he'd built up the courage to go. Before that year, he'd believed he'd needed to prove himself to Trevor before he could attend such an intimate event. Or any event Trevor had hosted. It had been an excuse, even his younger self had suspected, though for what, he hadn't been—and still wasn't—sure of.

That year he'd brought on his third and biggest client to Bishop Enterprises: Callahan Farms. Rumours had been going around for months that one of the biggest providers of pecan nuts to the Western Cape—and one of the biggest suppliers in South Africa—had been looking for someone to manage the exportation of their nuts abroad. Wyatt had known that if the rumours had been true, he had to score them as a client. His place at Bishop Enterprises would be secure then and he'd finally be able to thank Trevor for all the other man had done for him.

He'd done the work and found out the rumours had been true.

Weeks later, Callahan Farms had become a client of Bishop Enterprises.

So that year, he'd attended the Christmas party. He'd met Autumn almost immediately upon his arrival; Summer had been missing, which Trevor had seemed faintly annoyed by. But Wyatt had met her eventually, hours into the party, sitting on the steps in the west wing of the Bishop mansion.

She'd stood immediately. 'No one is supposed to be here.'

'I'm sorry, I was—'

He'd broken off, because the beginning of his excuse had already been formulated the moment he'd seen someone sitting on the stairs. That had been the part that had come out smoothly.

The rest had died on his lips because he had been too in awe of Summer's beauty.

'You were?' she prompted, taking the last steps down until she was on the ground level, walking to him.

'I was,' he repeated, before figuring out he was acting like an idiot. He cleared his throat. 'Sorry, I think I got lost.'

She dropped her head. 'On the other side of the house to where the party is?'

He winced. 'Fine, you caught me. I was exploring. This is—' He broke off, shaking his head.

She gave a sparkly laugh, though there was something hoarse in the sound that had his eyes resting on her face.

'Yeah, I know. It is…' Her mouth curved. 'Summer, by the way.'

'Yeah, I know.' He'd seen pictures, but it hadn't at all prepared him for the reality. 'You're the other sister.' He winced again. 'Sorry.'

'Don't worry,' she replied with a small smile. 'It's not inaccurate. Who are you?'

'Oh, yeah, sorry.' He cleared his throat. Again. 'Wyatt Montgomery.'

'Nut Boy,' she said with a smirk.

He blinked. 'I'm sorry—what?'

Her smile widened. 'You're the man who secured Callahan Farms for my father? You know, the man who charmed Pete Callahan into allowing Bishop Enterprises to sell his nuts abroad.'

He smiled. Stepped closer to her. 'I guess I am Nut Boy, then.'

'Nice to meet you,' she said, taking another step towards him.

It was the first time he'd seen her eyelashes were wet, clumped together as if she had been—

As if she had been crying.

His heart had collapsed at her feet.

She wasn't crying now though. He knew it because her body was absolutely still in his arms. The only reason he assumed she still wanted him to comfort her—*if* that was what she wanted—was the fact that she was still there.

Unable to resist, he rested his head on top of hers, taking in the smell of coconut and shea butter of her hair. She hadn't loosened it for her night-time stroll, though it wasn't in the stern hairstyle she'd worn earlier that day. She'd wrapped it in a silk scarf, so that the top of her curls was visible while keeping them away from her face.

The smell of her, the feel of her, sent an intense wave of longing through him. And now he understood some of the anger that had kept him from going to bed that night. A lot of other nights over the past two years, too, he thought.

She'd given up on this. On the fact that they could stand in each other's arms and not know what was wrong, but still comfort one another. It was a small thing, this, and it was one of many, but it cut through him easily. As if the thought had been specially designed to cut through him.

He pushed it aside when she pulled back.

'I'm sorry.'

She wasn't looking at him again. Which hadn't ever been something she'd done before, but he recognised as a tactic. A protective tactic; to protect herself from *him*.

'You don't have to apologise,' he said. 'I get it.'

'No, you don't.'

'No, I don't,' he agreed. 'But the chances of you telling me are slim, so I won't even ask.'

There was a long silence.

'I was…remembering.'

His heart thudded hard against his chest as he thought about the look on her face before she'd gone into his arms. The way her expression had twisted, tightened, and then fallen in what could only have been pain. What was she remembering?

Hope he hadn't known existed inside him inflated, swelling even more when she looked up at him and there was longing in her eyes.

They looked at each other for a long time, and though he knew it probably wasn't the best idea to let it linger, he did. He let the connection soothe the hurt inside him. Felt it skim over a deeper, darker hurt he'd refused to listen to.

Now wasn't the time to listen to it either, and yet he did, unable not to. The hurt about his father's abandonment was simple. One day Wyatt had come home from school and the man was no longer there. He'd always been there when Wyatt had got home. He'd worked the late shift at the pharmacy to look after Wyatt until Wyatt's mother had got home in the evenings.

That day, Wyatt had panicked. His father hadn't been there, but his clothes had been. At ten years old, Wyatt hadn't completely understood that someone could leave without their clothes. Then he'd found the note—the *Tell the kid I'm sorry* note—and even his ten-year-old brain had been able to comprehend that. It had even linked his father's behaviour the weeks before to his father leaving.

The coolness; the distance. Almost exactly how Summer had begun to act before she'd left, too.

Then there was the hurt about his mother. That was darker. More complicated. More...

More.

He couldn't think through it, or over it, as easily he did with his father. For some reason, it stuck in his head in the same way the hurt he felt about Summer leaving did.

Or perhaps, all the hurt had meshed together and now he couldn't figure out what was what.

He stepped back at the unexpectedness of it, the arms he hadn't realised were still around Summer's waist dropping to his sides as his hands clenched into fists. Suddenly it wasn't a summer's night at a lodge next to the beach. He wasn't holding his ex-wife under the stars with the sound of the sea crashing against the shore somewhere in the distance.

There was only the hurt.

It stiffened his body, had him straightening his spine. He gave a slight shake of his head when Summer sent him a questioning look. Her expression instantly went blank—the mask had returned.

They both took a step away from one another. He nodded his head now, and she turned, correctly interpreting his signal and moving ahead of him.

He swallowed, trying to ignore how it felt as if he'd been turned inside out.

It didn't work.

CHAPTER FIVE

It took Summer a full hour to get out of bed.

She'd struggled to fall asleep, and at some point during the night she'd opened her curtains so she could be calmed by the waves splashing against the pillars that held her cabin up. It was gorgeous, her cabin. It had stained oak laminate flooring; white wooden panels that formed the V of its roof; chequered carpets in the middle of each of the floors; and the glass sliding doors that made up the entire wall facing the ocean.

She and Autumn would be sharing for the weekend. Since Autumn was only arriving the next day, Summer had the room to herself. She was lucky. If Autumn saw her now, she'd take one look at—

Her phone rang. Autumn was video calling her.

Great.

Summer sat up, brushed a finger over her eyebrows to straighten them. She didn't bother with her hair; it was in her silk sleep scarf anyway. Attempts to fix it would be futile. At least if she wanted to avoid Autumn bombarding her with messages about why she wasn't answering.

'Hi,' Summer said when she answered.

'Hi,' Autumn replied. Summer recognised her sister's bakery in the background, which meant Autumn was likely calling during a coffee break. 'You've just woken up?'

'What makes you think that?' Summer asked. 'Is it my amazing outfit?' She tilted the phone so Autumn could see the nightshirt she wore. She tried to forget Wyatt had seen and held her in it, too. 'Or is it my fashion-forward headscarf?' She straightened the phone again.

'Both are fabulous, but I'm going to go out on a limb

here and say you're not wearing that to Mom and Dad's fancy breakfast?'

She groaned.

Autumn frowned. 'You forgot about it?'

'No,' she said defensively. A second later she said, 'I'm avoiding it.'

'Summer,' Autumn said in that tone she used when she was annoyed but pretending not to be. 'You can't be there and not attend the festivities.'

'Hmm.'

'Hey.' Autumn sat down on the bench outside the bakery. 'You said you were going to give this a try.'

'Because it means so much to you.'

'It doesn't mean anything to you?'

She didn't reply.

'Sun,' Autumn said after a moment, using her childhood nickname for Summer.

Autumn had come up with it after Summer had started calling her 'Wind'. It had been a joke because Autumn was a whirlwind of goodness. Successful, perfect. Determined to be the best at everything she did. Besides, it had seemed fitting, considering the season Autumn had been named after.

Her nickname had a similar origin story.

It had been their little joke, until one day Autumn had told Summer she felt as if Summer was the sun for her. Bright. Warm. Autumn was the only one who still described her that way. *Sun* was more suited to the person Summer had been before her father's deception. Before she'd been forced to lie to her sister.

'Mom and Dad are going to renew their vows tomorrow,' Autumn was saying. 'They'd really love for it to be a new beginning for our entire family as well. If you—'

'Wait,' Summer interrupted. 'Did you just say *they'd* really love it? As in, they spoke to you about this?'

Autumn's eyes widened. 'I… Well…' She went quiet

for a moment. 'We were out to dinner—' this part wasn't a surprise; Autumn had been honest about seeing their parents for a monthly dinner. Summer had politely declined her sister's invitation '—and they'd mentioned how much they'd missed you. The real you,' Autumn said when Summer opened her mouth, 'not whoever you are around them.'

Or around you.

'Dad, too?' she asked. Autumn nodded.

There was a pause.

'It's been eight years,' Summer said. 'Why now?'

'I don't know.'

'Do you really not know? Or did they ask you not to tell me?'

The confusion in Autumn's eyes was genuine. 'No, they didn't.' A beat passed. 'Why would you ask me that? They'd never expect me to keep something from you.'

Summer didn't reply.

'Sun,' Autumn said slowly, 'what's going on?'

'Nothing,' Summer said.

But if she needed proof this weekend was messing with her head, Summer now had it. Not once since the affair had she given any indication that she'd known about it before her mother and sister had. Not once in *eight years*. Within minutes into this phone call though, she had.

'Is this why you called?' Summer said, changing the subject. 'To check on my behaviour?'

Autumn searched Summer's face, then she shook her head. 'No, actually. I was wondering if you were okay. About the family stuff and the, um…' Autumn hesitated. 'The Wyatt stuff.'

'What Wyatt stuff?' Summer asked immediately. Brightly.

Autumn snorted. 'That's not going to work on me, sis.'

'What isn't going to work on you?' she asked in the faux bright tone that made her own ears bleed. 'I have no idea what you're talking about, Autumn. I am perfectly fine. But I must dash because I am terribly late for a fancy breakfast.'

She blew her sister a kiss before Autumn could protest, and ended the call. Seconds later her phone flashed with a message.

You used posh words. And a British accent. You're not fooling me.

And seconds after that:

I'll be there in twenty-four hours. Hang on until then?

Summer softened at the question, and typed back.

I can do that.

Autumn replied:

And don't do anything I wouldn't do while you do.

Summer smirked, and sent back a laughing emoticon, then a heart one.

Summer knew Autumn had been checking in because she was concerned. It was the same reason she was doing recon—reconciliation, in this case—work for their parents.

Autumn had never been able to understand why Summer couldn't move on from it as the rest of them had. It was because Summer couldn't tell her the truth: not only had their father cheated, but he'd asked Summer to keep it a secret for months. *Months.*

He'd told her it was because of business. He had an important deal to close, and he didn't want to complicate things by focusing on a personal issue. He'd put business above their family, and he'd had no reservations asking Summer to do the same.

It had made her physically ill. For those two months, Summer's stomach had twisted and knotted. She hadn't been able to eat. She hadn't been able to be in her family's company either. The affair had been an ominous cloud promising a storm, following her everywhere. And she couldn't warn the people she cared about to prepare for it. Every time she was with them, she wanted to tell them to check the shelter. To bring an umbrella at the very least.

But she was caught between the business and her family, too. No, not the business and the family; her father, and her mother and sister. At that point, she'd been closer to her father than to her mother. Maybe she'd still been protecting him when she'd agreed to keep the affair a secret. Or maybe she hadn't wanted to deal with the aftermath of her family finding out about her father's affair.

All she knew was that it was the worst two months of her life. So when her stomach had begun twisting and knotting again in her marriage—when she hadn't been able to eat and she'd seen Wyatt put business above his family, too—she'd tried to protect herself. She'd thought she had. But seeing him now didn't make her feel so sure.

In fact, it brought back all her memories of their marriage. At first, things had been good. They had spent time together, and Wyatt would easily put off work for another hour with her. But then Bishop Enterprises had nearly lost Wyatt's biggest client and things had changed. Wyatt had spent more time at work. When he'd been home, he was working. Talking to her father. And as Wyatt had worked himself into the ground to prove himself to Trevor—to himself, too, she thought—he'd changed.

She'd withdrawn into herself so she wouldn't feel how much it hurt. In some ways it had been easy. She'd already perfected the cool, disinterested mask with her family. Convincing herself that she had to be cool and disinterested with her husband, too, had been simple. Painful though, since he'd been the first person since her father's affair to see behind the mask she'd worn. She'd felt understood for the first time in years.

Until she hadn't been.

Her concern now was that this little holiday was cracking her mask. Hell, after last night, with Wyatt, she was worried it might have already broken.

But it couldn't be. She would have to glue any broken pieces back together, paint over any cracks. She couldn't let her family know the truth. She couldn't let Wyatt know the truth. She was more worried about that last part, because she'd always been vulnerable around him. Vulnerable Summer told Wyatt things he shouldn't know. Last night was the perfect example.

If she told Wyatt the truth, the work he'd found his purpose in would look different. And he needed that purpose. He hadn't had it growing up, and his life had looked dramatically different. He was proud of what he'd achieved now. She wouldn't tell him he'd achieved it at the expense of their family. She wouldn't taint that purpose for him.

She thought she did a pretty good job of fixing the mask when she finally joined breakfast. Her mother had arranged it for all their guests on the terrace of their significantly larger cabin.

'How lovely of you to join us, dear,' her mother said when Summer arrived.

The words would seem genuine to anyone who was not Lynette Bishop's daughter. Why would they be familiar with the *you've embarrassed me in front of people and we shall discuss this later* voice?

'I'm so sorry, Mother,' Summer said smoothly, pressing a kiss to her mother's cheek. After a brief moment of hesitation, she did the same with her father. The kiss, the hesitation, felt strange. Hopefully no one would notice. She intentionally avoided Wyatt's gaze.

'I struggled to sleep last night so I tried to catch an extra hour this morning.'

'Did you?' her mother asked, her voice softening as her eyes swept over Summer's face.

'I did,' Summer answered with a smile. 'Now, why don't you catch me up on what the activities for the day are?'

She listened to her mother's plans, ignoring the interested looks the other guests gave her. Most importantly, she ignored Wyatt's gaze. She could feel it on her as acutely as she could his arms around her body from the night before. It was almost as if his *look at me* bet had been issued again.

'Did you say— Did you say *disco*, Mom?' she asked, snapping to attention.

Lynette's smile brightened. 'I said some other things, too—' her eyebrow lifted, informing Summer she knew her daughter hadn't been paying attention '—but yes, we end tonight off with a disco.'

Summer wrinkled her nose. 'Can't we call it a dance?'

A chuckle went through the guests, and Lynette's expression turned into genuine amusement. Summer didn't even look at her father. Partly because she knew his reaction wouldn't be genuine, and partly because she was still angry about what Autumn had told her. How dared he tell Autumn he missed the real Summer? *He* was the reason that Summer no longer existed.

Sometimes she'd find herself staring at him, wondering if the man who'd so patiently taught her the ins and outs of the Bishop business was still there. That man had been honest. He wouldn't have lied. He wouldn't have asked her to lie.

She shook it off.

'You won't understand this, I'm sure, but discos were popular in my day.'

'Your day is right now, Mother,' Summer said sweetly.

'I've never met another woman as on top of current events as you are.'

'Oh, you're sucking up.' Lynette winked at her. 'I like it.'

There was another round of laughter before someone asked her mother about where the disco would be held. Summer let a breath out through her lips when the question distracted her mother, then made the mistake of looking at Wyatt. He was frowning at her. She immediately lowered her gaze, knowing what he must be thinking.

She was trying hard to make their family seem normal. She'd done it before. And she was sure that to most of her parents' guests, she was succeeding. But she could still feel Wyatt's gaze on her. He'd seen her let out that breath after joking with her mother, as if the joking hadn't come naturally. She was sure he'd noticed her hesitation before kissing her father, as if it was something she didn't do on a regular basis.

He'd already picked up on something between her and her father the day before. He was definitely looking. She thought he might be seeing, too…

It instantly had her wondering if she'd fixed the mask as well as she'd thought she had. But a deeper, more destructive part of her wondered if the old Wyatt was back. The man who'd seen through her façade. The one she'd fallen for in the first place…

Summer.

She had to up her game.

There was a break between breakfast and the lake cruise her mother had arranged. Summer used it to take a walk on the beach. She hoped it would give her back her steadiness. But when she heard footsteps behind her on the wooden path that led down to the beach, she gritted her teeth.

'Summer,' a voice said, and her feet stopped of their own accord. Then her father was next to her, and Summer didn't know what to do.

'Do you mind if I take a walk with you?'

Summer swallowed. 'I was hoping to have some alone time.'

'I won't keep you long, I promise.'

Unable to say no, she nodded, and they continued the walk down in silence. She wondered what he wanted, and, if it was nothing, why he'd come at all. She felt the tension grow in her shoulders with each step down; she could have done without that. In fact, she could have done without all of it, which was probably why she was hoping for something unrealistic like her father joining her without wanting to talk.

It hadn't always been unrealistic. She could remember instances when she and Trevor would walk together. Mostly during summer vacations. Largely to talk about the business. But it had been bonding time. And it had been enough for her.

She missed it.

Her heart ached at the surprise of it. At the longing of it.

She angled a look to the side. When she saw Trevor was looking out at the ocean and not at her, she allowed herself to look at him more freely. He'd grown older quickly. Or perhaps she thought that because she didn't dare study him if she could help it.

His grey hair was stark against his brown skin, his tall frame slowly hunkering over itself with age. He was still a handsome man, and one of those annoying kinds whose age made them more attractive somehow. She wondered if he'd be more or less likely to cheat because of it.

The thought caused a lump in her throat to grow, which, of course, was part of the problem with her relationship with her father. She'd found insidious little things like that creeping into her thoughts all the time. Even when she wasn't anywhere close to thinking about what her father had done. It made her feel as though she couldn't trust herself. Or him.

She rubbed absently at an ache in her chest.

'I wanted to talk to you about this weekend,' her father said finally. She made a non-committal sound. 'I know it's hard for you to be here.'

She still didn't respond; she knew this was a trick. No matter what she said, it would open her up to this line of conversation. The one about her feelings about what had happened.

Too little, too late.

'I've let this sit much longer than I should have,' Trevor said. 'I think a part of me hoped that we'd move past it like the rest of the family has.'

'Not a part,' Summer corrected. 'The whole of you, or it would have taken a lot less time than it has for you to mention this to me.'

Trevor sighed. 'Do you blame me for not wanting to relive the most shameful mistake in my past?'

'Yes, I do. But wait—which mistake?' she asked. 'Sleeping with a woman who wasn't your wife? Putting your business above your family? Or asking me to keep quiet about it? Doesn't matter,' she said over whatever he would have said. 'I blame you for all of it.'

She stopped walking, her feet digging into the sand. It was warm from the sun. Summer wished the heat could rise from her toes up, into her heart, so she wouldn't feel so cold.

'Are we done now?' Summer asked, turning to face her father. He'd stopped walking, too. She ignored the pain on his face. The surprise.

'I didn't realise...' He trailed off. 'You think I put the business over our family?'

She laughed, hard and harsh. 'You're not asking me that question because you want to know the answer. You already know it's true.'

He didn't reply.

She laughed again. 'Of course you know it's true. Because you remember what you said to me when I found out about the affair.' His eyes widened; he did. She would force him to hear it anyway. 'You told me you didn't want to focus on a personal issue like this when you had a business deal to concentrate on.' She paused. 'But, please, Dad, tell me how that makes me more important than work? Or Mom and Autumn, for that matter?'

Again, there was silence.

'Are you regretting telling Autumn you'd like to see the real me now?'

'Summer,' he said slowly. 'I didn't think... I didn't know...' He took a breath. 'I told you I was sorry—'

'No,' Summer interrupted, her eyes suddenly feeling hot. 'You actually haven't.'

Her father blinked. 'No, Sun, I... I did.'

'Don't call me that,' Summer said immediately, the heat prickling and her throat thickening again.

At what her father had said. At what she'd said. At the fact that she didn't mean it. Not really. Not when something inside her had turned at the name she hadn't heard come from his lips in over eight years.

'I'm sorry,' he said hoarsely. 'About everything.'

She stared at him, and a part of her wished she could accept the apology. But she couldn't. Not when he thought an apology like that was adequate.

Not when she doubted he knew what he was apologising for.

'The worst part is that you don't see why I can't move past it,' she told him, her voice breaking. 'You think it's because I can't get over the affair. But it's because I can't get over you asking me not to turn to the people I love after finding out. You pushed me to the outside of the family, Dad. Now you're wondering why I can't just step back in.' She swallowed. 'There are a lot of barriers keeping me from doing that. You built most of them.'

She took a deep breath.

'I'll see you at the boat,' she said. 'Don't worry. No one will suspect a thing.'

She turned and headed back for the lodge.

He hadn't meant to spy. That was what it was called, right? Watching people without hearing their words?

Though in all honesty, Wyatt didn't need to hear the words to know what was happening. From his position at the top of the pathway that led to the beach, he could see the tight hold of Trevor's shoulders; the angry expression on Summer's face. The sadness there, too, Wyatt thought. The hurt.

It hadn't been his intention to spy. He'd only wanted to talk with Summer about the night before. She'd been late to breakfast, which had prevented him from speaking to her beforehand. He suspected that had been the reason for her tardiness. Then she'd rushed off so quickly afterwards that he'd had to run after her—only to see Trevor had got there first.

He'd thought about waiting for them to be done before he'd been caught by the stiffness in Summer's posture. He forgot about his own intentions and watched as they spoke. As they *argued*. There was definitely something going on between Summer and Trevor.

He couldn't dwell on it when Summer turned around and began walking back to the lodge. He immediately turned and walked to the rendezvous point for the lake cruise, not willing to be caught in the act. He made it there earlier than the rest of the guests, and spent his entire time waiting wondering what the hell he'd just seen.

It was a refreshing difference from the thoughts that had kept him up the night before. Or was it the effort not to think about those thoughts that had kept him up? Probably both. Either way, this was much more interesting than the dark pits of his feelings about his mother. About his longing for his ex-wife.

Not that thinking about Trevor and Summer helped him figure out what was happening between them.

Summer's behaviour towards her father now was starkly different from when they'd been married. Or was it? Thinking back now, he couldn't remember too many occasions where he'd seen Summer and Trevor interact. When they had, he couldn't remember those interactions being anything other than respectful.

He hadn't paid that much attention to it, if he was being honest. A lot of the time his thoughts had been on work.

Because you know I was only taking my cue from you. Working hard. Focusing on building a name for myself.

Summer's words bounced into his mind, dribbling there until he paid attention to why he remembered them. Was it possible he'd missed something because of his work? Had he been so involved he hadn't noticed Summer didn't have a good relationship with her father, even then?

He dismissed the thought instantly. The Bishops didn't have bad relationships with one another. They were stable. They made jokes. Showed affection. None of that said *bad relationship*. And he would know. He had as bad a relationship with his family as they came. Besides, he'd been a part of the Bishop family. Whatever had happened must have been after his and Summer's divorce.

Or were you so enthralled by the idea of the Bishops that you didn't see the reality?

Lynette joined him then, smiling brightly when she saw him waiting, and he couldn't think about the answer.

But the question lingered.

'Bless you for being here before me, Wyatt.'

Wyatt tilted his head. 'You're...welcome?'

Lynette laughed. 'It makes me feel less embarrassed about how excited I've been feeling about this weekend. If you're here before me, you must be enthusiastic?'

Wyatt smiled. 'You have nothing to be embarrassed

about, Mrs Bishop. I think it's nice that you and Trevor are still so in love.'

Something on Lynette's face tightened, then softened. 'We've been through enough to know what's important.' Her gaze sharpened on his. 'Do you?'

Wyatt didn't get the chance to answer when Lynette's friend joined them. Lynette gave him a nod and began to talk about the cruise, leaving Wyatt to figure out—again— what had happened.

He thought about what he would have answered if he'd had to. Yes, he knew? Stability, security. Happiness, love. Lynette might have been happy with that answer. For some reason, he was not.

Because he'd tried it? Followed the example of the man who had it all and he'd failed?

But *he* hadn't failed. He just hadn't been good enough for the woman he'd thought he could find those things with.

He stopped himself. That line of thought was about as productive as what he'd been thinking about—or trying not to think about—the night before.

As if you weren't thinking about Summer last night, too.

The image of her in that loose nightshirt, the flimsy jersey over it, flashed through his mind. He tried to shake it off. It was successful only because she arrived then, in a bright dress that reminded him of the very season she was named after.

Her eyes fluttered over to him, and she gave him a slight nod. A surprise, considering how she'd avoided looking at him that morning at breakfast. Except for that one moment, which seemed similar to how she was looking to him now. As if she needed to. As if it…steadied her.

She stayed towards the back of the group, putting a solid distance between her and the rest of the guests. She had a large straw hat in one hand, which she clutched so tightly he thought she might break it. He walked over to her side, pretending not to hear her sharp exhalation when he stopped.

'I take it you're not looking forward to this?'

'What?' she asked, then gave him a smile so fake he expected it to appear on a plastic surgery TV show. 'I'm excited to be here. I love cruises.'

His lips spread as he listened to her. By the time she was done, he was chuckling.

'Man, you hate this so much.'

She gave him a look, before letting out a small laugh of defeat. 'Is it that obvious?'

'You mean is your extremely poor acting revealing your displeasure? Yes,' he informed her, without waiting for an answer. She looked up, shook her shoulders.

'Okay. Okay,' she said again. Then she hung her head before looking at him in sorrow. 'I will pay whatever amount it takes for you to distract me for the rest of the day.'

'You… Me…'

He stopped making a fool of himself, took a breath and tried to process what she was asking.

'Summer,' he said slowly, 'are you asking me to keep you company?'

'Don't make it sound like that,' she said irritably. Which, frankly, made him feel a lot better than thinking his ex-wife had been kidnapped by aliens. This was much more…on brand for her than asking something from him.

'I'm surprised.'

'Exactly. That's what you're making it sound like.'

'Because it's the truth,' he exclaimed and she swatted his arm with her hat.

'Keep your voice down,' she said in a low voice. 'I don't want the world to know I'm asking you a favour.'

'You're asking me a *favour*?'

Something remarkably like a moan slipped from her lips. She straightened her shoulders and looked him dead in the eye.

'I understand your surprise. Plus, you're correct; those words would never have left my lips if my sister was here.' She took a deep breath. 'Unfortunately, she isn't, and I cannot, for the life of me, pretend to be excited to attend a cruise with a bunch of people I don't particularly care for.'

She'd said all those words while exhaling, and was now taking another deep breath.

Wyatt braced himself for more.

'You're the only person I know here. Or I'm comfortable with.' She pulled a face. 'Relatively,' she added, before letting out a huff of air. 'It's not ideal, I know, but, for one day, can we set the stuff between us aside and be friends?'

She blinked—once, twice, three times—and opened her mouth. Closed it. Then met his gaze.

She was the one who looked surprised now. As if she had no idea what had come out of her mouth. As if she didn't recognise herself in what she'd asked him.

He felt the corners of his mouth tug up, and the *What the hell is happening?* feeling he'd had faded behind something more intense. Something that straightened out the bumps of hurt and anger that had initially kept him from saying yes.

Affection. And the desire to give her whatever she wanted.

Not that he'd make it easy for her.

'What is happening,' he said deliberately, 'is called humility.'

'What are you talking about?'

'It's this thing that allows you to ask other people for stuff, and not depend only on yourself.'

'Wyatt,' she said after a moment, 'are you really using this as an opportunity to teach me a moral lesson?'

'Hey—' he lifted his hands '—this isn't the kind of moment that comes around every day. I have to capitalise on it.'

She stared at him, slowing moving her head from side to side, though he didn't think she knew she was doing it.

'This is what I get for asking you for help,' she muttered.

He didn't resist the smile. 'It is.'

She glowered at him. 'You're not even telling me whether you're going to help me.'

'You still want me to?' he asked innocently. 'After what you just went through?'

'Wyatt,' she said, in what was definitely a moan. 'They're beginning to climb on the boat. If you don't give me an answer, I'm going to have to sit with someone I don't know and...' her voice dropped '...*socialise*.'

He laughed again, and a voice in his head told him to enjoy the feeling while he could. It probably wouldn't last long. Which gave him an idea.

'Fine, I'll do it.'

She brightened. 'Thank—'

'On one condition.'

What?' she asked flatly.

'I get to ask you one question.'

'What kind of question?' Her expression had gone careful, and now the voice in his head was telling him he was messing with things he shouldn't be messing with.

'Any question.' He lifted a hand before she could protest. 'Those are my terms.'

'Wyatt? Summer?'

They both turned their heads. For the first time, Wyatt saw that they were the only guests not on the boat. He also saw the interested expression on Lynette's face; the unreadable one on Trevor's, who stood just behind his wife.

'Are you two coming?' Lynette asked.

They looked at each other, and Summer sucked in her lip. What felt like an eternity later, she nodded.

'Deal.'

CHAPTER SIX

SUMMER DIDN'T KNOW what had come over her. Her first answer was desperation. It rang true, and louder, than any of the others, and she went with it. Which, all things considered, was a relief. She didn't want to think about the other reasons she might have asked Wyatt to be her friend.

Her friend. Oh, the sound of it made her cringe. But she'd been on a roll, and she hadn't paused to think about what she was saying. If she had, she wouldn't have done it. And he hadn't interrupted her—which made her wonder if he was giving her the opportunity to embarrass herself—so she'd kept talking and now she was sitting next to him on a boat.

It was actually nice. The boat had seats along its edge, with about ten more in pairs of two down the middle, separated by a bar. It seated all thirty of the guests—thirty-two, including her parents—comfortably, and the crew of three were in a small cabin enclosed by glass towards the back of the boat. She and Wyatt sat near the cabin.

Part of the deal, she thought, and relief flowed through her. She'd dreaded the socialising this weekend would include. The pretence, too. After speaking with her father, those feelings sat like stale bread in the pit of her stomach. And she'd sought comfort from the first person who'd come to mind when she thought she needed to be comforted.

She didn't dwell on that.

The point was, she didn't feel like being nice to people. She'd have to be nicer than usual, too, to prove to her father she could pretend everything was okay. So the desperation at turning to her ex-husband had been a reasonable kind. The fact that he'd said yes, though, was…interesting.

It wasn't new. The night they'd met at the Christmas party he'd helped her go into that room of people she didn't care about and pretend to be a happy family. Of course, she'd still had to go into the room and pretend, but Wyatt had made it easier.

When he'd asked her later why she hadn't been herself, she'd been stunned. No one she'd only just met knew she wasn't being herself. They almost always thought she was just the cool, aloof sister. The distant heiress to Autumn's warm persona. She'd played the role so well even her family believed it.

Wyatt seeing through her had felt significant in a way she couldn't understand then. But she'd felt understood. Which almost made up for all the times after when he'd let her down.

She'd asked him more times than she cared to admit to help her deal with social situations. Family obligations. Work meetings. He'd always say yes, and he'd keep his word…if it pertained to those family obligations. When it didn't, like clockwork, he'd call the afternoon of the event and cancel. Something important had come up at work, he'd always say. She didn't even think he realised it. But she had. And she'd learnt to stop relying on him.

Which meant his transition into her father had been like clockwork, too.

So the fact that she was sitting next to him now was so strange. It did feel as if he was the old Wyatt. The man she'd met that first night. Shaking her head—it was best not to go down that road—she stared out at the long reeds running along the river the boat was cruising down.

Beyond the reeds were hills of varying heights, covered in large part by bushes and the occasional tree. Every now and then, Summer would spy a house between the bushes; or at the top of the hills, though those were predominant and huge, with large windows and balconies to take full advantage of the view.

Though it was hot, the movement of the boat brought a welcoming breeze that cooled the sting of the sun. Laughter floated from the front of the boat down to them, light chattering adding to the ambience.

Summer closed her eyes, tilting her head up, and enjoyed the moment.

She had no idea when the last time was that she'd had one of these moments. Where it felt as if the world had slowed down and her mind stilled because of it. She'd spent the last six years building her own business. Making it a success had felt like a necessity after she'd given up the position waiting for her at Bishop Enterprises.

She'd been studying Finance when she'd found out about her father's affair, a degree she and Trevor had agreed would make her an asset to the company. After everything had happened, though, working for her father had seemed like a cruel joke. So she'd done her research and added Portfolio Management to her degree. Owning her own brokerage had seemed like a decent career change. But if she was honest, she hated that she wasn't working for the company that bore her name.

In the beginning, that hatred had fuelled her. Her marriage failing had done the same thing. When it had failed, she'd been determined to make her business a success. It soothed the ache that she wasn't working for Bishop Enterprises. And the strange burning sensation she got in her stomach whenever she thought that Wyatt had sacrificed their marriage for the sake of the job she should have had.

Regardless, it meant world-slowing, mind-stilling moments weren't easily found. She would enjoy this.

But she opened her eyes when she felt Wyatt's gaze on her.

It was interesting how she always knew it was him.

She shifted her head and their eyes met, and again it felt

as if the world slowed down. Except now, her mind didn't still, it froze. Handed over the controls of the situation to her heart, who took the reins gladly and guided Summer into noticing how handsome Wyatt was.

He wasn't the obvious kind of handsome. His face was…complicated. There were faint lines running across his forehead, his eyebrows were dark, almost severe. There was a dent in his chin that always made her think someone had pressed their finger into it and his skin had absorbed the pressure as if it were clay.

There were lines around his eyes, too, which told her his skin crinkled when he smiled. And between his eyebrows, that told her he frowned almost as much as he smiled.

There was the way his nose seemed as smooth as a slope in the Alps, leading to lips that were not quite as full as hers, but were sensuous. And the dents on either side of his mouth—his dimples—made her think she could fall into them every time they appeared.

It made complicated *very* sexy.

'You're staring at me.' His voice was lightly amused, and she lifted her eyes from his lips.

'You were staring at me first,' she said with a smile—and oh, no, she was becoming Marry-the-Man-Before-Thinking-it-Through Summer again.

'Only because I've only ever seen you with that expression on your face once before,' he said, distracting her.

'When?'

'The suntan session of two and a half years ago.'

'You mean the time I was having a relaxing afternoon on the beach and you poured a glass of ice water down my back?'

'I did not pour it down your back,' he retorted. 'I tripped over the bottle of champagne you'd left on the sand next to you.'

'So you say, Montgomery,' she said with a snort. 'But that water landed an awful lot quicker than you did, and, if memory serves me correctly, you weren't on the floor when I opened my eyes.'

'I wasn't,' he confirmed, 'because I have excellent reflexes.'

'Sure,' she said dryly.

He shrugged. 'That's my story, Bishop. It's never changed.'

'Hmm.'

She shook her head, though she was aware her lips were curved. Was even more aware his were, too.

She tried to remember the last time she and Wyatt had smiled at each other. Not grimaced, or exchanged fake gestures of politeness, but *smiled*. Genuinely, because they were amused with one another or just…comfortable. She couldn't remember, which did something terrible to her insides.

'What's wrong?'

'Nothing,' she said immediately, automatically.

There was a stretch of silence.

'When are you going to learn that you can't lie to me, Summer?' he asked quietly. 'When are you going to realise that I can see right through you?'

But you didn't, she nearly answered. *When it mattered, you didn't.*

She swallowed, clutched at her skirt, crinkling the material of it between her fingers. It was rather that than her lips, which was what she'd wanted to grip closed. To make sure she didn't say something she shouldn't. Like the fact that she hadn't wanted to divorce him; she just couldn't keep watching him turn into her father. Or feel as if he was turning her into her mother.

Or that she had felt more alone in her marriage than she had with her family.

When Wyatt had found her crying on the steps at her father's Christmas party, it was because she'd been tired of the pretence. A moment of weakness, she could admit, but it had been worth it because she'd found Wyatt. She'd kept him away from her parents in the six months before their wedding so she wouldn't have to pretend around him. And for those six months, she had been herself. She'd been happy.

She'd refused to compromise it with the truth of her father's affair.

At first, she'd made excuses. She hadn't wanted her father to be a part of her relationship. Besides, she and Wyatt had only just met. And he worked for her father, for heaven's sake. It had soon become harder. She'd fallen in love with him and had seen his respect for Trevor. After their wedding, when he'd told her about his parents, she'd realised it went far beyond respect. It was about purpose. About having something to work towards. And she'd understood that having a goal kept Wyatt moving forward instead of dwelling in his traumatic past.

She wouldn't take that away from him. No matter how much she wished his goal were better than having a life like Trevor Bishop's.

'I'll get us something to drink, okay?' Summer said, in desperate need of something to do.

Something that wasn't answering him.

Wyatt gave Summer a faint nod and watched as she moved towards the bar. She was stopped by a dark-haired woman halfway there. Her expression was pleasant—carefully so, he thought—as she leaned down to listen. A moment later she nodded, and stepped forward, before pausing and making her way to the front of the boat, where her parents were.

She spoke to them, nodded. Then she got her phone out of her dress pocket and began to type into it. She made her way down the entire boat, speaking to each and every person, her expression now of concentration as she tapped her phone.

Only when she reached the bar and spoke with the barman, showing him her phone, did Wyatt realise she'd started taking orders from everyone on the boat. He would have laughed if he weren't so surprised. Or if she weren't coming his way again, now speaking to the people on the opposite end of the bar.

One of the men said something to her and she laughed. His surprise moved up another notch. Who was this person? Certainly not the woman who had all but begged him to keep her from talking to people? Perhaps it was that alien again.

Or perhaps it was just her.

It reminded him of that night at the Christmas party. He'd spent pretty much his entire time there with Summer. At the end of it, he'd been so reluctant to say goodbye that he'd asked her out for coffee. She'd smiled at him—one of those heart-crushing genuine smiles she had; similar, he thought suddenly, to the one she'd given him moments ago—and told him she had somewhere else to be.

'Where?' he'd asked, desperate to stay in her company.

She'd tilted her head. 'Do you want to come with me?'

'Yes,' he'd answered immediately and that smile had widened, before she'd nodded and led him to the kitchen.

There, he'd helped her pack all the leftover food into containers that had been stacked in one of the cupboards. They'd loaded them into a van she'd hired, and had taken it to a shelter where people had known her by name.

That had been the moment he'd known he was a goner.

'Can I get anything for you, sir?' Summer asked, stopping in front of him and pulling him out of the past.

'I thought you already were,' he said dryly.

'I got distracted.'

'So it seems.' He paused. 'Sparkling water, please.'

'With lemon?'

'Just the water.'

'Okay.'

She widened her eyes before heading back to the bar, giving the other orders to the barman before taking the tray the man had set out and handing it out to the first half of the boat. She did the same with the second half of the boat. Then she returned the tray to the bar before taking their drinks.

'You okay?' he asked when she sat down and handed him his.

'Fine,' she replied. 'I was stopped before I could do ours. Figured I'd just do everyone.' She winced. 'You know what I mean.'

He laughed. 'Sure.' He took a sip of his water. 'You didn't have to though.'

'No,' she agreed. 'But this way it seems like I'm interacting with everyone without really doing so. Which keeps my mother happy and makes my father believe—'

She broke off, offering him an embarrassed smile before taking a sip of her own drink. He knew she hadn't meant to say the part about her father, and he had no intention of letting it go. But he would let her think that he did. He still had his one question, and he already knew what he was going to use it on.

'That wasn't the only reason you did it,' he told her. Gratitude flashed across her face like a shooting star. It was gone just as quickly, replaced by a careful expression.

'What do you mean?'

'You do things like that for people all the time.'

'No, I don't.'

'How about that time you paid for the groceries of the woman in front of you at the store?'

'She left her purse at home. It happens to everyone.'

'The beggar you gave your lunch to after he asked for money for a loaf of bread?'

'Which one?' She shook her head. 'Doesn't matter. Anybody would have done that.'

'Or that time you—'

'Wyatt,' she interrupted him. 'Surely you have better things to do than to repeat every good deed I've done in my life?'

He hid his smile behind the glass and watched the birds that flew over the river. He could have mentioned a lot more than he had, though he'd known she would stop him. It was as predictable as her helping people. Her generosity was rivalled only by her refusal to accept it as such.

That had been what had caught him that Saturday night at the party. The fact that she'd attended a lavish event that reeked of money and luxury, yet she'd thought of those without anything. Not only thought about them, but done something about it.

She was the most down-to-earth rich person he knew, and he'd come to know many of them in the nine years he'd built up his own wealth. She was better than even he was. That was saying something since he made sure the money he made went to helping the systems that had kept him alive when he'd been growing up.

Something inside him stilled at that thought, and he realised he needed to keep his head straight. He couldn't fall back into the man who'd spent a year falling in love with, marrying and then divorcing a woman. He'd tried that fantasy and it hadn't worked. Even realising it had him remembering that ball of pain that curled tighter and tighter into itself the more time he spent with Summer.

The time he spent remembering why he'd fallen in love with her in the first place. The time he spent watching her interact with people kindly, despite the way she felt about them. The time he spent being surprised by her, and delighted by her. The time he spent being attracted to her. Realising how perfect a match she'd been for him.

If only she'd felt the same way.

Just like that, the ball unfurled, spreading itself out in his chest and letting that pain and anger seep into his body.

CHAPTER SEVEN

WYATT STIFFENED BESIDE her. She looked over, catching her breath at the fierce expression on his face. It made his complicated features go from handsome to dangerous. It pulled at something low in her belly. Something that stretched out and purred for Dangerous Wyatt's attention.

She swallowed.

'What's wrong?' she asked, her voice hoarse.

He shook his head and she swallowed again, knowing that whatever had changed between them wouldn't get any easier if she pushed him for an answer.

She shifted, putting distance between them, but she could still feel heat radiating from his body. She could recognise it as anger, and she had no intention of putting herself in the firing line when she wasn't entirely sure what had caused it.

Though she knew it was her.

The rest of the boat trip was not as easy as the first half. She found herself looking for someone to talk to—*anything* to get away from the awkwardness happening beside her. But everyone who was available was far enough away from her that she'd have to move. Moving seemed like a concession of some kind, and she refused to concede. Even if she had no idea what she was conceding to.

Why did you have to have a wedding this weekend, Autumn? Summer asked her sister silently. She wished Autumn's bakery weren't as popular as it was. Then she felt bad, and immediately took it back. Her sister had worked her butt off to get the Taste of Autumn to where it was. Though that success wasn't a surprise. Autumn succeeded in almost everything she did. She was perfect like that.

What would Autumn have done if she'd been the one to find out about their father's affair? Would she have confronted him? Would he have asked her to keep it a secret? And would she have?

Summer stopped when the questions put a lump in her throat. When she found herself wishing it had been Autumn. She had no doubt Autumn would have done the exact right thing. She wouldn't have put herself on the outside while doing it either.

If it had been Autumn, Summer wouldn't have had a problem with Wyatt making her feel like an outsider, too. She would have put his desire to build the life he hadn't had growing up above her own hurt. Because she wouldn't have been hurt.

If it had been Autumn, Summer would have still been married.

She shut her eyes, fighting the heat of the tears that had been close ever since that conversation with her father. When she thought she'd succeeded, she opened her eyes, blowing out a small breath. But as she lifted her head, her mother looked back and caught Summer's gaze. Lynette frowned at whatever she saw on Summer's face, and suddenly the tears wouldn't stay where they were.

One trickled down her cheek, and her mother shifted forward. But Summer shook her head, offered her a smile, and then turned so that her body was facing Wyatt entirely.

'Summer?'

There was no longer danger on his face, but concern. Which made her tears want to come even faster, and she shook her head again, wiping voraciously at them before blowing out a breath and offering him a smile, too. She was suddenly immensely glad they were at the back of the boat. Not perfectly private, but enough that she didn't have to keep up with this ridiculous farce.

'You're crying,' he said softly. He brushed a thumb at a tear she'd missed.

'No, I'm not,' she corrected. 'I'm smiling. See.' She widened her smile.

His eyebrows rose. 'I don't think that expression is working as well as you think it is.'

She let out a small laugh. It sounded too much like a sob for her liking. 'A lot of things don't work as well as I think they should. As well as I would like them to.'

He studied her. 'What's wrong, Sun?'

It had been innocuous on her sister's part, using that nickname in front of Wyatt. They'd been at dinner with their parents and Autumn had used it. Summer hadn't even picked up on it, but Wyatt had asked about it after they'd given Autumn a lift home. Summer had explained it as quickly as she could.

He'd loved it. Said he felt the same way about Summer as Autumn did. Summer had no defences against it. And he knew it.

'No fair,' she said softly.

'What are you talking about?'

'Calling me that,' she said. 'You're not playing fair.'

There was a moment before he said, 'Like when you use my surname?'

'That's different.'

'How?'

'It just is.'

'Smooth.'

Summer gritted her teeth. 'Wyatt, I'm not playing a game. I'm—'

'What?' he interrupted. 'What are you doing, Sun? Because I can't see it. I don't think you can either.'

'I don't know what you're talking about.'

'But you do,' he disagreed. 'You must realise that asking me to be your *friend* today wasn't fair.'

'Now you're using my words against me.'

'Like you used what I told you about my parents against me?'

Her eyes widened. So did his.

'I'm sorry, I shouldn't have said that.'

'But you did,' she replied carefully. 'Clearly you feel it.' She paused. 'Do you feel it?'

'We shouldn't talk about this.'

'Or we should.'

'No,' he said, jaw clenched, 'we shouldn't.'

'Wyatt—'

'No, Summer,' he said in a tone inviting no discussion. 'This is not a conversation we need to have.' He met her eyes. 'It's too late. It's too late to matter.'

He repeated the words she'd told him the night before under the night sky, but he took no pleasure in doing it. Though he believed it.

What was the point in rehashing the circumstances around their break-up? It wouldn't change that they were broken up. As much as he wanted to believe that they could be friends, this boat trip had shown him why they couldn't be.

Friends couldn't be attracted to one another. They couldn't have the past hovering over them like an umbrella on a rainy day. They couldn't think about qualities that were appealing; they couldn't link those qualities to memories. To emotions.

Since all of that seemed inevitable for him around Summer, he knew they couldn't be friends.

And yet she only had to look at him, those brown eyes open wide, bright with emotion—exactly as she was looking at him now—and he seemed to forget all those reasons.

Thankfully, he didn't have to keep looking into those eyes when the captain announced the boat was once again at the marina. Since they had been sitting at the back, he and Summer got off first. He refused the crewman's help, and, despite himself, offered Summer his hand.

She looked between him and the crewman. Wyatt held his breath, as if her decision would affect the rest of his life. When she took his hand, he felt as if he'd won something. Even though the tingling in his hand had gone up his arm, straight to the most inconvenient places in his body, and told him it was not a competition.

Even though he'd just thought of all the reasons why it shouldn't be a game. Even though the fact that she'd asked for help meant nothing. Nor would it change anything. The time for change was over. She'd already made a decision that had changed everything.

Their divorce.

That decision had influenced the rest of his life. Not whose hand she took at the end of a boat trip.

'Thank you,' she said, letting go of his hand as soon as her feet were on the marina.

She brushed at that beautiful bright dress that stood out like a rainbow against her brown skin and looked at him. They stared at each other—heatedly, passionately, longingly, he didn't know—and she nodded her head to the side.

'We should probably get out of the way.'

'That would be nice, darling,' Lynette called from the boat.

Summer turned, laughed. But a blush crept up the elegant column of her neck, and there was a faint strain in her laughter. Seconds later, they both walked to an area a safe distance from the boat.

'This is getting complicated,' she said after a moment.

He angled his head, but she was looking straight ahead. Avoiding his gaze, he thought. Something about that pleased him.

It shouldn't.

I know. He nearly replied to the voice in his head. He

swallowed. He was slowly losing his mental stability. Because of it, he didn't reply to Summer.

'I'm not going to force you to keep to our deal,' she continued. 'I'll survive.'

'What if I want to keep to our deal?' he asked, even though the voice in his head was still screaming at him, asking him why the hell he wasn't taking the easy way out.

'Do you?' She looked at him now. He turned to face her.

'If you keep to your end.'

'One question?'

'Yes.'

She sucked her lip under her top row of teeth, nodded. 'Fine. But only if you stay by my side for the rest of the day. We don't have to talk,' she added. 'I just don't want to talk with anyone else.'

'Not even your mother?' Lynette asked, coming towards them.

Summer's face coloured, but she said, 'Are you always eavesdropping on me, Mother?'

'I think eavesdropping implies a level of secrecy. Or stealth. I've needed neither. You've been—' her gaze drifted over to Wyatt; something akin to satisfaction flared in her eyes '—distracted.'

The colour on Summer's face deepened. 'You're making me not want to talk with you.'

'But since I birthed you and your sister naturally, despite the repeated offers of a C-section, you will.'

'You don't get to hold that over my head when I'm pretty sure you put us all in danger with that decision,' she muttered, then said more loudly to Wyatt, 'I'll catch up with you at lunch. Keep me a seat.'

Amused, and desperately trying to ignore the pleasure that went through him at her request, he nodded and walked away. He made it two metres before Trevor fell into step beside him.

'Seems like you've cut Summer quite a bit of slack,' his mentor noted.

Wyatt felt his own colour rising. 'Just doing what you asked me to.'

'And a bit more,' Trevor said. It was all he said as they made their way back to the lodge.

Wyatt wasn't entirely sure how to reply to Trevor, so he didn't say anything. It was not the first time he'd chosen that option. In fact, he'd probably done it more often than not. Despite his relationship with Trevor—despite the respect and the loyalty—there had always been something inside Wyatt that was...careful.

He didn't know why that was. Trevor had never done anything to warrant it, and Wyatt couldn't blame it on the fact that Trevor was Wyatt's ex-father-in-law. He'd known Trevor long before he'd met Summer. Though, granted, those years hadn't exactly been a walk in the park.

No, they had been hard work. Wyatt had met Trevor when he had been in his final year of his degree at university. Trevor had singled him out in class for reasons Wyatt still didn't know to this day. After his blithe answer, Trevor had told him to stay for a moment after class. Wyatt had been braced for a scolding then. Had been prepared to brush it off just as he had all the others. Instead, Trevor had offered him a summer internship.

He hadn't been able to understand it, so naturally, he'd refused. But Trevor had asked him for one week in Wyatt's life. And because, back then, days had faded one into another, Wyatt had agreed. By the end of the week, Wyatt had fallen in love with the work. And the purpose.

Both had finally stilled some of the restlessness inside him. It had shunned the aimlessness he hadn't known had been there until it had disappeared. He'd decided to try harder at university, though it hadn't been easy after three years of messing around. When Trevor had asked him if he'd wanted to study further, he'd wanted to say yes. But he'd known his academic record would prevent that from happening.

Except he hadn't known the power of the Bishop influence then. He'd been granted entry to an Honours programme because Trevor had, as he'd put it, 'put in a good word'. Wyatt had no doubt that word had come with a serious donation to the university. But by then, he'd been able to recognise that the universe had given him an opportunity. He'd taken it.

He'd passed his Honours with distinction. Had got into the Masters programme on his own merit. He'd felt good—but indebted. There'd always been that distance in his and Trevor's relationship because of it.

Some of the distance had been bridged after he'd started dating Summer. More so after they'd married. He'd asked Trevor for a lot of advice during that time. About having a family; being a provider, though heaven knew Summer didn't need him to provide anything. Occasionally, he'd ask about Summer. He'd rarely got answers he agreed with then. Now he recognised it as a sign of a strained relationship.

His caution with Trevor had remained even in those moments. For the first time, Wyatt wondered what it meant.

'She asked me for a favour,' Wyatt blurted out suddenly. He was so shocked that he wasn't offended at Trevor's own surprise.

'She did what?'

'A favour,' Wyatt repeated. It was too late for him to stop talking now. 'You said I'm doing more than cutting Summer slack, but it's because she asked me a favour.'

'Summer did?'

'Yes.'

'Are you sure?'

Wyatt's spine stiffened. 'Yes, sir.'

Trevor's gaze swept over Wyatt. He sighed. 'I'm not

insulting you, Wyatt.' He paused. 'It's not like Summer to ask someone for a favour.'

Relaxing, Wyatt nodded. 'That's what I told her.'

'You told her that?' Trevor looked amused. 'What did she say?'

'She didn't like it.'

Trevor laughed. 'I don't imagine she did.' His smile faded after a moment. Wyatt watched with interest as Trevor's expression turned sad.

'Do you realise how much it must have taken from her to ask you for a favour?'

Wyatt stared straight ahead at the dining hall of the lodge, which they were metres away from. 'I do.'

'Do you, really?'

'Yes,' Wyatt answered solemnly. 'I'm her ex-husband.'

'No, I didn't mean that.' Trevor stopped walking. Wyatt did, too. 'Summer is…careful with people. Not unlike you,' Trevor said, quite simply stunning Wyatt. But he didn't stop long enough for Wyatt to work through it.

'I admit some of that comes from having money and influence. People tend to want to be in your life for those reasons, and not for the ones that count. Summer picked that up right away. She was shrewd when it came to who she let into her life. After—' Trevor broke off. Cleared his throat. 'Years ago she became even more careful, which was how we knew you were the right man for her. She let you in,' Trevor said, 'and that was significant to us.'

Trevor let that sit, then continued, 'If she asked you for a favour, it's significant, too. Particularly *because* you're her ex-husband.'

Wyatt swallowed, uncomfortable with the direction the conversation had taken. But he knew that Trevor was right. Perhaps that was why he'd softened at her request. Not perhaps, he corrected himself. That *was* why. He'd agreed because her asking had told him she trusted him. And if she trusted him…

Well, as Trevor said. It was significant.

'No more of this, I'm afraid,' Trevor said suddenly, saving Wyatt from having to answer. 'Here they come.'

Seconds later, Lynette and Summer joined him and Trevor. Lynette's face was tense, her eyes sweeping over her husband's as if she were looking for something. Wyatt felt Trevor stiffen; saw him look at Summer. She shook her head and looked down. And then Lynette was hooking into Trevor's arm, squeezing Wyatt's bicep, and the older couple was walking ahead, though the easiness he'd always seen between them was gone. Both he and Summer stood, watching them.

'What just happened?' he asked.

Summer's expression was stoic. 'Nothing.'

He studied her. 'We should get back,' he said after a while.

'Yeah. Yes,' Summer said.

And then they were walking up in silence, too.

CHAPTER EIGHT

SHE'D KNOWN THE conversation with her mother was coming. Had known it the moment her mother had made eye contact with her on that boat. *Might as well get it over with,* had been her philosophy when her mother had cornered her while she'd been speaking with Wyatt. Unfortunately, the conversation hadn't been as simple as the philosophy.

'Are you going to tell me how you've gone from not wanting to share a picnic basket with that man to sharing multiple intimate conversations with him? Not to mention a romantic boat cruise?' Lynette had asked shrewdly the moment they'd moved to a more private place.

'It wasn't romantic, Mother. There were thirty other people on that boat.'

'But there might as well have been none,' her mother replied. There was a pause. 'I take it your denial means no, you aren't going to tell me?'

'There's nothing to tell.'

'But he's upset you.'

The words were soft, concerned. Summer didn't respond. If she did, she'd have to talk about her marriage ending. Since her marriage ending had a lot to do with her husband trying to be like her father, she'd have to articulate why that was a problem. That would lead to the danger zone of her father's secret. Of keeping it.

No, it was best not to respond. Good thing she'd learnt that skill early on with the whole fiasco. Except that it had only added to the distant demeanour they'd already accused her of.

'Summer.'

'It's nothing, Mother.'

'Do not lie to me.'

Her throat thickened; her eyes burned. She didn't reply.

'Summer, darling…' Lynette sighed. 'When are you going to learn it's okay to confide in someone?'

A bark of laughter escaped from her lips. She almost covered her mouth from the surprise.

She cleared her throat. 'I'm sorry.'

Lynette sighed again. 'You can't keep running, my love.'

'I'm not running.'

'You are,' Lynette insisted gently. 'You have been for eight years.' Her mother's face suddenly became tight. She looked more her age than she ever had to Summer before. 'Your father and I hoped what happened… We hoped you wouldn't be affected like this.'

'Dad is concerned about this?' Summer asked, disbelief clear in her tone. 'Really?'

'Summer.'

This time her name was a warning.

'It's best if we don't talk about it,' Summer said, moving past her mother. A hand closed over her arm.

'You can't keep running.'

'But I have to!' Summer exclaimed. 'I can't talk about what happened. I have to keep running so I don't—'

She broke off, her heart beating hard in her chest. She took a breath.

'It'll be easier if you just let me go.'

She forced herself to look at her mother, whose expression was changing from confused to shrewd.

'You still love Wyatt.'

'What? *What?*' Her laughter didn't come as a surprise now. 'I do not.'

Ignoring her answer, her mother asked, 'Why did you end your marriage, Summer? And don't give me that nonsense about the two of you growing apart and focusing on your business,' Lynette said when Summer opened her mouth. 'Obviously that isn't true. Not after what I've witnessed this weekend.'

'You witnessed what we wanted you to witness,' Summer replied. 'We didn't want you and Dad to be distracted by our relationship during your anniversary weekend.'

Lynette studied her. 'You're lying,' she said with a perfect little scoff.

'I'm not.'

'You are. And you have been for—' Lynette broke off, her eyes widening. 'How have I not seen this?'

Summer nearly reached to her throat in an attempt to push her heart back down into her chest. Instead, she settled for that well-honed skill of not replying. It led to a long, awkward silence where her mother's eyes swept over Summer's face. She felt exposed by the searching, the studying. Felt as if her mother could see all the lies she'd been telling. The omissions she'd told herself weren't lies.

'Mom,' Summer said when the awkwardness became too much. 'We should go. They're going to miss you.'

'Okay,' Lynette said after a moment. 'Just answer me this.' She lifted her brows. Summer had no choice but to answer the unspoken question with a nod. 'Did you end your marriage because of your father's affair?'

Summer's tongue turned into lead. But the question was direct; there was no way she could pretend she hadn't understood. And heaven knew she was tired of lying.

'Wyatt admires Dad so much.' She spoke slowly, choosing her words carefully. 'He was turning into Dad. It made me feel...' She trailed off, unsure how to continue.

'Like me?' her mother asked.

'To some degree,' she allowed. 'More that he made me feel like...me. In our family.' She swallowed. 'Part of why I married him was because he had a way of making me feel different from what I was used to. I felt...understood.'

'Because we haven't.' Her mother's eyes were compassionate. 'Not for a long time.'

'No.'

'What changed?'

'I told you, he—'

'What happened,' her mother interrupted, 'that he went from being the man who understood you to being like your father?'

Her lips parted, her tongue lifted, all preparing to give Lynette an answer. Except she didn't have one. She didn't know what had changed. She only knew that something had.

'I don't know,' she told her mother honestly.

Lynette put her arm around Summer's shoulders. 'Perhaps now's the time for you to get some answers.'

Summer took a breath. 'Maybe.'

'Definitely.' There was a pause. 'If I can do it, you can, too.'

'Do— What are you talking about?'

Lynette dropped her arm, brushing her skirt with the back of her hand. 'There's more to this situation with your father than I previously thought. Or I allowed myself to think about,' Lynette corrected. 'We're going to fix that before the ceremony tomorrow.'

'No,' Summer said, panicking. 'No, I didn't say anything—' She broke off. 'There's nothing... I was...upset. I didn't mean to—'

'Summer.' Lynette took Summer's hand. 'I've known something hasn't been right in this family for a long time. I know you've been hurting.' She squeezed. 'I knew it had something to do with your father's actions, too. But I've ignored it for eight years because I didn't want to relive the nightmare of the hurt I went through when I found out.'

Lynette exhaled slowly. 'That was selfish. I left you alone with your hurt for far too long. I hoped you'd get over it. Clearly, there's more to get over than I thought. I'm going to find out what I've missed.'

'Please,' Summer whispered after a long while. 'Please, tell Dad I didn't say anything.'

She had no idea why she said it. Why it was important enough for her to say it. But she was relieved when her mother agreed and kissed her forehead. They walked to the dining hall in silence, and found Wyatt and Trevor waiting.

When her mother didn't offer her father the usual affectionate greeting, Summer saw the confusion on his face. Her parents exchanged a look, and Trevor looked at Summer in question.

Did you tell your mother?

She shook her head, looked down. It felt like decades later that they walked ahead, and her body loosened in relief. Just in time for her to evade Wyatt's question about the awkward interaction.

'I suppose the polite thing to do is to pretend not to notice how tense you are,' Wyatt said as they made their way to the dining hall. He angled a look at her. 'You know, how tense you are about *nothing*.'

She laughed softly, too tired to fight off her first instinct. 'So of course you're going to ask me about it.'

'I didn't say I was going to be polite,' he said with a sly half-smile. It faded. 'Are you okay?'

She heaved a sigh, pulling the hat from her head and patting her hair. 'Yeah. It's just been a hard day.'

He frowned.

'What?'

'You…answered me.'

'Don't act so surprised, Montgomery,' she said, rolling her eyes. 'You asked me a question; I answered.' Then she realised what she'd said. 'I'm sorry. I didn't mean to call you that.'

'Don't be sorry,' he said softly. 'I didn't say I didn't like it.'

'Oh.'

There was a pause, and thankfully she didn't have to

fill it when they reached the table. They were forced to sit in the only two vacant seats at the end. Her parents had wanted to sit next to one another at all meals, so they'd hired a long, rectangular table that extended wide enough in breadth for two seats to be at the end.

It was fine for them, since they were the anniversary couple. Though they probably regretted the decision now, she thought, taking in the tension between her parents. The seats were even more awkward for two ex-spouses. Especially after one spouse dropped a bomb on the other.

'I am surprised though,' Wyatt said after a moment, speaking quietly so that the guests closest to them wouldn't hear. 'You've been more cryptic this weekend than ever before.'

'And you thought I wouldn't be honest because of it?'

He gave her a look. 'The very definition of cryptic contradicts honesty.'

'I'm pretty sure cryptic means obscuring the truth. That's not the same as not being honest.'

'Isn't it?'

His eyes pierced through her. It was as if he knew about the conversation she'd had with her mother. As if he knew she'd realised keeping the truth from someone was the same as lying to them. But did he know that she'd kept something from *him*? Did he know about the affair? And how it had contributed to the end of their marriage?

For a second, she panicked. It took a long few minutes to realise she was overreacting. Her mind slowed down, giving her a moment to figure out what was happening.

When she'd asked for the divorce, she'd told Wyatt she needed to focus on her business. She hadn't mentioned that she'd much rather focus on their marriage. That she would have loved if he'd focus on it, too. But beyond asking her if she was sure, Wyatt hadn't done anything to indicate he wanted to fight for their marriage. In fact, he'd accepted the divorce so easily it was almost as if he'd…expected it.

Because of the pre-nuptial agreement he'd insisted on even though they'd eloped, things had been tied up fast. Just as quickly as Summer had found herself being a wife, she had been a divorcee.

'I don't think we should talk about this here,' she said quietly.

'No,' he agreed. 'Why talk about it here when you can postpone it till later and hope I forget?'

'I won't forget,' she promised. He looked at her. 'I haven't forgotten about the comment you made earlier about your parents.'

Wyatt's face immediately tensed. 'I didn't mean anything by that.'

'Now who's not being honest?' she asked lightly.

'Not fair.'

'I thought we already agreed things between us weren't fair?'

The waiter interrupted his answer by pouring them both a glass of champagne. Before he left, she got his attention.

'Sorry—is this non-alcoholic?'

'No, ma'am.'

'Could you bring us some?' she asked easily. 'Two glasses, please.'

'Of course.'

The waiter slipped away, and she looked back at Wyatt. There was gratitude in his eyes, but before he could say anything, one of her mother's friends, Pamela, who was sitting to their left, leaned over.

'No champagne for you, Summer?'

Summer smiled. 'Not today, no.'

'Any specific reason?'

'Like what?' she asked, frowning.

Pamela couldn't possibly know that she'd asked for non-alcoholic drinks because Wyatt's mother had been an alcoholic and he preferred not to drink. She hadn't wanted him to do it alone. It was always less conspicuous when two people weren't drinking, as opposed to one.

'Well, dear...'

Pamela's face turned knowing. After a few more minutes, Summer realised what she was talking about.

She burst out laughing.

'Oh, heavens *no*,' she said between peals of laughter. 'No, I'm not pregnant.'

'I don't see what's so funny about it.' The woman sniffed. 'You and Autumn are at that age where—'

Summer immediately stopped laughing. She had to stop herself from growling, too.

'I don't think that's appropriate to say,' Summer said with a stiff smile. 'Our childbearing abilities are no one's business but ours and the people we choose as our partners.'

Pamela blinked, her face splitting into a polite smile though her eyes were both embarrassed and annoyed.

'Of course, dear. You and Wyatt have seemed so close these last two days. And now both of you aren't drinking... I thought he wasn't drinking in solidarity.'

'Easy mistake to make,' Wyatt interjected, speaking for the first time. He sent her a look: *Let me handle this.* 'Summer and I made the decision not to drink when we were married, it's true. But since we've fallen into a friendship and the habit has stuck.'

There was a brief pause, during which Summer noticed they'd caught the attention of the couple sitting opposite Pamela. The Van Wyks were old school friends of her father's, who were apparently also interested in her childbearing state, taking their disappointed faces into account.

'I swear I saw you drink a glass of champagne at the picnic,' Mrs Van Wyk said with a shake of her head.

'Really?' Wyatt offered her his most charming smile. Summer was willing to believe anything he said next herself. 'Are you sure?'

'Oh, yes. She took the bottle—'

'You know,' Summer said, deliberately taking the baton in the imaginary relay race she and Wyatt were running. He had more to lose than she did. 'It's entirely possible that I *am* pregnant.'

She nudged Wyatt's shoulder with her own, trying not to laugh at the expression on his face. 'Friends sometimes do favours for other friends,' Summer added, winking at Pamela, since she'd asked the intrusive question in the first place. 'Anyway, we'll know in about two weeks. That's when I'm supposed to get my period.'

Summer made sure her face was perfectly pleasant and innocent, ignoring the shocked faces of her listeners. Saving them all from having to speak, the waiter arrived with two new champagne glasses, which he filled with the non-alcoholic champagne before removing the other glasses from the table.

Summer stood then, because, for the life of her, she wanted to make her mother feel good if only for that moment. It was a bonus that it meant the people around her would stop prying into things that were none of their business.

She picked up her fork, did the cliché tap on her now non-alcoholic glass of champagne, and prepared to give a toast.

She was amazing. Somehow, Summer had managed to put someone in their place politely, ensuring that they would never ask her—or anyone else, he bet—the dreaded *When are you having children?* question again. She'd also managed to refer to friends with benefits, sex, and her period while she did, all the while being perfectly respectful.

She absolutely deserved being called amazing.

He sat back as she clinked her glass, noting the way her fingers gripped the stem and knife tightly. It told him she didn't want to be giving a toast, and made him wonder why she was.

'Thank you, everyone,' Summer said with a smile that made her look as if she were a harmless little kitten.

Personally, he missed the claws.

'We're all here to celebrate my parents' anniversary. Thirty years together, no less.' She paused. 'Normally, I would leave this kind of thing to Autumn. Oh, don't pretend to be surprised by that,' she told the guests, and they laughed. 'We all know who the more charming sister is.'

Another wave of laughter went around the table, though Wyatt didn't see what was funny about it. He was perfectly charmed by Summer.

'But I couldn't let the second day of our celebration go by without at least saying on behalf of all of us—particularly from my sister and me—congratulations Mom and Dad. Your love for one another is beautiful.'

She looked directly at her parents. Though his gaze had been on her before, Wyatt now looked at Lynette and Trevor. Both of them looked more touched than such a toast should have warranted, though there was tension there, too. He couldn't explain any of it, yet Wyatt wasn't surprised.

'Here's to another thirty years.'

Summer lifted her glass, tilted it towards her parents, and sipped. Everyone at the table followed. Summer lowered back into her chair and let out a shaky breath. She immediately looked around, but the rest of the guests had turned their attention elsewhere. Except for him, of course, and she rolled her eyes when their gazes met.

'Glad that's over with.'

'So I see.' He angled his head. 'This is hard for you.'

She swallowed. 'Well,' she said with a strained smile, 'I wouldn't have minded some alcohol.'

'Why?' he asked, ignoring her comment. 'Why is this hard for you? I've never seen you struggle like this before.'

'I—I've never struggled like this before,' she admitted. 'At least not for other people to see.'

The sincerity, the pain in her eyes made him want to know more almost as much as he wanted to change the subject. Because he was keeping that as the question he wanted to ask her, he focused on the latter.

'Thank you,' he said sincerely. 'For doing what you did with the champagne. You didn't have to.'

She waved a hand. 'It's not like I'm a big drinker anyway.'

'You used to enjoy a glass of wine now and then, if I recall correctly. And—' he lowered his voice '—you did drink that champagne yesterday.'

She took her napkin and flapped it open, spreading it over her lap. It was another few seconds before she replied.

'I needed the courage yesterday,' she said, sending him a sly look.

His lips twitched, but he didn't smile. 'I don't think so. You're one of the bravest people I know.'

Her hands pressed against the napkin in her lap. 'I don't know what you're talking about.'

'You know exactly what I'm talking about. Starting a business outside of the Bishop name takes courage.'

'You can hardly call—'

'Standing up for someone when you don't have to takes courage.'

'You did it, too,' she said, brushing off his compliment. He wasn't surprised. She tended to do that. 'When you tried to save me from Pamela—' now her voice dropped '—and her inquisition.'

'I was offering you help because you were helping me out.'

'No, you weren't,' she said with a roll of her eyes. 'You were helping because that's what you do. You help people.'

He frowned, unable to reconcile that view of himself with his own. When had he ever helped anyone else? His entire life had been about trying to help *himself* out of the situations his parents' decisions had got him into.

'Wyatt,' she said on an exhalation of air, 'from what you've told me…' She hesitated. 'Most of your childhood was trying to make sure you and your mother were okay. You helped her even though you shouldn't have been responsible for that. You shouldn't be surprised by that.'

Except that he *was* surprised. When he and Summer had still been together, they'd never had a conversation like this. The night he'd told her about his parents had been tense and quick. He'd said what he'd needed to say and that had been that. He hadn't given her the opportunity to ask any questions; she hadn't tried. Then they'd pretended it hadn't happened—at least, they'd never spoken about it again—and so of course he'd never heard her opinion about how he'd taken care of their family after his father had left.

And how he'd had to make sure no one had known about his mother's alcohol problem. His mother had made that clear.

'Keep our business private, Wyatt,' she'd said with that mean look she got on her face when she was drunk. 'As long as I'm alive, we'll be okay.'

Which, he supposed, had been the reason for his *help*. He'd made sure nothing happened at school to make anyone suspect his mother had a problem. He hadn't invited friends over in case they'd see her drunk; he hadn't participated in after-school activities in case he got home and his mom had passed out. He'd been a star pupil at school, then he'd come home and made sure his mother kept breathing.

He'd done that for four years until he'd come home later than usual because of a compulsory school event. He'd found her passed out in her own vomit. That was when social services had become involved. After that, his mother had been in and out of rehab—had been sober and drunk almost as many times—and he'd been bounced back and forth between home and foster care.

How could Summer see *that* as helping?

His hand fisted on his knee. Moments later, Summer's hand curled over his, coaxing his fingers to relax. He looked down at it, then looked up into her eyes. They locked gazes, and he felt that tug in his chest. The one that told him she saw him. She understood. That was what had convinced him taking a chance on Summer would be worth it.

Look how that had turned out.

He broke the contact—of their gazes and their hands— and focused on the starter that had been placed in front of him.

'If it makes you feel less awkward,' she said, looking at her own food, 'you didn't help as much as you could have when we were married.'

'What?'

She offered him a smile he knew was meant to show him she was teasing. But her next words made that hard to believe.

'You were never home to help.'

He had no answer to that, so he left the conversation there. But all through his meal, he couldn't let it go. Then he remembered he didn't have to. He could ask her. Not now, he thought, nodding when the woman to his right offered him a smile when he looked up and directly into her gaze.

When she turned away, Wyatt leaned over to Summer and whispered into her ear.

'Do you want to take a walk on the beach after lunch?'

Her face angled towards him, confusion straining the beautiful lines of it, but she nodded.

'Sure.'

CHAPTER NINE

'Maybe we didn't think this through,' Summer commented after they'd taken their shoes off, and were forced to put them back on when the sand burnt their feet.

That was what she'd been talking about when she'd said it, but she realised the words worked for agreeing to walk with Wyatt at all. Particularly when her control had slipped and she'd told Wyatt he'd never been home to help her.

She'd known something had happened while they'd been looking at each other, their hands touching. It was probably the reason she'd lost control. Then his expression had gone cautious. Which would have been fine. They were divorced, after all. But the problem was she recognised that expression from long before their divorce. He'd worn it throughout their short relationship.

So why did it sting so much now?

It was the universe telling her to turn around and run away from him, she thought. Except, as it always was with him, she'd lost her ability to listen to warning signs and logic. To try and protect herself. Knowing *that* should have had her not only running, but sprinting.

Instead, she was walking on the beach with him.

'If you don't mind walking in your shoes until we get to that cliff—' her gaze followed to where he was pointing '—there's shade over there.'

'Sure.' When it sounded too eager, she cleared her throat. 'I mean, I'm in if you are.'

He gave her a strange look but nodded...

And held out his hand as if it were the most natural thing in the world.

She took it, as if it were the most natural thing in the world.

Oh, no, the sane part of her mind groaned, reminding her of how awkwardly tense things had been between them during lunch. Pamela and the Van Wyks had given up on making conversation with them. Summer hadn't minded, but it had made the silence between her and Wyatt more awful. She wasn't sure where the silence had come from, or why, after it, he'd asked to walk on the beach with her.

Or why she'd agreed, and was now walking on the beach with him, holding his hand.

She angled her face up to the sun, hoping the heat of it would slide into her body and soothe the parts that were jumping up and down with protest posters in hand. Or perhaps she was hoping for a measure of the peace she'd felt earlier that day on the boat. Though she wasn't sure whether that had come from the sun, or from the fact that things between her and Wyatt had seemed less complicated then.

She almost snorted.

'What?' Wyatt asked from beside her.

'What what?'

The side of his mouth pulled up. 'You looked amused with yourself.'

'I am,' she said, grasping at the first appropriate thing she could think of as to why. 'I was thinking about what I did in there. With Pamela.'

The other side of his mouth curved up, too. 'It was spectacular.'

Summer laughed lightly. 'Don't be too impressed. I've had years of practice.'

'It did seem to have that experienced kind of flair,' he agreed. Now she did snort. They took a few more steps before he asked, 'Was it all innocent, though? Telling her off?'

'Sure.'

'Why don't I believe you?'

'Because you've never been polite enough to accept my

answers at face value.' *Except our divorce.* The thought gave her pause, but she set it aside for later. 'There might have been a sincerer motive behind my impoliteness.'

'You weren't impolite.'

'I'm sure my mother will disagree with you once she hears of this,' she said dryly.

'And she will hear about it?'

'Almost certainly.' She glanced at him. 'You've been in these circles long enough to know nothing you say ever stays with the person you've said it to.'

His eyes met hers. 'That's not true.'

Her lips parted, and she slowly let the air release through them, as if she'd been deflated. She swallowed. Fortunately, she was saved from giving an answer when he asked, 'Are you worried about your biological clock?'

She blinked, then burst out laughing, just as she had with Pamela. *'No.'* She tilted her head. 'I've actually never given having children that much thought. I suppose it hasn't been one of my main priorities.'

'Hmm,' he said. 'I probably should have known that, considering I was your husband.'

She looked over. 'Do you want kids?'

'Not sure.' He gave her a dry look. 'I've never thought about it.'

She laughed. 'Oh, I see how it is. I'm a woman, so I must have spent all my time dreaming about the perfect wedding and the perfect family?'

'Didn't you?'

'My first—and only,' she added, 'wedding was arranged in the space of a week and happened in court. Does that sound like someone who imagined their wedding?' She didn't wait for an answer. 'There's no such thing as a perfect family.'

'Not even the Bishops?'

He'd asked the question deliberately, and something shifted inside her. She knew it because she hesitated—

even though her instinct was to lie. From the moment she'd heard about his parents, Summer had recognised that thing pushing Wyatt to work as hard as he did was an idea. An illusion. He wanted the ideal life; the life he thought Trevor had. But there was no such thing as an ideal life. And for once, she wanted to be honest about it.

Even if she had to tarnish the illusion.

'Especially not the Bishops,' she answered.

Emotion tried to claw its way from her heart up to her throat. All of her bravado faded, and she changed the topic.

'That hasn't stopped Autumn from wanting one. A family,' she said, when her mind told her her transition might have been too abrupt for him to follow. 'A wedding. It's always been part of her life plan.' She paused. 'Maybe that's why she loves baking for weddings so much.'

They reached the shady section, and she kicked off her shoes before she let him help her sit down. Moments later, they were lying on their backs, their feet in the sun and the rest of their bodies in the shade, staring up at the blue sky. Something about it made her feel nostalgic.

'I remember Autumn used to make these scrapbooks of what she wanted her wedding to look like.' She dug her heels into the sand, then pushed her feet out before sliding them back together, bringing new sand into the holes she'd created. She repeated the motion. 'And she used to use literally anything she could find in the house and pretend it was a baby.'

She thought of the time Autumn had used a two-and-a-half-kilogram sugar packet as her baby, had punctured it by accident, then fallen asleep with the packet in her bed and woken up to ants.

Her *I'm a mommy* game had been confined to dolls and teddy bears after that.

'Anyway, she's been a bit more sensitive to things like what Pamela said after the whole thing with Hunter exploded in her face.'

She placed the back of her hand onto her forehead, letting the other one slide out next to her. On the opposite side of Wyatt. She didn't need any accidental touching. As it was, she was already struggling with him being close.

With him being close in that white shirt that made him so devastatingly handsome.

'I heard about their break-up.'

'I'm not surprised. Bishop Enterprises is a hotbed for gossip.'

'Actually, your father told me.'

'Oh.' Her feet stopped moving. 'Of course he did.'

'That's hard for you to hear?' he asked softly. She could tell that he was looking at her.

'No.'

'He hasn't ever told me anything about you, if that's what you're worried about,' Wyatt said stiffly.

Her head turned before she could stop it.

'I'm not. I wouldn't have cared if you'd known something about me,' she said, testing it out in her head to be sure. She was. 'Besides, he wouldn't have known anything I didn't want you to know anyway.'

'You would have kept something from him because of me?'

'No.'

She wanted to roll over so she could brush away the line between his brows. Instead, she looked back up to the sky. When the silence stayed for much longer than she was comfortable with, she went back to talking about Autumn.

Using her problems to avoid your own. Nice.

'The break-up wasn't easy on Autumn,' Summer said, when the thought made her feel nauseous. 'I thought I'd take one for the team.'

'You're a good sister,' he noted, though his voice sounded strange. 'I'm sure you told her she has more than enough time to have a perfect wedding and family.'

'I have.' She cleared her throat. His *good sister* comment had done something to her insides. Probably because she didn't believe she was a good sister. Good sisters didn't keep secrets.

'She doesn't believe me.' Summer frowned slightly. 'It's hard to be somewhere other than where you thought you would be at a certain age. Especially for someone like Autumn. Her entire life's followed a plan.'

'Where did you think you'd be at your age?' he asked after a pause.

Her lips curved. 'Pretty much where I am right now.'

'Divorced?'

She grabbed a fistful of sand and threw it at his midriff, almost smiling when he twisted his body with a laugh.

'I was *kidding*.'

'Sure you were,' she said, giving him the stink eye. As he chuckled and brushed the sand off his shirt, she said, 'No, I did *not* imagine I'd be a divorcee at the age of twenty-eight.'

She hesitated briefly before settling on telling him the truth. 'Honestly? I thought I'd be somewhere in the management of Bishop Enterprises.'

He turned over onto his side, resting his head on his hand. 'Which is not where you are right now.'

'I'm in management,' she reminded him.

'Yeah, but it's not the family business.'

'No,' she agreed. 'It's not.'

His eyes searched her face. 'Why didn't you tell me you wanted to work for Bishop Enterprises?'

'I told you why last night. I thought it would mean more to build something for myself.' She took a breath. Answered his real question. 'It had nothing to do with you. And it wouldn't have changed things between us.'

He didn't reply.

'You more than anyone should know how important building is,' she said softly, turning to face him and mirroring his position. 'You've built an entire life for yourself. *By* yourself.'

He stared at her, then turned onto his back. Since she'd used the trick herself, she knew he was trying to avoid looking at her.

'Sometimes I find myself asking if that was worth anything.'

'What do you mean?'

'I've built and I've built but… I still don't have what I thought I would.'

Seeing the opportunity, she bit her lip. Sucked in air before diving in.

'Maybe… Maybe it's because what you thought you'd have wasn't realistic.'

He wanted to ask her what she meant, except that he already knew. At least in part. Having this conversation with her proved how unrealistic his wants were. And how he could never truly have what he wanted.

The opportunity to have these conversations with her whenever he wanted to. The pleasure of being the person she shared her thoughts and dreams with. The ability to listen to her laugh whenever he wanted to. To kiss her whenever he wanted to.

'It's not unrealistic because it's you,' Summer said, studying him. 'It's not realistic for anyone.'

'That's not true. It was realistic for your father.'

'No,' she said, her expression tight and pained. 'It's not. My father isn't—'

'It doesn't matter, Summer,' he interrupted.

'It *does* matter. This is part of what—' She broke off when he moved, staring incredulously when he stood. 'You're leaving?' she asked him. 'Wyatt, you're—'

Now she'd broken off because he'd lowered and scooped her into his arms, and was determinedly walking to the ocean. At least, that was what he wanted her to think…

'What are you doing?'

'Stopping you from talking,' he told her. He was rewarded with widened eyes and a curse so dirty he couldn't help but grin.

'I swear, if you throw me into the ocean, you will live to regret it.'

'I won't throw you into the ocean,' he assured her. 'I'll gently place you—'

She interrupted him with another curse.

'Wyatt,' she said through her teeth, 'please, for the love of all that is good in this world, put me down.'

He stopped abruptly and did as she asked, enjoying the surprise on her face.

She sniffed. 'Thank you. I assure you this was the best decision you could have made.'

'I'm not sure I agree with that,' he told her. 'But at least it gives you the opportunity to run.'

'To run? What does—?'

'Three—'

'Wyatt?' she asked, her eyes wide, which told him she'd finally comprehended what he'd meant. He didn't think she knew it, but she'd taken a step back.

'—two—'

'Wyatt Montgomery, don't you dare think this will scare me into—'

'One!'

She shrieked and began to run, and, with a grin, he followed.

Perhaps he would look back at this moment and wonder if he'd really wanted to avoid talking about his unrealistic dreams so much that he'd picked her up. Perhaps he'd wonder what had possessed him to put her back down and start chasing her. Or perhaps he'd just look back at this moment and see himself having fun for the first time in for ever.

Hell, he felt like a kid, running around freely, chasing someone he liked. Except he didn't know if that was true. He'd never had the opportunity to run around freely or play games when he'd been a kid. He'd been too busy taking care of his mother. Too busy being responsible and figuring out which steps he needed to take to get them a life she'd denounced as unrealistic.

Stability and security wouldn't have been real for him and his mother anyway. He'd tried hard during his teen years to get them there. To create a routine for them every time she left rehab. Even after her first few relapses and he'd begun to anticipate the moment he'd find her drunk again. Even after he would and he'd be forced back into foster care until she was sober again.

He tried again—and again and again—to turn their lives into something. He'd even thought he'd succeeded, when he'd turned eighteen. The routine had finally stuck. Things had been steadier. Weeks without drinking had turned into months, and he'd let himself believe it would be different this time.

He'd let himself believe it was safe to go off to university with the part-bursary, part-loan he'd taken out to live on campus and study. He'd returned to a 'For Sale' sign on the front lawn with his mother nowhere to be found.

He'd called the estate agent, who'd told him his mother had chosen to sell the very month he'd left for university. The house had been cleared out of everything, including his own things, and the agent had been in contact with his mother through a lawyer. When he'd called the lawyer, he'd got a bunch of nonsense about attorney/client privilege and he'd got the picture. His mother hadn't wanted him to contact her. She'd purposefully made it hard so he wouldn't.

He hadn't. He still didn't know where she was.

The experience should have taught him that, no matter how hard he tried, he'd never have the true stability and happiness he wanted: a family. People who cared for him unconditionally. Who wouldn't leave him.

Yet he'd still allowed himself to hope with Summer.

He'd allowed himself to trust her. And just like his mother, Summer had shown him what a mistake hoping, trusting had been. So obviously, too. She'd been just like his father, pulling away from Wyatt first, then leaving. Because there were conditions to her love. She wanted someone who didn't come from a broken home. Someone who fitted her idea of the man she should be with.

He'd thought that idea was her father. When he'd sensed her pulling away, Wyatt had tried to be like Trevor. In some stupid way, he'd thought it would be enough to keep her from leaving.

Now he wondered if he'd got that wrong. And asked himself whether he'd ever learn.

He looked at her, running ahead of him, skirt flapping around her shapely legs, hair tumbling out of its confines at the nape of her neck. He pushed forward, enjoying her shriek, feeling it smooth something inside him even though he was sure she'd caused that something to crease.

Today wouldn't be the day he learnt anything.

He caught up to her easily, then ran a few metres ahead before turning to face her.

With a frown, she stopped, too, and said a little breathlessly, 'Aren't you supposed to do something once you catch me?'

'No.'

She tilted her head, waiting for more. But he got distracted by the curls that had escaped and were now wildly framing her face.

'Wyatt?' she said impatiently. 'Are you going to tell me why you've stopped playing a game you started?'

'Okay.' He frowned, trying to formulate a valid reason. 'It felt inappropriate.'

'What did?'

'Picking you up, then setting you down and chasing you.'

'What are you talking about?'

He sighed. 'I'm your ex-husband. What I just described could easily have been a plot to a horror movie.'

'You're my friend,' she corrected, 'and we were having fun.'

'Fun?' he repeated. 'You swearing at me and then running away was *fun*?'

'Well—yeah.' She pushed absently at the curls of hair that had bounced over her forehead. 'Weren't you having fun?'

His lips curved. 'Yeah, I was.'

'Okay.' She nodded, putting her hands on her waist. 'Okay. That's fine.' He wasn't sure who she was talking to. 'That's perfectly fine. We're allowed to have fun with one another.'

He smirked.

'Even if the fun came because you wanted to change the subject of a conversation we were having.'

His smirk died a swift death.

'I think we should get back. They'll start to wonder about us.'

'So let them wonder,' she replied, moving closer to him. 'You can't keep running, Wyatt.'

'I don't have to think about why you left if I keep running,' he said, the words slipping off his tongue. He couldn't bring himself to regret them.

Her expression tensed. 'My priorities changed.'

'Right after you found out about my parents,' he retorted, the anger he'd felt moments ago reigniting.

Their eyes met. It felt as if a flare shot up and into the sky.

'Yes,' she said after what felt like an eternity. 'I found out about your parents and I realised that I would never be what you wanted.'

'You… No,' he said with a shake of his head. 'You realised I wouldn't be what *you* wanted.'

'What? No.' She paused. 'That's what you think?'

'You started pulling away from me after that.'

'Because I realised I wasn't what you wanted, Wyatt,'

she repeated. 'You told me about your parents and I realised all the work you were putting into your life... It was so you could have a life I could never give you.'

He shook his head, unable to speak.

'I don't blame you.'

'But you did,' he said automatically. 'You left.'

'Because the life you want doesn't exist,' she cried. 'I couldn't watch you strive for something that isn't real.'

'Why didn't you just tell me?'

Her eyes searched his face. 'You're angry. I'll tell you—'

'Summer,' he said, his voice low, 'why didn't you tell me?'

There was a long pause.

'It gave you purpose,' she told him softly. 'Before you met my father you didn't have that and your life then...' Her voice faded. She cleared her throat. 'I wasn't going to be responsible for pushing you back into a life that made you miserable.'

His mind raced at the new information. There was too much of it, and too many emotions accompanying it, and yet he knew she wasn't telling him everything.

'There's more.'

She lifted both her hands and placed them on either side of his face. 'Yes.'

'Tell me.'

'I can't.'

His jaw locked. But then her fingers moved, resting over the swell of it, lingering at where the muscles tensed, kneading them gently. Almost without realising it, he relaxed. Seconds later her hands lowered to his chest.

They were shaking.

'It was never because you weren't what I wanted,' she said in a voice that did the same. 'You silly man.'

He almost laughed. 'What was I supposed to think?'

'You were supposed to accept what I told you at face value.'

'That you were too busy for a marriage?'

She lifted a shoulder. 'You were,' she admitted. 'You were so busy trying to build your ideal life that you didn't have time for your wife.'

'Summer,' he said, his voice hoarse.

She didn't reply, and he lost his mind.

'I thought… It doesn't matter.' He shook his head. 'You were always going to leave. I just pushed you to do it sooner.'

Her eyes widened, before her face crumpled in emotion that broke his heart. Which made no sense. Her *actions* had broken his heart. Not her emotions. He stepped away from her when he couldn't make sense of it. Away from the heat of her hands, which felt as if it had seeped into his chest, reviving parts of him he'd thought had died when she'd left.

'You can't really believe that,' she said, folding her arms around herself. It made him angry, though heaven only knew why.

'It's the truth.' His voice was hard; it was the only way he'd get through it. 'Everyone leaves. My father left. Pulled away like you did before, too. Though thinking back now, I shouldn't have been surprised.' He took a breath. 'And my mother…'

He trailed off when his throat tightened. Besides, talking about her would only serve to upset him more.

'Those were the two people who were supposed to believe in me the most. And they gave up on me.' His eyes met hers. 'Maybe I could explain it by saying they didn't get to choose who I was. Maybe they didn't want me because they didn't like me.' He swallowed down the pain. 'But *you* chose me. You chose me, Summer, and then you left. Just like they did. Even though I tried—'

Suddenly his face was clasped between her hands again and she was staring at him intently.

'Don't you dare say I didn't believe in you, Wyatt Montgomery,' she said sternly. 'I did. I do.'

'But you still left.'

'So you wouldn't go back to the life you had before.'

'That wouldn't have happened.'

'It would have,' she said, eyes bright. 'If I'd stayed, I would have had to tell you...' She swallowed. 'It was the best thing for you, Wyatt. And it was because I believe in you.' She held his gaze. 'I would never give up on you.'

His heart felt as if it had been dipped into warm water after battle. He was stung, and bruised, and yet somehow still felt comforted.

'Okay.'

'Okay?' she asked. He nodded. She dropped her hands. 'This is so exhausting.' She blinked. 'Not you,' she said. 'Well, not entirely—' She broke off. 'I'm not making sense.'

'No.'

She let out a little huff of air, and her lips parted. For some inexplicable reason his eyes dipped to her throat as she swallowed.

His gaze lifted to meet hers. 'But that's okay. For now.'

She nodded, and the air between them changed. A pang went through his body as if it had recognised a piece of itself that had gone missing.

She edged closer to him. 'Really? Or are you just saying that?'

'No,' he said, and found it to be true. 'It's enough for now.'

'Okay.'

They stood like that for the longest time, looking at one another, barely any space between them...

And seeing each other for what he thought was the very first time.

So when she moved even closer to him, standing on her toes, bringing her lips a breath away from his, he answered by dipping his head to hers.

CHAPTER TEN

SHE'D BRACED FOR the contact, so much so that when their lips touched, she felt nothing—heard nothing—except for her heart pounding. She wondered if she'd see it beating in her chest if she looked down. Or if she'd be able to see it beat outside her chest since it felt exposed.

Then everything faded except for the feel of his lips on hers.

They were soft, tentative, and so wonderfully real. She felt the contact in her heart and down to her toes and, for some cliched reason, right to her soul. His lips began to move against hers and something sparked. Lust, desire. Whatever it was, it had her body sighing in relief. With pleasure. She had begun to worry the only thing this kiss would result in were emotions.

Then she felt as if she'd been plunged into the coldest depths of the ocean beside them. Her skin shot out in gooseflesh—each cell of it hyper-alert, hyper-sensitive—so that when his hands rested on her waist, she felt it throughout her body.

She paid no attention to the crashing of the waves next to them, or to the breeze that somehow both smelled and tasted like the ocean. She didn't think of the sun beating down on them, or how her toes were sinking into the sand.

No, there were only his lips on hers; his hands now roaming her skin; and the warmth of his tongue sliding against her own.

It felt as if she were a tourist in a different country, homesick and finally seeing someone from back home. It felt as if she'd been alone for years and were finally being reunited with her closest friends. And yet despite that, there was uncertainty. Caution. She didn't know whether it came from him or from her; either way, she was sure it came from curiosity.

Curiosity about whether anything had changed since they'd last kissed. About whether the emotions—the deep and raw feelings they'd shared with one another—would have any effect on the mating of their mouths.

When he moved closer, her body sighed *yes* and moulded itself to his. The uncertainty, caution, curiosity faded.

Her hands slid up, over his chest, and back down again, savouring the feel of his muscles beneath her fingers. When she'd seen him in that white shirt, she'd thought him handsome. It had hit her in the stomach, really, and she'd vaguely wondered what he'd have done if she'd gone into his arms before she could stop herself. Then she'd been distracted and she hadn't had to actively stop herself from being tempted by that face. By that body.

But she wasn't distracted any more.

She opened the buttons of his shirt at the middle of his torso, moaning when it gave her access to his skin. The moan came again when he deepened the kiss, and she was lost in the sensation of their tongues tangling and the pleasure and heat it had tumbling down her body.

They stayed like that for what felt like for ever. Kissing. Exploring. And though she knew her legs weren't working any more and that he was holding her up, she still kissed; she still explored.

Finally, they broke apart. And they stood there.

Breathing.

Standing.

Until finally he said, 'Are you okay?'

Her heart, which up until that point had still been thumping in her chest, melted. His own emotions were likely up in the air about the kiss, but he was still asking whether she was okay.

That was the thing about Wyatt. He never did put himself first. He'd put his mother before himself when he'd been growing up. After his rebellious years at university, he'd put her father and the Bishop business first. For a brief—and, yes, wonderful—time, he'd put her first. Then, the idea. The illusion.

He was hurting himself by doing it. By putting himself second. His mother; her father; herself; the idea... They were all unreliable. They weren't worth prioritising. Not even her.

Wyatt had already found that out with his mother. With her. If Summer told him about her father, Wyatt would realise it about Trevor, too. And the idea would unravel naturally, as he seemed to have linked it to her father...

Still, even after all they'd shared before that kiss, she couldn't bring herself to tell him the truth. Even after she'd repeated her mother's words to him about running, *she* was still running. From this. From hurting him.

Even if it meant hurting herself in the process.

She stepped back. 'I'm fine.'

'Are you sure?' he asked, his voice not giving away any of the emotion he must have been feeling.

'Perfect.' She cleared her throat when the word came out strangled. 'I'm just... I'm thinking about tonight. About the dance. The disco. Whatever.'

Oh, no, she was rambling. That never ended well.

But she was still talking.

'I don't particularly want to go. Not because of this,' she added quickly, 'but I... My parents... It's complicated.'

There was a long pause.

'So don't go.'

'Do you know who my mother is? She will find me and drag me to that disco.'

'What if I cover for you?' He stuffed his hands into his pockets.

'You—you'd do that for me?'

He lifted his shoulders.

'You don't have to, Wyatt.'

'I know.' His eyes met hers, which made her realise that he'd been avoiding looking at her since they'd stopped kissing. 'I want to.'

'You want to cover for me? Or you don't want me to go?'

She winced at the accusation in her tone.

'What do you want, Summer?' he asked, though the question was heavy and didn't at all feel as if he was asking about the dance. 'Do you want me to cover for you, or do you want to go?'

She studied him. And realised what he wanted her to say.

'Cover for me. Please. Thank you.'

She turned on her heel and left.

He'd offered to cover for Summer for his own selfish reasons. He knew it; she knew it. And she'd chosen to let him cover for her because of it.

It had taken him less than a minute to realise that after she left. It had taken more time to realise he had to come up with a reason why Summer wasn't at her parents' dance. And that he'd have to spend the dance mingling when that was the last thing he felt like doing.

But he couldn't bail, too, regardless of how tempting the prospect was. He made his way down to the private beach that would be used for the dance. It was on the opposite side of the lodge to where his cabin was, and would be the venue for the vow renewal ceremony, too.

He shouldn't have been surprised when he walked into the large room, then. When he looked through glass doors out onto a patio that opened to the most idyllic stretch of beach he'd ever seen.

The patio and beach had been decorated for the evening's event. Colourful lights had been draped around pillars; both those supporting the patio, as well as the makeshift ones in the sand forming a dance floor. A bar stood to one side of the dance floor, lined with coconuts he assumed held alcohol. Considering the number of people on the dance floor who were swaying, holding their coconuts tightly, he was confident in that assumption.

The beach section was uncovered and open under the moonlight, which somehow made it romantic. He hadn't expected that. Or perhaps he was projecting how he'd felt the night before. When he and Summer had stood under the moonlight on that bridge, the sound of the ocean—

He stopped his thoughts in their tracks. He had to stop thinking about her like this. It was a mistake to indulge in fantasies about her. It had been a mistake to kiss her and discover that those fantasies had a foundation. Because she still wasn't telling him the whole truth.

Though what she had told him hadn't painted him in the best light. He'd made her feel as if *she* weren't what *he* wanted! He could still feel the shock vibrating through his body at hearing those words. But he understood them. Could see how the time he'd spent at work had led her to believe that work was more important.

What she didn't see was that he'd been working for her. Or he thought he had been. He'd wanted to give her the life he knew she deserved. If he couldn't be what she wanted, maybe he could give her what she wanted. What a stupid thought, he realised now. And he could have realised it earlier if he'd spent more time at home. If he'd paid more attention to his wife.

He'd been in his own head about how he thought she would respond to what he'd told her about his parents... He'd let it obscure how she really felt: that no matter what she did, she wouldn't be able to give him the life he wanted.

But it wasn't the life *he* wanted. It was the life *she* wanted...

Unless it wasn't?

'Wyatt?'

He turned, saw Lynette. Relief flooded through him when he realised he wouldn't have to think about it any more.

'What do you think?'

'Looks good. People are already enjoying it,' he said, nodding towards the dance floor.

Lynette smiled, though there was a tightness on her face that dimmed it. 'I think that has more to do with the alcohol that hasn't stopped flowing since yesterday.' She gestured to the bar. 'Can I get you something? We have many mocktails available. Or would you prefer something else?'

Wyatt smiled uneasily, wondering how she'd known about his non-alcoholic preferences. Had Summer told her?

'I don't have anything against mocktails.'

'Good,' Lynette said. 'I made a special request after lunch today. Which, according to my understanding, was quite interesting?'

His smile was more genuine this time. From relief, and that Summer's prediction that her mother would know about lunch had come true.

'Things always tend to be interesting with Summer around.'

Lynette tilted her head.

'Yes,' she eventually replied, quite slowly, 'our Summer does tend to make things more interesting.' She paused. 'I don't think I've seen her this evening. Have you?'

'I— No.' He cleared his throat, trying to remember what he'd come up with as an excuse for Summer not being around. 'She actually wasn't feeling well after our walk on the beach—'

'You two walked on the beach?'

Feeling heat push up his neck, Wyatt nodded. 'Yes, ma'am. We…had a talk.'

'People don't tend to have talks with their exes, you

know,' she noted softly, her eyes both curious and...
strained.

'I—'

'Nor do they sit next to one another on boat cruises. Or
at lunches. Or ask favours.'

'Oh, leave him alone, Mother,' someone said from his
side.

It took a moment for his brain to reset after it had
scrambled with mortification. When he looked down and
saw Summer, his mouth opened, just a little.

Summer looked amused. 'You've broken him,' she told
her mother. 'Which means you likely gave him a much
harder time than what I overheard.'

'Oh, there's been no hard time at all.' Lynette waved a
hand. 'Has there, Wyatt?'

He shook his head, not trusting his voice.

'Anyway,' Lynette continued, 'how are you feeling?'

Summer frowned. 'Fine?'

'I...er...told your mother you weren't feeling great after
the beach walk,' he jumped in, not wanting her to get
caught in the web of lies.

Summer raised a brow at him, then looked to her
mother. Her expression immediately changed. It took
Wyatt a second to realise it was because Lynette's expression had, too. It had gone from easy, teasing to...strained,
he thought again. Concerned even.

'I was tired,' Summer said, softly. 'But I had a nap. I'm
feeling refreshed.'

If it hadn't been for her expression, he might have believed her. She was wearing a red dress that looked as if
it had been made with summer nights in mind. It had cap
sleeves that exposed the elegant curve of her clavicle and
shoulders. Its neckline offered the slightest—though no
less enticing—view of her cleavage; and it stopped mid-
thigh, showing off shapely limbs that made him remem-

ber what it had felt like to have them wrapped around his waist.

Besides all of that, she was there, instead of in her cabin. She was with him, instead of far, far away.

Despite what he'd thought on the beach, he was glad for it.

'Well, darling,' Lynette said, her lips curving though Wyatt wouldn't call it a smile. 'I'm glad you could make it.'

'Is everything okay, Mom?' Summer asked, her own lips curving, mirroring her mother's not quite smile.

'Everything's fine.'

Lynette pulled Summer into a hug, pressed a kiss into her hair before patting Wyatt's shoulder as she walked away.

'For the second time today, I'm going to ask—what just happened?'

'I'm not sure,' she said, her expression pensive. 'I think…' She shook her head. 'It doesn't matter.' She smiled at him. 'What matters is that my mother just teased you.'

He winced. Lifted a hand to the back of his neck. 'I'm aware.'

'It's not a bad thing, Wyatt,' Summer said, her smile growing genuine. 'It means she sees you as family.'

He opened his mouth.

It stayed open.

Summer laughed. 'Almost a decade of creeping into her heart and you're still surprised?'

'I'm not family.'

'Not legally,' she agreed. 'Not any more. But you were invited to this weekend. And she's teasing you. Clearly she's realised there's no point in denying your relationship with the family is more personal than professional.'

'I'm not—it's still professional.'

She patted his shoulder, much as her mother had.

'If that makes you feel better. But my father wouldn't be grooming a man he didn't think of as family to take over the family business.' There was barely a beat before she said, 'Drink?'

She was already walking to the bar before his mind caught up.

Before his mind caught up, got distracted by the fact that she wasn't wearing shoes and that that somehow made her sexier, and then focused again.

'You're talking about this very nonchalantly,' he commented once he joined her at the bar.

'How am I supposed to talk about it?'

'I don't know.' He shrugged. 'I would think there'd be more emotion about your ex taking over your family's business. That he's seen as family.'

She ordered some tropical mocktail for herself, glanced over her shoulder for his order. He asked for the same.

'You've worked hard,' she said quietly, turning back to him. 'You deserve this.' There was a pause. 'And since it's not me, I'd rather it be you.'

He didn't have any time to process before she was moving on.

'Besides, my father's seen you as family long before our relationship. He's not going around offering internships to every bad-tempered university student.'

The barperson set down their drinks and she grabbed them both, offering his to him with a sly smile.

'I was not bad-tempered,' he said, choosing the most innocuous of what she'd said to focus on.

'You're right. I made it sound like it was in the past.'

He refused to smile at that. 'Did you come to this dance specifically to annoy me with perkiness?'

Her eyes narrowed. 'Don't you dare call me perky, Montgomery.'

He lifted his free hand in surrender, and suddenly realised the other patrons of the bar were staring at them, watching their interaction with unabashed interest.

'Want to find a place closer to the water to finish these at?'

Her eyebrows rose, but she turned, scanned the room

before lifting her coconut. He followed her gaze and found Trevor and Lynette standing on the patio. Lynette responded in kind, but Trevor only nodded.

When Wyatt turned back to Summer, her eyes were tense. She covered it up with a smile.

'Sure. They've both seen me now, so I can abandon ship.'

He followed as she led the way past the dance floor, stopping right at the edge of where the waves crashed on the beach. She sat on a dry piece of sand, away from the view of the dance, extending her legs. He couldn't bring himself to care about the privacy she'd anticipated though when he couldn't stop staring at her legs.

It was fascinating, seeing the brown of her skin against the almost identical brown of the sand. He wanted to touch her legs; to take the sand and spread it over them to see how different they truly were.

Which was nonsensical, and more erotic than he should have allowed his thoughts to indulge. He drank deeply of the sweet drink in his coconut, relishing the burn of the sugar in his throat.

Perhaps it would burn away his insanity.

'Why did you come?' he asked, desperate to get out of his own thoughts.

She set her drink down. Began drawing circles around it in the sand.

'It didn't seem fair,' she said after a pause so long he'd thought she wouldn't respond, 'to force you into explaining my absence.'

'You weren't forcing me.'

'I would have been.' She carried on drawing circles. 'And now I'm forcing you to be here with me.'

'How are you forcing me when I asked you to come down to the beach with me?'

'Because…you don't put yourself first, Wyatt.'

'What?'

'You agree to share a blanket with me at a picnic because of my father. You agree to keep me company on the cruise because I asked you to.' She didn't look up. 'Were those really things you wanted to do? Or did you do them even though you'll regret them?'

'I didn't regret them,' he said after he'd processed what she was saying. And realised she was right.

'Not even that kiss?' she asked softly, abandoning her sand drawing.

'It was probably a mistake, but I don't regret it.'

She rolled her eyes. 'They're the same thing.'

'No, they're not. Regret is wishing you hadn't done something. I don't—' he hesitated '—I don't feel that way.'

Her eyes were full of emotion he couldn't describe.

'And a mistake?' she asked, her voice husky.

'A mistake is…knowing you did something wrong.'

'So our kiss was wrong, but you don't regret doing it?'

'Exactly.'.

'Why not? Why don't you regret it?'

Up until that moment, he hadn't thought about the kiss. Or he'd tried not to, except to acknowledge that it had been a mistake and he couldn't repeat it. But not once had he wished he hadn't done it. Even now, when his mind told him it would be for the best to regret it, he couldn't bring himself to.

'I don't know, Summer,' he replied honestly. 'I guess it was nice to remind myself that our marriage wasn't a fluke. That there was a real, honest attraction between us before everything… Before.'

'You doubted it?'

He gave her a steady look. Her cheeks pinkened.

'Fair,' she said. 'But now you know the divorce wasn't because of that.'

'I still have questions.'

Her fingers curled into the sand beside her.

'So ask them.'

He hadn't expected that, but it didn't take long to come

up with a question. He'd been wondering it ever since their discussion.

'How could you have ever thought you weren't what I wanted?'

There was a long silence.

'Because you kept looking for more.'

'At work?' he asked. She nodded. He sighed. 'I wasn't looking. I was…hoping. If I could give you what I thought you wanted, maybe you wouldn't leave.'

She blinked. 'Why didn't you ask me what I want?' When he didn't reply, she said, 'The answer would have been simple: I wanted you. The man I fell in love with. The man you already were. Not who you were trying to be.'

My father.

He heard the words as clearly as if she'd said it.

It felt as if his heart had been torn out of his chest and lifted into space. It was too tight, too sluggish, too exposed. He waited for the feeling to pass, and when it didn't, he stood and began to pace.

'Wyatt—'

'I wanted to give you the life you deserved,' he interrupted.

'I didn't deserve you turning into my father,' she said so softly he might have missed it if he hadn't moved forward.

'You didn't deserve the instability I'd grown up with either,' he said through his teeth.

'Were those our only two options?'

'One of them wasn't as bad as the other.'

Abruptly he turned and walked towards the ocean. Almost immediately a wave washed over his feet. It happened again when he didn't move. And again, when still his feet remained rooted in the sand.

'Wyatt,' Summer said from behind him.

When he turned, she was standing a metre away from him. Gently, she took his hand and pulled him out of the water, closer to where they had been sitting.

'I'm sorry,' she said. 'I didn't mean to make you think about it.'

'No,' he said. 'It's not your fault. It's…always there. Hovering over my head. Work helps to keep it at bay.'

She dropped his hand. 'I didn't know.'

'I didn't want you to… I didn't want you to think I was broken. Or remind you I wasn't what you wanted.'

'I wouldn't have.'

'You wouldn't have,' he repeated, agreeing. Finally seeing. 'There's a reason I want that life you say is unrealistic, Sun,' he said softly. 'Realism wouldn't have got me out of my situation. I had to work towards something. My job… It allowed me to do that.'

Her eyes were wide, bright even under the night sky. She nodded.

'I thought,' he said after a moment, 'that I was working towards a good life for the both of us.' He looked down. 'I guess I was doing the opposite.'

'It's not your fault,' she said after a moment. 'I should have said something. I would have…'

She trailed off. He waited for more, but there was nothing, not for the longest time. Eventually, she said, 'This is my fault, too, Wyatt.'

'Why?'

'I—' She exhaled sharply. 'I can't tell you.'

He studied her. 'What am I supposed to do with that?'

'I don't know,' she said.

Her hand lifted, her fingers curling into a fist before it dropped. But then it lifted again, almost as if she couldn't help it, and cupped his cheek.

'I don't know.'

CHAPTER ELEVEN

FEAR PULSED INSIDE her chest.

She wanted to tell Wyatt the truth so badly, but that fear confirmed the only thing telling him would bring her was heartache. She felt torn between the two desires: tell him, or protect him. Or protect herself. The turmoil almost caused her physical pain.

A part of her suspected things would change soon anyway. Something had happened between her mother and her father. Summer could see it in the stiff way her mother held herself up; in the sharp glances her father sent her.

Even if Summer hadn't seen those signs, she would have known something was wrong based on her mother's behaviour. Lynette was acting strangely. Apologetically. And that could only mean her mother knew the truth.

So maybe she *could* tell Wyatt and finally get it off her chest.

But that wouldn't change the reasons she hadn't told him in the first place. She still wanted to protect him. She wanted him to keep his purpose. Except that felt up in the air now. Things had changed with him, too. They'd been honest with one another, and it hadn't destroyed him. It hadn't destroyed her either. Maybe she could—

The fear bounced inside her, demanded her attention. She dismissed the possibility. No, she needed to keep this a secret. And she'd just have to deal with Wyatt walking away from *her* this time...

Except he wasn't.

He should have. Her hand was cupping his face, and she was seeking comfort from him for her own selfish reasons. He should have been walking away from her.

He wasn't.

All she could think was that it felt good. Touching him felt good. Being there, practically alone in the dark with him, felt good.

She kept expecting him to push her away. To tell her that she didn't deserve to touch him, or feel good about anything that had to do with him. She held her breath, waiting for it. Waiting for the moment he'd realise he didn't have to stay there with her. The moment he'd realise his life would be so much easier if he left.

But it didn't come.

The longer she waited, the stronger the spell of the moment wove around them. The fact that the ocean was only steps away from their feet. The fact that the moon shone down over them, and the stars twinkled above them. Like the night before, when they'd met on that bridge.

Except it felt different now. As if the obstacles that had kept them from talking the night before had suddenly been overcome. Which they hadn't been, she knew, and yet it didn't change that things felt different.

Music drifted down towards them, mingling with the sound of the waves crashing in a seductive tune that made the spell impossible to bear.

Soon she wasn't thinking about what Wyatt should be doing. Or about what she should be doing. She was only thinking about her hand on his face. If she wanted to, she could slide it to the back of his head, apply pressure, and bring his lips down to hers...

It didn't help the fantasy—or delusion—when he turned his head to press a kiss into her palm. It seared her skin, so that when he tugged her hand away from his face, she looked down to check for a scar. She barely had a moment to see her hand before his fingers twined with hers. His free hand slid around her waist, pulling her gently towards him as he began to sway.

'Wh-what are you doing?' she asked.

'Dancing,' he replied, lifting a brow. 'Clearly I'm not doing it very well if you had to ask.'

'No, I—' She broke off when she realised how unsteady she sounded. 'I'm surprised.'

'That I'm dancing with you…at a dance?'

'That you're not running away from me.'

The light amusement on his face faded. 'If it helps, I'm wondering that same thing.'

'It does, actually. Not that I can tell you why.'

'Misery loves company,' he replied, the amusement creeping back into his voice.

'Loneliness, too,' she commented.

He looked down at her. 'You're lonely?'

She blinked when her eyes heated. Said, 'Yes,' before she could help it.

'But you have a family.'

'Doesn't mean you don't feel lonely,' she told him. 'Doesn't mean you feel like you belong.'

He searched her face. 'How did I get this so wrong? Your relationship with your family?'

'Is this your question?'

He blinked. 'What?'

'Your question. Your payment for keeping me company earlier.'

'Oh.' A puzzled look settled on his face, then his eyes sharpened. 'You'd like it to be, wouldn't you?'

'Just paying off a debt.'

He studied her. 'Fine. You've given me plenty of other questions. I suppose this one can be official.'

Something settled inside her.

'Well, then.' She cleared her throat. 'The answer is simple. You didn't know how I felt about my family because I hid it away from you.'

Wyatt stiffened. Her expression told him she'd felt it, but she continued as if neither of them had noticed anything.

'You know how, when you have someone coming over to your place for the first time, you make sure everything's in place?' she asked. 'You stuff the cupboard with your clothing, pack away the dishes, make sure all the surfaces are nice and tidy before they get there so you can impress them?'

He nodded, unsure of where she was going with it.

'That gives you a pretty good idea of what happened when I met you. Which is strange, because you were the only one who could see past what I was showing to the world.' She shook her head. 'The point is, I wanted you to see what you thought existed. Me, the perfect partner. My perfect family.' She paused. 'But I couldn't keep pretending like the clothing wasn't a jumble behind the cupboard doors. Or that I hadn't packed the dishes away into the wrong places, or that the surfaces stayed nice and tidy. What you've seen this weekend is...behind the pretence.'

'You're saying you stopped tidying up?'

She nodded. 'I'm sorry for it.' Her voice, her expression were sincere. 'I see now that I added to the idea of the life you wanted. But it's not real, Wyatt. I just pretended it was. At least, what you hadn't seen through.' She paused. 'I'm not perfect. Neither is my family.'

'Why? Why did you hide it?'

'Ah, that's a lot more complicated,' she said, her face sad. 'I've already told you some of it.'

'Purpose?' he asked. She nodded. 'We've already spoken about that. What's the rest?'

She shook her head, her face anguished, and he couldn't bring himself to ask it again.

He should have. Maybe he would finally get the answers he needed. Except he already had them. Some of them, at least. He saw that part of why she'd left had been because she believed she was doing the right thing for him. He couldn't blame her for it when he *had* needed a purpose. He'd needed something to work towards.

He didn't regret that desire when it had lifted him out

of his broken childhood. But he could see how the idea of
an even better life had ended his relationship. He'd had
more than what he needed when he'd been married. Hell,
he'd had everything he'd ever wanted. Still, he'd wanted
more. He'd worked for more.

Not for Summer, he realised now. Summer had had the
life he'd thought she deserved before she'd even met him.
But he'd let his feelings about his parents cloud his vision.
He'd let the brokenness they'd left inside him block his path.

And he'd hurt her because of it.

He should have been content with those answers. He
wasn't. He wanted to know everything that had contributed to the end of their marriage. He needed to know in
case he didn't have to accept that he'd allowed his parents
to rob him of his happiness.

But he couldn't ask her directly. Not when it had put
that look on her face. So he hedged.

'For someone who doesn't feel like they belong to a
family, you do a lot for them,' he remarked slowly.

'What do you mean?'

'Standing up for Autumn today. Making that toast.' He
paused. 'Being here at all.'

'This is my parents' anniversary. I couldn't not be here.
I tried, remember?'

'Summer, you can't deny you care about them.'

She shrugged. 'Caring about them doesn't mean I belong. In fact, it makes it clearer that I don't.'

'Did they do this to you? Did they make you feel this
way?' he asked. 'I can't imagine Autumn or your mother—'

'Because it wasn't them,' she interrupted. 'Not intentionally.'

'So it's your father.'

'Wyatt,' she said, her voice low.

'It is.' He stared at her. 'Your father made you feel like
you don't belong? How is that possible?'

'What do you mean?'

'How is it possible that he could make me feel a part of something bigger than myself, but he made you, his own daughter, feel this way?'

'Because you've put him on a pedestal,' she said darkly.

'He earned his way onto that pedestal,' he retorted. 'You know how much your father has done for me.'

'But he's human, Wyatt,' she said, stepping out of his embrace. 'Just make sure you have some steps for him to reach the ground. So he doesn't fall and hurt you both.'

'He won't,' Wyatt said stubbornly.

She snorted. Shook her head. 'One of the reasons I love you is because of your generosity. Your willingness to do things for people who don't deserve them. But this? This is— What?' she asked, interrupting herself. 'Why are you looking at me like that?'

He wasn't sure how he was looking at her, but it must have been some kind of combination between surprise and the warmth spreading through his veins.

'I—' He cleared his throat. 'You… Er…you said you love me.'

She frowned. 'No, I said—' She broke off, and all the colour drained from her skin. She shook her head slightly, then more vigorously as she took a step back.

'I obviously meant *loved*. Part of the reason I *loved* you is because of—' She waved a hand. 'It doesn't mean— *I* didn't mean—' She sucked in a breath. 'Look, tonight was a mistake. A mistake,' she repeated, 'not a regret. And I'm going to— I just need to—'

She turned away before she could form a coherent sentence. He stared after her as she walked, wondering if he should follow her and force them to talk about what had happened.

Except he could barely think it through. The uncertainty of it weighed down his legs, rooting him to the spot. So he kept watching, trying to figure out what the hell was going on between him and his ex-wife.

CHAPTER TWELVE

SUMMER COULD NOT fall asleep for the life of her. Which turned out to be handy, because when Autumn snuck in early Sunday morning, Summer was already awake.

'I told him I love him,' she said when the door to their cabin shut behind Autumn.

Her sister gave a shriek before a bump sounded. A few more joined that one before the lights went on.

'What the hell, Summer? Were you waiting up so you could scare me?'

'No,' she said defensively. 'I wasn't waiting up for you…per se. I couldn't sleep.'

'It's five in the morning!' Autumn interrupted in exclamation. 'The sun's coming up.'

As if hearing Autumn's words, the purple-blue sky began to turn orange.

'Is there a reason you're telling me these things?' Summer asked.

'You've been up all night?'

'Yes. Because last night I told Wyatt I love him.'

Autumn's eyes widened. She took off her jersey, kicked off her shoes, and curled up on the bed in front of Summer. She took Summer's hands in her own.

'What happened?'

'I don't know.' Summer tightened her grip. 'One moment we were dancing on the beach, the next I was saying "one of the reasons I love you". Not loved, Wind, *love*. Like, in the present or something.'

Autumn's face was carefully blank. 'Did you…? Did you just say you were dancing on the beach with your ex-husband?'

Summer pulled one of her hands out from Autumn's grip and put it on her forehead. 'Yes, but it was Mom and Dad's disco. Really, that's not the important part of what I told you.'

'It sounds important to me.'

'More important than the fact that I told him I *love* him?' Summer's voice was incredulous.

'Of equal importance,' Autumn replied, unfazed. 'The person I spoke to on Friday—or Saturday, for that matter—would not have danced with her ex-husband, let alone tell him she loved him. Love, sorry,' Autumn said when Summer opened her mouth. 'What happened to *that* Summer?'

'I don't know.' Now Summer stood and began pacing. 'I'd like to know, too. I'm freaking out.'

'Yeah, I can see that.'

Then Autumn stood, too, and took Summer's hands in hers again. Summer allowed it because that was their thing, holding hands. Something inside her eased.

'We'll figure it out, Sun,' Autumn said. 'But first, we're going to have a cup of tea because some of us got no sleep for normal, practical reasons. Like the fact that I've been driving for six hours through the night to get here in time for Mom and Dad's ceremony.'

'Which might not even be happening,' Summer said with a groan. She turned the armchair next to the bed so that it faced her sister before sinking down on it. And found Autumn staring at her.

'I'm sorry,' Autumn said. 'Did you say the ceremony might not happen?'

'Oh.' *Damn.* 'No. I'm sure it will.'

'Explain.'

'Mom and Dad had an argument yesterday,' Summer said, knowing Autumn wouldn't let it go if she didn't have some form of an answer. Summer would have preferred not to lie, but she'd been so caught up in her own drama that she'd forgotten herself.

'About what?'

'You know they don't tell me things like that.'

Autumn's eyes narrowed, but she began the motions of making tea. 'I take it there hasn't been a big reconciliation this weekend, then?'

'Sorry.'

Autumn didn't say anything, only finished making the tea. After she handed Summer a cup, she sat down on the bed and curled her feet under her again.

'It wouldn't be the end of the world if you put this behind you,' Autumn said softly.

'Except that I can't,' Summer replied sadly. 'Things are…different for me.'

'Why?'

She sighed. 'They just are.'

Autumn sighed now, too. 'Sun, you've let it affect so much of your life.'

Summer didn't reply.

'You were so afraid of being hurt that you divorced the man you love—'

'Excuse me?'

Autumn sipped her tea, eyes sharp on Summer's. 'Oh, I've forgotten what you said ended it? Your work?'

'I didn't want to hurt him by telling him about Dad,' Summer said tightly.

'You didn't want to *be* hurt by telling him about Dad.'

'You don't understand.'

Autumn studied her. 'I know I don't.' She paused. 'But Wyatt did, when you first got together. He understood you. Maybe you should trust that he will again.'

Summer's heart ached. She should have known that Autumn had seen through her. Especially after that conversation with her mother, when Lynette had admitted to knowing something was wrong with Summer, too. If Lynette knew, Autumn did, too.

It was worse that Autumn was right. Wyatt had understood her once. And she desperately wanted him to again. But...

'He'll hate me.'

'He won't.'

She looked down. 'Dad will.'

'Dad's an adult,' Autumn said softly. 'He can take responsibility for himself.'

She closed her eyes.

'Wyatt's an adult, too, Sun,' Autumn reminded her gently. 'Whatever his reaction is, he has to deal with it. Or you can do it together. But at least if you're honest with him, you won't have to keep wondering what would have happened if you'd told him. Maybe you'll finally be able to move past what happened with Dad, too.'

Summer didn't have the heart to tell her sister that that wouldn't happen. Not unless she could go back to eight years ago and change how everything had transpired.

But Summer smiled, and said, 'I'll think about it.'

'Okay.'

They sat in silence, drinking their tea. Eventually Autumn said, 'If you do still love him, and there's a chance you two can be together...' She trailed off, her face going sad. 'It's worth taking that chance.'

Summer knew Autumn was talking about her own relationship that had ended. She leaned forward and gripped her sister's hand. And though it was selfish, Summer thought it almost felt like before.

Wyatt didn't consider himself a fan of weddings. In fact, besides his own, he hadn't actually attended one. Which made sense. He hadn't made enough connections in life to be invited to weddings. No, invitations required friendships. Wyatt Montgomery had no friends.

Not even Summer, he thought, gritting his teeth. He'd thought they'd developed a truce of sorts. Then he realised that that didn't quite make sense, considering they hadn't been in a fight. She'd left, as he'd known she would. He'd accepted it, because he hadn't had a choice.

Except that didn't ring true any more, and he was too annoyed with himself—with her—to try and figure out why that was.

Instead, he made his way to Trevor's room, where his boss had asked to see him the night before when he'd said his goodbyes.

'Wyatt,' Trevor said when he opened the door. 'Come in.'

Wyatt walked past Trevor, his eyes widening slightly as he took in the large room. It was double the size of his own, with glass walls that offered a view of both the ocean and the steeps hills and mountains at the edge of the island. The interior was modern, with a touch of classic, its wooden floor panelling covered in parts with plush red carpeting, the walls decorated with antique African art and bright colourful paintings.

'It must have been a hardship for you to stay here,' Wyatt noted with a smile.

Trevor's mouth curved. 'Indeed. It almost made me regret picking this place to renew our vows at.'

Before Wyatt could ask why they'd chosen the place, Trevor's face fell. The older man walked to the decanter, put ice into two glasses. In one he poured sparkling water; the other whiskey. He handed Wyatt the water.

'I called you here for a reason, Wyatt,' Trevor said quietly. 'But I'm afraid that reason might no longer be relevant.'

'I'm not following?'

'I wanted you to be my best man.'

Wyatt wasn't sure how to reply. It was as if his brain had packed a suitcase, hitched a ride to the airport and was flying away. Far from where Wyatt could reach it to demand it give him something to say, apparently.

Anything to say, he thought, his skin growing clammy. His heart was thudding as the time went by and, still, he couldn't think of anything.

He opened and closed his mouth multiple times. A part of him was certain Trevor would retract his offer as he tried to figure out what was happening. Finally, his ability to speak returned.

'You said "wanted"?'

'Yes.' Trevor drained his drink, setting the empty glass on the table. 'The ceremony might not happen.'

'Why not?'

Trevor heaved a sighed. 'It's a long story.' His eyes narrowed as he looked at Wyatt. 'Summer hasn't told you?'

'Told me what?'

'She didn't, then,' Trevor said after a moment. 'I'm not sure if I should be content with that, or frustrated.'

'I... I don't know what you're talking about.'

'I'm sorry,' Trevor said. 'I thought—' He lowered himself into a nearby chair, looking older than Wyatt had ever seen him. 'Not sure why I thought it,' Trevor continued, almost as if to himself. 'She hasn't told anyone anything. Which is why things are such a mess.' He rubbed a hand over his face. 'No, things are a mess because I did what I did. I can't blame her for it. I shouldn't have asked her to do it in the first place.'

Wyatt wasn't sure what he should do. Trevor was clearly not speaking to him. And the things he was saying... They had nothing to do with Wyatt. They did have something to do with Summer though, which was why his feet were rooted to the spot. His curiosity, his concern didn't allow him to leave.

'I'm sorry,' Trevor said again. 'You shouldn't have to listen to my ramblings.'

Wyatt's spine straightened. 'Would you like me to leave?'

'No,' Trevor said immediately. 'No, I…' He let out a humourless laugh. 'Son, I don't know what I want.'

Wyatt's stomach curled into itself, then dropped to the bottom of his body. He swallowed. Breathed. But his head was swirling and his stomach was still in the vicinity of his shoes and he couldn't figure out what was happening.

'Lynette and I aren't on speaking terms right now,' Trevor said slowly. 'I'm not sure we will be by the time the ceremony rolls around.' He looked at his watch, laughed that sharp laugh again. 'In ninety minutes.' He paused. 'But I can't regret asking you, Wyatt. If there is a ceremony, I'd want you to be my best man.'

'I would be honoured.'

Trevor brightened for a beat, his face shining with approval. 'That means more than you could possibly know.'

'I could say the same thing,' Wyatt replied, though he wasn't sure he could. But he should have been able to.

Why did this interaction feel so…strange?

'You should go, Wyatt,' Trevor said, looking tired again. 'I'm not the best company at the moment.' He tried to muster what Wyatt assumed was a smile; he failed miserably. 'I'll let you know if things change.'

Wyatt nodded, leaving the room more confused than anything else. The one thing he was certain of was that he needed another shower. Sweat cleaved to his skin, making the one he'd had that morning feel as if it had been months ago.

He'd thought it a natural reaction to Trevor's question at first. He'd been put on the spot in an unfamiliar situation. But his skin still felt sticky, and his heart was still beating rapidly. And he could still hear Trevor calling him *son*. The term echoed in his mind as if it were a drop of water in an empty chamber.

His throat had begun to tighten at some point, too, and

he was eager to get to his room so he could down a bottle of water. It would help with the tightness, he was sure. It would also protect him from dehydration because of all the sweating.

As he crossed the wooden bridge separating the two sides of the lodge, he saw two figures walking towards him. They were identical in height, and from this far there weren't many distinctions between them. Except his eyes immediately settled on the one on the left. His body's reaction to Trevor's question was timid compared to what it was doing now.

He swallowed. Did it again and again when that didn't take the tight feeling in his throat away. He forced air into his body with a deep breath, exhaling slowly before he was close enough for them to notice.

'Morning,' he offered when they were metres away from one another.

His eyes were still on Summer. She nodded, the colour on her cheeks deepening before she looked away. He dragged his gaze to Autumn.

'It's nice to see you again,' he told her, blinking when she walked up to him and brushed a kiss on his cheek.

'It's nice to see you, too, Wyatt,' Autumn said pleasantly.

'You were missed,' he said, when the silence extended long enough for him to think about Summer not looking at him. For him to realise he desperately wanted her to.

'You missed me?'

He smiled. 'That's not what I said.'

'No,' Autumn assured him, 'it's just what I heard.' She gave him a bright smile. 'I do enjoy hearing what I want to.'

'Autumn,' Summer said mutedly. 'Mom's waiting for us.' When he looked at her, she nodded again. 'Sorry, Wyatt. We have to go.'

'Of course,' he replied, embarrassingly grateful she'd

said something to him. 'I'll see you there.' Then he remembered his conversation with Trevor and felt like a fool for not bringing it up earlier. 'Or you might not. I had a conversation with your dad that…'

He trailed off at the expression on Summer's face.

'Wyatt?' Autumn said in a tone that made him think it wasn't the first time she'd called his name. 'What happened with my father?'

'Summer knows.'

Summer was shaking her head before he could finish. 'I don't know anything.'

'Summer,' he said softly. His next words came from a place he had no idea existed inside him, but his gut told him she needed to hear them. 'It's time to stop running.'

Her eyes widened, became glossy. He ignored the frown Autumn sent him, and the way she looked from Summer to him and back.

'Be honest, Sun,' he said. 'Let them in. Let yourself belong.'

He nodded at her, then at Autumn, and walked back to his cabin. Once there, he stripped off his clothes and went straight to the shower, hoping the cool water would calm him. Or at least, help him think.

It had started with Trevor's question about Wyatt being his best man. Wyatt wished he could blame it on not having been in a wedding before. But this wasn't nerves. If it were, he'd feel calmer now. He'd only get nervous again when he was standing in front of the guests at the wedding. But he felt as if he was in some fresh new hell *now*. His skin felt as if it had been sunburnt—sensitive and prickly—and he still had to force his lungs to do their damn job.

But it had something to do with the wedding since that had started it all. It wasn't because he didn't want to be Trevor's best man. He did. Not because he felt indebted, but because…he wanted to.

He saw now that it hadn't been a lie when he'd said it meant something for Trevor to ask. It took him a moment, but he realised that admission changed his relationship with Trevor. He didn't know what had changed; only that something had.

And *that* was what felt strange. The fact that Trevor had asked at all. That he had called Wyatt *son*. Wyatt had thought about weddings and connections before, but what did this mean? If attending a wedding simply meant having a connection, what did being in one mean? What was deeper than having a connection with someone?

Family.

Summer had told him her parents considered him family the night before. It had been unsettling hearing it then, but he only now figured out why.

He didn't know how to be family. He'd never had one. Certainly not one like the Bishops. Though he didn't really know what that meant now. He'd idealised their family; Summer had made that clear. And he'd seen it himself.

But they were still more of a family than he'd ever had. His only example of familial relationships had been his parents' abandonment. His first and only attempt at creating his own family with Summer had failed.

Why did thinking about that make his heart ache? Why did it make fear thrum in his veins?

He didn't know. But as he got out of the shower, Wyatt was determined not to think about it.

CHAPTER THIRTEEN

EVEN IF WYATT hadn't warned her, Summer would have known something was wrong the moment she walked into the room.

The lodge had prepared a room for Lynette to get ready in, but it looked as if it had been used for more than that. The bed was unmade; her mother's suitcases were in the corner. Lynette was sitting in a white nightgown on a chair, staring into the cup in her lap. Summer couldn't tell if anything was inside it.

'Mom,' Autumn said after taking everything in. 'Are you okay?'

Lynette's eyes lifted lethargically, as if she hadn't re-alised they'd walked into the room. Her expression soft-ened when she saw Autumn.

'Honey, I didn't know you were here.'

'Of course I'm here,' Autumn said, sitting on the chair next to her mother. 'You and Dad are renewing your vows.'

Lynette looked down again, but not before Summer saw her mother's eyes fill. She stood, unmoving, before lift-ing her shoulders when Autumn shot her a look. *Help,* it screamed. But how could she help when this was her fault?

'I'm not sure we'll be doing that, Autumn.' Her moth-er's voice was soft but firm. 'Your father and I are...not on the same page any more.'

'What does that mean?'

Lynette's head lifted, and she looked directly at Sum-mer. 'Why didn't you tell me, darling?'

Her legs began to shake, though Summer couldn't be sure that hadn't started the moment she'd seen Wyatt. If not then, surely when he'd told her to be honest. To let herself belong. She'd been hopeful in that moment, thinking about the possibility of belonging again. But she was sure now it wouldn't happen. Keeping her father's secret had already brought such destruction. How could being honest be any different?

The look on her mother's face told her she no longer had a choice though.

She took a deep breath. 'He asked me not to.'

'And you listened to him?' Lynette asked. 'I raised you better than that.'

'But the man who raised me alongside you asked me to do this. It wasn't…' She blew out a breath. 'This wasn't a failing in how you raised me, Mom. It wasn't my moral decision. This wasn't my decision at all.'

'That,' Lynette said, her fingers tightening on her mug, 'is not true.'

'Okay,' Autumn said into the tight quiet that followed their mother's words. 'Clearly I'm missing something here.' She looked from Lynette to Summer. 'Care to explain?'

'I knew about the affair,' Summer said, tired of the secret now. 'I found out before the O'Brien deal went through. Dad asked me not to tell you and Mom until the papers were signed.'

'*What?*'

Summer didn't answer. Instead, she walked onto the patio, resting her forearms on the balcony railing. She took a deep breath, letting the sea air soothe her. Except it reminded her of Wyatt now. Of when he'd chased her along the edge of the water. Of when they'd kissed. Of when they'd danced.

Let yourself belong.

She walked back into the room.

'Sun,' Autumn said as soon as she did, 'how long did you know?'

'Two months,' she answered. Inhaled. Exhaled. 'That's

when I started separating myself from the family. I wanted to tell you both so badly. I didn't want to be alone in it. I know that sounds selfish—'

'It doesn't,' her sister interrupted. 'Part of why I could get through it was because I wasn't doing it alone. We all were. At least, I thought so,' she added, pained.

'No, you didn't think that,' Summer said. 'You knew I was struggling. You both did.' She paused. 'And this is why, by the way. Not because I was clinging to the past, or because I couldn't get over Dad breaking our trust—'

She stopped at that. Took a moment to figure out why it felt significant. She'd spent so much time resenting him for asking her to keep the affair a secret that she hadn't truly thought about the affair itself.

No, that wasn't true, she thought immediately. She had thought about it. And she had felt betrayed—about both things. Her father cheating on her mother *and* asking her to keep it a secret.

She shook her head. She'd think about it later.

'I couldn't forgive him for breaking up our family,' she continued quietly. 'Not only because of his affair, but because of what it did to me in our family. It…pushed me out.'

Both Autumn and Lynette moved towards her, but Autumn fell back and let Lynette pull Summer into a hug. Summer heard the sob that came from her mouth as if it were in the distance, but she managed to stop any more from escaping. She didn't want to break open now. She still wasn't sure what would spill out.

But she clung to her mother, needing the comfort. Feeling, for the first time in for ever, as if Lynette finally understood.

Lynette pulled back. 'I'm sorry you went through that.'

'Thank you,' she said, sincerity coating her words.

'I wish you'd told me.' Lynette brushed Summer's hair away from her face. 'Then we wouldn't be here.'

'Wouldn't we?' Summer asked.

'No,' Lynette said decisively. She went back to her seat, lowering down regally. 'I wouldn't have said yes to your father's proposal if I'd known.'

'Dad proposed?' Summer tilted her head. 'Why didn't I know that?'

Lynette lifted a shoulder. Something jiggled inside Summer's chest.

'Anyway,' Summer said, ignoring it, 'you know you would have said yes, Mom.'

'No, I—'

'This isn't worse than him cheating on you.'

Lynette's face tightened. 'So you say.'

'Because I know,' Summer said. 'I know you and Dad. If you could work through the affair, you can work through this.' She paused. 'There was no real damage, Mother.'

'You must be joking,' Lynette said, straightening. 'You've spent the last eight years in pain. And your father knew it. He did nothing about it.' She pressed a hand to her stomach. 'You should never have felt like an outsider to this family, Summer.'

'But that was just as much me as it was Dad,' she said, realising its truth. She swallowed. 'I think Dad did a cost benefit analysis and realised he'd rather hurt me than you.' She took an unsteady breath. 'Which would have happened if he'd told you the truth, clearly.' She paused. 'I understand why he did it.'

'I don't,' Lynette said stubbornly.

Summer looked at Autumn then, tilting her head towards their mother.

Autumn lifted her brows. *Are you sure?* she was asking. Summer nodded. When Autumn wordlessly asked why, Summer shrugged.

She didn't know why she wanted to make things right. Maybe she was tired of a broken family. Now that Autumn and her mother knew the truth, she wouldn't have to hide anything any more. They could move forward. She could belong.

She wasn't sure she could tie this up so simply, particularly when she hadn't even thought about where her father fitted into all of it. But she didn't want her mother to hurt. Not for her sake, anyway. Not when her mother was right: she'd made a choice to keep the truth from them. By doing so, she'd continued to play the outsider role. She'd had a say in that, too.

She couldn't quite wrap her head around it though, so she pushed it aside. Pushed the emotions down, too.

'I think Summer's right,' Autumn said, on cue. 'You've spent the last eight years working through this. You've built a marriage that's stronger.'

'And yet I still can't trust him.'

'Of course you can,' Summer said, waving a hand. 'Dad's changed in the last eight years.' She frowned. 'More than I realised.' She shook her head. 'He's put you first since then, Mom. Wyatt has more responsibility at Bishop Enterprises now because Dad's spent more time at home. With you. Working on rebuilding that trust. Your marriage is important to him.'

Defending her father felt strange, but the words weren't lies. She still didn't know what to do about that knowledge.

'What happened with me… He was wrong, Mom, but I don't think he was trying to hide it from you. He just didn't want to jeopardise what you've worked so hard to rebuild.'

Silence followed Summer's words. She held her breath, trying to anticipate her mother's next argument.

'It ruined your marriage, Summer,' Lynette said. Summer certainly hadn't anticipated that. 'You clearly still love Wyatt. The reason you two divorced isn't because of your work, like you told us.'

'No,' Summer agreed, speaking over the lump in her throat. 'It's because I…was afraid of being hurt like you were,' she said, grasping the reason Autumn had given her that morning. She leaned more heavily on the crutch. 'I was afraid to trust someone again.' She sucked in air. 'But I'm an adult, Mom. It was my choice. It's my responsibility. I've accepted that.'

'What about—?'

'No,' Autumn interrupted. 'Now you're just looking for an excuse to get out of this.' Autumn took Lynette's hands, drew her up. 'I think you're getting cold feet.'

'I am *not*.'

'Great.' Autumn grinned. 'You have no more reason to delay this wedding.' Autumn looked at her watch. 'With thirty minutes to spare, too.' She paused. 'Can I tell Dad you've forgiven him?'

Lynette's eyes swept over Summer. Summer nodded, giving her the most genuine smile she could manage. When her mother's face brightened, Summer thought she deserved a prize for acting.

'Tell him the ceremony will continue,' Lynette said. 'Don't let him know I forgive him yet.' She sniffed. 'He can spend some more time being miserable. It can be his penance for doing what he did to Summer.'

Summer's smile came more naturally now.

CHAPTER FOURTEEN

HER MIND WAS still a mess by the time they made their way down to the beach for the ceremony. Fortunately, Autumn was walking in front with Lynette, chatting about nothing in particular. Summer knew her sister was doing so purposefully. Autumn had sent her shrewd looks the entire time they'd spent getting ready; she knew how much Summer had borrowed from their conversation to make their mother feel better.

If they both hadn't been determined to get Lynette down the aisle, Summer was sure Autumn would have said something. But they were, thankfully. And Autumn was nothing if not a team player, so the chattering's intention was to keep Lynette from noticing Summer's silence.

It was a relief when they finally reached the beach. It was the same venue as where the disco had been the night before. This time, the inner venue had been transformed into a dining hall. Three long tables were arranged at an angle in the room, with one smaller table on one end.

All the tables were decorated with white cloths and yellow runners. A bright, bold flower arrangement stood at each end; tea-light candles had been placed on top of white petals running between the arrangements. The smaller table had 'Mr and Mrs, Again' carved in wood at its front. Fairy lights hung down the wall behind the table.

The patio was void of any lights, and had been softened with vases and pots of white, yellow, and pink flowers. A carpet extended from the sliding doors of the venue down, over the patio to the front of where Summer assumed her parents would be renewing their vows. She had to assume as her view of that area was currently obscured by a large arch of greenery and white, yellow, and pink flowers that had been placed at the beginning of the beach.

'Wow,' Summer breathed. 'This is… Wow.'

'Thank you.' Lynette smiled thinly. She'd recovered enough to be nervous. 'Your sister and I have been working on this for months.'

Lynette put an arm around Autumn and squeezed. Something inside Summer squeezed, too.

'You've been helping with this?' she asked Autumn. 'Why didn't either of you tell me? Or ask me to help?'

Lynette and Autumn exchanged a look.

'We thought you wouldn't be interested, dear,' Lynette said. She took a step forward, brushing a curl from Summer's forehead. 'But you're here. And we're a family again. That's enough.'

She kissed Summer's head and took a deep breath. The show of nerves made Summer realise now wasn't the time for her emotions. She could be offended at how low the bar was later. She could think about her mother being pleased that she'd simply *attended* a family event later. She wouldn't think about how it showed how much of an outsider she'd allowed herself to become now.

No, now, she'd offer her mother a smile.

'You look breathtaking, Mom. Dad isn't going to know what hit him.'

Her mother smoothed down the front of the simple white dress she wore. It had sleeves and lowered into a modest V at her neck. There was a yellow belt at its waist; the rest of the white material fell down to her bare feet. Her curls were tamed into a bun, though some strands of them had escaped and sprung around the yellow flower Summer had tied in her hair minutes ago.

For some reason, the picture of it had Summer blinking back tears. She forced her smile wider instead. Autumn gripped her hand, squeezed. Then it was time for them to walk down the aisle.

Summer had never been more grateful for the beach than at that moment. The wind was blowing lightly, and the sun wasn't strong enough to do anything other than tenderly warm the earth.

She took a deep breath of salty fresh air and followed Autumn down the aisle.

The first thing she saw was the white arch at the end of the aisle. It had been made of wire, and had greenery and flowers curving around it like the first arch. The second thing she looked at was her father. He looked…grateful, she thought. When her mother started the walk down the aisle, Summer watched him blink back tears.

It felt like proof her father had changed. Or become a better version of himself. A combination of the good things of the man she'd thought she'd lost all those years ago and someone who was trying. That last part made a difference, she thought. Trevor had always been a good man. His priorities had been skewed, and that had led him down a dark path. But he'd changed those priorities. He was trying to put his family first this time. And he'd succeeded… With Autumn and Lynette.

It still stung that he hadn't tried with her.

She believed everything she'd told her mother. She knew her father had weighed up hurting his wife against hurting his daughter. His daughter had lost. Which, she supposed, was to be expected. She couldn't even blame him for it.

What she did blame him for was teaching Wyatt to do the same thing.

It was my choice. It's my responsibility.

The memory of her words forced Summer into remembering she'd contributed to the end of her relationship, too. Hell, she'd just realised she'd contributed to isolating herself from her family as well. There were myriad examples of times when she'd excluded herself. Enough that her mother hadn't even asked her to help plan the vow renewal.

She'd told herself her father had broken their family. And that Wyatt's actions had ended their marriage. She'd conveniently removed her own culpability in the process.

Watching Summer walk down the aisle had given him chills.

The chills hadn't been the bad kind. They hadn't been because he'd been frightened by seeing his ex-wife walk down the aisle. Seeing her hadn't caused his stomach to turn. It hadn't caused nausea, nor the hundreds of other reactions he should have had at seeing a woman he'd divorced walk down an aisle again.

No, his chills had been of the good kind. They'd accompanied the thought that he'd lost out by suggesting they marry in court. And *that* thought had been accompanied by a longing he'd felt so rarely in his life he could count the instances on one hand.

Like the time he'd seen a father and son having a meal together in a restaurant when he'd been sixteen. Or when he'd been twenty-four and he'd seen a man and his mother reunite at the airport.

The longing always—*always*—came with regret. He didn't care for it.

So Wyatt desperately tried to ignore Summer altogether. He was determined not to think about her standing on the opposite side of the aisle. It should have been easier than it was considering she barely looked at him. He knew that because his efforts were failing. He tried to focus on the ceremony again.

Again, he did not succeed.

His eyes slid over to her and he thought that, perhaps, he was being too hard on himself. Almost everyone else in attendance must have felt the same way. The Bishop sisters made a startling picture as the maids of honour— titles Trevor had informed him of with great amusement.

Though Trevor's smile could have come from his relief that the ceremony was on again.

Both sisters were dressed in yellow. Autumn's dress was a bright shade that looked as if it had been made for a summer wedding; Summer's a much lighter colour. The styles of their dresses were also different, though this time Autumn's seemed demurer and Summer's more audacious. It was intricately designed, so naturally he couldn't describe it. All he knew was that he could see a leg and an arm and he felt lucky for it.

Then there was her hair.

She wore it in one big mass of curls around her head, accentuated by a large yellow flower, slightly smaller than the one that had been pinned to Lynette's hair. He was sure Summer had teased those curls so that they looked bigger and bolder than what he'd seen before. It was the first time this weekend he'd seen her hair loose, too, and his fingers itched to pull at the curls.

Her face went from tortured to carefully blank, as if she'd realised people were watching her. He still saw the torture reflected in her eyes though. He wondered what could possibly have happened in her relationship with her father to put that hurt there.

He was so deep in thought about it that he missed his cue to hand Trevor the rings. He frowned when he caught Summer looking at him. It took him an embarrassingly long time to realise Summer wasn't the only one.

'Sorry,' he mumbled, handing Trevor the rings.

Trevor chuckled, winking at Wyatt as he took them. Wyatt purposefully avoided looking at Summer after that. Before he knew it, Trevor and Lynette were sharing a kiss.

Almost immediately after, the guests were told to relax while photos were taken. He followed the guests until Trevor called him to be a part of the photos. Somehow he hadn't realised that was part of the best man duties. After an inordinate amount of smiling, he was back to being grateful he and Summer had decided on a court wedding.

Summer looked as if she were grateful for that fact, too.

When they were finally given permission to leave so Lynette and Trevor could take solo photos, Summer turned on her heel and walked off. They all watched, though it was Trevor Wyatt glanced at shortly after. The man's gaze was pinned to Summer's retreating figure, before he exchanged a look with Lynette.

'She's fine,' Autumn said brightly at his side. Wyatt opened his mouth to contradict her, but was silenced with one look. 'Go ahead, Mom and Dad. Enjoy.'

She waited until her parents were gone, then turned to Wyatt.

'Shouldn't you go after her?' he asked after an awkward silence.

Autumn's expression turned pensive. 'No,' she replied. 'No, I don't think she needs me right now.'

'Who else is there?'

Autumn lifted a brow. It took a thudding heart to realise she was talking about him.

'Oh.' He paused. 'No.'

'No?'

'She's not my responsibility.'

It felt like an excuse.

It felt like a lie.

'Not legally, no,' Autumn said. 'But apparently things have happened between you two this weekend?'

'Not things that make going after her my responsibility.'

'Really?' she asked dryly. 'Dancing on the beach doesn't carry emotional strings for you, then?'

His face grew warm, and he rubbed a hand along the back of his neck. 'I didn't realise you knew about that.'

'That you're a romantic?'

'I'm not—'

He broke off when he realised she was teasing him. Besides, it did sound romantic.

Did Summer think so too?

'Anyway,' he said, deliberately changing the topic, 'I don't think she wants me.'

'Maybe not.' Autumn's face softened. 'But I think she needs you.'

He wanted to ask her what she meant, but she squeezed his arm and walked away.

He stared after her. When she didn't turn back, Wyatt sighed and went in search of his ex-wife.

CHAPTER FIFTEEN

SUMMER WATCHED THE waves crash against the rocks that created the natural boundary of the private beach where the ceremony had been held. It made her feel trapped. For a minute, she fantasised about climbing over the rocks to escape the feeling. Surely being able to breathe properly would be worth her dress? Her hair? Her make-up?

Another part of her wanted to walk into the ocean. To feel the cool water flow over her skin that suddenly felt too hot. To feel the waves carry some of the weight that was pressing on her shoulders, her chest. To have the salt burn her eyes instead of the tears.

She knew leaving as soon as she could would probably worry her mother. And her sister. But Summer couldn't stay there with her too-hot skin and her weighed-down shoulders and chest. She sure as hell couldn't stay there when it felt as though the tears would fall down her cheeks at any moment.

But crying felt like an admission. Instead of giving in to the temptation, Summer closed her eyes and pressed a hand to that spot just beneath her breasts that expanded with air. She let herself breathe. Let herself feel the air move in and out of her lungs. It helped her feel steadier, until she felt the air shift around her. She opened her eyes and found herself looking directly into Wyatt's.

'How long have you been there?' she asked unsteadily. 'Not long.'

He put his hands in the black trousers he wore. They were rolled up at the ankles, revealing his bare feet. They looked out of place with his white shirt and yellow bow-tie. But the whole thing reminded her of how cute he'd looked when she'd first seen him. As soon as she'd thought it, the demons of regret kidnapped her thoughts.

'I see you were forced to participate in this, too.'

'Not forced,' he disagreed.

She nodded. Took another breath. 'Why are you here?'

'You're upset.'

'I am,' she said, ignoring the tightening of her throat at how vulnerable admitting it made her feel. 'But it isn't your responsibility to come after me.'

'Autumn seemed to think it might be.'

'She's wrong.' And Summer would speak to her about it. 'I'm not anyone's responsibility.'

'You are when people care about you,' he said swiftly.

She snorted. 'People don't care about me. I'm not a priority—'

She stopped. 'I'm sorry,' she said. 'You didn't deserve that.'

'Except I think that I did,' he said softly. 'I'm sorry I made you feel that way.'

'I wasn't talking about you,' she said, raw.

'Doesn't mean it's not true.' He paused. 'I've spent my entire life knowing what it's like not to be a priority. I'm sorry I did the same thing to you.'

'You're not the only one.' She released a breath. 'I prioritised my own issues over our marriage.'

He nodded, acknowledging it. Then his face tightened. 'We don't have to talk about this. I just wanted to know that you're okay.'

'I am,' she said. 'I'm fine. So... I'll see you back at the party.'

She'd dismissed him—plainly and somewhat embarrassingly—and yet he didn't move. Instead, he kept his steady gaze on her, watching her. *Seeing* her. Just as he had the night at the Christmas party.

It broke something inside her, thinking that. She wished she could go back and start over. That they could start over.

It was a futile fantasy. The only reason she was thinking it at all was because she was free of her father's secret with her family.

But she was still caught in it with Wyatt. She might think that he could get over her father's affair now, that it wouldn't affect what he was working towards, but it didn't change that she'd let it eat at their marriage. She'd let her feelings about being isolated in her family isolate her in her own marriage. Yes, Wyatt wasn't innocent in it, but neither was she. And it was time she took responsibility for it.

She'd broken the relationships in her life. She'd lost the man she'd loved—the man she still loved—because of it.

The realisation was too much for the pure will that had been holding back her tears. She felt her face crumple, heard her throaty sob, before she realised what was happening. She turned her back to him and pressed a fist to her forehead, embarrassed beyond measure that she was breaking down in front of him. That she felt safe enough to show him behind the mask now. *Now.* When she didn't know what he'd see.

Warm arms pulled her in before she knew he was even in front of her. His hand pressed gently against her head, encouraging her to lean against him.

She did.

Embarrassment fizzled as emotion took over, her mind once again handing the reins to her heart now that she felt secure. Her heart had no problem with breaking down from all the pain it had felt the last eight years. Pain that had started the moment she'd found out about her father's affair. Pain she'd stuffed down to the bottom of her heart. Pain that would no longer allow itself to be ignored.

She hadn't cried when she'd found out. Or after, when her father had made his request. But she did now. She realised how much she'd lost now. How much her carrying that secret had cost her.

She'd thought she'd been protecting Wyatt by keeping the truth from him. She still believed that, though she recognised it as an excuse, too. Autumn was right, she had been afraid of getting hurt again. Not because she believed Wyatt would cheat on her. Not entirely.

She just didn't want to be left alone by the man who'd always managed to make her feel included. She didn't want to be cast aside, only to discover one day that her husband had replaced her with someone else. Most of all, she didn't want to lose being understood. Being seen. Especially after the years she hadn't been. She'd shut down when she'd thought that had happened. She'd thought it would be better if she chose it. But it wasn't. The defence mechanism had simply isolated her further.

She pulled away from him with that thought. She didn't deserve that he comfort her. She pressed her hand to her mouth, wishing she had a tissue so she could, at the very least, blow her nose. A handkerchief appeared in her line of vision. She mumbled a 'Thank you' before cleaning her face, and tried not to notice the make-up smudges on the white material.

When she looked up, his expression was kind.

'Don't look at me like that.' Her voice was strangled.

'Like what?'

'Like you feel sorry for me.'

'Not for you,' he disagreed. 'For what you're going through.'

'Well, don't,' she told him, straightening her shoulders. 'I deserve to feel this way. I put myself in this situation.' She paused. 'With some help from my father. But these were my actions, and—'

'Summer, I have no idea what you're talking about.'

She looked at him, and something inside her said, *Screw it*.

'I know. It's time that you do.'

* * *

Seeing Summer cry had shaken him. So had feeling her trembling body in his arms as the tears worked their way through her. Now she was staring at him with those big brown eyes wide, her mascara smudged, and her expression determined.

His stomach twisted at her beauty.

'Wyatt,' she said. He forced himself to focus on what she was saying. 'You're probably going to hate me after telling you this. I'm sorry.' She paused, bit her lip as tears gleamed in her eyes again.

Then she shook her head and swallowed.

'I'm sorry for what I've let it do to our relationship. And what it might do to how you see my father.'

'Your father? I don't—'

'He cheated on my mother,' she blurted out. Took a breath. 'Eight years ago, I found out before he told my mother and... He asked me to keep it a secret. From my mother and Autumn. Until the O'Brien deal went through, which was two months later.'

Her chest expanded and contracted. For some reason he found himself watching that instead of looking at her face.

'For two months, I watched my family be a family without me. I couldn't participate knowing what I knew. Even after they found out about the affair...' She took a breath. 'We didn't tell them I knew. It became this weight I carried with me. Like I was watching my family move on, move forward without me, and the weight kept me behind.'

It took a long time for him to reply, mostly because he hadn't realised she'd stopped talking. His brain had selectively taken in the information she'd told him. Now, it was playing it back so he could have all of the facts before he replied. It seemed like a safe way to do it. Yet when he spoke, he could have sworn he hadn't made any attempt at processing at all.

'Your father *cheated*?'

She gave a stiff nod.

'He asked you to keep it from your family?'

She nodded again.

'And from me?'

Her eyebrows rose, and she shook her head.

'Why didn't you tell me?'

'I—I didn't tell anyone.'

'I was your husband,' he said in a hard voice. 'I told you things I didn't tell anyone else.'

'Which made me realise I couldn't tell you!' she exclaimed. 'You were aiming for my father's life, Wyatt. It gave you purpose. A way out of what you went through with your parents.' She stopped to take a breath. 'How could I tell you that life didn't exist?'

'So your leaving wasn't because you thought you weren't what I wanted.'

She closed her eyes with a shake of her head. When she looked at him again, he felt the emotion there as if it were his own.

'It was a combination of the two. I knew I wouldn't be what you wanted because I knew that life didn't exist.'

'That's not the only reason you didn't tell me, though.'

'It's part of it.' Her eyelashes fluttered. 'The rest is… My father's secret isolated me from my family. Your determination to become him isolated me from—' She hesitated. 'From you.'

He saw that. Along with everything else he'd realised, he could see how she must have felt as though she'd had no choice but to leave. But it didn't keep him from getting angry that she hadn't told him the truth. That she'd made decisions for him. That she'd tried to protect him when, really, he'd needed her honesty.

'My father isn't someone you should look up to, Wyatt.'

'That isn't for you to say.'

Her head dipped. 'Do *you* say so?'

He took a moment to figure out the answer, then shook his head.

'I don't think I care.'

'You don't...' she repeated softly. 'This doesn't affect the way you see him at all? The way you see his life? The one you so desperately wanted to have?'

'No,' he said dismissively. When a tear trailed down her cheek, he clenched his jaw and tried to answer. 'It makes me see your father's human, like you tried to convince me last night.'

'You didn't believe me then.'

'I didn't know this.' He thought about it. 'In all honesty, it makes me like him even more. I don't like what he did,' he added quickly, when the colour disappeared from her face, 'but he made a mistake. Clearly he's made up for it or today wouldn't have happened.' He shrugged. 'He made a mistake and he still has a good life.'

'You respect him even though you know what he did? To my mother—to *me*?' Her voice was small.

He ran a hand through his hair. 'I don't know what you want me to say, Summer. He's been the most consistent presence in my life in the last nine years. Hell, he's been more consistent than my own parents were when they were still in the picture.' His hand dropped. 'This news... It's disappointing, sure, but it doesn't change our relationship.'

'But...'

She stopped, her face twisted in pain, and enough sympathy pooled inside him that he said, 'Summer.'

She didn't reply, just pushed that gorgeous mane of curls back and stared up into the sky. When she looked back at him, her eyes were steady.

'When you told me about your parents, I realised how significant your relationship with my father was. Is. I didn't want to be the one responsible for disillusioning you. Clearly I was wrong.'

'You were,' he said uncompromisingly.

'Because this doesn't change the way you think about my father?'

'No.'

She nodded, pursed her lips. 'Well, it did for me. I wasn't interested in repeating my mother's life. You were turning into my father,' she continued at his frown. 'What stopped me from turning into my mother? The woman who was second-best to my father's business? Who eventually slipped so far down on his list of priorities that he cheated?'

'You did,' he said after a moment. 'You stopped yourself from turning into her.'

'Damn right I did.'

'You thought you were protecting me, but you were really protecting yourself.'

'Clearly I needed to.'

He stared at her. 'I can't believe you'd say that.'

'I can't believe what my father did to me doesn't faze you in the least.'

'Because you did it to yourself.'

He saw her wince, but he refused to let it soften his heart.

'You chose to leave me instead of talk to me about this. You didn't even think about needing to protect me from *that*. From being abandoned one more time.' He barely paused to take a breath. 'I told you about my mother and father leaving and your first thought was about you.'

'I... No. I didn't want to hurt you.'

'No, you didn't want to hurt *yourself*,' he retorted. 'All because *you* couldn't face that your father was human.'

He was right.

The knowledge was worse than how coolly he'd responded to her father's affair. Or how he was focusing on the wrong thing in it all. No, not the wrong thing, she thought. The *right* thing.

She'd accused Wyatt of placing Trevor on a pedestal because that was what she had done. She'd told him to see her father as human because she hadn't. She hadn't allowed Trevor any space to make mistakes. To *be* human. She hadn't truly known him; only the version of him she'd created in her mind.

That version had been based on the man who had always been there, even if he'd been distracted. Who'd showed her such patience when teaching her about the Bishop business. Who believed in her enough to want her to take over. Who cared for her enough to show her how.

It hadn't considered the distractions when he was around. The focus on the business. She'd only seen her father's priorities after she'd discovered his affair. Realising that had opened her eyes to all of his weaknesses. And that had thrown her life into disarray.

Because she'd seen what she'd wanted to.

She'd done the same thing with Wyatt. Her actions in her marriage had been because she'd thought she knew how things would go. She'd projected so much of her father onto Wyatt she hadn't given him a chance to prove her wrong. She'd seen what she'd wanted to and acted according to that. His unexpected reaction now proved it.

She was wrong. Had been for so long.

How could she trust herself after that?

Her eyes fluttered to Wyatt's face, and she knew with certainty that, subconsciously, she hadn't trusted herself for the longest time. She'd fooled herself into believing she could because that was how Wyatt made her feel. He saw through the pretence and the hurt. Because of it, she saw through it, too. Enough that she'd agreed to marry him.

But that feeling hadn't stayed for long. When she'd realised what Wyatt had wanted, needed, she hadn't trusted herself to be able to give it. And her trust in herself, in her feelings for him, had diminished even more. So she'd used her father's affair to protect herself. She'd used her own response to it to anticipate what Wyatt's response might be, as if it were a test.

One she now knew she'd failed.

Her stomach churned. And though, logically, she knew it wasn't possible, her heart churned, too. It was so disappointed it couldn't trust its feelings for the man that filled it with warmth. The man it had never stopped loving. The man she'd never stop loving.

But that love didn't matter because it came from her. She couldn't trust that she hadn't fallen in love with someone who might hurt her. And she couldn't spend her life or their relationship trying to anticipate that hurt. Trying to protect herself from it. Trying to protect herself from *herself.*

She couldn't put Wyatt through that either.

'To think,' Wyatt said softly, oblivious to her inner turmoil, 'if you'd told me the truth, we might have still been married.'

She stared at him, and it was as if scales had fallen from her eyes.

'No,' she said. 'I don't think we would have been.'

'What?'

'You said you felt me pulling away from you. Which is true, I did. I didn't trust that I could give you what you needed from me.' She paused. 'But you pulled away from me, too, Wyatt.'

He frowned. 'I was…responding to you being distant.'

'I was responding to *you* being distant,' she shot back. 'You know that. But telling the story that way keeps you from being a hypocrite, doesn't it?' She didn't give him a chance to answer. 'You used your reaction to your parents' abandonment to anticipate my reaction, too. You thought I'd respond by telling you that you weren't what I wanted, so you pushed yourself harder to give me the life you thought I wanted.'

She shook her head.

'But that's not my point.'

'You have one?'

She ignored the jibe. 'If you felt me pulling away, why didn't you say anything?'

Confusion settled over his features. 'I thought…it was always going to happen, I guess.'

'But you tried to keep it from happening.' She paused. 'Why not just talk to me?'

'Are you punishing me?' he asked after a moment. 'Because I said you should have talked to me?'

'No,' she answered. 'I think you're right. I should have spoken to you. If I could go back and change that, I would. But that doesn't mean we wouldn't have ended up here.'

He didn't reply. She sighed.

'Our relationship wouldn't have lasted, Wyatt. I can't be in a relationship. I don't trust myself. How can I expect to trust you?' She took a breath. 'But also because you don't want to be in the relationship. Not with me, not with anyone.'

CHAPTER SIXTEEN

'THAT'S NOT TRUE.' He shook his head vehemently. 'I asked you to marry me. Of course I wanted to be in a relationship. With you. How did this become about me anyway?' he asked. 'How are you blaming me?'

'We're both to blame for our relationship ending, Wyatt.'

He shook his head again.

'You just said you always thought I was going to leave,' she pointed out. 'How can you start a relationship expecting that?' And then she saw it. 'But you did. That's why you asked me out after knowing me for a few hours. That's why you asked me to marry you after knowing me for six months.' She almost laughed. 'You were setting our relationship up to fail.'

She waited for a reply. It didn't come.

'You didn't even fight when I asked for the divorce.'

'I asked you why,' he said mechanically.

'And accepted the obvious lie I told you.'

She removed the emotion from her voice, speaking coolly to try and combat the heat in his eyes. She had no intention of fighting with him. She was too tired. Tired of what the conversation had forced her to face. Tired of pretending: to herself, to the world. To Wyatt.

Pretending she didn't have feelings for him would likely be the death of her.

'Look, we should probably get back—'

'We're not done,' he interrupted.

'What more is there to say?' she asked, no longer keeping the fatigue from her voice.

'What about an apology?'

'I'm sorry.'

'What are you apologising for?'

'What do you want me to apologise for?'

'Summer—'

'No,' she cut him off. 'I'm done. We wouldn't have worked out. I don't know if I can trust who I think the people I love are and you're...' She lifted her eyes. 'You're far too afraid of someone leaving you to be fully invested in any relationship.'

'Why are you saying these things?' he asked. 'They're not true.'

She studied him, saw he believed what he was saying, and threw caution to the wind.

'Okay, then. Actually, it's perfect for me because I'm tired of the turmoil of keeping things to myself.' She paused for a second.

'I meant what I said on the beach last night. I... I love you. I love your work ethic and your loyalty. I love how freely you give of yourself to other people. *For* other people. I love how you see me. How you've always been able to see me. I love this feeling—' she pressed a fist to the base of her stomach '—right here that heats and trembles whenever I'm near you.'

'Summer.'

His voice was breathless, his face stricken, and her mouth curved. She walked towards him, rested a hand on his chest, over his heart. Feeling the rapid beat of it, she exhaled shakily.

'Your heart's beating much too fast.' Her hand lowered to his stomach. 'And there's panic turning your stomach.' The hand lifted to his neck. 'Your throat's thickening, too.' She waited a beat. 'Am I right?'

He nodded.

'That's because you don't want me to be in love with you,' she whispered. 'You're terrified of being in a relationship.'

'This is not fair,' he rasped.

She studied him, then rose up on her toes and pressed the lightest of kisses to his lips. The feel of it sank right down to her toes.

'No, it's not,' she said gently. 'But it is what it is. We weren't meant to be, Wyatt. We won't ever be.'

With the pieces of her heart trailing behind her, she made her way back to the wedding.

After his conversation with Summer, Wyatt was tempted to let Trevor down.

He wanted nothing more than to go back to his cabin, pack up his things, and return to Cape Town. In fact, he made it halfway to his cabin before sanity prevailed and he dragged himself back to the celebrations.

He couldn't disappoint Trevor, no matter how strong the temptation was. To him, that felt like proof Summer was wrong. He wasn't afraid of relationships. He'd had a long, stable one with Trevor for years.

His conscience had chosen that moment to remind him of the caution he'd exercised in that relationship. And how he'd panicked when Trevor had asked him to be in the ceremony. When Summer had told him her father saw him as family.

It might have been proof that he'd forged a relationship over the years, but it also proved that every step he'd taken had felt like a tremendous feat. A compelling argument in favour of Summer's words.

It had hooked into his brain, that thought—that realisation—so the reception was not a pleasant experience. He managed to avoid most of the chit-chat because of his conversation with Summer, but caught enough to be relieved when dinner was served.

He was seated at the same table as Summer and Autumn, though he'd been relegated to the opposite end of where they sat. Summer studiously avoided his gaze.

When he made eye contact with Autumn, she mouthed the word 'sorry'. He nodded, though he wasn't sure what she was apologising for. The celebrations dragged out, though the formal part had been mercifully quick, so he had no reason to stay after the dessert was served.

When he was sure no one would notice his departure, he sneaked out of the venue and made it all of five metres before he heard his name. He waited when he turned and saw Autumn running towards him. He waited some more when she caught up with him, but not her breath.

'Running in sand is really *hard*,' she huffed, and his smile grew.

'Apparently.'

'Please, have some empathy.' She braced on her knees, then straightened. 'Not all of us are perfect human specimens.'

His eyebrows lifted. 'Was that meant to be a compliment?'

'It was a compliment, but it's kind of an insult, too, mainly because your tone suggested you were making fun of me. But it doesn't matter,' she said, waving her hand, placing both of her hands on her hips now. 'I'm not here to give you compliments.'

'How disappointing,' he said dryly.

She gave him a look. 'I wanted to say sorry about the tension during dinner.'

'It's not your fault.'

'I feel like it is,' Autumn admitted. 'I told her to tell you the truth… I encouraged you to go after her… I feel like I facilitated it somewhat.'

'Why?'

'I told you—'

'No, I mean why did you tell her to tell me the truth?' he interrupted.

'Oh.' She frowned. 'You guys still have feelings for one another.'

'I don't—' He broke off. 'I don't have feelings for her.'

Autumn's eyebrows lifted so high he was surprised they didn't disappear into her hair.

'Oh. I didn't realise we were ignoring the real world,' she commented. 'But her annoyance with you kind of makes sense now. She tells you she loves you, and—'

'She told you that?' he asked, his heart doing a strange skip in his chest. 'She told you she loves me?'

'Yes. Not that she had to,' Autumn said. 'She's never stopped loving you.' She made a face. 'Why are you pretending not to know this?'

'She said she loves me,' he replied slowly. 'She didn't say she's always loved me.'

Autumn snorted. 'Were your moves that good this weekend you thought you'd convinced her into falling in love with you again?'

He didn't know what to say.

She laughed, then her face sobered. 'Look, I know things are complicated. But the thing with my father, and the secret? It hurt her. We hurt her.' Autumn's face tightened. 'Despite that, she still told you she loved you. Tell me you don't think that means something.'

He couldn't.

Not that it mattered. He'd dealt with everything so poorly. Part of that had been because he'd wanted to tell her he loved her too.

He took a deep breath. 'You don't have to apologise,' he said to Autumn. 'None of this is your fault. Not really.'

She threaded her fingers together.

'I know I'm going to be out of line with this, but if you do have feelings for Summer—' her tone made it clear she believed he did '—you should prove it to her. Be there for her. Prove you are who she thinks you are.'

He nodded, but things were happening in his body again. The same things Summer had pointed out when she'd said she loved him. The pumping heart, the panicked stomach, the thickening throat. He ignored them and said goodnight to Autumn before making his way back to his cabin.

It was a peaceful walk, mainly because all the lodge's guests were still celebrating at the beach. It had taken him a while to realise no one other than the Bishop party was staying at the lodge for the weekend. But then, the Bishops were known for their wealth just as much as they were for their close-knit family. He supposed that was part of what upset him about Summer's secrets.

His entire career at Bishop Enterprises, he'd idolised Trevor Bishop. Not only because of what the man had done for him, but because of what Trevor had achieved. He'd turned the company his father had started into one worth billions. All with a solid marriage and a happy family in tow.

Except hearing about Trevor's affair hadn't surprised him. Wyatt didn't care much for the moral implications of it, but he wasn't surprised. Which told Wyatt he'd suspected the life he'd idolised Trevor for couldn't be real. It proved he'd been after an illusion. An unattainable idea. Just as Summer had said.

Had he been so desperate for a better life than what he'd grown up with that he'd made up the one he was working towards? Or had he just allowed that illusion to obscure how much he wanted a family?

A little of both, he thought, though it was the last one that stung. It forced him to recognise what longing for a father-son, mother-son relationship meant. It forced him to face how much his parents had hurt him by leaving. How much Summer had hurt him by leaving.

Facing it made him realise how upset he was with himself. For creating the illusion. For believing it existed. He knew it didn't. But he'd needed to believe it did to get him out of the hole he'd been in during university.

He saw that now, clearly. Which meant he knew that

part of why Summer had left had been valid. If she'd told him the truth, he would have been disillusioned sooner. Or he would have had to face the truth sooner. Would it have caused him to devolve into angry, aimless Wyatt? He didn't know. He supposed that uncertainty had prompted Summer into avoiding even the risk of it.

But if there'd been something inside him that had believed the idea didn't exist, shouldn't it have steered him away from relationships? It might not have been conscious, but considering his own relationship experiences, shouldn't he have run away from Summer?

You were setting our relationship up to fail.

Summer's words echoed in his head. They had that same heartbreaking quality to them as when she'd said them the first time. He'd been offended by the accusation then. He'd been angry and not thinking straight, and his instinct had been to lash out. But she was right. And so was he. There had been something that had steered him away from relationships. It hadn't been conscious, or mature, and so it had manifested itself in exactly the way Summer had said.

He *had* set their relationship up to fail.

He reached his cabin as that thought allowed a flood of emotions, of questions in. The last thing he wanted as that happened was to be confined between four walls. Before long, he found himself on the path leading down to the beach where he'd kissed Summer what felt like a lifetime ago.

It seemed right to be there. This was where things had changed between him and Summer. Or had that happened that night on the bridge, where he'd seen her vulnerable for the first time since she'd asked for a divorce? Where he'd allowed *himself* to be vulnerable for the first time since telling her about his parents?

Perhaps that was why he hadn't stopped feeling since that night. He'd opened the door and had forgotten to close it. Or had been unable to close it. Spending time with Summer seemed to have that effect. It scared him. Same as when he'd fallen in love with her all those years ago.

He'd gone into defence mode then. Or self-destruct mode. And he'd sabotaged his relationship with her. He'd proposed after six months of dating. He'd told her about his parents knowing it would change things for him. He'd spent their marriage pursuing a life he knew didn't exist. He'd let her down, countless times.

His heart ached at the way he'd treated her. Though he supposed there was something significant about that. He'd never felt the need to sabotage his relationships with other women in the same way. Not that he'd stuck around long enough to. His longest relationship before his marriage had been a year and he'd spent more than half that time travelling for work. He hadn't even considered feelings then. Now he saw he'd purposely orchestrated his life so he wouldn't have to.

Then Summer had come along. What he'd felt for her had been different. More intense. Scary. Instead of taking a step back and dealing with that fear, he'd identified all the exits and sped through the closest one when she'd presented it as an option. Hell, he hadn't only identified exits, he'd *built* them. Because of that fear.

That fear that had awoken in his veins when his father had left. That had taken residence when his mother had gone to rehab for the first time. That had dug in its roots and grown freely every time he'd had to go into foster care. That had overtaken everything when he'd come home that day and realised his mother had left for good.

He should have known the remnants of his past were still there. He should have seen his aversion to long-term relationships as a symptom of it. Should have seen his caution in his relationship with Trevor as a part of it. The fast pace of his relationship with Summer, too.

He should have realised he was protecting himself. Preparing himself. If he could protect himself—if he could prepare himself—maybe it wouldn't hurt so damn much when the people he cared about decided to leave.

Wyatt lowered to the sand, grabbed a fistful of it, and threw it into the receding waves as if somehow it would help him throw away his issues. Or the guilt that realising them brought.

He'd denied that he hadn't wanted a relationship with Summer. He stood by that. Because the truth wasn't that he didn't want it; he hadn't been ready for it. Everything that happened with Summer proved his feelings for her had been special. Considering that the fear was still throbbing heavily through his body, beating loudly in his ears, he thought those feelings might not only be in the past...

He looked around, saw the spot where he and Summer had lain in the sand. Where they'd shared things with one another. Where they'd opened up.

His eyes shifted to where he'd chased her on the sand. He could still hear her shriek of laughter. Could still feel the grin it had brought to his face.

And where he was standing had been where they'd kissed. Where he'd felt her soft body under his fingertips. Where the perfection of her lips had touched his.

There were other things racing through his mind, too. Like how Summer always put others above herself. Like how, despite how wealthy her family was, she hadn't sat back and enjoyed that wealth. How she'd gone out and made a name for herself. How she was the most down-to-earth person he knew.

She was the most caring person he knew, too. She loved deeply; hurt deeply. Having someone she cared about betray her trust must have stung. Feeling like an outcast because of it, though she'd done nothing wrong...

He could see how he'd made her feel isolated in their marriage. And how feeling that way with him must have hurt her.

He could also see why she'd want to protect him from that kind of hurt, too.

He stilled as warmth spread through his body at that. At how her thinking about wanting to protect him at all was more than either of his parents had done. She might have been misguided in her motivations for leaving him, but they were nobler than either of his parents', he was sure. And she'd done it all in spite of how he'd hurt her.

Besides, it wasn't a small thing that she wanted him to have the life he'd always wanted. She believed in him. Not in the way Trevor did, for his smarts or capabilities, but for who he was. For the person he was. Most of all, for who he had the potential to be.

It complicated things, these realisations. It complicated...feelings. He knew what those feelings were, but he didn't know what to do about them. Especially not when his fear still mingled with them. When he was still afraid of being abandoned.

When the sun started to light the sky, he wasn't any closer to knowing what he should do about them. Or the urgency accompanying them.

CHAPTER SEVENTEEN

SUMMER HAD PACKED her stuff before Autumn returned to the cabin after the wedding. When her sister walked in shortly after midnight, she greeted Autumn with her luggage.

'What's going on?'

'I'm leaving.'

Autumn's brows lifted. 'Right now?'

'I would have left much earlier if I hadn't waited to say goodbye to you.'

'Thank you for being so considerate,' Autumn replied dryly. 'Seriously, Sun, you can't leave now. It's after midnight.'

'You drove after midnight last night,' Summer reminded her.

'Because I needed to be here for Mom and Dad today. Not because I was feeling emotional and had to escape my ex.'

Summer's back went up. 'Really?' She narrowed her eyes. 'How is Hunter, by the way?'

Autumn's straightened. 'He's fine.'

'Hmm. Your friendship is going well, then, is it?'

Autumn folded her arms. 'Yes, actually it is.'

'So you wouldn't even be tempted into running if you told him you loved him? And he didn't reply,' she added flatly, when Autumn opened her mouth.

There was a pause.

'Fine, I supposed I'd be tempted to.' Autumn threw her clutch onto the couch. 'But I wouldn't let him ruin the time I got to spend with my family because of it.'

'Of course you wouldn't, Autumn. You're perfect.'

Autumn tilted her head. 'Not sure I deserved that.'

Summer exhaled. 'No, you didn't.' She cleared her throat. 'But spending time with the family isn't exactly a pleasure for me.'

'I know,' Autumn said, her face softening. 'I'm sorry you went through that. I should have—'

'It's not your fault, Wind,' Summer interrupted, mostly because she didn't have the energy to dive into it. 'Look, I just need some space. And since there's little chance of me getting sleep tonight, I might as well make the best of the time.'

'Sun,' Autumn said slowly. Summer waited for the lecture. 'I don't want you to drive in this state. You didn't have any sleep last night either. At least try to get some rest. If you can't, I'll drive us home in the morning.' She put her hand on Summer's arm. 'Please, don't go.'

Summer studied her sister's face, saw the genuine concern there, and heaved out a breath. 'Fine. But first thing in the morning...'

Autumn crossed her heart, brought two fingers to her lips, and then lifted them to the air in the salute they'd created when they'd been kids.

Six hours later, Summer was kissing her sister on the forehead while Autumn slept, rolling her bags out the door.

She hadn't made the promise, she told herself when her conscience poked at her. Besides, she didn't want to cut short Autumn's time with their parents because of her emotions. She'd done that far too many times in the past. Things would change in the future. She'd make sure of it.

She packed her luggage into her boot. When she closed it, she jumped when her father appeared at her side.

'What are you *doing*?' she asked, pressing a hand to her heart.

'I saw you making your escape.'

'How?' Summer looked around. 'Your cabin is on the other side of the lodge.'

Trevor pursed his lips; Summer rolled her eyes.

'Autumn.' Summer frowned. 'She sent *you*?' She winced at the incredulity in her voice. Then, with a shake of her head, said, 'I'm sorry, I didn't mean that.'

'You did. It's fair.' Trevor gave her a steady look. 'How about we take a walk down to the beach before you go?'

Again? Summer wanted to ask, but caught the question before she could. Clearly Autumn thought she needed to speak with their father, which wasn't untrue. Summer had planned to have a conversation with him as part of her 'things would change' resolution. Although she hadn't counted on it being so soon.

When their feet touched the sand of the beach, Summer said, 'I have something to say to you,' at the same time her father said, 'I'd like to apologise.'

Then they both said, 'What?'

'Let me go first,' Trevor told her, 'since I need to say something I should have years ago.'

Summer nodded and put her hands into her jersey's pockets.

'I'm sorry, Summer. For the affair. For asking you to keep it a secret. For seeing what it did to you and not doing anything about it.'

Summer swallowed, shutting her eyes against the tears that immediately began to burn there.

'I should never have asked it from you. Or let you suffer for it as long as you did.'

She felt her father's hand on her wrist, and she stopped walking, opening her eyes. The sincerity on his face soothed her; the sadness unsettled her.

'I know I hurt you.' He cleared his throat. 'I thought it would be easier if I ignored—'

'Dad,' she interrupted. 'You don't have to explain. I know why you didn't do anything about it.'

'You do?'

'Yeah. It was easier to hurt me than to hurt Mom again. I get it.'

Trevor's face tightened. 'I'm so sorry, Summer.'

'I know.' She took a shaky breath and looked up. 'But I did some of it to myself, too.' She met his gaze. 'You hurt me. I felt...betrayed. About everything.' She started to look down, then forced herself to keep eye contact. 'I stopped trusting you because you weren't who I thought you were.'

Trevor's eyes gleamed, but the nod of his head was firm.

'I stopped trusting myself because of it. I thought you were one person, and you turned out to be another, and I didn't know how I missed it.' His eyes widened, but she kept talking. 'It's messed me up. I only saw how much this weekend.' She took a breath. 'I have a long way to go before I can put it behind me.'

Trevor looked down.

'But I'm willing to try.'

His head shot up. 'You are?'

Something similar to a smile touched her lips. 'Yeah. I'm taking responsibility for our family, too.' She waited a beat. 'So you can go back and tell Mom you apologised.'

His lips curved, but it wasn't a smile.

'I wanted to do this,' he said. 'I didn't do it because she told me to.'

She studied him, and saw a sincerity in his eyes that she hadn't for the longest time. She nodded, then stepped closer to him. Carefully, she wrapped her hands around his waist, rested her head against his chest. She felt his hesitation before his arms went around her, and they stood like that for a moment before stepping away.

She pretended not to notice the tears that trailed down her father's cheeks.

'I'm going to make it up to you,' Trevor promised.

She nodded, folded her arms. His eyes shifted to be-hind her.

'Starting now,' he said, moving forward and kissing her on the forehead. 'You should try with him, too, Sun.'

She frowned, opened her mouth to answer, but he was already walking away. When she turned, she saw Wyatt a few metres behind him.

Wyatt braced when he saw Summer's body tense, though he wasn't sure why. Would he chase her if she tried to run? Or would he have let her go, considering not five minutes ago he wasn't sure what he'd say to her when he saw her?

His heart immediately steeled with resolution, his mind following.

No more letting her go.

'You're up early,' she noted demurely.

'Not up early,' he told her. 'Going to bed late.'

An eyebrow quirked. 'You couldn't sleep?'

'Not after what happened last night, no.'

She studied him. 'Don't let me stop you.'

'Actually,' he said softly, 'I think I have to.'

'What?'

'You were here with your father,' he said, ignoring her question.

'Yes.'

'Everything okay?'

Her arms tightened at the front of her chest. 'It will be.'

'Good.'

A long pause followed his pathetic answer.

'Well,' she said, when the awkwardness reached peak level. 'I guess... I'm going to leave.'

'No, wait,' he said before she could, panic spurring the words. Then, when she didn't move, only looked at him expectantly, panic turned into fear. He'd never been more terrified in his life.

'Wyatt?'

'I built exits,' he said, 'in our relationship. I built…
exits.'

'Am I supposed to know what that means?'

'Yes,' he replied. 'And you do.'

She bit her lip, then inclined her head in acknowledgement. 'You were looking for a way out.'

'I started our relationship knowing exactly where the
ways out were. I… I helped create them. I pushed us both
towards them with the way I behaved. So,' he added measuredly, 'you were right last night. We probably *would*
have ended up here anyway.'

'You know,' she said after a few seconds, 'if you built
the exits, I handed you the tools.' She paused. 'I was always afraid I wouldn't be able to trust you. Because I
didn't—don't—trust myself. Or my belief of who you
were. Because of what happened with my father. Or whatever,' she ended on a mutter, her face turning red.

Seconds ticked by.

'We were both wrong, then,' he said.

She lifted a shoulder. 'Or we were both right and this…
didn't have a future.'

'Does it now?' he asked, through numb lips—and with
a numb mind, since he had no idea where that question
had come from.

Or no, wait, he did. It had come from the fact that she
loved him. That he'd never stopped loving her. Suddenly it
became clearer than it had ever been. That this was more
important than the fear. That this was worth the chance.

'How can it?' she interrupted his thoughts. 'I still don't
trust me. And you… You still don't want a relationship.'

A brand-new fear began to thrum through his body,
more urgent than the other he'd let control his life. Finally
he realised his past fears had been so extreme with Summer because he knew she'd be the most important person
in his life. Which was why it had hurt so damn much that
she'd given up on them.

Yet he'd given up on them, too.

But no more.

'What if I prove that you can trust you?'

She laughed softly. Heartbrokenly. 'How are you going to do that?'

'By showing you that you can trust who you think I am.' He reached for her hands. 'No matter how long that takes.'

Summer couldn't believe her ears. But there was warmth spreading through the icy coldness of her body; of her heart.

This is really happening.

Even in her worst nights after the divorce, when she'd missed him with everything inside her, she hadn't allowed herself to think about getting back together with him. Now that the possibility was here, she couldn't believe it.

'What if it never happens?' she asked.

It was easier to dread the worst than to hope for the best.

'Worst-case scenario?' he asked, brow furrowed. 'We spend our lives enjoying each other.'

'That's a big ask from someone who's spent his life running from commitment.'

'We prefer "fearing abandonment",' he said dryly, before his expression sobered. 'I know. So I suppose we won't only be proving you can trust me.' He paused. 'We'll be proving I'm… I'm safe with you.'

She studied him. Saw the passionate, resolute answers he'd give her if she asked him every question going through her mind on his face. In the light shining so fiercely in his eyes.

'That's a big ask from someone who doesn't love me,' she said quietly.

His eyes swept over her face. 'Are you fishing for compliments?'

'Why would I—?'

'Because you want me to tell you that I like you. Your

dry humour and the way you put rich people in their place.'
He plucked a stray curl and pulled it down, before letting
the spiral bounce back up. 'I like how you get annoyed
with me. With people. And with yourself. And your feelings.'

Her lips twitched, but he continued before she could
say anything.

'I like how you care about me,' he said. 'That you tried
to protect me, even if being honest with me would have
been better.'

'Wyatt—'

'You should have been honest with me,' he interrupted,
'but I shouldn't have let you leave. I should have fought.'
His lips curved, then straightened. 'I'm fighting now.'

Her eyes welled up with hope—that damn *hope* that
wouldn't go away—but she shook her head. 'We haven't
changed, Wyatt. I haven't changed—'

'That's not true,' he said, his fingers gently holding her
chin. 'You've realised things about yourself. I've realised
things about myself.' He paused. 'Are you telling me that
hasn't changed you? Because it's certainly changed me.'

She thought about all the things she'd learnt after this
experience. Like how she'd been too hard on her family. How maybe…maybe she'd been too hard on herself,
too. And that she'd let both those things control her life
for too long.

Which probably meant she had changed.

'You really want to try?' she asked huskily. 'You're not
afraid any more?'

'I'm terrified,' he said with a raw laugh. 'But I'm more
afraid of losing you.'

She blinked rapidly, but it did nothing to deter the tears
that fell down her cheeks. 'I like you, too, for the record.'
She cleared her throat. 'I like that you made something
of yourself. I like how funny you are. I like that you see
me. No,' she said, 'I *love* that you see me.'

She lifted a hand and cupped his cheek, then brought her lips up to his, kissing him with the rest of her answer. With the simple *I love you*. There was passion and romance and happiness in that kiss. When they parted, they were both breathing heavily.

'I love you, too,' he said with a breathless laugh. Her eyes filled again. 'Hey,' he said, 'hey, that's a good thing.'

'I know,' she said with a little sob. 'It's just that you knew exactly what I was saying with that kiss and I haven't slept properly in weeks and I'm so tired.'

He laughed and pulled her into his arms. 'I know, baby.' He kissed her head. 'How about we get some breakfast and then some sleep?' He paused. 'Then make our way down to reception to extend our stay here.'

She pulled back. 'Why?'

'I don't know.' Colour curled up his neck, and Summer hid her smile. 'I thought it might be nice to stay here and get to know one another again. It's an idea. A terrible one, it seems, but...' He trailed off. 'Why are you looking at me like that?'

'I'm waiting for you to tire yourself out,' she said with a smile. 'I like the idea, Montgomery. It would be kind of nice to have a little holiday at the beach. If you promise to keep the water to yourself. I'm not having you "accidentally" throw it on my back while I'm suntanning again.'

He grinned. 'No promises.'

'Mont—'

He silenced her with a kiss. And for the first time in for ever, Summer felt like the sun.

EPILOGUE

'FIVE YEARS LATER, and still as beautiful as ever.'

'Why, thank you,' Summer said lazily, not bothering to open her eyes. 'Anything is possible with a balanced diet and exercise regime.'

'You know I wasn't talking about you.'

'And yet I answered, Montgomery,' she replied, opening her eyes and pushing herself up on the beach towel she was suntanning on. 'Probably because I'm tired of you saying how beautiful this place is. We've been here for three days. It's time to get over it.'

'Don't sound so bitter,' he told her with a grin. She used the moment to enjoy him standing shirtless in front of her. 'This is our special place.'

Before she could respond, he was scooping her into his arms.

'I'm not bitter,' she continued as if he hadn't picked her up. 'I just don't want you to turn into that person who repeats the same things. By the way, what are you doing?' she asked calmly.

'What I should have done five years ago.'

'To clarify—that would be to drop me into the ocean?'

'Correct.'

Accepting her fate with a nod, Summer threaded her fingers behind Wyatt's neck. She couldn't even muster up annoyance that Wyatt was threatening to throw her into the ocean. Again. Every time they got near a body of water, Wyatt went through the same routine. Not once had he thrown her in.

Though this was different, Summer knew. For the first time in five years they'd returned to the lodge where they'd rekindled their relationship. Where Wyatt had threatened to throw her into the ocean that very first time. It was enough to make her nostalgic.

It wasn't an emotion she felt regularly; her present was much better than her past. Though she did have a fondness for the last time they'd been on this beach together. They'd recommitted to their relationship. And every day in the last five years, they'd grown stronger.

They hadn't rushed into their relationship this time. There had been no jumping past important steps. No spontaneous engagements. She and Wyatt had taken the time to build something beautiful. And they'd succeeded.

The first thing Wyatt had done when they'd got back to Cape Town was hire an assistant. It had helped him with the pressure at work, which left most of his evenings free. He and Summer spent their free time together as far as was possible, and Summer had no doubt Wyatt had prioritised her. She made sure she did the same for him.

The slogan for their rekindled relationship was that work was important, but the other was more important. Cheesy, but it worked.

The time they'd spent together had allowed them a safe space to work through their issues. Summer had learnt to explore her trust issues; Wyatt, his fears. Acknowledging that they had issues had been an incredible step forward. As had being honest with each other. There was communication and laughter. Disagreement and arguments. Make-up kisses and...more.

They'd forged a different relationship with her family, too. Wyatt had become more realistic in his expectations, which had allowed him to bond with her family. And Summer had allowed herself to be...herself. To be *freely* herself. There were weekly family dinners; business consultations with the previous and current CEOs of Bishop Enterprises; spa dates and event planning with her mother and sister.

So much had changed in the last five years. Summer couldn't imagine her life getting any better.

The thought stilled something inside her and Summer leaned back, content in Wyatt's arms.

'You aren't concerned about this at all, are you?' Wyatt asked, glancing down.

'Nope,' she said brightly.

'That takes some of the fun out of it.'

'Why do you think I'm approaching it this way?'

'Calling my bluff?'

'Even if you throw me into this water, my love, I will forgive—'

The rest of her sentence was engulfed by the water. She could still feel Wyatt's arms around her, which then dragged her up before she could fully process what had happened.

'What were you saying?' he asked with a grin, wiping the water from his face.

'Nothing,' she said through clenched teeth. She pushed her hair out of her own face. 'Though I'll admit, I didn't think you'd do it.'

'But you forgive me.'

She grunted, and he laughed before picking her up again. He stopped and set her down where the waves could only reach their feet.

'If it makes you feel any better, I did it for a reason.'

'Yeah, I know,' she said, folding her arms over her chest when a blast of wind made her shiver. 'You were being a jerk.'

'No.' His voice had thinned. Almost as if he were nervous. 'I didn't want you to expect this.'

'I didn't expect it,' she said dryly. 'I thought you were—'

That was when she saw him kneeling on the ground.

It took her a long time to find her voice.

'Well,' she said, barely louder than a whisper. 'You're right. I didn't expect this at all.'

Now the nerves danced across his face.

'In a good way or bad way?'

'Which way do you want it to be?' She laughed at his expression. 'A good way. Of course a good way. As if you didn't know,' she scoffed lightly.

He nodded—still nervous, which made her smile—before taking a box out of his pocket.

Y'You've wet it,' she said before she could help herself.

'It's sealed.'

He opened the box, took a small plastic bag out and reached inside it to reveal the most beautiful diamond ring. It was nothing like the one he'd first got her. That one had been large and ostentatious; part of what he'd thought she'd wanted, he'd told her later. This ring was a simple solitaire design.

It was perfect.

'So,' she said after a moment. 'Are you going to ask me?'

'I'm trying to figure out whether you want me to.'

'The past five years that I've stuck around haven't been enough to convince you?' she asked gently.

'No, they have,' he said, his teasing expression sobering. 'They absolutely have.' He took a shaky breath. 'I've felt safe with you for every day of these last five years. Every time my mind would expect you to leave. If we had an argument, or a disagreement. Or things went from easy to hard. But you didn't.' His eyes shone. 'And my heart told my mind it was a fool for thinking it.'

Another breath.

'I waited much too long to ask you this, especially considering I bought the ring a month into our new relationship.' He smiled. 'Will you marry me, Summer Bishop?'

Summer took the ring, slid it onto her hand.

'Does that give you your answer?'

He laughed and stood, pulling her in for a kiss. She put every single thing inside her in that kiss. When he leaned back, his eyes told her he knew all the things she wanted to say to him. There was time to say them all out loud later.

'Yes,' she said, reaching down and taking the plastic bag and ring box from him. 'In case you need to hear it.'

'I do.'

'I know.'

She took the ring off, put it back into the bag. Then she put the bag in the ring box and slipped the box into his pocket.

'What are you doing?'

'It's called payback, darling.'

'Pay—'

She didn't hear the rest. She was too busy tackling him into the ocean.

* * * * *

THE BABY ARRANGEMENT

TARA TAYLOR QUINN

For Finley Joseph.
May you always be aware how very much
you were wanted.
You've filled holes in many hearts, Little Man.

Chapter One

She didn't want dinner. She wanted his support of her plan to buy herself some sperm.

Excited in a way she hadn't been in far too long, Mallory Harris calmed herself as she waited for Braden to join her at the upscale, quiet restaurant he'd chosen for the meeting he'd called. Staring out the wall of windows toward the harbor, watching people walking along the decks of a cruise ship that had docked, she turned her attention to the pink skies beyond, the miraculous beauty of the sun's final rays gracing the Pacific before it would drop beyond the horizon for another day.

Wishing she'd ordered a glass of wine, she changed her mind and did so. A glass of her favorite California-grown Sauvignon Blanc. Braden would be expecting her to have one and she didn't want any raised eyebrows until she was ready to deliver her spiel.

A little liquid courage didn't hurt, either, though she wasn't normally one to seek sustenance from anyplace except inside herself. And somewhat from Braden. She and her ex-husband might not be simpatico, but she still trusted his judgment on most things. Things that didn't deal with actual emotions.

He'd had a reason for the upcoming dinner. Though they ate out together on a fairly regular basis, it was never just to eat. There was always something to talk about requiring them to come together.

Speculating about the reason for the meeting was wasted energy, she'd decided long ago. After three years of being post-divorce friends, she and Braden had found a groove with which they were both relatively comfortable. At least she thought so.

One was never quite sure how Braden felt—probably not even him. If ever a man was disconnected from his emotional side, it was Braden.

All water under the bridge. Not her problem anymore.

He was probably going to tell her he was seeing someone. Why he felt the need to confess to her every time he saw a woman more than once was beyond her. They were divorced. Technically, she no longer had a right to know.

Or even a desire to know.

Her wine arrived and she took a sip. Okay, maybe a little piece of her, way deep inside, liked that he told her about his relationships. Like she was in one step deeper than the women he told her about. Shaking her head, she pushed the thought away—as far as she could get it.

Wanting to be inside Braden's deep places wasn't healthy. She'd very purposely and specifically chosen, through much personal work and counseling, to get herself outside of him. To stay outside of him. Lest she waste her life in a vortex of void and unfulfilled need.

Or feel like she had to hide every time she had a tear to shed. Being ashamed of her grief was something she'd worked long and hard to get past.

Braden had never meant her to feel shame, she knew that. But when someone got uptight every time you cried, or, worse, walked out when you cried, you ended up with learned reactions that weren't necessarily accurate. Humiliation. Mortification. Guilt. And a host of other words she'd heard bandied about during her group grief sessions.

So yeah, wine was good. If he thought her idea was nuts, she wasn't going to cry. Or even be embarrassed. She was going to remind herself that they were divorced and that she had every right to pursue single parenthood. That, for some women, it was not only the best choice, but the only real workable choice.

When the waitress came by again, she ordered a beer for Braden. She'd purposely arrived early enough to not risk walking in with him—looking or feeling like a couple. When they were meeting others, it didn't bother her to travel together, but when it was just the two of them, she had her rules. Her boundaries.

They never spoke of them, but he respected them just the same. She always got there at least fifteen minutes early. He'd arrive exactly five minutes before the designated time.

Unless he texted to say he was going to be late.

Or she did.

They had the friendship down to a science.

Now if only she could be certain that he was going to be friendly about the new direction her life was about to take. With all of the preliminary testing and physical exams done, the paperwork filled out and money paid, all that was left before the actual procedure was letting him know. She could do it without him. Would do it without him.

But life was still better with Braden in it.

She'd changed after work. It wasn't a big deal for her to have done so. Her house was only a couple of miles from the daycare—and from the harbor restaurant he'd chosen for dinner. Braden just noticed, as he was walking across the room to meet her, that she looked phenomenal in black leggings and that tight-fitting cream-colored shirt. He'd been expecting jeans and a Bouncing Ball polo shirt. After all, she didn't know that this meeting was major, as opposed to the more general passing of news for which they normally came together.

She didn't need to know that the sight of her still turned him on.

Working in the same high-rise executive office building as they did, albeit with his property management and real estate business taking up the top floor and her daycare housed in a double suite on the ground, they could chat there any day they chose. They just, by some unspoken agreement, didn't choose to.

No point in having people who shared their professional days gossiping any more than necessary about the couple who'd divorced after their five-month-old baby died.

The pity, even after all this time, was hard to take. He had no desire to feed the trough.

He was hungry, though, and ready, as he slid into the booth across from his ex-wife, to order a big juicy steak. She'd have some kind of meal-sized salad.

He'd never been a salad kind of guy.

Taking a long sip of the beer she'd ordered for him, he smiled at her, liking the warm gaze she sent back in his direction. Maybe he was making a mistake, transferring himself a little further out of her life, but he had to do something or they were both going to stagnate and die.

By the end of their smile, the waitress was standing there, tablet in hand ready to take their order. Without looking at the menu, they both told her what they wanted. She thanked them, took their menus, turned around and he all but pushed her away from the table.

He had to get this over with. Plans for his move to L.A. were moving rapidly. He needed Mallory to know.

And to fully understand, from the outset, that he wasn't selling the building in San Diego or in any way changing their business arrangement. It had been in effect before they were married and would remain for as long as she wanted The Bouncing Ball, her highly successful daycare, to be housed in the executive office building that used to be his only commercial holding but was now one of many.

He raised his beer to her glass of wine and sipped it, words spilling in his head, unable to utter them. Not at all like he'd decided this would go.

He knew he just had to say what he'd come to say. That he was acquiring land north of L.A. to build a professional complex similar to the one they now shared in San Diego, and he would be moving there for the foreseeable future.

"I'm going to have a baby."

Good thing his beer was close to the table. When it slipped out of his hand, it didn't break. And barely spilled.

Mouth hanging open, he sat there, too dumbfounded to say anything.

"I just wanted you to know."

He stared. White noise from the room around them faded.

"I'd kind of hoped you'd be supportive, but if you'd rather not know about it, hear about it, I completely understand."

He didn't move.

She did. Standing, she touched his arm. "I'm so sorry, Bray. I had no idea the news would upset you so much. I guess… I mean, in light of the fact that the last time we did it together… I mean…with losing Tucker… I should have been more sensitive. I just… I'm the one who's been dragging us both down with my inability to move on and I'm really excited about this. I just… couldn't wait to let you know that I…"

Her fingers on his arm were nice. Familiar. Tender and light.

"Sit." He got the word out, then followed it with, "Please."

He took a full breath when she quickly slid back into her seat.

"I'm sorry," he said. He'd broken an understood rule— one was never to make the other unduly uncomfortable or bring an overabundance of emotion into their joint atmosphere.

He could blame it on her for laying something like that on him, but they were allowed to tell each other anything they wanted to share. That had actually been a spoken agreement. Reiterated more than once, by both of them, in the early days of their post-divorce relationship.

Hell, for all he remembered they'd said it to each other like a vow during the actual divorce proceedings. They'd said several things meant for their ears only when they'd sat before the judge that day, holding hands.

He shook his head and sipped his beer.

"You're pregnant." He got the words out and he wasn't cut as sharply by the sound as he'd expected. Who in the hell had gotten his ex-wife pregnant?

The unwelcome words kept repeating, like an annoyingly bad rhythm, in his mind. He wouldn't speak them. They weren't cool.

"Not yet." From the crease in her brow, the way she leaned toward him slightly, the hint of an upward curve on those beautiful lips, he knew she was placating him. Dammit.

And yet…she wasn't pregnant?

Holy damn. Relief eased the sweat that had popped up all over his suited body.

"But you've met someone."

The truth still loomed. She was going to have another man's baby. Start a family separate and apart from him.

The implication he was to draw from that followed almost immediately.

She was moving on.

This was good news.

Very good news.

Exactly-what-he-wanted news.

But he wasn't smiling anymore.

Mallory had someone else to watch her back now. She was finally over the past enough to start anew.

He was free.

Chapter Two

Braden was going to give himself a crick in the neck if he didn't quit the exaggerated nodding.

Prior to that, he'd sipped his beer a couple of times and some expressions had flitted across his face. She wasn't going to put herself back into near suicidal mode by trying to decipher them. Or make more of the hint of despair than was meant to be there.

Braden didn't allow himself to acknowledge despair, nor was he all that comfortable around those who did. For all she knew, he honestly didn't get the feeling. Not like she did.

He'd gotten the love, though, hadn't he? Back before Tucker died. No one could deny, seeing him with their son, that he'd adored that boy.

Tears stung her eyes while welling emotion clogged her throat. She took a sip of wine, forcing her muscles to relax. She was not going to do this. She would not fall

prey to feelings of inadequacy around her ex-husband—
which meant she couldn't cry in front of him.

It had been an unspoken rule between them since
they'd decided to stay friends after the divorce.

And the best way to not burst into tears was to think
happy thoughts.

He was wearing one of her favorite Braden ensem-
bles. Dark grey suit with just a hint of lighter thread-
ing, the striped shirt in grey, black and white with the
maroon tie. At six-two, with that lush, thick, dark hair
and those baby blue eyes, Braden could easily have been
voted sexiest man alive.

"No, I haven't met someone," she said after the silence between them had stretched a bit too long. "I'd
have told you if I had. You know that."

There were some things they counted on from each
other. Telling him if she was moving on was one of
them.

Which was probably why he was always informing her when he was seeing someone. He hadn't ever
seemed to get to the point of seriously moving on,
though. He dated, he fizzled, he dated, he fizzled.

His frown brought back a wave of tension. "I don't
understand, then."

"I'm going to be artificially inseminated," she told
him. And then, before he could voice an opinion of any
kind, she barged full force ahead with the spiel she'd
practiced in bed the night before and in the car on the
way over, too.

"With the advance in research and technology, and
with changing lifestyles, more women than ever are
using sperm banks to have children. There's even an
acronym for us, SMC, Single Moms by Choice," she
said—not at all what she'd practiced. "I've already had

all of the exams and testing done. I'm using a facility in Marie Cove, forty-five minutes south of LA. They're fertility specialists, not a sperm bank. I met with the owner when I was looking at places and I just really like her. I got a good feeling when I was there.

"It could take up to six tries, and I'm prepared for that, financially and emotionally," she continued, speaking to the man she knew him to be—one who dealt with facts, with reality, and shied away from the emotional aspects of being alive.

She didn't blame him. She'd met his mother and his sister many times. She had sat next to him through countless phone calls where they'd tried to get him to side with them against whoever they felt had slighted them, from something as menial as someone using a hurtful tone of voice against one or the other of them, or their claim that someone had been deliberately manipulative or demeaning. As the only male influence in their home growing up, he'd spent his youth learning how to bypass the drama to get to the truth of whatever might need attention.

"Way back in the '80s, more than 30,000 children were born as a result of donors," she told him. "There hasn't been any numerical research collated since then as there's no one body of collation, no database. But judging by the sheer volume of clinics today and the number of clients they have, you can logically guesstimate that the number of births has risen well into the hundreds of thousands."

She'd gotten out of bed the night before, in the middle of preparing her spiel, to do that particular research. For him. She really wanted him to be okay with her choice.

He was still sipping beer. Watching her.

"I'm going to do this, whether you approve or not,"

she told him. "I'd love your support. It means a lot to me." She paused, sipped her wine and hoped dinner didn't come for a while because her stomach was in knots. "It means a whole lot to me," she added. "But my decision is made."

Because she'd had to be certain that she was doing the right thing for her life. She hadn't even told Tamara yet. But she was fairly certain her friend from grief counseling would approve. Though Braden hardly knew the woman who'd lost four babies—three to early term miscarriages and one a viable birth but too premature to sustain life—Mallory felt as though she and the other woman were soul mates in a lot of ways.

His expression gave away very little. He was studying her.

Was he trying to figure out how to diffuse this emotionally wracked tangent she was on?

She watched him back, knowing her last thought wasn't fair. Not to either of them. Braden had always shown her the utmost respect when it came to her life choices. And he had often times sought her advice when it came to his own matters. Still did.

Their waitress stopped to say their dinners were almost ready and asked if he'd like another beer. He nodded. Her wine glass was still more than half full.

"Say something," she told him when the waitress walked away.

"There's a light in your eyes I haven't seen in…well, too long."

She smiled. "I've found my future," she told him softly.

Then he shook his head. And she braced herself. She wanted his support, so she had to listen to his concerns.

It wasn't like there weren't any. She had them, too. She readied her answers as their waitress delivered his beer.

"Being a single parent, Mal, having to work *and* take care of a child all on your own... We were exhausted when there were two of us."

Meeting his gaze, she took him on.

"I grew up with a single mom who not only worked and tended to me but regularly opened our home to other children, as well. Troubled children."

He knew her history, starting with the high-end prostitute mother who'd tried to keep her but who'd eventually realized what her life was going to do to her daughter and had given her up. Mallory had been almost three then. She didn't remember the woman who'd later died of AIDS, contracted after Mallory's birth. She remembered having to be tested, though, just to make certain she wasn't carrying the HIV virus.

By the time Mallory went in the system she'd been too old to be immediately grabbed up like a newborn. There'd been a couple who'd wanted her, though. And after almost a year in the courts while living in their home as their foster child, they'd gotten pregnant on their own and changed their mind about the adoption.

She remembered them.

And then Sally had come into her life. A social worker in another county, who had her own professional caseload of children, Sally was also a licensed foster parent in the county where Mallory had been living. She'd taken Mallory in and kept her until she'd gone off to college. There'd been children in and out of their home during the entire time she'd been growing up, but she'd been the only permanent foster Sally had had. The other kids had been like a shared project between them, with the two of them doing what they could to love the foster children during the time they were in their home.

Mallory had always loved caring for kids. Nurturing came naturally to her. She was meant to be a mother.

"Have you talked to Sally about this?" Braden asked. He'd met the woman a couple of times, but she'd retired, moved to Florida, met a man and married—her first marriage, late in life. He had a big family that she'd taken on as readily as she'd taken in all those children over the years.

"Not yet," she said. "But I'll let her know at some point. You know she's going to tell me to adopt, rather than birth, and while you'd think, in my position, having grown up as I did, that I'd be looking in that direction, I just want a biological family of my own."

"So find a man to share it with you."

Her heart lurched. And quieted. She shook her head.

"You've hardly dated, Mal. I'd hoped that guy at Thanksgiving—that dad—was someone you were getting interested in."

"I have dated," she told him. And she listed four men in three years. He nodded as each name rolled off her tongue. She'd told him about every one of them. "There's been no spark." She could have left it there, but for some reason, didn't.

"You know as well as I do, Bray. The magic is so great in the beginning, but there's no guarantee it will last. Look at us. Tragedy happened. You changed, I changed, or we found different parts of ourselves that hadn't had reason to present before." She shook her head. "I just don't trust the whole magic, in love thing. Besides, you said yourself many times that I changed even before tragedy hit. I loved motherhood more than I loved being a wife."

His words, not hers, but she wasn't sure they were wrong. She'd loved being his wife more than she could ever put into words. And yet, being a mother...it was like an empty cavern inside of her had suddenly been filled to the brim.

"The Bouncing Ball takes up twelve hours a day of your time."

She was proud of her daycare. It had a waiting list now, since she'd made the news the previous summer when a couple come to her for help in finding their kidnapped child. She was even, at Braden's suggestion, raising her rates for new clients. She'd put her foot down when it came to charging her current clients more.

"I spend my days taking care of children, Bray," she said now. "And I have a fully trained and certified staff who also specialize in child development."

Yes, she spent twelve hours a day at the center, doing what a mother does. Now, instead of just doing it for other people's children, she'd be doing it for her own, as well. And then getting to spend the remaining twelve hours a day doing the same.

"There'll be no more empty hours," she said aloud.

Braden seemed to be searching for words, and for the first time in a while she hated what they'd become. Hated the friendship that kept so much inside, erecting an invisible and completely safe barrier between them.

"Tell me what you're really thinking." She blurted the words.

And, of course, their waitress chose right then to deliver their dinner.

She could hardly eat. But because he was devouring his steak, she forced herself to go through the motions. Was she being way too insensitive here? Telling her ex-husband that she was having a baby when the loss of their own child was what had driven them apart?

Telling him she was having a baby when she knew he blamed himself for their loss?

"You wanted me to move on," she said, putting down her fork when she couldn't pretend to eat anymore. "More and more I can feel your tension, Bray. You need me to get a life."

"I never said that."

"You didn't have to."

He didn't deny her accusation.

"I'm right, aren't I? You feel responsible for my unhappiness, which means you can't move forward until I do."

Putting a forkful of meat in his mouth he chewed. His lack of response infuriated her. And yet, not as much as it might have done six months ago. Just because Braden didn't respond didn't mean he had no response.

"SIDS is not something you can predict," she said. "And if we'd been home, Tucker still would have died."

That's what the doctors told her. And the counselors. She still didn't totally believe it. If she'd been home, if Braden hadn't pressured her to leave their son with a nanny so that he could have some one-on-one time with her and spend most of the night making love with her, she might have heard a change in his breathing on the baby monitor. Might have been able to get to him in time.

To do what, she didn't know. At least she could have had a chance to breathe her own air into him.

To hold him.

Feeling herself sliding backward, she took a sip of wine. Four years of counseling, of recovery, and then she could so quickly be right back there.

"If you'd really believed we did nothing wrong by being gone that night," he said, "you'd have been able to have sex with me in the months that followed."

His softly spoken words hit her with a ferociousness she knew he hadn't intended. She sat back, hands shaking, trying to get control of emotions that just didn't die.

Her inability to want sex with him, even after the immediate blow of grief had worn off, had been a final nail in their marriage's coffin.

Their lovemaking the night Tucker died had been incredible. She'd even admitted, sometime during it all, that Braden had been right to insist that they have that time alone together. She'd missed him so much. Had half forgotten how incredible he made her feel, how right it was to be locked body to body with him, riding the crazy crest together.

And afterward…

"I felt so guilty for being so into you that I'd actually forgotten about him, on and off, for those hours when we were together. I was having the orgasm of my life while he was dying."

She could feel the tears pooling in her eyes and knew she'd gone too far.

She expected him to motion for the bill and almost reached for her purse.

"You aren't supposed to think about your children in the middle of sex, Mal. Or be turned on when you're thinking about them. It's a God thing, I'm sure. A shut-off valve that's embedded in us to keep the parent-child relationship sacred and on track."

She stared at him. Had he just said that? Were they really having this conversation?

Now? After all this time?

"My current concerns don't stem from anything to do with me," he told her then, getting them back on topic.

She sat back, the threat of tears gone. "I'd like to hear them," she told him honestly.

He cut a piece of steak, ate it. She broke off a piece of bread, played with it, making a pile of crumbs on her plate.

"I'm worried about you being alone and facing all of the things that could possibly go wrong."

"You don't think I'm strong enough to deal with life on my own?" That was a new one to her. She'd grown up in foster care, caring for foster children. She knew a hell of a lot about what could go wrong.

"I do. It's just that when it comes to mothering, Mal, you're so all in, and losing Tucker just about killed you. The idea of you having another baby… I figure it needs to happen for you, but are you sure you're ready? And doing it alone. What if—"

She shook her head. "No what-ifs, Braden. Not unless you want me stuck with no life forever. There are always what-ifs. I've chosen to tackle them one by one as they come, if they come. As a part of living."

He put down his fork, not quite through his steak. He'd barely touched the potato.

"You've really thought this through," he said, meeting her gaze head on.

"For months," she told him. "Remember last November I told you about Tamara referring that man to my daycare whose mother had died in prison giving birth, and he suddenly found himself with custody of a newborn without even knowing that his mother had been pregnant?" This was how she'd practiced telling him how she'd arrived at her decision.

This was what Braden would understand.

He nodded. "I kind of thought you and he would hook up."

"Tamara tried her best to get me to think that way, for a minute or two. I knew all along she had a thing for the guy."

Her friend had been unable to so much as hold a baby, however, which had definitely been a major roadblock for the couple. Still was, sometimes. But they were working on it. And there was no doubt in anyone's mind that Tamara loved that baby girl. Mallory could see it when Tamara came in to The Bouncing Ball, sometimes with Flint, sometimes not, to pick up little Diamond Rose after work.

"The thing is I've learned from seeing her courage, seeing how she forced herself to fight her way out of hell to give herself a chance to be happy, to make others happy. I have to do this, Braden. I can't let the past prevent my future."

Which was why she'd agreed to spend the previous Christmas on a yacht with some old friends from college instead of with Braden, as they'd done in the past. He'd gone home to North Carolina to be with his mom and sister, but up to the last minute had tried to get her to go with him. He'd been worried about her spending the holiday alone.

It hadn't been her best Christmas, but she'd done just fine.

"Okay." Hands on the table, he looked at her. Then loosened his tie and motioned for the check.

"Okay, what?"

"Okay, you're going to do this."

Her smile broke through with more of a rush than the tears. "And I have your support?"

"Of course. I told you the day we divorced that you'd always have that. It wasn't conditional, Mal."

Tears filled her eyes. "Thank you." She nodded and left him sitting there, credit card in hand.

Because she knew that was the way he'd want it.

Chapter Three

Holy hell, Mallory's going to have a baby.

Up at one in the morning, walking naked to the kitchen of the upscale high-rise condo he'd purchased on the beach not far from the harbor, Braden couldn't get the thought out of his brain.

He'd gone straight to his office after dinner to look over figures that had been coming in for a couple of days regarding his real estate interest north of L.A. He'd put out a contractor bid request and was going over every submission line by line. He'd put a call in to his architect, too, the same man who'd designed the complex where Braden Property Management had first begun and still resided. Some changes would be needed to suit the L.A. property, but the basic plan would be the same.

And it would bear the same name: Braden Property Management. Once upon a time he'd envisioned his second big venture to be titled a bit differently: Braden and Son Property Management. Once upon a time.

He hadn't told Mallory about his move. Hadn't even realized that he hadn't told her until after the check had been paid and he was heading out to the parking lot.

Holy hell. Mallory's going to have a baby. Alone.

He'd been prepared for her dating. Getting serious. Eventually marrying. All of which would have led to a very different future for her. Then he'd have prepared for her having another family. One that worked for her this time.

At thirty-three she was getting closer to her biological safety zone. She hadn't brought up that point at dinner but he was certain it had been on her mind. She was a child-development guru and firmly believed that her best chances for conceiving a healthy and robust child were before she turned thirty-five. Back in their other lives, she'd hoped to have at least two and maybe four by then.

Always in evenly numbered increments. She didn't want a family with an odd man out.

In his know-it-all, youthful arrogance, each time she'd mentioned her "clock goals" he'd pointed out that women were having babies successfully in their forties now. His way of deflecting the tension she'd begun to bring to their marriage after three years of still using birth control. They'd been establishing their businesses, and both had wanted to wait for children until they were secure.

It might have been more manly to deal with the tension. To acknowledge the validity of her feelings and sit with her as she felt them.

Sit with her. She wasn't the only one who'd had some counseling after Tucker's death. *Sit with her.* It had been what his counselor had told him he should have done when Mallory's grief had flooded their home to the point that he'd had to escape.

He hadn't been able to fix things. Hadn't known how to help. What to do.

What she'd apparently needed was for him to sit with her. Just be there while she grieved. *Be willing to be in her grief with her.* Whatever that meant. He got the words but he'd never completely figured out the concept.

Nor the next one. *Let her into your grief.*

The whole counseling thing hadn't lasted very long.

Wandering to his desk instead of heading back to bed, he sipped from his milk and stood in front of his computer—an identical setup to the one he had at his office and linked to it.

But work wasn't calling him.

Insemination was.

For a few minutes, earlier that night, he'd been with the old Mal. The one who didn't carry grief with her everywhere she went. From the way her eyes had lit up, even the way she'd held herself, it had seemed at first that he'd been sitting with the woman who'd blown his life away with her beauty, her contagious good feeling. He'd been in love all over again, there, for just a second.

For just a second he'd forgotten that he'd robbed her of the chance to kiss her baby good-night for the last time. To change him for the last time. Bathe him. Feed him. Hold him. Rock him to sleep. That had all been done by the nanny.

The next morning, the coroner had already been to the house by the time they'd arrived home. And Mallory's breasts had been leaking Tucker's food all over the place.

No matter how many times you relived it, the picture was always the same. He sipped his drink.

For just a second, earlier that night, Mal had seemed to be soaring again, instead of sagging.

He couldn't take that from her. No matter what misgivings he might have. No matter how valid they might be.

He was still staring at his computer, his milk almost gone.

If he was going to support Mallory in this venture, he needed to know everything there was to know.

Heading off for some boxers he came back and set to work.

An hour later, he had her on the phone.

"Braden? It's two in the morning! What's wrong?"

"You never said when you were going for your first procedure." *Or what kind it was going to be.* "For all I know, it's first thing in the morning. I wanted to chat a second before it happens."

"Tomorrow's Saturday," she reminded him. "My appointment's on Monday, after work, unless I don't ovulate as expected."

Not that far off, then.

"I called tonight's meeting. When were you planning to tell me about this?"

Whoa, buddy. You don't sound like a friendly and supportive ex-husband.

"Before tonight...or last night, now," she said. "But when you called Wednesday, asking to meet, I figured Friday night was fine."

He moved on, letting himself slide on the over zealousness of his questioning due to the lateness of the hour and shock of her news.

"I assume, given the circumstances, your ability to

conceive, your age and your excellent health that you're considering either ICI or IUI," he said, looking at the screen of statistics in front of him. Intracervical insemination. Intrauterine insemination. And there was intravaginal, too.

"Really, Braden? At two in the morning?"

"IVI is cheaper, by far, less invasive and less painful, but chances of conceiving the first time are considerably lower. ICI is still cheaper and less uncomfortable. But IUI has a slightly higher success rate. I think you should go with that. The less raised hopes and disappointment here the better."

"I'm fully prepared for this to take several months." She yawned. And sounded slightly amused, too.

It *was* two in the morning.

His nearly naked body yearned during the second it took him to remind himself that it was Mallory he was talking to. The woman who had no interest in being a wife once motherhood was in the picture.

Mallory, who'd been unable to feel any desire for him at all since their son died.

Because she felt guilty for how great it had been for her that night.

That was new knowledge that he'd process at some point.

That night had been the best sex of his life, too. He didn't feel bad about that.

"How about a meet-up sometime this weekend?" he asked.

"Fine." Another yawn.

"I'm taking the boat out on Sunday," he told her. "You want to go fishing?"

"I'd rather lie on the deck and soak up some spring sunshine."

Right. He knew that. She'd gone out with him plenty of times. She'd never caught a fish and had only tried once or twice after he'd bugged her to the point where she'd given in.

If she had a boy, who was going to teach the kid to fish?

Knowing Mallory, she had some kid's fishing development group already lined up.

"Seven too early for you?" They'd have plenty of time on the boat for talking.

"Nope."

He could tell her about his L.A. plans, too. "Meet me at the dock?"

"Yep."

"Okay. We can—"

"I'm going back to sleep now, Braden. Good night."

He caught her chuckle just before the call went dead.

In leggings, a short-sleeved, oversize black shirt and tennis shoes, her dark hair tied back in a ribbon, Mallory boarded the fishing boat Braden had already owned when she'd met him eight years before. She carried a plastic bowl of cut fruit in her hands.

He was on board with a plate of doughnuts.

Looking at each other's goods, they laughed. "Some things don't change," she said, not as worried as she might have been about spending leisurely time with her ex-husband.

Surely, after three years of successful friendship, she and Braden could handle a few hours alone on the ocean. He probably wouldn't even leave the harbor.

He'd set a lounger for her on the deck, maybe the same lounger she'd used in the past.

She'd brought her own towel and dropped it on the lounger while he did what he did with his bait.

She opened the food, set it out on one of the benches with the little disposable plates, napkins and plastic forks she'd brought. He started the engine, fixed himself a plate and backed away from the dock. The boat had a little cabin and, noticing the travel mug he had next to him at the helm, she went below, found the coffee he'd made and poured herself an insulated cup full. With doughnuts and fruit on a plate, she pulled on the hoodie she'd brought aboard and settled in her lounger. When the sun was fully above them, she'd be hot, and she'd take off the hoodie and get some color on her skin.

And at some point, Braden was going to want to talk. Apparently to make certain that she knew she was doing the right thing and to tell her he was seeing someone again, she supposed.

Which was fine.

She'd listen, as she always did, and support him in his endeavors, as she always did.

Until then, she was going to relax into the bliss.

"Can you come up here?"

Drifting off to sleep, the rising sun's warmth cozy in the cool San Diego spring air, Mallory heard Braden. Not in the mood to hear about his new girlfriend, she took a second to decide whether or not to acknowledge that she'd heard.

The engine had stopped. She'd heard him moving around, getting his rod and casting his line. He'd be sitting up on the bow, watching the boats on the horizon as much as anything. She'd always said he did more relaxing than fishing when he went out, but hadn't seen that as a bad thing.

Thinking he had to carry the whole world on his shoulders as he did, Braden didn't relax enough.

And then she quit picturing it. Braden on the bow of the boat, wind in his air, was just...hot. A part of them that had to be dead to her now.

"Mal?"

"Yeah, I'm coming," she said, repositioning her sunglasses as she opened her eyes. They'd only been out half an hour. So much for her bliss.

But, hey, by the following night she might be pregnant. Braden could get remarried and it wouldn't be enough to snap her out of her good mood.

Joining him on the bow and sitting with her back propped on the small rail, she faced him, her feet in front of her with knees bent. His jeans and tennis shoes were new since they'd been divorced. The forest green T-shirt she'd washed before. A breeze blew his hair and he didn't seem to notice.

It made him look free. And just a touch wild.

The impressive breadth of his shoulders...that was the same as it had always been.

"You said you wanted my support in this venture of yours."

She wouldn't call having a baby a "venture" but understood that he would. And that what he called it didn't have to matter to her anymore. She nodded.

"Then I have some concerns I'd like to address."

He wasn't going to spoil her good mood. Not that he'd ever want to. Or intend to. He was trying to help. She got that.

"What are they?"

Throwing up one hand, he glanced at the line hanging placidly over the front of the boat.

"Most of them—" He stopped and shook his head.

"There's one major one, but I have a plan that can tend to it."

Did Braden just have a hitch in his voice? Heart beating faster, she studied her ex-husband. This mattered to him.

A lot.

Which warmed her. A lot.

"What's your plan?"

He frowned. "I'd like to present the concern before I move forward to the solution."

Had they been married, she'd have felt rebuked. She smiled, instead, finding his predictability, his need to keep things in order and under wraps, kind of endearing. "Of course."

"I'm concerned about the Y component," he told her, catching her completely off guard. She'd been expecting something more along the lines of her being a single parent. Taking on a two-person job all alone. Concerned that if she had a son, the boy would have no father figure.

Or anyone to take him fishing.

"You won't know family history," he continued, when she decided silence was the best answer until she could figure out where he was going with the conversation. "According to the National Human Genome Research Institute there are forty-eight known and listed genetic disorders that could be passed on to your child. That doesn't include the ones that occur when certain genes meet with inhospitable partner genes. If that were to happen, your likelihood of miscarriage would increase greatly, but I'm not even there yet."

It sounded like he was right there. Some more of her bliss faded. She wouldn't let go, though.

She was going to do this.

"Women have been having healthy donor babies for decades."

"And they've been having children with disabilities, too."

"So have married couples." So could they have had.

"But at least when you know the Y component, you have more of a chance to prevent something or to catch it in its earliest stages."

She didn't have an immediate answer to that. Except what she'd already said.

"You've been through so much, Mal. I applaud what you're doing here. I'm elated to see you taking up the reins of your life again. Moving on. Creating a future where you'll be happy."

Elated and *Braden* weren't words she'd put together. At least, not since Tucker died. Before that she'd seen some elation. More than he'd probably realized. But not as much as after she'd found out she was pregnant.

Was the pregnancy what had changed him? At least somewhat? Was there more to their divorce than just their dichotomous ways of dealing with life's tragedies, which ultimately blew their emotional trust in each other?

"I'm concerned, Mal," he said after a lengthy silence had fallen. "Really concerned. All weekend, the more I think about it, the more concerned I get. To the point that I'm not sure I can give you my support. Not with such a huge unknown."

So she'd do it alone. She'd already made that decision. And she'd known from the beginning that she might not win his buy-in.

Still, she could feel the weight of sadness come back, trickling into the outer recesses of her heart.

"I'm worried about what you'd do if you lost a second

child." The depth of compassion in his tone was something she hadn't heard in a long, long time.

"There are never guarantees, Braden. He or she could be hit by a car or a bolt of lightning. The point is, I'm not going to let the past rob me of my future."

Which was exactly what she'd told Tamara she shouldn't do.

Exactly when the words had become her mantra, she didn't know. She just knew that she felt the truth on a soul level.

"But why play with fate when you have a choice?"

Again, she had no ready answer so she thought about what he was saying, instead. She'd asked for his input. Having his support meant more than him just agreeing with everything she said and did.

She valued his opinion and she wanted him to care enough to speak up.

"You need a full family medical history," he said. "Or as complete of one as you can get. Way more than the general things the sperm bank provides. You need to know if his grandfather was prone to anxiety attacks or his entire family were unmotivated sloths."

"Right, so what do you suggest I do, Bray? Put an ad in the paper for sperm that comes with that kind of extensive history?"

"Of course not."

"Then what?"

It was only when she asked the question that she remembered he'd said he had a solution to her problem. A plan that would tend to his concern.

"You let me be your donor."

A wake from an incoming cruise ship in the distance hit the boat and she grabbed the rail, holding on so tight her knuckles turned white.

Chapter Four

She was staring at him, clutching the rail, mouth open, looking at him like he'd lost his mind.

He hadn't. Exactly the opposite, in fact.

He had to do this. He might not want to do it. Didn't like the messiness.

But he had to do it.

He owed it to Mallory.

"You're already going to be fighting the fear of another loss," he said, keeping things practical because he knew that was the only way to get through this. Through any tough situation. "You'll need all of the reassurances you can get. During your first pregnancy, you worried about the fact that you don't know your own family history. Knowing mine helped calm those fears."

She'd closed her mouth but was still staring.

"It's not conclusive that genetics have any link to SIDS, but we know that there is no evidence of it whatsoever in my family."

Shoulders drooping, she'd lost all appearance of happiness. Though that was not his goal, it was often the outcome whenever they had a real conversation. Still, he couldn't drop this.

"There are no guarantees, Mal, we both know that, but I'm as close to a guarantee as possible when it comes to healthy genes."

After Tucker's death, he'd had complete genetic testing done on himself, including familial screening, which he'd paid for. The results had shown that he and his family had absolutely no predispositions for any of the maladies such tests could indicate. He'd shared the news with Mallory.

And it had been the absolute wrong thing to do at the time. She'd taken his information to mean that she was to blame for their son's death.

"We also know that our reproductive environments are compatible." They'd conceived Tucker the first month they'd tried. "The sooner you conceive, once you start trying, the less stressful that portion of the process will be."

He saw her blink and took that to mean she was hearing him.

"Further down the road, if the child were to develop an illness or sustain a severe injury, something that needed a blood transfusion or donor of any kind, you'd have both parents to pull from."

She let go of the rail, wrapped her arms around her knees and looked out to sea. Was she going to turn him down?

"We can get everything drawn up legally," he continued, figuring that he'd covered all of the bases in his mind since Friday night, and if he just kept talking, he'd allay any concerns she might have. "You'd be the sole parent, just like you want. I'd have no say in anything, no legal rights, no more than any anonymous donor."

He drew from the thoughts that had consumed his weekend. "It would save you money, as well," he said. "You wouldn't have to pay for the sperm."

Her glance, when it swung back his way, had his heart palpitating for a second. He wasn't sure why.

"You're actually suggesting that we have sex?" The sentence ended almost on a squeak. He wasn't sure if she was offended or simply appalled and shocked.

At least she'd spoken.

"Of course not," he quickly reassured both of them. Yeah, he'd been cursed with an apparently lifetime attraction to his ex-wife, but she cringed at the idea of sex with him, and there that possibility ended. "I'd leave my specimen at the clinic, but I'd do so as a non-paid donation specifically for you."

She'd have to pay for the procedure, just not the sperm.

"If you go with IUI your chances of conceiving the first time would be better than with sex."

Mallory was shaking her head.

"What?"

"Do you realize the mess we'd be making if we did this?"

Sitting on the bow of his boat, her little feet in ridiculously small-looking tennis shoes, the woman made him nuts and peaceful at the same time. Helping Mallory was the right thing to do. Tucker would have expected it of him.

Hauling her downstairs to bed was not even in the realm of possibility.

Nor did he want it to be, anymore. Sex with Mallory came with a whole knotted ball of strings attached.

"That's the beauty of it, Mal," he said, glancing over as his fishing line grew taut. There'd be no fish there. He hadn't baited the damned thing.

He could just imagine being in the middle of presenting his case and having to stop to reel in a slippery, smelly, great-tasting piece of fish.

"We're in complete control here, Mal, and we've got the perfect vehicle. We've spent three years building a friendship that would allow the peace of mind you need for this venture. It couldn't be better if we'd planned it all along."

"We live on the surface," she said. "A baby won't stay there. Nor will all of the emotions attached to having one. I'm fully prepared for that. Are you?"

She wasn't getting it. "That's just it! I won't be emotionally involved. I'll be going on with my life, as planned, while providing you the means to go as safely as possible on with yours."

Frowning at him, her eyes only partially hidden by her sunglasses, she said, "You honestly think you can father a child without feeling anything?"

Sure, there'd be some feelings attached, at first probably, until he fully adjusted the changes in their lives. "No more so than any other sperm donor."

"They don't ever know if their sperm is even used, let alone have a relationship with the recipient."

"Some do." He'd researched that one. "Men donate to gay women friends. Women are surrogates for gay men friends. I read about a man who donated to his best friend, who was celibate, so he and his wife could have a baby. And a mother who carried for her barren daughter and son-in-law—"

"We were married, Bray. We had a son together. Lost

a child together. And you think you can father my second child and just walk away?"

"I do." He really did. "When I'm ready to have a family of my own, I know full well I can do so. I'll meet a woman, the desire will be there and I'll have my family. I'm not there yet. But you're ready to have your family, and I can help ensure that you have the best chance at doing so happily." He didn't waver as he met her eye to eye. The plan made perfect sense.

"I need your support during the pregnancy more than I need the sperm," she said. "Sperm I can buy. But you're right, it's going to be hard. I've done all the reading, too, and giving birth after SIDS is hard. Your head plays with you, makes you afraid what happened before can happen again. I blame myself, like my body is broken somehow because it produced a child with a faulty breath regulator. What I was hoping to have from you was the common sense reminders that calm my fears."

"And you'll have them."

"It would be much easier for you to give them with more detachment," she said, the steady look in her eye and the calm tone of her voice making him listen to her. "Having no intimate involvement will better ensure you getting through this with the least amount of discomfort. You know, if the child isn't yours…"

"He won't be mine in an emotional or legal sense," he said immediately.

She was making a point. He got it. When the kid was born, wouldn't Braden need a second chance, too?

He shook his head, adjusted his baitless pole. "I'm giving away my sperm, Mal, not becoming a father." The designation was key. "It's all in how you process it."

But if she truly didn't want his biological component in her child…if, in spite of the testing he'd had done, she still thought his genes were partially to blame for what had happened, then he wouldn't force her. Couldn't force her. And he didn't even want to try. He just wanted this to work out for her. Most of the process was completely out of his control, except for this one small area where he could possibly positively affect her chances.

"Can I think about it?"

Her question came right when he was giving up.

"Of course."

"On the deck? In the sun?" She was already crawling her way off the bow, giving him too good a view of her ass as she did so.

Way too good.

Hard in the wrong place, he set about baiting his line. It was time to do some real fishing. And not for the things he couldn't have. Or things that no longer existed.

Weak in the knees, Mallory made it back to her lounger without incident. Sinking into the woven chair, she kept on her sunglasses just in case Braden was looking. And she refrained from wiping the tears from her cheeks for the same reason.

She'd just been given a second chance. From the minute she'd met her ex-husband she'd known that she'd wanted him to be the father of her biological family. To someone who'd grown up an orphaned foster kid, whose own mother hadn't even known who'd fathered her, biology was important.

So important.

As important as Braden Harris was to her.

She couldn't let him do this. Couldn't use him this way. It was his guilt playing with him. She knew that.

Just as she knew that keeping your baby in your room was a key SIDS preventative. She'd studied them all, from the Mayo Clinic to the American Academy of Pediatrics and every blog or message board she could find in between:

Place baby on back, not side or stomach.

Remove all fluffy bedding.

Keep crib as bare as possible.

No prenatal smoking.

Good prenatal care.

Pacifier at night after four weeks of age.

Breastfeeding.

And baby in your own room for a minimum of six months, better if it was twelve.

Not in your bed but in your room. It had to do with waking more easily, among other things. Logic then followed that if she'd been home that night Tucker would have been in his smaller crib in their room, where he'd been every night since his birth. She'd have been there, too. Which could have prevented SIDS.

Braden had done his own reading. He had to know this, too. And he was offering to give her what she wanted in order to appease his guilt.

Maybe it would be kindest to give him a way to atone and move on.

How could she put him through fathering a child he didn't want? How could she ask him to experience the pregnancy with her, knowing what it would probably cost him? How could she hurt him any more than he'd already been hurt, loving him like she did?

Unless…if atoning set him free…

She tried to doze, to let the sun take her to the peaceful place outside of pain, and ended up thinking about Tucker instead. The sound of him laughing. The first time he'd laughed Braden had been at work. She'd been alone with the baby, coming at him again and again with funny noises, stopping just short of reaching him to pull back and start again, reveling in the way his eyes had followed her every movement.

Braden had missed the whole thing. Tucker had been asleep when he'd arrived home that evening and though Braden had gone to wake him, she'd told him not to. It would have been too hard to get the baby back down. Feeling as sleep deprived as she had been, the admonition hadn't been completely without warrant, but what would it have hurt in the long run? Yeah, she'd been exhausted, but it wasn't like she'd had to get up to go to work. She'd still had another month of leave ahead of her. Even if the baby hadn't laughed again that night, Braden would have racked up more minutes of memories to feed him in the years that followed.

Someone like Braden probably wouldn't access those memories like she did. And when they came to him, calling up a wealth of emotion, they might be more a hindrance than anything else.

So maybe someone like Braden, someone who was happier shutting out emotion than letting it in, would be the perfect sperm donor—if he really didn't want another child of his own.

But what if he only thought he didn't? What if, once they got into it, once she heard a heartbeat and then started to show, once the baby started to kick, he found out he really wanted it all again, too?

She tried to find the idea abhorrent but couldn't.

Because if Braden could be the man she'd thought he was, there'd be no more perfect scenario than having his baby.

Which was the true problem, she acknowledged, lying there with her eyes closed, the sun beating down on her, the gentle sway of the boat rocking her.

The real problem was her. What if she got pregnant, heard the heartbeat, started to show, felt the baby kicking her...and wanted Braden to get excited about all of those things because it was his baby, too? What if she fell in love with him all over again?

What if she started to fall back into who she'd been? A woman who'd been ashamed to cry because her husband didn't like emotional outbursts. One who'd curtailed her most exciting moments when he was around for the same reason.

One who'd grown to relish her time alone with her baby so she could gush and be all intensely moved by the miracle of him and just feel complete.

No, she couldn't do it. Couldn't have Braden's baby.

That settled, she concentrated on the slow rhythm of the boat's movement and tried to drift off with it.

But she lay there, wide awake as a thought struck her.

She had to put the baby first.

Always.

In the end, she didn't matter at all. What mattered was her baby's health. His or her best chance at a long and happy life. Braden was right. With a sperm donor there were many unknowns.

She herself was an unknown, too. Yes, she'd had her own genetic testing and didn't carry any alarming signs, but her family might. She had no way of knowing if there was a history of cancer. Or liver or kidney disease. Or slowly developing areas of the brain that regulated breathing.

Not only could her baby develop something, but she could, too. What if kidney failure ran in her family? Or car accidents?

Sitting up, Mallory opened her eyes, taking a minute

to bring herself back mentally to where she was. The ocean. The boat. Fresh sea air and sunshine.

Car accidents weren't genetic.

But they did take people unexpectedly, leaving loved ones behind to fend for themselves.

In her case, it would leave her little one with no known family at all. He or she would be just like Mallory, a foster.

Rising, she made her way back to the front of the boat. Braden was sitting with his forearms resting on raised knees, looking in her direction. His line lay limp before him. There wasn't a single fish in the basket close by.

With a raised brow, he seemed to ask if she'd reached her decision.

"I have a question."

"Okay. If I don't have the answer, I'll see what I can do about finding it."

The reply was so Braden she almost teared up again. And smiled, too. He tried. He really, really tried hard.

"If something were to happen to me, would you be willing to take the child, to raise him or her?"

"Of course."

It wasn't so much his answer—which she'd have expected if she'd given herself enough time to think about it—as it was his lack of hesitation that set her suddenly frightened heart at ease.

"Then I accept your offer."

"Good."

He was looking at her. She looked back at him.

They'd just agreed she was going to have his baby.

And it felt as though they'd never been further apart.

Chapter Five

Feeling not the least bit relaxed, Braden gave up any pretense of enjoying a Sunday morning fishing jaunt. Mallory seemed to share his eagerness to get off the boat, based on how quickly she'd agreed with his suggestion that they head back to shore.

It was as though once they'd made their decision to give her another child, they couldn't stand to be around each other.

The idea was ludicrous, and yet, it held a strong ring of truth, as well. Strong enough that he couldn't just let things go as they were. If he and Mallory couldn't be friends, if he didn't have the access to help her out when she needed him, the entire point of his involvement was moot.

Luckily he knew exactly how to fix that problem.

"I never did tell you why I called Friday night's meeting," he said, planning to finally tell her of his pending move. He'd lowered the throttle and headed a little more slowly toward the private marina where his dock was located. In the seat next to him, she'd been silently watching their progress.

Now she glanced at him, waiting for him to continue. He wanted to know what she was thinking—a husband's desire, not a divorced friend's one. Cutting the throttle completely, he let them bob on the water.

"What's her name?" she asked. And then, before he could answer, she added, "And are you sure she'll be okay with this? Because if you need to reconsider, I fully understand."

Staring at her, he wasn't sure whether to grin or be pissed. About to embark on a huge and potentially frightening life change, considering the demons that would be on the trip with her, Mallory was sitting there thinking about him. Letting him off the hook.

Just as she'd always done.

Why the thought pissed him off, he wasn't sure.

Or maybe it wasn't her at all.

"There is no 'her,'" he said. But he didn't like how available that made him sound, so he added, "At least not at the moment. And when there is, in order to qualify, she'll need to be okay with the fact that my ex-wife has a child that is biologically mine and that I am her friend."

Yes. That was it in a nutshell. All clean, wrapped up and completely doable.

"She'll have to be one special woman." Her grin made him think of how special she was.

Right.

And, of course, any future relationship he might have would be with someone else who was special to him. That was the nature of hooking up. It would be that way whether he donated sperm or not.

"I can put off my appointment," she said, making him aware that he hadn't responded to her earlier comment.

The ocean's vastness called to him. And yet, there he sat in the harbor. The story of his life. At sea, but missing out on a world of possibility.

No. What was that nonsense? His life was a damned good story. He got up every morning, eager to get going. His work didn't just earn him loads of money; it energized him.

"I think you need time to seriously reconsider," Mallory said, turning that warm, concerned gaze on him. How well he recalled that look. He'd almost been jealous of his own son once, when he'd been trying to talk to Mallory about a particularly testy client and a lucrative deal that had almost gone sour, and instead of hearing him, she'd heard Tucker sneeze and had immediately turned that same look on the baby.

Hard to believe he even remembered that.

"It will just be too messy."

Whoa. She wasn't changing her mind, was she?

"Only if we make it so," he said, jumping in before the deal went south on him. "It will be what we make it," he continued, looking her straight in the eye. "We're friends. Your child will be your child, just as though you had an anonymous donor. I will be there for both of you, as a friend of the family, in the same way as I would be if you purchased the sperm." He'd spent much of the previous day getting straight with it all. "The only difference will be the biology—a scientific component that no one will ever need to know about—that will make you and the child safer than if you did it anonymously."

She still looked as though she needed reassurance.

"It's not like we just divorced," he said, putting every

ounce of confidence he had into his words. "We're three years in, Mal. We've got this down."

She nodded.

"If anyone can do it, we can."

She watched him, saying nothing.

"It's perfect for us, really," he said, continuing to fill the silence. "You said multiple times that I'm detached. So here's where my detachment works for us."

He hadn't been detached when they'd been married. But he was now. Somehow he'd become what she'd thought she'd seen.

"I still think I should cancel my appointment to give you more time."

"I don't need any more time. If you do, if you want to think about this some more, then by all means, postpone things. But you don't need to do it on my account."

Her response was quick. "I'm not worried about me. My mind is fully made up."

"I meant about using me as a donor. If that's going to be a problem for you."

"I think it's fraught with potentially difficult situations, most I fear that we can't even see right now, but, honestly, I'd take on any of them to have the peace of mind of knowing that if something happened to me, my child would have biological family willing to welcome him."

"But he would only know about that biology if such an occasion arose." They needed that clear. They were proceeding as if this was an anonymous sperm donor. For her sake, more than anything. It was what she needed.

"Correct." She nodded but then glanced out to sea.

"Maybe you do need to take a little time," he told her, not wanting to rush her. Mallory had never been

one to jump into anything. Because she gave her all
when she got there.

She looked at him. "I told you, my mind is firmly
made up."

He nodded, believing her.

"So, do you need me tomorrow, then?" He'd never
been to a fertility clinic, but he'd heard his share of
do-it-in-the-cup jokes. Seen sitcom episodes on TV. It
wasn't his style, but what the hell.

"I thought I'd call in the morning and see what they
suggest. With the change of plan, they might want to
reschedule."

He met her gaze and held it. "So, I'm good. Are
you?"

Her smile rocked him more than the incoming wake.
"I'm good."

He wanted to believe both of them.

Mallory didn't contact Braden again until after she'd
spoken with the clinic Monday morning. Because of the
different procedure, they would need to reschedule if she
took Braden up on his offer. Though they almost never
sought each other during the business day, she took a
quick break from The Bouncing Ball to ride the elevator up to the top floor. William, the receptionist who
kept Braden Property Management running smoothly,
looked surprised but not unhappy to see her.

"Mrs. Harris!" He stood, coming around the built-
in counter to take her hand. She'd kept Braden's name.
Her business had been established in that name. The
hassle to change everything hadn't seemed worth it.
Particularly since she had no ties, emotional or otherwise, to her maiden name. But the Mrs... Most people
just called her Mallory. Or Ms.

"It's so good to see you," William's smile was genuine and his pleasure at her sudden presence gave her pause.

She shouldn't have broken her and Braden's unspoken protocol by showing up at his office suite. But the clinic only had a couple of openings. She had to call them back to let them know if she'd be keeping her afternoon appointment.

And she'd needed to see Braden one more time, to make certain that he knew what he was getting into before they did something irrevocable.

"Good to see you, too, William." She smiled back at the man who'd been with Braden since college and was more of an office manager than a receptionist. William just liked to be out front, keeping an eye on everything that went on. From out here he knew which agents were present, which mortgage brokers were on time and which clients appeared nervous when they arrived.

But he couldn't know why Mallory was suddenly visiting her ex-husband.

"Is he in?" she asked, nodding toward the hall that led to Braden's huge, luxurious office suite.

"An hour ago," William confirmed.

He didn't ask her to wait while he let Braden know she was there, but she knew he'd call to inform him she was on her way back.

"I'm sorry," she blurted as he opened his door just as she was approaching. "I shouldn't be up here, but—"

"Of course you should be up here," he said, closing his door behind her as she entered the rooms she'd helped him decorate.

They'd christened each one with lovemaking a long time before. An inappropriate memory to be having in that moment.

He motioned toward the couch in the main room—which also housed a massive teak desk, an entertainment center with a large-screen TV and a wet bar.

"I only need a second," she said, shaking her head at his offer to sit. "I have to get back."

He slid his hands in his pockets, drawing her attention down there. To the part of him that he'd be using on her behalf if they did this.

Oh, God.

Could they really be considering such an asinine choice?

Glancing up, she felt the heat rise up her neck to her face. He'd caught her looking.

Of course he would. Braden missed very little.

Unless it came to emotions. Then he managed to bypass pretty much everything.

Or at least he seemed to.

The man she'd married, the one with whom she'd shared the best years of her life, had shown her a different side. He'd been verbally reticent, not one to express emotion in words, but he'd definitely known them. And shown them. He'd also been able to sense even the slightest change in her, it had seemed.

At least that was the way she remembered it, looking back. Who knew how it had really been?

"I called the clinic," she said, hoping she sounded as confident as she wanted him to think she was. About the procedure, there was no doubt.

About using him, there was tons of it.

But knowing her baby would have family if something happened to her simply meant too much to her to decline his offer.

"And?" he prompted her.

"If we... If I... I'd have to reschedule," she found her

point eventually. "The procedure is slightly different. They have one opening on Wednesday morning and one Thursday, late afternoon. They need an immediate call back if I'm going to cancel this afternoon's appointment."

"'If?' Are you reconsidering again? I thought we'd been through all of that."

So much for her giving him time to change his mind. He wasn't being open-minded enough to do so.

"We have been. But I just don't think you realize what you're putting yourself in for. The possible ramifications. You'd have a child you could never acknowledge, Bray. Think about that. I mean, if we lived on opposite sides of the country, maybe that wouldn't be such a critical consideration, but I'm right downstairs. My baby will be right downstairs. Every single day."

Right now they didn't see each other on a daily basis. But knowing that he had a child so close and that he couldn't be a part of its life might drive him over the edge.

"Which brings me to the reason I called Friday's meeting," he said.

For a second there she thought he was losing it. He hadn't known her plans, nor made his offer when he'd called the meeting. What could one possibly have to do with the other?

"I'm confused."

"I'm moving, Mallory. So, you see, I won't be upstairs from the baby every day."

She went cold. From head to toe, everything about her was cold. She stared at him, trying to assimilate what he'd said.

She headed for his couch and sat.

"You're moving." It wasn't a question, and yet...he was moving?

When Braden sat next to her, closer than he'd ever been when alone with her since their divorce, she knew that his news was big.

Serious.

And it was coming at her whether she wanted it or not.

Just as she knew that she did not, in any way, want him to leave.

That one was as unequivocal as their divorce.

Chapter Six

"You own properties in several different cities now. Why would you have to move to purchase another?" she asked when he told her about buying the L.A. property.

She'd gone white. Braden hadn't expected that.

He'd figured she'd be upset at first. Mallory wasn't a huge fan of change. But she always saw reason. Always supported his choices. Encouraged them, even.

Perhaps he should have been a bit more conscientious in telling her his big news.

"I don't have to move to buy the L.A. property," he told her. "I want to move." Maybe that was it. He'd misrepresented the plan. He'd come at it from the business end of things. "The other properties all were purchases of existing buildings, with tenants," he explained. "The L.A. one is going to be like this one here, Mal. I'm going to make a second Braden Property Management building, starting from scratch. I'll be using renditions of the same plans. To anyone just driving by, the properties will look pretty much identical. I'll need to be on hand, much like I was here, during the entire process." He heard himself and corrected, "I want to be there."

"This building is your baby." She'd spoken softly, looking at him with that tender gaze that seemed to see more than was there. "And as such, you have my full support."

"I wouldn't put it that way."

"I mean…the new project is you building your own life separate and apart from me. Braden Property Management in San Diego, with The Bouncing Ball on the ground floor, is us, Bray. You love this place, but you need to make a life of your own. That's as it should be."

He shook his head. She was making way more of this move than was there. Except for one key point.

"I'm a developer," he said. "The project will be a challenge and I look forward to that," he agreed. "I also think maybe it's time for us to live far enough apart that we aren't in each other's spheres all day every day."

Her lips pursed, she nodded, then stood.

"That's it? You're just going to go?" he asked her.

"I have to get back downstairs," she reminded him. "I don't like to be gone long, you know that. And I have to call the clinic." She was walking toward the door. All he could see was her back.

He had to let her go. This was their life.

"Thursday afternoon would work better for me," he shot out at her.

She stopped, nodded, then reached for the door handle and was gone.

Leaving him, once again, feeling like a jerk.

* * *

Mallory was more excited than nervous—and eerily calm, too—for most of that week. Her plans were solid. Right. She had no doubt about that.

Just as Bray's new plans were right for him.

She didn't doubt that, either.

Hence the calm. Three years ago they'd chosen to live life on individual paths, rather than one path together. It had been the right choice for both of them.

No doubt on that score.

So why was she so incredibly sad all of a sudden? Not overall. Not all day. Or every minute. But in bouts. Unexpectedly throughout the day, for a minute or two.

L.A. was only two and a half hours away. Knowing Braden, he'd still be in San Diego at least once or twice a week. He wasn't going to leave the San Diego headquarters hanging.

Unless…

Was he planning to sell the complex? Would the new owner raise her rates to something she couldn't afford without passing on higher fees to her clients? Many of her clients worked in the building and couldn't afford any higher fees. Would some of the smaller businesses be forced to move? Would she?

She couldn't believe he'd do such a thing.

And yet, things were changing so drastically. She was taking very real steps to have a family again. To be a mother.

Braden was not only supporting her, but doing everything he could to make the way easier for her.

She had no business putting any kind of a guilt trip on him about his plans.

But maybe she was a little more on edge than she might have been when they met in the parking lot of

Braden Property Management Thursday after lunch. He'd suggested they drive to the clinic together. Considering the distance, she couldn't come up with a reason why they shouldn't. It made absolutely no sense to take two cars from San Diego all the way to Marie Cove.

Coming from work, he was still in his suit, looking confident—and too sexy for her immediate peace of mind. She'd changed from jeans and a Bouncing Ball polo shirt to a calf-length, colorful, flowing skirt and a short-sleeved, figure-hugging purple shirt with sandals.

The ladies who worked for her knew she had a doctor's appointment. They didn't know why. No one did. Not even Tamara.

When she was pregnant, she'd share her news. Until then, she needed to keep things low key.

They got in Braden's dark blue luxury SUV without discussing whose car they'd take. The vehicle was new since their divorce. She'd ridden in it a handful of times. The tissue holder attached to the passenger-side sun visor was one she'd purchased for him years before.

Kind of ironic, considering that her crying—and thus needing tissues—had contributed to the reasons for their divorce.

"Thank you for doing this," she said as he maneuvered through traffic and pulled onto the highway heading north.

The appointment ahead was bound to be awkward for him, going into a room with the express purpose of...

Yes, well, she wouldn't be there and needed to steer her mind away from that thought. He'd be having a somewhat personal medical procedure. Administered by himself.

Details not her concern. But she couldn't help thinking about that particular part of his anatomy. She knew it well. Had loved it well.

Again, not her business.

Her business came immediately after his. A short procedure. And then, by the time she was on the opposite side of that very highway later that afternoon, she could be pregnant!

She wouldn't know, of course. It would take a couple of weeks before she could hope for accurate results from a home pregnancy test.

"You nervous?" Braden asked as he set the cruise control and settled back.

"A little." Not as much as she'd have thought. She was creating her future, one step at a time. Just one step. That's all she was facing that day. That's all she'd ever have to face. One step. Before she'd have to deal with the next.

Or get to celebrate the next.

One thing she'd learned from losing Tucker, from the grief counseling, was to live in the moment. To enjoy every single moment as best she could. The moment was all anyone ever had at any given time. And then, God willing, they'd have another one moment.

They'd been on the road half an hour and said two words a piece.

"This isn't a bad drive," she offered. She'd made it a few times in recent months.

"No, it's not."

He'd obviously been making the trip, too, adding on the extra forty-five minutes further north to L.A. At least, enough to pick the property he was considering for his new venture.

Odd how their attempts to get on with their lives apart from each other had led them both to the L.A. area.

Difference being, of course, that she only visited. He was moving.

"Maybe we could drive by your new property," she offered, hoping he never knew how difficult it was for her to support him. She was being selfish and wasn't proud of that. "You know, when we're finished at the clinic. We'd be almost there and I'd like to see it."

More like she needed to know where he was going to be. Just so she could relax and let go.

He glanced at her. She could tell but didn't look over at him.

"I'd like that, actually, if you're up for it," he told her. "I'd like your input."

Warmth flooded her.

All of these changes were a good thing.

Maybe everything really would be okay.

Braden didn't need the magazine. He'd been apprised of its availability. Knew exactly where and how to access it, but didn't. All he had to do was picture Mallory their last night together, naked and wild in that hotel room, as hot for him as he had been for her.

The whole thing was over in less than a minute.

Which was a good thing, considering the night that did it for him was also the night their son had died.

She couldn't have sex again after that.

The memory of their time together that night turned him on. If that made him a sick bastard, then, he supposed it did.

For Mallory, the two were indelibly tied into one.

For him, they were two completely different things. For her, losing one meant losing both. In his mind, their togetherness as a couple could have been something that saw them through the loss.

But then, his tendency to live in his mind had been a big part of their problem.

He made business calls and answered email from his phone while he waited out in his vehicle for Mallory. He'd been told it could take six or more tries for her procedure to take. This was the only time he'd need to be present. He hoped it worked out for her quickly.

If this was what she really wanted.

Maybe after trying, she'd have second thoughts. This attempt wouldn't take, and she'd forgo another.

Maybe.

Staring at email he wasn't comprehending, Braden had to stop himself a second. Was he hoping Mallory didn't get pregnant?

Did he want this venture to fail?

He wanted her happy. That answer came to him quite succinctly and he recognized the absolute truth of it.

And if it took a baby to make her so?

He wished it didn't.

But if it did?

He wanted her happy.

Satisfied with where his internal dialogue ended, he answered three emails in as many minutes. One from an investor. Two from contractors regarding the L.A. property.

Mallory was making her new life.

He was making his.

She didn't look any different. Logically he'd known she wouldn't and yet, as Mallory climbed back into the passenger seat next to him just as the sun was starting to set, he was struck by how normal she looked.

As though he'd expected her to sprout horns or a baby rattle or something.

She strapped herself in and as the seat belt crossed over the front of her body, he remembered another time, another doctor's office parking lot. They'd just come from her thirty-nine-week checkup. She'd begun to dilate. They'd had an ultrasound and Tucker had been head down and in position. Mallory had been talking nonstop as she'd guided the seat belt beneath her belly bulge and clicked it closed.

He'd looked at the huge belly sticking out there and for the first time had had a sense that there was going to be another human being in his family. That stomach wasn't just Mallory's thing. Just something she wanted and would be great at. It was a human being, ready to join them.

Them, not her.

He'd been scared to death. Afraid of what the change would do to the "them" that worked so perfectly, in his opinion.

And afraid that he wouldn't be as great a dad as she'd be a mom. Afraid that he'd disappoint her.

He'd also been strangely elated. And uncomfortably moved. That bulge was about to become his son. Having never had a dad or a brother, that new male advent into his family had suddenly been huge. Visions of fishing and sports and doing business together had started to pop up at the most unexpected times.

They'd always made him grin inside. Lifted the weight of the loads he carried. He'd never had another man to step in and be the man of the house if the need ever temporarily arose.

"What?" Mallory's voice broke into his thoughts, bringing him back to the moment. She was looking at him, concern on her brow.

"What, 'what?'"

"You're staring at me. And you had a funny look on your face."

He could tell her the truth. But then things could get messy.

"I'm just wondering how it went," he improvised. It was the truth. He had been wondering about that, in the midst of the rest of it.

"Good," was all she said.

He wanted more.

But didn't ask.

Braden didn't say a whole lot as he pulled onto the vacant property he hoped would be the newest Braden Property Management acquisition, and put his SUV in Park. Motor still running, he kept the headlights on, shining toward the center of the property. It wasn't quite dark, but almost.

Mallory looked around, noticing the lake across the street. They'd just passed a gated community, and across the other way was a fine dining restaurant with green grass and landscaping that could have been on the cover of *Better Homes and Gardens*.

Just outside of L.A., it was the most spacious area she'd ever seen so directly attached to the crazily busy metropolis.

"It's perfect, Braden" The words didn't quite catch in her throat. Only because she got them out before the deluge of emotion hit.

His new place would be better even than the San Diego version. Of course. Braden was a lot wealthier now than he'd been then. The first building had gone up with loans, not investors.

"You really think so?" He was watching her and she looked back at him.

"I do."

Her eyes glistened, but she smiled.

Looking satisfied, he nodded. "I was thinking the front of the building would face south," he said, going on to describe his vision for the complex.

She added a few suggestions, which drew other ideas from him. All in all, they sat there for almost half an hour.

Mallory was proud of how well she managed.

His new life was going to be great.

And she resented the hell out of it for taking him away.

Because somehow over the past three years she'd become completely selfish where Braden was concerned. Counseling, both grief and marriage, had taught her to focus on herself—the only thing she could control or fix. Maybe she'd gone a bit too far with that.

"Do you think it's wrong, me having a child?" If they'd been sitting in a restaurant with people buzzing around them, or in the broad light of day, she might not have asked.

In the dark in the enclosed and private comfort of his vehicle, with jazz music playing softly in the background, the question slipped past the barriers that guarded their friendship.

"I wouldn't have participated if I did."

She'd probably known that. And wished she'd asked a different question. Maybe more to the point would have been, *Do you like the idea of me having a child?* Or, *Do you want me to have a child?*

No. Neither one of those worked.

Do you feel good about me having a child?

Maybe that one was more what she wanted to know.

Was he hoping, secretly maybe, that she wouldn't conceive?

Now she was treading on minefield territory.

"Are you planning to sell the complex in San Diego?" Sitting back, she stared at other headlights on the road in the distance and watched the rhythm of their passing, one after another.

"Of course not. Why would I do that?"

She shrugged. Trying to keep her tone even, non-committal, she said, "You don't need two headquarters."

"Braden Property Management can have more than one office. It needs more than one, actually."

Thinking about what he did, all of the people who worked for him, she could see that.

"Is William going with you to L.A.?"

"No. I need him right where he is, doing what he does."

She could see that, too.

"Don't worry, Mal. Everything is going to remain exactly the same as far as The Bouncing Ball, and the entire complex for that matter, is concerned."

It wouldn't be the same without him there.

"I'll still be around, at least once a week, if not more," he continued.

So what, he was reading her mind now, like he used to do when they were one? Two parts of a same whole so closely entwined that they knew what the other was thinking.

When had that stopped? Traveling back in her mind, she tried to pinpoint exactly when she'd stopped knowing what Bray was thinking. Or when she'd felt as though he didn't get her anymore.

She landed...nowhere.

She was probably just too tired.

The day had taken more out of her than she'd thought. Not physically. The procedure had been mildly uncomfortable and over more quickly than she'd expected.

But emotionally.

If all went as expected, she was going to be a mother again. Maybe not this time. Or next. But soon.

And Bray...he was going to be a business owner again. Same plans, same look, same top floor. If not on the current property he was considering, then on one like it.

It was kind of ironic. It seemed like in moving on, neither one of them was actually doing that. They were doing just as they'd done in the past—only this time they were doing it separately.

Mallory had no idea what to make of that.

Chapter Seven

One step, one minute at a time. Mallory spent the next two weeks living her life only in the moment. She might be pregnant; she might not. Didn't do any good to dwell on it, either way. If she was, great.

And if she wasn't, she'd try again.

Braden might be leaving soon; he might not—depending on how quickly things came together for him. He was going. She just didn't know when. Watching for his parking spot to be empty didn't serve any purpose, either. It would be at some point.

They met for lunch once. He told her that he'd made an offer for the property he'd shown her. He still hadn't chosen a contractor, but he'd narrowed it down to two.

And he wasn't buying a place to live right away. He'd be renting a suite at the hotel half a block away at first, and then looking for something nearby to rent until he had the building up and running. He'd be keeping his condo in San Diego, regardless, and planned to be in town, at the Braden Property Management office, at least one day a week.

So, for all intents and purposes, not that much would change as far as the two of them were concerned. They rarely saw each other more than once a week anyway. And sometimes less than that.

Overall, she was doing just fine. If you didn't count those moments when she imagined the spare bedroom in her little house as a nursery or touched her stomach and thought about bonding with a new baby.

Oh, and the time she'd lain in the dark and thought about being uncomfortably huge with baby and not having Braden's back to prop up against. It had taken her half an hour to figure out that she'd use pillows instead. A body pillow. She'd picked one up the next day and she had started using it, too.

On the thirteenth day after her procedure she still didn't get her period. While that didn't mean she was pregnant, her nerves tingled with energy all day long and into the evening. So much so that when she was mixing a bowl of tuna salad for a late supper and a knock sounded on her front door, she jerked so hard tuna flew off her spoon onto the counter and wall.

She wasn't expecting anyone and didn't usually have people just stop by. In the jeans and purple Bouncing Ball polo shirt she'd worn to work that day, she left the mess and went to look out from the corner of the front window. Her house wasn't big, but it was in a nice, predominantly crime-free neighborhood. Still, she was a woman living alone.

And she might have a baby to protect.

The thought was right there.

She recognized the SUV immediately and pulled open the door.

"Bray? What's up?"

He'd been to her home. Had taken a look at it with her before she'd purchased it. But he didn't visit.

"I called first but you didn't pick up."

Her phone was still in her bag, where she'd dropped it before a late meeting with a prospective client couple expecting their first child. "It's still on silent," she said aloud, taking it out and holding the screen up for him. He didn't step in, just stood there in his suit and tie and held out a key.

"I'm heading to L.A. and just thought, with me moving down there, you should have a key to my condo. Just in case."

He was moving? At eight o'clock on a Wednesday night?

She reached for the key. "Your offer was accepted on the property?"

"Not yet, but I have every reason to expect it will be, I want my guys there Friday morning. We'll need to apply for permits and want to get that process going immediately."

Oh. The whole contractor thing, getting going on an actual formation of a building—making it real—had come fast.

He'd be out of town when she took the pregnancy test the next day. They hadn't talked about her plans, or his part in them, since the day they'd visited the clinic together, but he knew the process, the timing.

He knew that tomorrow was her big day.

And yet he chose that day to go to L.A. and buy his property. His statement couldn't be clearer: he was moving on.

Which was good, because so was she.

"When will you be back?"

"Friday night or Saturday."

Mallory blinked. "That's only two days."

Chin jutting, he nodded. The porch light was bright, putting his dark hair in a spotlight but leaving his face in shadow.

"So, you aren't moving yet."

His shrug was so...him. It left her needing more. "I'm not going to be moving much of my stuff, just some clothes and personal items, but since I'm keeping my place here, I figured I'd buy new there. When the time comes."

Made sense, she guessed, though she didn't think she'd like having two sets of belongings. She'd want the red sweater with the crop sleeves that didn't itch, and it would be in her other place. The truth settled on her, though. She was a homebody. Braden was not.

Maybe that had been part of their problem without either of them knowing it. Or acknowledging it if they had.

"Okay, well, I'm heading out," he said, leaning in to give her a kiss on the cheek. She almost turned her head and opened her mouth.

And she was shocked by the sudden instinct to do so.

Must be hormones.

If she was pregnant.

"Be safe," she said to his back.

"Always," he called with a raise of his hand and was gone.

Leaving her standing there holding his key, wishing she'd had that kiss.

He was going to be back Friday night or Saturday, but he'd brought her a key to his place. Presumably to be able to let someone in if he had a problem, needed service or something sprang a leak.

He hadn't said. She could only guess.

So, did that mean that he'd be back over the weekend but leaving again almost immediately?

She should have asked. The real Mallory would have asked. Friend-instead-of-lover Mallory couldn't.

Cleaning up tuna from the wall, she told herself that she didn't care where Braden lived as long as he was healthy and happy. Needing to keep herself that way, she ate. Then she worked on spring-into-summer decorations for the daycare reception. She liked to change them every month, to keep things feeling fresh and happy. Crafting of all sorts made her happy.

Twice she went in to the bathroom, thinking she might take the pregnancy test a day early. It wouldn't hurt anything. Worst case, she'd be out the money it would cost to buy more. Considering that she'd purchased a case of them off the internet because she could get them so much cheaper, she wasn't all that worried about buying more.

Twice she went back to the third-bedroom-turned-craft-room in her house without taking the test. Chances were it would come up negative, which would only upset her. Still, it could just mean that it was too early to take the test, not that she wasn't pregnant.

If it came up positive she'd get all excited and might then find out she wasn't pregnant because it had been too early to take the test.

Logic told her twelve hours shouldn't make that much difference.

Braden had left town without even wishing her luck for the outcome of a test he knew she'd be counting the hours to take.

That hurt.

There. She'd admitted it.

He didn't have to be personally invested or anything. He didn't need to care for himself whether or not the insemination of his sperm into her body had created a new life. But she'd hoped he'd care for her sake, no matter whose sperm she'd used.

He wouldn't be back until after she'd had a day to deal with the results. Either way, she was bound to be a bit emotional over them. Elation, disappointment... either reaction would most likely be intense at first.

And Braden had purposely taken himself away.

So typical. And why had she expected any different? Of course he'd be there in a heartbeat if she called. But his choice was to be absent.

Her intensity made him uncomfortable.

She cut and glued—burning herself on the glue gun—embellished, trimmed, embossed, traced, drew faces, even did a bit of calligraphy with big thick strokes. Pulling supplies from various white plastic drawers stacked all along one wall of the room, she had her eight-foot worktable filled with papers, cardboards and pencils in various colors, an electronic cutter, paints, hole punches in several shapes, plastic pieces for 3-D effects, and yet she still saw Braden everywhere she looked.

How could he be so present in her mind, even after three years of divorce?

It wasn't until she was lying awake in the middle of the night that it hit her. He'd left her his key. Something he'd never done before—and he'd certainly been out of town for longer than two days on numerous occasions.

He'd left her his key.

Giving her access to him when he couldn't be there.

It hit her like a warm breeze on a cool day.

He was staying connected to her in his own way. And that was good enough.

Or at least good enough for her to settle into sleep. If, deep down, she needed more, wanted more, she'd let that go.

It was a learning process.

One minute, one step, one day at a time.

Braden checked on his offer first thing Thursday morning. The owner had phoned in a positive response, but it wasn't yet officially accepted. He made arrangements with the hotel to secure a suite for a monthly rate, good for however long he needed it, and got himself settled in. It would be fine for now. He was going to be ungodly busy, not only with contractors and building details but with filling twelve floors' worth of office suites.

That's when it hit him that he should have a daycare on the first floor. Being able to offer on-site childcare at a reduced rate was a great selling point. One that Mallory had come to him with. He'd trusted her judgment and she'd been right.

So, morally, he owed her the opportunity to open a second business if she wanted it. Practically, he didn't see it. The Bouncing Ball in San Diego took up all of her time as it was. And with a new baby, she'd have even less time. He couldn't support her taking on any more. She'd be stretched too thin, get stressed and lose sleep and not be happy.

Mallory was Supermom. She'd only be happy if she had ample time to spend with her new baby.

If she got pregnant. When she got pregnant.

She could already be pregnant.

And if she was, she wouldn't be in any position to join him in opening a new business.

He knew how she was. He remembered the way she'd buzzed through every hour of every day spouting off crib prices, watching sales, conversing on anything baby. He knew more about differences in breast pumps than he'd ever need to know. He could do a pretty good commentary on the benefits of disposable diapers, the differences between brands, even the comparable pricing on them from local stores. He remembered the calm glow about her, the light in her eyes and the joy in her smile when she'd told him the first time around that they were going to have a baby.

He'd whooped right along with her, grabbing her up and swinging her around until they were both dizzy. He'd made sweet love to her, taking it easy, and yet finding no less fulfillment for having done so. She'd been so beautiful that night, more than she'd ever been. Being pregnant had completed her.

He'd been certain back then that having Tucker had completed them.

He'd been all caught up in her excitement. Letting himself get carried away with the emotion of it all. Had allowed himself to wallow in the emotional high.

But emotion was fickle. It misrepresented facts. Made things seem different than they really were.

A second daycare would provide more financial security for Mallory. She could hire someone to run it for her if she didn't want to split her time between L.A. and San Diego. She'd have him in L.A., able to pop downstairs and check on things for her.

He wasn't her husband anymore.

He had no right to make her decisions for her.

Which meant that he had to call her and make the

offer. If she asked for his opinion, as a friend, he'd talk over her choices with her.

Decision made, he watched the clock until the half hour she usually took her lunch break, then called her. He'd had her on speed dial since he'd got a smartphone. He'd seen no reason not to continue keeping her there when he switched to newer versions.

She didn't pick up. Not even when, fifteen minutes later, he tried a second time.

She'd have taken the test that morning. Not the previous evening. Not the next day. On this, Mallory would be following every dictate to the nth degree. She was determined and she'd do all she could to get her part exactly right.

She'd also be tending to the emotional struggles that having this baby would be sure to bring her. It wasn't going to be easy. Fighting off fears. But she'd do what it took to be happy. She was that strong.

Which was why he loved the heck out of her.

Since waking that morning he had, on and off in the back of his mind, wondered about the results. He knew she'd call when she was ready to share them with him.

She hadn't done that yet.

And she wasn't answering his call. Or calling him back.

His realtor did, though, with the news that his bid had been accepted.

Sliding his phone in his jacket pocket, Braden went out to start his new life.

Chapter Eight

Though it was a difficult choice, Mallory didn't take a pregnancy test Thursday morning. The morning was hard, and yet she'd been energized, filled with a renewed sense of purpose.

She'd been going at Mach speed so that she didn't have time to think about the fact that her ex-husband—one of her best friends—was making an offer that, if accepted, would take him away from her.

She didn't want to know if the test was negative. Not yet.

It wasn't critical, either way. They'd told her that, commonly, it took more than one try. She had enough money already put aside to pay for six attempts.

She just didn't want to be disappointed. Not on that particular day. Her mental and emotional health was something she managed carefully. It had been a tough battle for her—learning to be kind to herself. To expect enough of herself, but not too much. To accept that she didn't have super powers that made her more accountable than anyone else.

For moral support, she called Tamara, her other best friend, and asked for a lunch date.

They met at a diner on the harbor, Mallory in her jeans and polo shirt, Tamara in a slim skirt and fitted jacket that made her look more like a glamor model than an efficiency expert.

"So?" the auburn-haired beauty said, looking Mallory straight in the eye after their hug. "What's up?"

They hadn't even been seated yet.

"Bray's making an offer on a property in L.A.," she said. This was their way, their pact. Born from a desperation to own their own lives after grief. To have a full and happy life after the loss of a child. Or as much of one as was possible.

Having met in grief counseling, the two had been deeply drawn to each other—and away from the group. They were alike in so many ways—and different in a lot of ways, too. But their spirits…it was like they'd been sisters in another life.

Or, as Tamara had once claimed, their babies in heaven had become best friends and were angels tending to the mothers they'd left behind.

There was no subterfuge. And no holding back.

They were each other's nonmedicinal medication.

"He's moving," Mallory continued.

"He's moving? To L.A.?" Tamara's eyes were wide.

The hostess stepped up to seat them, so all Mallory got in was a nod, but she felt better already. Tamara would see through any self-lying she might be doing. By asking the right questions, she'd lead Mallory to the truth.

Just as Mallory had done for Tamara last fall when she'd held a stranger's baby and fallen apart. And had done several times since as Tamara adjusted to loving with a whole heart again.

"You still love him." They'd ordered salads and tea, which sat untouched in front of them. Tamara wasn't letting Mallory pay attention to such mundane things.

She did love him, of course. It wasn't news. She nodded.

"No." Tamara shook her head. "You're still *in* love with him."

She wasn't. How could she be? "He's so wrong for me. On elemental levels."

Tamara's nod wasn't encouraging at all.

And she'd yet to tell her friend about the baby she might have conceived with Braden's sperm. Or about her plan to conceive at all. She hadn't needed Tamara's help on that decision.

Which had been one of the things that had told her so clearly that she was ready. It wouldn't be easy. She wasn't kidding herself. She knew her road ahead as a working single mother, one who'd lost a child and would forever carry the fear of losing another, would be tough. She also knew it was right for her.

And that she was ready.

The fact that she'd let Bray talk her into using his sperm, she was a little less comfortable telling Tamara about that...felt a bit more defensive about doing so...

"I think maybe I've been using him as a crutch all these years," she said. "I never really gave him up, in terms of my personal security. I didn't have to worry about being alone in times of trouble because he'd always have my back."

"And that's going to change when he moves to L.A.? You think he's suddenly going to desert you?"

"No. It's just... I don't know what it is. This sad, sick feeling inside, that's what it is. And I can't figure out why it's there. What it means."

She picked up her fork and Tamara followed suit. They ate a few bites and drank tea like they were just two friends out for lunch. Except that there was silence between them.

"He's been dating other women for years, so I know it's not that I'm worried that he's starting a new life," she finally said. "He did that long ago."

"You said once that you don't know why he bothers telling you that he's going out with someone because it's not going to last."

That was true.

"So his dating isn't really moving on and starting a life without you, is it? It's just living his own life with you in it."

"But this move to L.A. is moving on to a life without me. I won't have any part in it." She'd known that already but she hated saying the words.

"Sounds that way." Tamara was watching her, her food apparently forgotten.

"And that makes me incredibly sad."

"Maybe because you're still in love with him."

She didn't want that to be true. Didn't think it was. She needed a man who could support her when she showed some emotion other than passion.

One who didn't make her feel ashamed when she burst into tears or got all excited about something.

Like she knew she would when she finally heard that she was pregnant again. Once she got over the initial spate of anxiety.

The thought struck her in the heart. She didn't want to know for sure if she was pregnant because then there'd be something to lose.

Fear was an insidious beast. It had snuck up without her knowing. And being with Tamara, her free zone where whatever thoughts she had were safe, had let her see something she'd been trying so desperately to avoid…as much as she wanted the baby, was willing to go it alone, she was scared to death, too.

"It's not a crime, you know," her friend said, bringing her back to their current conversation about Braden and still being in love with him.

Which she was not.

But she was afraid to take that pregnancy test. Maybe as much as she was excited to do so. And not just because she might be disappointed with a negative response—though there was definitely that, too.

She was a cesspool of emotion. It was a good thing Braden was out of town.

Her expression must have been giving away some of her thoughts because Tamara spoke up.

"If you're in love with him, you are. It's nothing to feel badly about," she said.

"I'm not still in love with him. We've hurt each other too much. It's there between us—this mistrust of each other in an emotional sense. I trust him to die for me, but not to hold me if I cry."

"Has he ever?"

She thought back through her memories.

"When we were first married, he used to hold me when we watched sad movies and I started to cry. It wasn't a big deal. He never said a word. He'd just move closer and hold me."

Where had that man gone? And when?

Before Tucker died, she knew that for sure. It wasn't just their son's death that had come between them. Losing Tucker had been the trigger, but things had already been coming apart.

Why hadn't she known that?

"I let him down, too," she said now. "He doesn't trust me to meet his needs in the moment, or in a relationship sense."

Not just sexually, but in other things. He wanted to come first.

It wasn't an unnatural desire.

She just hadn't been good at putting two people first. In fact, she'd sucked at it. Strange, because she tended to thirty kids in any given hour and made them all feel special.

"Besides, he's too unemotional, you know that," she said now. And she knew why. Understood why. Growing up as he did, the only male in the house with two drama queens—his mother and sister—had forced him to be the practical one at all times.

She didn't blame him.

She just wasn't good for him. Or he for her. She was truly more at peace, less stressed, when she didn't have to worry about his reactions. And she knew it was the same for him.

Which was why their friendship had such clear boundaries.

"And yet," Tamara said, "his moving leaves you with incredible sadness."

She couldn't explain it. Or lie about it, either. Which meant she had to deal with it. Tamara wouldn't let her hide or kid herself or pretend.

Stabbing lettuce with her fork, she bowed her head.

* * *

Braden called twice while she was out to lunch. Having already taken a longer break than normal, Mallory didn't take the time to call him right back. She threw herself into caring for the children, playing with them, watching over them, evaluating and helping her teachers wherever she could. She did what she did and she did it well.

Braden hadn't left a message. There was no emergency. He was probably calling to tell her his offer had been accepted. She wasn't ready to hear the news. Didn't trust herself to sound happy about it. She truly wanted him to get on with his life, because she wanted him to be happy. He was a good man, always giving of himself where he could, reliable to the core, conscientious and tending to those in his world—tenants included. He deserved to be happy.

By his definition, being happy meant being busy doing what he was driven to do.

So, yes, he needed to get on with his life.

And she needed to take her pregnancy test. If she wasn't pregnant, she wanted to get another appointment scheduled as soon as possible. So, thinking, she didn't even stop at the end of her drive to check her mail when she got home. After heading straight into the garage, she let herself in through the kitchen, dropped her bag on the counter and without bothering to turn on lights made her way to the bathroom in her master suite. The test was on the counter where she'd left it after the morning's mental debate, waiting for her.

She read the box first, then opened it and read the pamphlet inside. It had been five years since she'd done a home pregnancy test. Not much had changed.

The one difference was this test would show her

how many weeks it had been since conception with 90 percent accuracy. She didn't need that information as she knew conception and time, down to the minute. If she'd conceived.

But she could at least vouch for the test's accuracy. Maybe.

Or be more certain that it wasn't a false positive if it also got the conception right. Right?

She had to quit vacillating on when to take the damned test. She had to get on with her life.

Make it what she wanted and needed.

Stalling was done. And in less than thirty seconds so was the test. She'd waited all day to do it, and now the wait for results seemed to take a year. Weak in the knees she sat on the closed commode, picked up her phone and returned Braden's call.

His news would distract her. Put things in perspective.

It wasn't like this was her only shot to have a baby. A no answer just meant she'd have to wait another month.

He didn't pick up.

And she wasn't pregnant.

As soon as Braden could excuse himself from his business dinner at his hotel with a couple of key investors, he took the elevator straight up to his suite and called Mallory.

Was she pregnant? He was expecting a yes. They'd had no trouble getting pregnant the first time. To him the conception part was a given. How she felt about it was the question. Now that it was happening, was she sure she could handle it?

Or was she worrying already about the future fate of her unborn child?

And if she was, what could he do about it?

She picked up on the fourth ring. "The test was negative, which was to be expected," she said in lieu of hello. "I'll call the clinic in the morning and schedule the next procedure."

She said it like she was discussing having the carpets cleaned.

"I'm sorry." He was, for her. And sorry for the relief he felt, too.

"They said to expect up to six months for it to take," she reminded him.

"You're taking it well." Why that surprised him, he wasn't sure. Other than Tucker's death, Mallory had always taken life in stride. It came from growing up in foster care, he'd figured.

"It's a process," she told him. "I knew that going in. I've had all the tests. There's no reason to believe I won't conceive."

"Still... I'm sure you were hoping the baby was already on its way." Why was he doing this? Trying to get emotion out of her when she knew it was exactly what he didn't want and, therefore, would withhold it from him?

"Of course I'd hoped, but I didn't get all worked up about it. I knew the chances were good it would take more than one try."

Walking over to his bar, he pulled out a shot bottle of expensive scotch, emptied some into a glass and took a small sip.

"My offer was accepted."

"Oh, Bray! I'm glad." The sincerity in her tone warmed him. The scotch probably helped, too. "So did you get your permits going?"

"Yes." He took a couple of minutes to tell her about

the meetings he'd had. Which was more than they usually did—other than by general mention. But then, this wasn't normal—him in L.A. starting a new venture and her in San Diego trying to have a baby without him.

He took another sip and then he launched into another topic.

"I have something to discuss with you. An opportunity," he said, wandering over to the window with his glass in hand, staring out at the lights of L.A. in the distance.

"What kind of opportunity?"

"I told you I'm intending to make this L.A. project as much a replica of Braden Property Management as possible."

"Yeah." He couldn't tell by her tone if she was focused or distracted. He reminded himself she'd just suffered what had to be a crushing disappointment. No matter what she said. He knew how badly she thought she wanted another baby.

And he hoped she was distracted enough to politely decline the offer he was about to make.

"One of the things that helped make us such an instant success was our ability to offer tenants in-house daycare at a reduced rate."

He couldn't judge her reaction from her silence, but that was all she gave him.

"Since the idea was yours, and because The Bouncing Ball plays a part in the success of Braden Property Management, I'd like to know if you'd be interested in expanding, if you'd like to open a second daycare, here in L.A."

"I…"

She stopped, as if she was thinking it through. He tried to wait her out but couldn't.

"You don't have to give me an answer right now. Just think about it, would you?"

He wanted an immediate no, not more time to fret about the ramifications of the plan.

"I don't need to think about it," she said. "Of course, I'll need time to get plans in place, but I can tell you right now that I'd be honored to be a part of the L.A. venture, Braden. Thank you."

His heart sank.

Chapter Nine

Was she nuts? She couldn't be a single mother and run two businesses.

What in the heck had she been thinking? *I'd be honored to be a part of the L.A. venture, Braden. Thank you.*

Had those words really come from her mouth?

Without a moment's hesitation?

Mallory passed through the next couple of days in a blur. She made her next appointment at the Elliott Clinic in Marie Cove, assuming she ovulated as expected, and then didn't let herself think about not having another baby. It wasn't a matter of if, it was merely a matter of when.

Instead, she lay in bed Sunday night and scared herself into wondering if she was really capable of letting Braden move on without her, being his friend and supporting him while he did it. Why else would she have told him she'd be a part of his new venture?

She had absolutely no desire to own an empire. Or to live in L.A. Those were Bray's dreams, though the whole L.A. thing was new even for him.

Yet she'd jumped at the chance to join him. All weekend long she'd been reeling with the facts. He'd called once, asked her to lunch to discuss business, but she'd made an excuse, and he hadn't pushed.

Was he having second thoughts, too?

Were they back to him going and her being no part of his new life?

That thought brought back the incredible sadness she had felt at the mention of his moving.

The thought of opening a second daycare that far away brought panic. And no less desire to have her baby and get on with her life, either.

So what gave?

What was driving her?

Years of counseling and taking accountability for her own emotional health made her seek out the elusive answers.

Was she really in love with Braden still, as Tamara had said?

She had to ask.

And the answer was still the same. There was a bond there, of course. They'd been in love, had a child together and lost that child. But she didn't think she was in love with him. Anytime she tried to get there she arrived right where they'd ended—at complete odds with each other, letting each other down emotionally.

She still felt ashamed at how wild she'd been in his arms at the same time her son had died.

Still hated that she'd been away from home.

After four years it was a pretty good bet that those feelings weren't going to go away.

As night gave way to day, she got up, showered, got herself to work and greeted her children. Her days were about them, fully and completely. And yet, on Monday she was stopped in her tracks by an expression on the precious face of one of her four-year-olds. Liam was precocious and about as happy as a little boy could be. He'd come up and offered her a picture he'd drawn of a heart and told her he loved her.

She could barely hold back her tears but she pulled it off for Liam. She hid her emotion in the hug she gave him, telling him she loved him, too, and escaped as quickly as she could.

Did Braden ever think about what Tucker would be like if he'd lived? Did he ever see a four-year-old boy and wonder if Tucker would have been like him?

Her thoughts from the night before were there again, in the middle of her day. She had to tell Braden she couldn't accept his L.A. offer. She had to let him go.

She took a couple of minutes locked in her private bathroom to let the tears flow.

After having a weekend to think about it, Braden was looking forward to the idea of Mallory's daycare in L.A. He couldn't envision how it would work exactly, but he had a few ideas to run by her, ways she could manage her business, expand her business and have the life she wanted, as well. By Monday he was congratulating himself on coming up with the idea. The Bouncing Ball supported her comfortably, but with a baby to raise, the added security of a second business would further cultivate her emotional health.

Though there might be more on her plate on a day-to-day basis, at least at first, she'd have less to worry about in the big picture.

Mal had always been a big-picture girl. He'd been all about making the moment count. She'd been on the forever plan.

She didn't have time to meet him for lunch on Monday, either, and because he was leaving Tuesday morning to head back to L.A., he waited for her after work. Nothing overt; he just watched from his window for her to be heading out to her car and then called her and asked her to wait a second.

She said she had to get home to return calls she'd promised would be made that day, but when he pushed, telling her he was heading out in the morning, she relented.

If he didn't know better, he'd think she was avoiding him.

He shook his head at the thought. That was his sister's way of thinking, not his. She built a mountain of drama out of putting imaginary negative thoughts about herself in other people's heads. Mallory had no reason to avoid him. They'd established that neither of them had to worry about speaking with the other ever again.

No more hurt feelings or tense silences between them.

They weren't married anymore. They couldn't disapprove of each other's plans, thoughts, wants or desires. It had been established the day they'd divorced. Right along with the fact that they'd always be friends and have each other's backs. Or some such thing. He couldn't remember the exact words that had been said, but the understanding had been there. They had three years of proof to substantiate it.

She was sitting in her car when he got downstairs.

"Follow me home," he suggested. His place, a luxurious high-rise condo, was only a few blocks away.

When she looked ready to argue, he said, "I'll order dinner delivered and you can be home making your calls within the hour."

He was pushing too hard. But they were building their future here—futures apart from each other, while still offering friendship and support. He needed every detail laid out.

He needed this to work.

He'd been living in limbo too long and was beginning to feel like he was wasting his life.

If it was just a feeling, he'd move on. Braden tried never to build plans on something as unreliable as feelings. But when it was feeling and fact combined, he knew to push.

In her jeans and polo shirt, with her dark hair swirling around her face and shoulders, Mallory looked tired as she preceded him through his front door. And hot as hell, too. Braden liked women and got turned on as easily as the next guy. But Mallory pushed a button in him no other woman seemed to know how to push.

Probably because he had to get her out of the way before another woman could find her way in.

You'd think her continued physical rejections during the last year of their marriage, including a show of out-and-out aversion to him touching her, would have done it.

You'd think. But it hadn't.

He'd called in an order of lasagna and salad from the wine bar on the bottom floor of his building and it arrived right behind them. Mallory was looking around the condo as though something might have changed since she'd last been there three years ago, shortly after he'd moved in. She should know him better than that. She was the one into aesthetics. He liked his surround-

ings nice and clean, and then he just lived in them—
used them for their purpose, took them for granted.

With Mallory, her surroundings were almost like a
living entity, a partner in her life. She tended to them
on a regular basis, changing things up, adding stuff.

He used to look around when he got home from a
trip, testing himself to see if he could figure out what
she'd changed while he'd been gone.

She'd challenge him and if he could work out whatever it was, he'd get sex before dinner rather than afterward.

He'd almost always had the appetizer sex.

"You want a glass of wine?" he asked, pulling the
bottle he'd ordered out of the bag. He had to get his
head in the game.

And get her out of his head.

"Tea's good, if you have some."

Of course he had tea. It had always been a staple for
both of them. He poured a glass for her, added ice, then
opened the wine for himself.

She found plates and silverware, took them to the
table in the dining room, in front of French doors that
led out to a balcony facing the ocean in the distance.

She'd loved the view the moment she'd seen the
place. He'd known she would.

"We could have just gone to a restaurant," she said
as they sat down. She hadn't looked at him since they'd
been inside.

"It would have taken twice as long and you're in a
hurry. Besides, we can get through more business if
we aren't constantly being interrupted by wait staff."

He'd wanted their talk to be private. What they were
doing, her having a baby with his sperm, that was about

as private as it could get. And now, they were about to enter into a second business agreement.

"I thought maybe you wanted to show me things," she said. "You know, where things were in case you needed me to tend to them in your absence."

That was logical, he thought, since he'd given her the key.

"Like maybe how the thermostat works or where the water shut-off valve is," she continued.

Good points, both of them. "I'll do both before you leave," he said, digging into his lasagna. She'd served herself a big bowl of salad with a small slice of the lasagna, forgoing the garlic bread.

"We should have been doing this all along," he told her, at ease with her in a way he hadn't been sitting across from her at their various restaurant haunts.

At least, he felt at ease until he met her gaze across the table and all the blood in his body surged to his penis.

For a second there he froze. Did she know? What was she thinking?

No, she couldn't possibly know. His pelvis was under the table, out of her view. And far hungrier than his stomach. Lasagna wasn't what he wanted.

"I wanted to talk to you about the daycare in L.A." Mallory stabbed the lettuce delicately, chewed, then took a sip of tea.

The daycare. It was what he'd been trying to talk to her about.

It was the purpose of the meeting, he reminded himself. Not taking her to bed.

Restaurants didn't have his bed just down the hall. Was that why they met in them?

"You know, in your new complex," she said, fork suspended as she frowned at him.

He nodded and wiped his mouth with his napkin. "That's the purpose of this meeting," he said, attacking his lasagna with a vengeance. "I have several ideas that I think might give you a lot of added security for your future, you know, with a child, and yet wouldn't run you ragged, trying to keep up with it all."

Barely giving himself time to chew and swallow, he suggested that they use The Bouncing Ball name, set it up with the same room configurations and colors, use all of the same philosophies and paperwork, apply one accounting system that would be run online to keep both facilities connected in real time, but hire a manager to run the L.A. branch.

"You could install cameras, like the ones people put in their homes to be able to see what's going on inside when they aren't home," he continued while she silently ate her salad and then finished her piece of lasagna—all four bites of it.

"That way you can monitor what's going on in every room, all day if you want to, to make certain that the children are being treated with the loving discipline that has earned you so much respect."

She wasn't really nodding, but he could tell by the expression on her face that she was interested.

"And to make certain that the philosophy stays solid, you could offer the management position to Julia, maybe. You said since John died she's been fading. Maybe a change would be good for her."

Julia, Mallory's second-in-command, had lost her husband to a motorcycle crash the year before. They were in their forties and had never been able to conceive children. Rather than adopting, Julia had chosen to work in the childcare field. She'd applied to work with Mallory before The Bouncing Ball had even opened.

"She's actually just started seeing someone," Mallory told him. "A single dad with two kids, a boy and a girl, both under ten."

"Someone from The Bouncing Ball?"

"No. She met him through a friend of a friend. He's an engineer."

He should have known that. Why hadn't he known that? It wasn't like he and Mal didn't talk regularly.

With a shrug, he took another bite of food. And then said, "So maybe Donna or someone else would be up for the move," he said, making a mental run-through of her remaining eight employees and what he knew about their qualifications and living situations.

Mallory reached her fork over toward his lasagna and they both stopped moving, staring at each other.

Eating off each other's plates had been common once upon a time. Mostly him finishing up whatever she'd left. But not once in the last few years had either of them crossed that boundary.

"I'm sorry," she said, putting her empty fork down beside her plate.

"No," he pushed his plate toward her. "Please. I'm not going to finish."

She looked at him for a few seconds. He held her gaze. He kept telling himself he should look away, that staring into her eyes was only stirring his penis even further, but he couldn't turn away. Eventually she picked up her fork and helped herself to a bite from his plate. Watching her put it into her mouth, he dropped his napkin in his lap.

It was a good thing he was moving to L.A.

A damned good thing.

Chapter Ten

She had to tell Braden that she wasn't going to open a second daycare. All that week and into the next, Mallory told herself that she'd make the call tomorrow. Each day, it would happen tomorrow.

She had to distance herself from him. They'd proven that they weren't good for each other as more than friends. After Tucker's death the ashes of their marriage had almost destroyed her.

They were just too different in the basic way they approached life. They needed different things to make them happy.

So why hadn't she stopped his talk at his condo the week before? Told him that she'd changed her mind about joining his L.A. venture?

She didn't know, really.

It wasn't like he had to know right away, she'd told herself. He'd still do the daycare with or without her.

Any work she'd need to be involved with wouldn't come about for months.

But he should know.

Driving into Marie Cove for her appointment at the clinic, exactly one month after she'd made the same drive with Braden, she settled into the rhythm of the road, wrapped in the protective silence of her car, and let her mind relax. To relive recent business with Braden step by step. She thought back to the time he called her to ask her to wait for him. No, wait, she skipped backward to when she'd avoided his attempts to meet up.

Because she'd known she needed to tell him.

Then, that Monday night, a week and a half before, he'd asked her to his condo. She hadn't even argued. Because it had made sense, with her watching over the place for him, she should probably acquaint herself with it, learn its unique foibles.

She'd been planning to take the opportunity to tell him that he'd be doing the L.A. thing without her. She'd actually been ready to do so. Having played around with the idea, she knew that it wasn't right for her.

And then he'd sat down with her, the two of them alone at the table, with that view, in his place, and he'd started talking about the daycare. And she had kept quiet.

He'd given it so much thought. Pointed out that the added security would give her extra peace of mind as she set out into single parenthood.

He'd made sense.

He'd been supporting her in her new life.

And then he'd looked at her...more than once.

Did he know that his blue eyes darkened when he was turned on? Had she ever told him?

She'd seen that look from him thousands of times

before. Had recognized it with a shock that sent ripples through her entire system.

And for a second there, she'd received an answering call from places within her she'd thought dead and gone. At least where he was concerned.

And that was why she hadn't told him she'd changed her mind.

Shaking with the truth, Mallory missed her turnoff.

Though he'd been in San Diego twice since he'd had Mallory in his condo, Braden hadn't seen her. Purposely. He needed time to get himself under control, to be mentally prepared against flashbacks before he saw her again.

He'd met a woman in L.A., an architect colleague of Don Miller, who'd done the drawings for San Diego and was already modifying them to fit the L.A. property. Don had called Anna in for consultation on a couple of points having to do with building around the natural landscaping that they'd like to keep if they could. The three of them had had lunch.

Braden had since had dinner with her. Twice.

He liked her. A lot. More than any other woman he'd dated in the past three years.

Business-minded like him, she lived alone, visited her family in San Francisco enough to be diligent and had a beautiful smile. She laughed often. And she didn't appear to have a dramatic bone in her body. From the signals she was sending, he was pretty clear that she liked him a lot, too.

He'd made a date to have lunch with her on Thursday, a week and a half after his dinner with Mallory, but had been toying with the idea of canceling all morning. When he'd spoken with his ex-wife the night before she'd mentioned her second clinic visit, scheduled for eleven that morning. She'd had a positive ovulation test.

He'd yet to tell Anna about Mallory, other than to say he was divorced and he and his ex had remained friends. The rest was left to be shared with someone when he took their relationship to the next level.

In his hotel "office," going over the final drawings to be turned over that day to the contractor, he figured he and Anna might be headed to that next level in the very near future.

But he still figured he should cancel lunch.

Mallory would be in Marie Cove.

He could text her to meet him for a quick bite by the clinic. She'd need to get back; she never liked to take time off during the day, though, as the boss, she was free to do so. Regardless, she'd need a meal.

And he needed to tell her about Anna. He could be there and back before his next appointment.

Picking up his phone, he sent the text.

Sitting alone on the table in a paper gown, with a blanket wrapped around her to ward off the chills she'd suddenly developed, Mallory waited for her doctor. Phone in hand, she tried to distract herself with one of her favorite puzzle games.

She'd been weighed, had her blood pressure checked, peed in the cup, and all that was left was the few minutes it would take for the injection of Braden's sperm into her uterus.

It was all procedure. She'd been through it before. And she didn't have a single doubt that she was doing the right thing.

What bothered her far more was the fact that she'd

failed to distance herself from Bray in the daycare venture. Because she'd been attracted to him?

It had come and gone so quickly she'd closed her mind to the possibility instantly. But she'd worried about it ever since.

She'd been turned on by her ex-husband.

Looking back, she thought maybe she was imagining the whole thing. Maybe she'd just reacted so strongly because she'd been shocked that he'd been turned on. Shocked to see that look in his eye. Or maybe she was hormonal, her body raging with the need to be a mother again.

Maybe it was because she was using his sperm.

Her phone vibrated with a text. The message flashed up on her screen.

Meet me for a quick bite?

The timing was no mistake. She was certain of that.

Yes.

She was going to tell him she was out of the L.A. deal.

"Mallory? You can get dressed," Dr. Sharon Miller said as she came into the exam room and closed the door.

Last time a nurse had come in before the doctor with a tray filled with procedural materials. She'd been expecting the nurse first.

"Get dressed? I don't understand."

Surely she didn't have the wrong time. They'd checked her in like they were expecting her. Put her through the pre-insemination rigmarole.

Dr. Miller's smile threw her off a bit. And then she heard, "You're pregnant!"

Everything inside her stopped and then restarted in double speed. Her heart pounded. Her breathing quickened. Her stomach jumped. It was like she could feel everything individually. In slow motion.

"I..."

She didn't know what to say. Was afraid to believe it.

"Your urine test came back positive. That's why, once we've started the monthly injections, we always check."

"But I had a period." A light one. Really light. But that wasn't all that unusual for her when she was stressed.

Putting a hand on Mallory's, Dr. Miller said, "You're pregnant, sweetie."

She was pregnant? As in...right then, right there, inside her, she had a new baby? She wasn't just Mallory Harris, divorced mother of a deceased child anymore?

She was an expectant mother?

"I ovulated," she said through a dry throat, swallowing to try to fix that malady.

"An ovulation test will commonly show up positive if you're pregnant."

She hadn't known that.

"I'm pregnant?"

"Four weeks," Dr. Miller was still smiling. "That's one benefit to insemination—no guessing as to gestation timing."

Mallory sat there in her gown, the blanket wrapped around her, hugging her stomach, and nodded.

"You'll need to see your OB as soon as possible," the doctor continued, talking about vitamins, prenatal care, the rounds of tests she'd be going through. Most of which she'd done with Tucker, too. "I'm recommending that they do a six-week ultrasound," she said. "It's common with fertility and insemination procedures, just to make certain that everything is okay."

She added Mallory's projected due date: December 10th. And then said, "I'll leave you to get dressed. It was nice meeting you, Mallory. Good luck and Merry Christmas!"

The woman was out the door and Mallory sat there with her mouth hanging open.

Merry Christmas! Last Christmas she'd been on a boat with friends, feeling more alone than she'd ever felt in her life.

By next Christmas she was going to be a family again. A mother. With her own baby to hold. Assuming everything was okay.

I'm recommending that they do a six-week ultrasound...just to make certain that everything is okay.

As she remembered Dr. Miller's words, fear struck. Instantaneous and sharp.

Assuming all went well with that, she'd have to get past the five-month mark before she'd really be home free.

No. Shaking her head, she slid to her feet, reaching for her clothes with shaking hands. She wasn't going to let fear rule her life. Her past would not steal from her future.

She was going to be a mother again! That was this moment's truth.

Her mind would remain firmly on what was, not on what could be.

She would control her fear.

Reality was she had a baby growing inside her!

Holy crap!

* * *

The Elliott Clinic was not far off the freeway. Using his GPS to find a nearby place for a quick lunch, he'd texted Mallory with the address. She was already there when he arrived. Already seated among a far wall of booths, all filled with well-dressed, mostly business-looking patrons. The two men right behind her seemed to be in serious discussion.

Just as he'd been the day before when he'd met with his top investor.

At the moment, he envied those two men. He'd much rather be talking money than telling his ex-wife that he was dating again. If he and Anna did hook up on a more serious basis, he'd need to make certain that he didn't have to dread an emotional conversation like the one that could be potentially ahead.

Him dating wasn't that big of a deal. He'd told Mallory half a dozen times about going out with various different women.

But Anna was different.

She was L.A. The start of his new life.

At least that's how he feared Mallory was going to see it. She'd make a bigger deal of it than it was at the moment.

She'd ask him if her suspicions were true.

And he wouldn't be able to deny them, because, at some point in the future, they might be.

She'd already ordered their tea. It was sitting on the table as he slid into his side of the booth. Not able to meet her eyes, his gaze dropped to the table and met her breasts just above it. They looked fabulous in a purple shirt. Just fabulous.

"I ordered you a grilled chicken sandwich with sweet

potato fries," she told him. "Sorry, but I need to get back."

"No, that's great." Lifting his gaze, he smiled at her. She looked radiant and for a second his penis came more fully to life. Was she that happy to see him?

Then he caught himself.

She'd just been inseminated again, so of course she looked radiant.

What was with all of his overreaction around this woman? Was her emotional approach to life contagious? Something he'd caught when they'd been married, like some disease he couldn't shake?

It had been three years, and now he'd suddenly had a relapse?

"Look, I know we don't have much time, so I just need to tell you right away. I can't do the L.A. day-care thing, Braden. I appreciate the offer so much. And you're right, it could be a great thing, but I've decided to pass on your offer."

Everything settled inside him. He was calm. Analytical. Himself again.

"Why? Other than the initial investment for start-up, which I told you I'd loan you at today's rate minus a percent due to the fact that I stand to benefit from the deal, this won't be a drain on you. Especially if you let someone else manage the place for you, with cameras installed so you don't keep feeling like you have to run up and check on things. And it will ensure your future security."

He thought it had all been worked out. The idea made sense. He was going to do the daycare. The business plan had already shown itself highly successful in San Diego. Someone was going to benefit. Might as well be someone he cared about.

"Besides, with your philosophies, your hiring of employees, your oversight, I know that the daycare will be the asset I need it to be so my future tenants feel comfortable leaving their kids there. And you have no problem offering the lower rates for tenants because you've already seen how, in the end, you benefit financially from the built-in clients.

"Added to that, we've got the success of The Bouncing Ball in San Diego to show them. Prospective tenants who would be daycare clients can drive down and visit you there to see the great environment you have to offer them."

He might have kept right on talking if their food hadn't been delivered.

She'd ordered half a grilled chicken sandwich with a cup of soup and dug right in.

"So?" he asked after he'd taken the edge off with a couple of bites.

She shook her head. "It sounds good, Bray, but I can't."

The woman wasn't budging. Studying her, he didn't get it.

Which was probably why they were divorced.

He wanted her to get it.

He wanted her to be part of the L.A. venture. It made practical, financial sense.

She'd be taken care of. And he could move on more easily.

"I'll be there to check on things," he told her. "You know I wouldn't let anything untoward happen. I've got your back. I always have."

Her smile made him hungry for sex again.

"I know, and that's why I can't do it."

Throwing a hand up he said, "I don't get it."

"The whole point of your move to L.A. was to start your own life. To move on. We both know that means moving on from me. From us. How are you going to do that if I follow along with you?"

"I'll have an entirely new life in L.A. Living in a new place, hanging out with new people." Like Anna. And others he'd met in the past weeks. Guys who'd invited him to play golf. A bar he'd found where there were high-stakes dart tournaments. He'd been pretty good at darts in college.

Her look had him stumped. Was it pity he saw on her face?

No, but…something.

"Answer me this. If it wasn't for the fact that we both know life was growing stagnant and had to change, that we needed a break between us…if this was just a business venture, would you accept the offer?"

"Probably. As you said, it makes sense in a lot of ways."

"So let's table this for now, okay? Think about it some more. See how it goes with me in L.A. and you in San Diego. I think you'll see that the distance we need will be there."

She shook her head. "I know I need to say no, Bray."

"Please," he pushed. Because he couldn't not. The plan made perfect sense for both of them. And then something occurred to him. She'd had to fight hard to recover from the panic attacks and fear that had beset her in the early days after Tucker's death. They'd only lasted a month or two, but the fact that they'd happened at all had scared her. "Are you afraid you can't let go of me?"

Her gaze shot up. He got hot again.

"I'm pregnant, Bray."

He dropped his sandwich. At first he didn't even notice. All he could see was the glow in her eyes, that odd look again. It wasn't pity. It was compassion. Her "mother" look, he'd once dubbed it. He should have known.

"But you said you had your—"

"I did. But they did a test this morning and it turns out I'm pregnant."

Hmm.

Well.

Whoa.

He nodded a bit.

And when he thought maybe he had assimilated the situation he said, "I'm seeing someone."

Chapter Eleven

That first weekend Mallory was consumed with baby buying. She'd done Tucker's room in yellows and greens, giraffes, elephants and monkeys. This time around she chose primary colors, balloons and bears, mostly. And she bought a new crib—she'd gotten rid of Tucker's the day he'd been taken from it—in a new style, too; instead of brown, white this time with a changing table to match. She filled her car and went back a second time, filling it again.

If you build it, they will come. The phrase came to her from somewhere in her past. From a movie about baseball fields. She couldn't remember when she'd seen it or with whom, but since the words presented themselves out of the blue, she took them to heart.

She'd build the nursery and her baby would come.

And then she was done.

There'd be more to add as the months passed. Outfits, diapers, cute things she'd pick up for the room as she saw them. And a rocker—she was thinking old-fashioned this time, not the glider kind she'd had before. But, for the most part, what had taken her months the first time around was done in three days.

No researching was necessary this time. She knew what kind of swing she preferred and why; she had them at the daycare. Car seat, portable crib, bouncy seat and high chair, too. She was a woman who knew pretty much everything about baby paraphernalia—down to the style of breast pump.

By Sunday afternoon she was satisfied with how the room across the hall from hers looked. Liked how the portable crib fit into her room's decor.

And then she panicked. What if something happened? What if she miscarried? Should she have waited until she'd passed the critical three-month stage? What if she'd jinxed things? Like she'd left Tucker that night?

If you build it, they will come.

She wasn't jinxing; she was building.

Heart pounding, she concentrated on slowing her air intake so she didn't hyperventilate. She drew in deeper breaths as she thanked God that Braden wasn't around to witness her weekend.

Then she called Tamara.

Having driven to San Diego on Saturday to retrieve his boat and dock her in her new home not far from the hotel where he was staying, Braden took Anna out on the water Sunday. She wasn't into fishing—or sunbathing, either, for that matter. But she had a great time captaining the boat when he offered her the wheel, laughing when she hit a wake. Right behind her, his arms wrapping her as he taught her, he laughed, too.

And he told himself that this was living.

But later that afternoon, when they docked and she made it clear that she was open to them spending the rest of the day—and the night—together, he chose to get back to work. He had meetings in the morning—Braden Property Management business, not new build business—and needed to prepare.

Mallory was pregnant. It was right that he let Anna know before he had sex with her. Just in case she had a problem with it.

He didn't expect she would. Didn't see why she would.

Still, with Mallory's news still so fresh, he was pretty certain the decent thing was to let Anna know.

He called Mal on the way back to his hotel, figuring he'd get her opinion on the matter. She was a woman. She'd probably know better than he how to present their situation to his potential girlfriend. She didn't pick up.

Out baby shopping, he was sure. Ever since she'd told him she was expecting again, he was remembering how she'd been the first time, so he was certain he could predict her actions, even down to the stores she'd visit. It would take months. She'd think of nothing else outside of work.

At first, he'd been as bad as she was. The memory creeped in as he pulled into the underground parking garage and took the elevator up to his suite. He'd heard of an out-of-the-way spot that sold handmade nursery furniture and he'd called Mallory, convincing her to go with him to see if they could get the crib she wanted.

He'd been willing to play hooky but she'd made them wait until Saturday.

They'd painted the nursery together. He'd accidentally bumped into her with the roller. She'd given him such a saucy look he'd slid it up her shirt. And then dropped it. And his pants. About as quickly as she'd dropped hers.

Lovemaking had always been like that with them. Spontaneous. Intense. All the time.

Until she'd started to pull back. He'd understood. It had been getting harder and harder for her to find a comfortable position just to sit or lie down. Having him in her space, on her space, hadn't helped.

He'd told himself that after the baby was born things would return to normal.

Instead there'd been a new normal. Mallory had become a mother.

Being a wife didn't seem to interest her anymore.

Until that last night.

Maybe he'd been too impatient and hadn't given her enough time to adjust. It was the first time in her life she'd been aware of being with biological family. Of course that had to have had an effect on her.

She'd needed him to sit with her.

He'd needed her to have sex with him. Or even just sit with him.

To matter.

He couldn't blame her for how she'd felt, how motherhood had completed her. None of what she had done had been wrong. She'd been a great mom. A working mom.

And it wasn't like she hadn't still talked to Braden, asked about his day.

It hadn't just been the lack of sex, either, though.

When she'd looked at him, it had been like she wasn't really seeing him. She was seeing whatever Tucker was doing, even if he was in his crib asleep.

And when he'd talked, at least one ear had always been listening to or for the baby. She'd carried that damned monitor everywhere.

He'd started to resent the thing. Which was why he'd pushed so hard to have her to himself for one night.

It had been quite a night. The best sex ever. And

more, Mallory had seen him again. Heard him. She'd cared that he was there seeing her, loving her. He'd thought that night had solved their problems. He'd been ready to head back home to their son and give her the time she'd needed to adjust, figuring that she'd be paying more attention to him, too.

Instead, they'd gotten the call…and after that, everything just went from horrible to worse.

With a glass of whiskey in hand he stood at the window of his hotel suite, disgruntled, a sense of dissatisfaction settling over him. In his mind he returned to an earlier time. The moment he'd known that he and Mallory were heading for divorce. He'd been in a hotel similar to the current one, away on business and dreading going home.

He'd had a woman invite him to spend the night with her earlier in the evening. He hadn't done so, of course. He'd taken his marriage vows seriously and would never have cheated on Mallory, just as he'd been certain she'd never cheat on him.

But he'd been tempted. God, he'd been tempted.

Which was how he'd known.

Sipping from his glass, he dropped down to the sofa, still facing the window.

In the beginning, though, when they'd first found out they were having a baby, there'd been nothing like it.

She was experiencing that same feeling now.

While he was back in a hotel room. Planning to sleep with Anna as soon as he told her that Mallory was pregnant.

Funny how life seemed to go in circles and still got so screwed up.

The first thing Mallory told Tamara about, when the woman showed up at her door Sunday rather than just returning her call as they'd discussed, was Braden's offer for expanding The Bouncing Ball business with a second daycare in his L.A. complex.

Tamara hadn't needed to come, but Mallory understood why she had. Mallory had made similar visits to the home Tamara shared with Flint Collins and the precious little baby sister he'd inherited, and she would continue to do so whenever Tamara called her.

They were two strong women who'd suffered debilitating grief but were determined to live happy lives. They shared things that most people who'd never lost a child would ever fully understand.

"Did you tell him you'd do it?" Tamara's expectant expression settled her a bit. She could have looked worried. Or horrified.

Bringing glasses of tea out to the small patio off her kitchen, she handed one to her friend and sat down with her at the round glass table. "I told him no," she reported happily. Then she amended her response. "At first I said yes, but when I thought about it and the things we'd talked about, I knew that I was doing it for the wrong reason."

"Which was?"

"To continue to be a part of his life. I'm using him as a crutch. Preventing myself—and him—from moving on."

She had more to say. A lot more. But she wanted this part cleared up first.

Because it really mattered.

Being a mother was only part of her life. Something else she'd learned the hard way. When she'd lost Tucker, she'd lost herself. She'd had her own identity so wrapped up in his—her only known biological person in the world—that she'd almost lost her own life. Had her son lived, her being so consumed by him would not have been good for him. Though she didn't ever see herself marrying again, didn't see herself being successful at being both mother and wife, she still needed to have healthy adult relationships. For her own sake and that of her child.

"When he made the offer, I wasn't sad anymore about his plans. Which told me that I'd wanted to be a part of them."

Tamara was frowning now.

"And before you say it, don't," Mallory said. "He wasn't offering for the same reason. We aren't two people who are still in love and meant to be together." Ever since Tamara had opened up her heart and fallen in love again, she was seeing true love everywhere.

Mostly, Mallory found the characteristic endearing. Except for now, when it was turned erroneously on her.

"Braden was just being Braden. He had a whole list of reasons why joining him would be good business. Good for me financially, too."

When Tamara asked what they were, she listed them all, almost verbatim as Bray had presented them to her. "Besides," she added, "he's seeing someone again."

Tamara frowned again.

"What?" Mallory asked her.

"If he's involved, and his reasoning is sound, are you sure you aren't letting your past rob from your future?" she asked, her gaze steady.

"I'm confused." Mallory stared back. "Isn't that what I'd be doing if I accepted his offer?"

"Is it?"

She'd like to have been able to get irritable with her friend and move on. But that wasn't why she'd called Tamara.

"I don't know," she said. "I turned him down. Thursday, at lunch. He told me he was leaving the door open. He reiterated all the reasons it was a good idea. He said nothing had to be done for a few months and just wanted me to think about it."

"So are you?"

Obviously she was. She had some pretty incredible news to share, and here she was, rehashing the whole Braden thing again.

"I want to do it," she said. "I just want to make certain I'm doing it for the right reasons."

"Then take the time he's given you. Revisit it from time to time over the next couple of months. See if your feelings change."

She smiled, feeling her clarity returning. "Thank you."

"Of course." Tamara smiled back and made a crack about being glad to have the excuse to get away from cleaning out the shed. The baby, Diamond Rose, was spending the afternoon and evening with her paternal grandparents. Tamara just wanted to be home in time for bath, bottle and bedtime.

Mallory grinned. Hugely. She couldn't help it.

"I have other news," she admitted, sitting forward. "I'm pregnant."

"You're what?" Tamara squealed loudly enough for all of the neighbors to hear. Jumping up, she tilted the table and spilled tea from both of their glasses. "You're pregnant?" She stood there, hands on her hips, staring at Mallory, who nodded, still grinning inanely.

"But...who's the father?"

She didn't even hesitate as she told Tamara about her plan to have a child. The trips to the fertility clinic. The decision to use insemination.

"You've been working on this for months and never said a word?"

"I didn't need clarity," she said. "When I was ready, I just knew I was ready." She stood and Tamara grabbed her up in a nice long hug. One she'd been craving since she heard the news.

"You want to see the nursery?" she asked, taking her friend's hand and leading her back into the house, through the living room and down the hall. "It's been hard not telling you, but I wanted to wait until I was pregnant first. They said it could easily take up to six months and there was no point in anyone else wondering and waiting every month."

"Except that I would have been happy to share that with you, so you weren't going through it alone."

She hadn't been. Braden had known.

But Braden's part in the process was the one thing she hadn't shared. Nor did she share it as her friend oohed and ahhed over the nursery, lingering a bit as she touched the crib, the swing cover, causing Mallory to wonder if maybe Tamara was thinking about trying one more time to have a child of her own.

"Just don't hold out on me when the fear hits," Tamara said, standing close as she held Mallory's gaze. "You know it's going to come."

"It's already started."

"Don't go through it alone."

"I won't."

"No matter what time of day or night."

She'd answered a couple of middle-of-the-night calls from Tamara during the past months.

"I promise."

She swore she'd call her friend anytime she needed her, then answered all of Tamara's questions about the insemination process, the doctor's instructions, her due date. The one thing she still didn't do was tell her friend that Braden was her sperm donor.

Because it wasn't critical. The sperm was from a donor. She'd just chosen to use a donor whose family history she knew. For safety's sake. And one who'd offer another kind of insurance as well—a biological family for her child if anything should happen to her.

It was all just science and legalities.

She had clarity on that.

Chapter Twelve

Braden was on his second whiskey, paperwork spread out in front of him on the coffee table in his suite, staring out the window as dusk fell over the city, casting shadows on mountains in the distance, when Mallory called him back.

"Sorry. Tamara stopped over," she said, dissipating his growing sense that she really was avoiding him.

Nonsense was what that was.

But Tamara… Mention of the other woman made him tense. Mallory and Tamara didn't go shopping or to the theater like other friends. No, they only got together when one or the other of them was on the brink of an emotional meltdown.

It wasn't like he found anything wrong with that. In truth, he found it admirable. It just made him uncomfortable to the point of drinking more.

"Is she okay?" he asked because it was his duty to be polite.

"Yeah. I called her."

Oh.

"You're struggling?" *Already.* "Because of the baby?"

"No."

Oh. Well then... "I was calling to ask your opinion on something," he said, watching as lights slowly popped on in the distance, thinking it would be one hell of an onerous task to count them all.

And then he wondered what it said about him that he spent so much time paying attention to the lights outside his window.

"Of course." Mallory's reply was steady. Easy. Kind. She didn't sound like she was close to any kind of breakdown at all.

Relieved, he took a sip of whiskey and said, "I think it's only right that I tell Anna that you're pregnant, and that I am your sperm donor. I was hoping you might have some suggestion about how I do that."

"You don't do it."

"Of course I have to let her know that—"

"Braden, the whole point here is that you just donated sperm. Period. I'm not having your child. I'm having my child."

Standing, he left his glass on the table and walked over to the window. "Yeah, I wanted to talk to you about that."

"What?" A definite tone of wariness entered her voice.

"I think you should put my name on the birth certificate."

"Wait. Are you're trying to tell me that you want to be the baby's father?"

"No! Of course not!" Dear God, no. But he couldn't help wondering... Had her voice changed yet again, as though she was open to the possibility? Or had that just been incredulity at his presumptuousness? "I'm not going to renege on my agreement to support you in raising a child on your own," he quickly assured her. "But I was thinking about what you said, about knowing that I'd take the child if something ever happened to you, so that your child would have biological family other than you."

"What does that have to do with your name on the birth certificate?"

"I wouldn't have to prove paternity. The child would come to me immediately."

He didn't know if her pause was good or bad and he didn't like not knowing. He probably should have waited to have the conversation face-to-face so he'd at least have a chance at reading her expression.

"We could have papers drawn up immediately with me giving up all custodial rights to you—"

"I don't—"

"Think about it, Mal. What if down the road something happens to you and I'm not in the picture? I don't know about it and they give the kid to social services." The idea set off a maelstrom of quandary inside him.

He didn't do quandary. He found logic, made plans, acted.

"You're planning to lose contact with me?"

That wasn't what he'd said. She was doing that thing again where she read emotional impact into words that weren't at all intended to deliver a punch.

"I was thinking more along the lines of you choosing not to be in touch, for whatever reason. Or the two of us drifting apart as a mutual thing."

Another pause. How had things gotten so out of hand?

He returned to the couch and took another sip of his

second shot. He'd probably be feeling a whole lot better if it was double that.

"Look, it just occurred to me that my name on the birth certificate would give you further peace of mind," he told her. "Because you put such weight on the fact that I'd be willing to step in in case of emergency. I was just trying to make that a foregone conclusion for you. You'd never have to worry about me changing my mind or getting married and having a wife who talked me out of keeping my word to you. Which is also why I thought I should tell Anna."

"You're thinking about marrying her?" The question ended on a high note.

"No! Not anytime soon at any rate. We've only been on two dates. I just… I like her. And my point in being here in L.A. is to get on with my life. I made a promise to you that I would be a father to that child if anything happened to you. Which means that any woman who is sharing my life would have to be willing to take that on."

Or she wouldn't be sharing his life.

"If you're on the birth certificate you'd be responsible for child support."

He didn't give a damn about the money.

"We could set up a college fund."

"You can't pay for my baby's college."

"I'd have to pay if something happened to you. Consider it the alimony you wouldn't take during the divorce."

He'd offered. Many times. Pushed, even. And lost unequivocally on that point.

"Give me time to think about it, okay? I've got another eight months before the birth certificate will be an issue."

"But you'll think about it?" He dumped the rest of his glass of whiskey down the sink at the bar and grabbed a bottle of tea from the refrigerator.

"Of course. You've asked me to, so I will."

So Mallory. She'd accommodate a scorpion if it had a way of communicating its needs to her.

"And, Bray? Seriously, I'd hold off on saying anything to Anna. At least until you know that you want to marry her. This is my business, too, and I definitely don't want every woman you date to know about it. I don't want anyone to know, which was the whole point of insemination to begin with. I get your point. You're right that your wife would have a right to know about your promise to me. But can we at least wait until you know for sure you want to get married before you say anything?"

She hadn't asked him to donate his sperm. He'd pushed. The ball really was in her court.

"Fair enough."

Mallory thanked him, wished him good-night and hung up.

So did that mean he was now free to sleep with Anna?

She'd made it clear she was free that evening. And open to deepening their relationship.

Setting the tea on the table by his business papers, Braden sat down and got to work.

Other than Tamara and Braden, Mallory didn't tell anyone she was pregnant during the next two weeks. The ultrasound with her own OB in San Diego loomed and she wanted to make certain that everything was okay before she spread her news.

There'd be a lot of questions, "Who's the father?" being number one, she was sure. And, if something was awry, there'd be a lot of sympathy. She was prepared to answer the questions when the time came. She'd made a conscious choice. There would be those who didn't understand. She wouldn't hold their lack of understanding against them.

She talked to Braden a few times during those two weeks. Mostly just touching base. He'd mentioned Anna a time or two, so she knew he was still seeing the other woman. Might be a record for him, she thought.

Not that it concerned her.

And yet…she found herself obsessing about the other woman when she was too tired to control her thoughts. Who was she? Where did she come from? What did she do? What did she look like? Was she good enough for him?

Of course not. That last answer she had, unequivocally. She didn't know how she knew the answer, she just did. And she would be relieved when he called to say that it was over.

He always did.

But what if this time he didn't? He'd been staying in L.A. almost full-time. What if dating this Anna person really was him moving on with his life?

Well, she was moving on with hers, she reminded herself as she checked in for her ultrasound that third Thursday in April. At only six weeks she wasn't showing at all, nor did she have any signs of morning sickness yet, either.

She'd had it bad with Tucker, for about a week. Hadn't been able to keep anything down. Poor Bray had been so worried, standing there over the toilet with her, holding her hair back, giving her cool washcloths when she was done puking her guts out.

He'd tried. He'd really tried.

She hoped Anna got that about him. That he tried.

So what was wrong with her that trying wasn't enough? What had she expected—perfection?

"Mrs. Harris?" the technician called her name. Mallory saw no reason to correct her title to Ms. Harris was her married name.

Thinking about names got her to the hallway. Then she had little to distract her from the fact she was about to go in for a test that could show something wasn't okay.

She'd built her nursery. She was building her new life. So "they" would come, right? Her baby—he or she—would have a safe little home in there.

"If we're lucky you'll be able to hear the heartbeat this morning," the technician—*Adelaide* her nametag read—told her as they entered the room. "I don't know if they told you that or not."

She shook her head as she climbed up on the table as directed.

"We can record it," Adelaide continued as she lifted Mallory's shirt high enough to completely expose her stomach and then rolled under the waistband of her jeans, as well. "That way the father can hear it, too."

Recordings weren't her concern at the moment.

And...the father?

As Adelaide spread cold gel all over her stomach, Mallory stared at the ceiling and thought about the first time she'd heard Tucker's heartbeat. It had been during her normal prenatal check. Braden had been at work and she hadn't thought to ask if he wanted to come along. Those early doctor visits, they'd felt...feminine. Between her, her doctor and her baby.

They hadn't offered to record it, either.

Braden hadn't seemed to think anything of it. He'd

been super excited to know that she'd heard it. He'd asked her how it sounded, and when she'd said it was fast, he'd looked worried, asking questions until she'd assured him that the doctor had said it was perfectly normal.

The technician put a handheld device on her belly, started moving it around.

Why hadn't she thought to invite Braden to hear Tucker's heartbeat for himself?

"Okay, you can look right here and see..." The technician's voice fell off. She adjusted the transformer, and Mallory turned her head to look at the screen.

She'd told herself she wouldn't. She'd just let them do their work and assume everything was fine. It wasn't like she'd know what she was looking at anyway. Not this early.

"See...right here," the technician said. "This is your baby."

She didn't see a baby. She saw something that looked kind of like a peanut still in the shell. A really small one. If she looked really hard at the differences in the shadows, she could almost make out a bunny head, too.

"Is there a heartbeat?"

"Not yet," the technician said, moving her apparatus around. She'd grown quiet. Her tone more business-like than chipper. Honing in on one part of Mallory's stomach, she put more gel on her and stared at the screen.

Oh, God. Everything wasn't okay.

She couldn't do this. No. It wasn't right.

She took a deep breath. She had to handle what life gave her. There simply was no other choice. Tucker had taught her that. Her sweet baby boy. He'd be in heaven, watching over her.

"There..." Frowning, Adelaide held the transformer still.

"Is that a heartbeat?" It sounded different from what

she remembered of Tucker's. Of course he'd been older.
But the sound was so...jumbled. Not a regular rhythm.

There was something wrong with her baby's heart.

"It's two actually," the woman said. "I wasn't sure at
first, but there are definitely two babies there."

Two babies?

But...

"Do twins run in your family?"

She had no idea. And Braden's? Did they run in his?
She didn't know that, either.

But she knew she could find out.

And she would.

As soon as she got a hold of herself.

She was having two babies? Kids who'd always have
each other. Who'd never know what it was to grow up
alone.

Two little ones to hold. To raise. To watch grow.

Twice the love.

Lying on the table with her smeared belly exposed,
Mallory burst into tears.

Chapter Thirteen

Braden was getting ready to go into a theater with Anna to see a touring Broadway production of *Hamilton*, something she particularly wanted to see, when his phone buzzed with Mallory's call.

"I'm sorry. I have to take this," he told her, leaving her to find their seats on her own while he stepped out into the lobby.

"Everything okay?" he asked. She almost never called in the evening.

"I just…was wondering…when you're going to be in San Diego."

"I can come tonight if you need me. What happened?"

"Nothing happened. I'm just calling to arrange a meal. You know, lunch or dinner, so we can talk."

Her words said one thing, her tone of voice another. His concern turned into something more.

"Is the baby okay?" He knew she couldn't handle another loss. Didn't deserve it.

"Yes."

"You're sure?"

"Positive."

Did she just chuckle?

The lights blinked, signaling that the play was ready to start. He made a quick mental review of the next day's calendar. Fridays were usually lighter than Mondays, but still booked. He'd been planning a trip home over the weekend. Had even thought about maybe inviting Anna to accompany him. But then there'd be the whole overnight thing.

He was pretty sure he wanted sex as badly as she seemed to. He just wasn't ready to take a chance on sex making them more committed than he was sure he wanted to be. Yet.

"Can you do lunch tomorrow?" he asked. And then amended, "Or dinner would be better so I could have a full day of business."

"You're going to be here tomorrow?"

Now he was.

"Yes." A couple of his meetings were over the internet. He could do those from his San Diego office. And reschedule other things.

His mind raced. Mallory only called if it was important. "You're sure everything's okay?" He hated not knowing what was going on with her. How could he stay on top of things, make certain that he was giving her the support he'd promised, if he didn't know what he was dealing with?

"I'm sure, Bray." She sounded sure.

Walking back toward the hall that led to his entry into the theater, he relaxed, made arrangements to meet his ex-wife not far from work for dinner the following evening and went in to enjoy an evening of Broadway with his girlfriend.

Life was moving on.

Just as he'd planned.

Mallory was both gleeful and scared to death as she dressed for work on Friday. Instead of her normal pants and polo shirt, she wore one of her many light cotton skirts—this one in shades of burgundy with beige flowers—a beige top and a three-quarter sleeve, lightweight maroon sweater. Her jeweled flat sandals matched perfectly and completed the comfy but feminine feel she was going for. Because she had a late parent meeting to discuss a precocious three-year-old who belonged in a four-year-old class academically, she wouldn't have time to go home and change before dinner with Braden.

It was just a normal dinner, she told herself, at a restaurant they frequented often.

Except this time they were talking about her twins.

Did he have twins in his family?

It didn't really matter; she was having them whether he did or not. But the doctor seemed to want to know. Something to do with the insemination process.

She'd been assured there was no danger to her babies, either way, but they wanted it on the record, if possible.

Her babies.

She was having twins. Of all things.

All by herself.

It stood to reason that they'd both be hungry at once, need to be changed at the same time. How would she choose who to tend to first?

Up late looking on the internet the night before, she finally nixed that endeavor. There were more horror stories and warnings, parents talking more about the challenges than anything else. She could come up with her own list of potential problems without any help, thank you.

And she was a certified child-development specialist with a college degree in the field who worked with dozens of children, not just two, every single day.

She could do this.

Arriving at the restaurant her usual fifteen minutes early, expecting to have a good ten minutes to acclimate herself to a friendly conversation minus any of the drama rambling through her, she was surprised to see Braden already there. Stepping away from the wall off to the side of the hostess's desk, he greeted her with a kiss to the cheek and, with his hand at her back, walked with her as the hostess showed them to their table.

It was a booth by a wall, with no window to look out. No ocean to see. Leaving her staring at him as she reeled from the touch of his hand at the small of her back. It had been so long since he'd touched her there. She was making too much of it, she was sure. Totally overreacting.

As was her want for more. Like a kiss full on the lips instead of the cheek. Maybe with some tongue touching.

What was wrong with her?

It had to be the pregnancy. Or, worse, perverseness because she knew he was seeing someone. She hoped to God it wasn't that. She wasn't that small, was she?

She wanted Braden happy. That's all she'd ever wanted for him.

Yeah, she'd love it if they could still be married, but they'd torn each other apart. It was much better to be friends than to lose him completely.

Glancing over, she caught him looking at her with

that darker blue shadow in his eyes. The one that told her he'd rather have sex than dinner.

Again, it had to be her misreading the look.

"I didn't really plan to be in San Diego today." His voice was soft, taunting her, though there was no way he'd know that.

Pray he never knew that. She'd be so humiliated. And he'd feel badly, as if it was his fault and as if he owed her for the fact that her body suddenly seemed to be coming alive for him again.

It *had* to be the pregnancy, and that had been totally her fault. Her choice.

"You didn't?" she asked when she could trust her voice not to crack.

He shook his head. And she wasn't sure what she was supposed to make of that.

They ordered and as they ate, Braden talked about the progress being made on the new L.A. build and the pros and cons of living in a hotel. He missed his own bed, his own bathroom and closet more than he'd thought he would.

She wondered if he missed San Diego, too, but didn't ask.

He didn't ask why she'd called the dinner meeting. Needing some time to get over her emotional reaction to seeing him, to him touching her lower back, she didn't tell him. She didn't trust herself not to gush. Or cry. And she definitely didn't want to add those flames to a relationship that seemed to be changing in spite of their desires and efforts and promises to not let that happen.

When their plates were cleared and he was paying the bill, she figured she'd ask him about his family's twin history as they were parting at their vehicles. Make it just a quick oh-by-the-way thing.

He asked her to go for a walk with him, instead. They were downtown, one block from a row of shops and hotels along the ocean. With the balmy May evening air feeling good to her heated skin and her fears right there ready to mock her, she agreed, thinking a walk with her ex-husband was better than fighting with her own mind.

Their hands brushed and she immediately stepped to the side, adjusting her walk to prevent another touch.

"I want to apologize," she said, when she'd meant to ask about the history of twins in his family.

"For what?"

"When we had Tucker I didn't even think to include you when I went to the doctor, you know, hearing the heartbeat and all that."

"I didn't ask to go."

"But you'd have gone if I'd asked, wouldn't you?"

"Of course."

"I've been thinking about it all day." The words poured out even though she'd promised herself she wouldn't do this to him. Wouldn't drag him back into the emotional quagmire he detested. "I wasn't fair to you, Bray. I excluded you from things that maybe you didn't necessarily care about or think were a big deal, but if you'd been there...well, maybe they could have been."

"You were having a baby. I wasn't. Of course there were things only you got to experience."

"But I didn't even try to make you a part of them." And after Tucker was born, she'd never once asked him to rise in the night to get the baby. She'd been breast-feeding, so she'd had to get up anyway. Besides, he'd been working while she'd taken four months off.

"We painted the nursery together," he said, and out of the blue she was suffused with heat again. She'd forgotten about that and how that venture had been interrupted with sex on the floor of the nursery.

Her nipples tingled and liquid pooled below. *Hormones, all hormones*, she assured herself. With a little dab of memory mixed in.

"I just… I'm sorry I robbed you of the chance to fully experience the birth of your first child."

There. She'd said it.

And she felt better. Sort of. She could never give those experiences back to him.

"I missed you." Hands in his pockets, he stared ahead of them.

"What, this week?" she asked. "We talked twice." But she knew that wasn't what he'd meant. He was wearing the purple tie, and she wondered if he'd chosen her favorite color because he'd known he was having dinner with her.

Like she'd chosen her outfit for him.

"Back then. It wasn't so much that I couldn't experience everything you were experiencing. It was that you didn't seem to need me around."

She felt as though she'd been softly and kindly slapped. If such a thing could happen.

Truth was, she hadn't needed him, not in the way she should have. She'd been deeply in love with him, hadn't wanted to lose him. But on a day-to-day basis, she'd been in heaven those months she'd been a mom— before and after Tucker's birth.

"I don't know how to be all in with two different people," she told him. "And Tucker was incapable of taking care of himself."

She'd chosen her son over her husband. The truth was between them, like a third walker in their party.

There'd been no aloofness in her baby boy. He'd been

all about love and hugs and cuddles. "I guess I needed more touching than just for sexual purposes," she said aloud. But she knew it was more than that. She'd been swamped with emotion and had needed to be able to express herself naturally, fully, without fear of judgment. Bray had always loved that she was a practical woman. He'd told her so many times.

But even practical women had feelings. A wealth of them. And expression of emotion was a natural need. A mandatory one if you were to remain healthy.

She truly didn't know how Braden did it, going through life without any ups and downs as he did. She'd never seen him cry after their son died. Even at Tucker's funeral he hadn't shed a single tear.

"I'd have held you without sex, Mal. It's just that every time I touch you I want you."

Want. Not *wanted.*

There they were, back in dangerous territory again. Made completely so by the fact that she was pretty certain that she wanted sex with him again, too. Just because of hormones. Otherwise she'd have wanted it two months ago, wouldn't she have?

Sex wouldn't solve anything. It would be great to be in his arms again, to lose herself to the magic of his touch, to feel his lips.

But when it was done, they'd still have their problems.

The one thing she knew, without a doubt, was that she couldn't go through losing him again. Their friendship might not survive another divorce.

Chapter Fourteen

He wanted to sleep with his ex-wife. Even more than he wanted to have sex with Anna. Walking beside her that Friday evening, he had to face the fact.

And to figure out if he could possibly be reading her correctly because he was definitely getting vibes that she wanted him, too. Like she had before Tucker.

"I need to know if you have a history of twins in your family."

"I don't know, but I can ask my mom. Why?"

The question made it out just as he stopped cold and stared at her.

The grin on her face and the glow in her eyes in the fading dusk were brighter than any streetlight would have been.

"You're having twins?"

"Yep." She nodded and kept grinning.

Braden grabbed her, hugged her, started to swing her around and caught himself. Putting her down abruptly, he said, "I'm sorry, but I'm so happy for you, Mal. That is, if you're okay with it."

"I'm great with it. A little worried," she said as she started walking, being kind enough to ignore the way he'd just grabbed her. "I have no idea how I'm going to handle two middle-of-the-night feedings every two hours, but I know I'll figure it out. I want to figure it out. It seems so perfect to me. Birthing best friends."

"They're going to fight."

"I'm sure of it. But from what I've read, a vast majority of twins are really close. I love it that my children will grow up with built-in playmates and confidantes."

She'd talked some about her years in foster care, about the kids who came and went. Some she'd missed horribly, others not as much.

And it occurred to him that Mallory wasn't used to having someone hang around forever. Had never had that. Even her foster mom had faded away when she'd started a new life with a new family.

Everything seemed to stop for him. Right there.

Was that why she'd pushed him away after Tucker came along? Or, rather, had given everything she had to their son? Because she'd never really expected Braden to be around forever?

But being a mother, biologically connected to Tucker, she'd finally felt that she'd found that forever person?

He had no idea if he was right or not. But the thought made sense. A lot of sense. It didn't change anything, other than to give him some understanding.

He still wasn't the man she needed. Wasn't ever going to be able to "sit in her tears," or whatever the counselor had said. He didn't have it in him. And he wasn't ever going to be able to make up to her the fact that he'd robbed her of her last minutes with her son.

Living with her anger afterward had convinced him of that one. It wasn't something he'd ever choose to repeat.

But…twins. She was having twins.

Braden was still chewing on the thought long after he'd left her at her car and returned to his condo for the night. He'd half thought about driving back to L.A., seeing if Anna was available for a drink. But he didn't really feel like entertaining or being entertained.

What he felt was empty.

Which told him he needed a good night's sleep in his own bed.

So he got one.

The world and its problems could wait until morning.

Mallory didn't see Braden before he left to head back to L.A. He called her, though, to let her know that twins did indeed run in his family. His paternal grandmother had been a twin. Having never known the father who'd run out on them, he hadn't known that.

She'd asked if his mother had made a huge deal out of him asking, but he'd had that covered, as of course he would have. He'd told her that he was having his DNA ancestry run and the question had come up. He'd said his mother tried to press him, but he'd made shutting down his family's drama an art form. One at which he excelled.

Braden checked in with Mallory a lot more often after that night. By text, if not a phone call.

At her eight-week checkup she heard two heartbeats very clearly and sent him a recording. And by sixteen weeks she was showing. Braden was still seeing Anna, but he hadn't slept with her yet. Why he'd felt the need to tell Mallory about that, she wasn't sure, but she reacted as she always did around him—with kindness and support.

Though how you supported your ex-husband on choosing the right time to sleep with his new girlfriend, she wasn't sure.

The whole thing was starting to drive her nuts. To the point of wondering if she should offer to sleep with him just so he wouldn't do it with Anna. The fact that she'd had the thought scared the hell out of her. But she had it more than once as May moved into June.

San Diego's weather didn't vacillate drastically, but it was a hotter-than-normal summer so far and Mallory had taken to wearing sundresses to work. Her employees and parents all knew she was expecting. In the newsletter she handed out to parents as they dropped off and collected their children, she'd written a note explaining that she'd made the choice to be a single mother and had opted for insemination. For the most part, she'd been met with congratulations and support. Any who hadn't understood seemed to have kept their comments to themselves. She certainly hadn't lost any business over the matter.

To the contrary, her waiting list for students was growing.

Which made her think more and more about expanding with a second site in L.A. Not that her San Diego requests would get use out of an L.A. facility, but if she could double her income, she'd be a fool not to. She was having double the babies she'd originally intended, which meant double the future financial need.

It would take extra time. She wasn't kidding herself about that. She wasn't going to be getting a lot of sleep in the foreseeable future. Nor would she have much time apart from work and babies, but she didn't want or need any, either. She loved her career and she needed a family. Those two things were her joy.

She was reminding herself of that fact as she ran out to her car the first Wednesday afternoon in August to retrieve from her trunk the month's decorations she'd made the night before. She wanted to get them up that evening so she could sleep in a little later in the morning and not have to come in early.

"Hey, I was just getting ready to call you!"

She jumped, hitting her head on the roof of the car as Braden's voice sounded behind her. She'd seen his car in the parking lot that morning, but it hadn't been there when she'd headed outside just before.

Turning, she saw him, still in his SUV, stopped in the aisle behind her, calling to her out of his window. He always let her know what city he was in. That night he was supposed to be back in L.A.

"What's up?" she called over her shoulder.

Instead of answering, he pulled around and parked, getting out and reaching to help as he saw her lifting things out of her car.

She wasn't ready to take them in. She was sorting through them, arranging, so when she got inside she could go directly to the room for which the decor was intended. She'd have done so before she loaded them into the car if she hadn't been so darn tired the night before.

Carrying two babies was vastly different than having just one growing inside her.

She turned as he approached and saw him staring. "You're huge!"

"Hardly," she chuckled.

"You barely showed at all last time when you were

four months." He stopped talking but kept looking and coming closer.

Before she realized what he was doing, he'd put his hand on her stomach. "Can you feel them yet?"

Their eyes met and though neither of them looked away, his hand dropped away.

He used to love feeling Tucker kick from inside her. She'd forgotten that until right then. The look on his face the first time he'd felt their son had been like he'd seen God face-to-face. He'd been so fascinated by that proof of the life growing in her and he'd wanted to know how it felt.

Was he remembering that now?

"I haven't felt them yet," she said. "But the doctor says it could be any time."

He nodded, looking uncomfortable, so she did what she knew to do.

Bring them back to his comfort zone. Business.

"I've reconsidered and I've decided to accept your offer to take The Bouncing Ball with you to L.A."

"Oh, good!" He grinned. "I'm glad to hear that. I'll have my contractor contact you with any questions he has when he gets to that part of the building. It's being framed now, but the basic building will be just like here, and electric will run the same as well, so your outlets will be in the same places. But if you'd like door placements changed or anything, you'll have a chance for input on that."

She cared about the fact that he'd instinctively wanted to feel her baby kick. Not about doors. She cared that his lips looked like she had to touch them with hers.

And while he talked about countertops and light fixtures, she wondered what he'd do if she quieted him with a kiss wet and hot.

Then he reached into her car for the entire pile of decorations, lifting them up and out, waiting for her to lock up before he followed her inside.

Braden was halfway back to L.A., looking forward to a quiet dinner with Anna, when Mallory called.

"You said you were just getting ready to call me, but never said what for."

He had, in fact, said that when he'd seen her in the parking lot earlier. But all too soon what he was about to say hadn't mattered as much as getting the hell out of there. He wasn't sure what it was about her these days, but every time he saw her he was out of sorts. Not himself.

She was having a baby without him. Kind of what she'd done the first time around, too.

"I was going to ask if you'd had any further thoughts about putting my name on the birth certificates. I know there's still plenty of time to decide, but if we're going to have legal things drawn up, we should probably start thinking about hiring someone to do that."

He'd just lied to her. That wasn't what he'd intended to call her about at all. He'd been going to tell her that he'd be back in town midweek if she'd like to schedule a meal together. And at the meal he'd have brought up the other topic.

"Now that there are two babies, it just seems more pertinent that we get this settled. You don't want to take any chances that they get split up."

He was pressuring her. He could see it, but it kept coming out.

"I'm just not sure it's fair to you," she said. "It leaves the door open for all kinds of things to get messy down the road."

"Not if we neatly and legally tie up all ends before-hand."

"What happens when one of them needs to see their birth certificate for something, like getting a marriage license or a driver's license or a passport, and sees your name? What if he or she decides they want to meet you?"

She was planning to tell her children that they'd been conceived by artificial insemination by a donor. How confusing would it be to have a father's name on the birth certificates?

"I was thinking about that, too," he said, tense and wanting a shot of whiskey. Since he was driving, he'd have to settle for ordering one at dinner.

That would amount to him having more whiskey in the last four months than he'd had in the last four years. This woman and her babies were driving him to drink.

"You were thinking about them wanting to meet you?" she prompted him.

"Thinking about them not knowing about me. Don't you think, if something ever happened to you, it would be better for them to have heard that I exist before they're suddenly faced with being uprooted and having to come live with me?"

"If they know about you they'll want to see you. This is why I didn't want to do this to begin with. It's already getting too complicated."

He'd talked her into it. Promised her it wouldn't be complicated. That he'd let her do her thing.

"You're right," he said, and meant it.

But he couldn't stop thinking about the fact that he was going to have two children in the world who might one day find out that he'd known about them and then think, by his lack of participation, that he hadn't wanted them.

True, he'd had no plans to have children, at least not then, and not with their mother. He'd donated his sperm for Mallory because she'd wanted a baby and his sperm gave her the security she wouldn't have had with an unknown donor.

His intentions had been good, but he couldn't have his own children thinking he didn't want them.

Except that he had no other choice.

He had to find a way to let this go.

The nights were the worst. She knew this. Clarity was less prevalent in the dark. When one slept, one let go of one's control of rational thought. And Mallory's uncontrolled, irrational thoughts were the stuff nightmares were made of.

She'd had more than she could count since she'd found out she was pregnant.

She'd been prepared for them, she'd thought.

But the night after she saw Braden, after his phone call, she had a doozy of a nightmare. The twins—they'd been a boy and a girl—had disowned her because she'd smothered them. At first the smothering had been emotional. She'd just been trying to be a good mother, but somehow she'd become needy and controlling, with no life but them. And then suddenly she was outside with flashers blinking around her house—rescue and police vehicles—and her babies were inside, smothered in their cribs. She'd been sobbing, looking at their window, knowing that she'd done it.

As soon as she woke up, trembling, sweaty, with her heart pounding fast and hard, she got out of bed and went to the kitchen to brew a cup of chamomile tea.

She grabbed her phone as she sat down at the table with her drink. This was a time to call Tamara. But her friend would be in bed with Flint. The call might wake up little Diamond Rose.

And she didn't really need Tamara. She knew what was going on. The fear didn't have her in its grip.

She was in her own grip.

Braden wanted to have a place in the lives of his children. She didn't know how she was so certain, but she knew.

She'd cut him out of Tucker's pregnancy and much of the five months of his life, too. Not purposely. Not knowingly. Not even wanting to. But she'd done it.

It hadn't been healthy for her or Braden, and had Tucker lived, it wouldn't have been healthy for him, either.

Most likely he'd have been the product of divorced parents, living in two households.

She didn't want that for any child. And certainly not hers. She'd always promised herself, if she ever had a child, she'd make certain that home was one place that didn't change and that didn't end. For as long as she lived, her child would always have a home to come to.

Somehow she'd failed to include Braden in that plan.

He'd failed her, too, in many ways, but this…this was on her.

Braden might not have planned to develop feelings for the babies she was carrying. And maybe saying he had feelings was going a bit far. But he felt a responsibility toward them. Felt accountable to them.

Legally she had every right to deny him access, even with the birth certificates. Even ethically she probably had the right, based on how his sperm had come to be involved.

But morally?

Could she deny her children the right to know their

father when the man was someone who would bless their lives? Someone who would always be there for them? Whether she met an untimely demise or not.

Certainly they were going to know Braden. It wasn't like the two of them were going to suddenly stop being friends.

Sipping tea, she shivered. Everything was such a mess.

As she'd known it would be.

And she'd agreed to use his sperm anyway.

Because in the long run, what had mattered was the security of her children. And two biological parents who'd want them were better than one.

Braden had been right about that.

Picking up her phone, she dialed him. He was keeping her up nights, so he could get up, too. It was only when she heard his sleepy hello that she wished she'd thought a little longer before making the call. Like maybe until he was back and they were having lunch?

She didn't want to give herself time to change her mind.

But now a thought struck her. "Are you alone?"

His pause told her he was not and she hung up.

Chapter Fifteen

Pulling the hotel coverlet with him, wrapping it around his boxers like it mattered if the world saw him in them, Braden went out into the living room of the suite and called Mallory right back. She wouldn't have called if it hadn't been an emergency.

His head pounding, he cursed the fact that he'd allowed Anna to talk him into drinking more than he knew he should. She'd met him at his hotel for dinner and then engaged him in a where-is-this-going conversation. That had led to the fact he'd just seen his ex-wife and had some things to work out with her first, at which time she'd started drinking more than she should, too.

"Mallory, pick up," he said when her machine answered, aware that Anna was probably awake in the bedroom behind him. "Please. It's not what you think. Call me." He ended the call.

It's not what you think? Like he was some cheating husband who'd just been caught?

He was divorced for Christ's sake. Had been for years. It wasn't like he hadn't had sex during that time.

But he hadn't had it with Anna that night. Or yet.

Back in the suit she'd worn from the office to his hotel, she came out of the bedroom, looking better than he felt.

"I'm sober enough to make it home," she said, going for her purse. "I'm really sorry to have passed out on you. That's just not my style."

He'd carried her from the couch to his bed, thinking she'd be closer to the bathroom if she got sick, and he'd be close enough to help her get there.

"It was a rough night," he conceded, speaking as much for himself as for her.

"So…is this it, then? I shouldn't sit around expecting a call from you?"

Watching her, he wanted to be able to give her what she wanted. Thought he'd be able to. As soon as he got the thing with Mallory under control.

And he told her so.

"So…call me," she said.

"I will."

He meant what he said, but didn't bother going to the door as she let herself out.

Embarrassed beyond anything she could ever have imagined, Mallory didn't answer any of Braden's calls over the next couple of days. She texted him to let him know that she and the babies were fine. And almost texted to cancel their lunch set up for the following Tuesday.

They'd been through much worse. Their friendship, which had taken three years to build, was the envy of many. She wasn't going to lose him now.

But the thought of him with another woman cut deeply. All she wanted to do was cry. In fact, she was afraid that she would do exactly that when she saw him, which was why she seriously considered canceling.

It was just because she was pregnant. She knew that. She'd been extra teary with Tucker, too, and figured, carrying two, maybe she'd be twice as bad this time around.

But how humiliating to be calling him to give him what he wanted and have another woman in bed with him.

Every time she thought about it she wanted to curl up in a corner and hide her head.

In one sense, her life was fuller than she'd ever thought it would be again. And in another, she'd never felt more alone.

She'd be a mother, but not a partner.

Her choice, she reminded herself. And knowing herself, she figured it was a good one.

So why did it hurt so much?

She was trying to tell herself it didn't when she entered the restaurant where she and Bray had agreed to meet. It was a different place—Mexican, which she loved—and a bit further from work. He'd had an appointment nearby and had thought it looked nice.

He'd been right. Inside, the decor was colorful and bright, and the people were friendly. She felt at home as, at her request, they walked her through the inside to a private patio off the back. Completely enclosed by trees and greenery, the area hosted eight or so tables, with umbrellas over them. In the middle of them, a tall rock fountain, with flowing water, gave a feeling of privacy and peace.

All but one of the tables was full, so she knew where

she was going. She'd barely settled in her seat before Braden was there, asking for two glasses of ice tea and then privacy until they motioned for service.

She'd never heard him be quite so forceful. He wasn't impolite, but his usual easygoing, friendly demeanor was definitely not present.

"I'm sorry I didn't return your calls," she said immediately, trying to ward off any undue tension between them before it got out of hand.

He leaned in toward her, his tie caught between the wrought-iron table and his chest. "I did not have sex with Anna."

Waving a hand as though she wasn't suddenly lightheaded with relief, she said, "It's none of my business, Bray. You can sleep with whomever you like. You know that."

"The point is, I didn't."

He was serious, looking her right in the eye. For some reason this was important to him. "Okay."

As he sat back, their tea was delivered, as though their waiter had been watching and waiting for his cue.

When the man left, Braden leaned in again. "And I'm sorry for pressuring you on the other stuff. These are your children. We were very clear from the first about that. My participation was my own idea and—"

She almost held her tongue. Because she thought ultimately it might be the best way to preserve their friendship. But it wouldn't be best for their children. Or for either of them.

"I'm going to put your name on their birth certificates, Bray," she said. "That's why I was calling the other night. I'd just woken up with this horrible dream and—"

She stopped. She couldn't tell him her nightmare.

They seemed to be reaching some new understanding, a more honest understanding perhaps, but there were some things that didn't change.

Braden's abhorrence of drama and emotion of any kind being one of them.

Her obsession with having a biological relationship above all else being another.

"Anyway, you're right," she said. "It will be far better for the kids. And as long as you're willing to have them know about you, then they should know."

Everything about him seemed to change. He sat back. His expression settled. It was as though she could see the tension physically slide from his body.

And she knew, in spite of her apprehensions to the contrary, she'd made the right choice.

Life was good. His building was going up. All initial inspections had passed. Potential tenants were putting in applications and things with Mallory were finally resolved. She was going to bring The Bouncing Ball to L.A. Braden was satisfied that all was as it should be.

Driving back to L.A. that evening, he was looking forward to the future. Mallory was happier than he'd seen her in a long time. As the legal father of her children he'd have a solid place in her life and the right to take care of her or her children if the need arose.

He was free to pursue a more committed relationship with Anna. If she was still interested.

Yes. Things were working out according to plan.

Except...

They'd talked over lunch about having a legal custody agreement drawn up. He was taking charge of it, paying for the attorney, everything. She'd have full custody and he would be signing away any rights during her lifetime. The children were going to be added to his will. She was going to set up a trust for the children, leaving them all of her worldly goods, and stipulating him as legal guardian of them in the event that anything happened to her.

He would not contact the children outside of his friendship with Mallory. If they wanted to see him, separate and alone, he would make himself available to them pursuant to arrangements made through Mallory.

The one thing they hadn't thought of was his mother and sister. The children were going to have a grandmother and an aunt who would adore them.

Dote on them.

Biological family to love them.

He dialed Mallory through his steering wheel, activating Voice Command.

"I just thought of something," he said when she picked up. It wasn't six yet. She'd still be at the daycare, but would most likely be alone.

"What?"

"My mom and sister. As much as Mom drives me nuts, she also loves like the gush of the ocean."

The pause on the end of the line didn't seem good.

"Just think about it," he said. "A biological grandmother could be something you want for them. If you do, let me know. I'll take care of it."

"Bray?"

"Yeah?"

"When do we realize that this is getting too complicated?"

"It won't be complicated," he told her, refusing to get sucked into the mire. "We make the choices here. Or rather, you do. You're in complete control."

He'd do what she wanted, even if he disagreed.

"I'm signing away all rights, Mal. But you asked for my support, which means you get my opinion." They'd established that from the beginning.

"I know."

"The second you no longer want that, all you have to do is say so." It wouldn't be all bad if she did, he told himself as he made the offer. He'd be completely free of entanglement from the past.

"I want it."

"So, think about it?"

"Of course."

Good. Yeah, so, life was all good.

Morning sickness didn't happen. Not even as she moved toward her fifth month. But she was tired. Sometimes it was all she could do to get through the workday, make herself a sandwich when she got home and then plop down on the couch.

She'd ordered a second crib, exactly like the one she'd bought.

The girls at work were throwing a shower for her.

Tamara and Flint and Tamara's parents had already given her a year's worth of disposable diapers through an open credit account at a local box store.

Tamara had news of her own to share, as well. She and Flint were going to try to have a baby. Her doctor had said there was no reason that she couldn't try to carry to full term, as long as she was emotionally strong enough to handle it if she miscarried again. With Flint and Diamond Rose there, loving her, Tamara was ready to try.

It was enough to make one believe in happy endings.

Yet as each day passed, Mallory was less and less happy. She wasn't unhappy. She was deeply, deeply thrilled to be having her babies. Thankful beyond any measure.

She'd made the right choice to have them.

And yet, she lived on the verge of tears. Pregnancy hormones, she was sure. But that wasn't all of it. Maybe she was more apt to cry because of them, but the source of the tears was real.

She wept for Tucker. For the shortness of his sweet life.

Sometimes she cried out of stark fear. What would she do if she lost either of the two precious beings growing inside of her?

And she cried for Braden and her. She remembered his reaction that day at lunch, when she'd told him he could be on the birth certificates. She'd felt him so acutely. And she'd known. Just clearly, calmly known. Tamara had been right. She was still in love with him.

It didn't change anything. He wasn't good for her and she made him a tense mess, too. The sadness of that weighed heavily on her. She carried it with her every second of every day. And she worried that she was going to pass it on to her babies. "A mother's emotional state as she carries her children has an effect on the unborn children." She'd read that.

Promising herself she'd work at being calmer, for her babies' sakes, she focused on the paperwork on her desk. Till the phone rang.

It was her OB. The week after her four-month visit, the week after lunch with Braden, she'd been in the doctor's office for a standard blood test, one that could indicate that one or both of her babies had one of several possible genetic disorders, Down syndrome being one of them. And with a few words—"We got a positive"—her life imploded again.

Her first thought was that she'd done it. Something was wrong with her.

She listened while the doctor assured her that they weren't worried. They'd done another ultrasound during that visit as well and all measurements had been normal. The blood test in question came up with false positives more than any others, the OB assured her. But she'd need to have more in-depth blood work done as soon as possible.

Mallory had to leave work, she was sobbing so hard.

She couldn't believe it. Just couldn't believe it.

In her car, she drove around the corner from the business complex and then stopped. She shouldn't drive in her condition but she had to get to the doctor's office. They had an opening at their on-site lab that afternoon and she'd taken it. She had to know.

Had to be able to do whatever was possible to help her babies if they were in trouble.

The thought drew her up. With a hand on her already swelling belly, she made them a promise that she would do whatever it took to give them the best life they could possibly have. This wasn't about her. It was about them.

The doctor had said she wasn't worried. And now it was Mallory's job to stay positive. To do all she could.

And she would.

But as she drove to the office she wished she wasn't doing it alone.

She needed Braden. Wanted so badly to call him.

But she didn't.

Chapter Sixteen

Sometime after midnight that night, Mallory sat in the old-fashioned wooden rocker with the brightly colored cushions, a teddy bear clutched to her, and looked at the identically adorned, empty cribs on either side of her.

She'd fallen asleep on the couch earlier and had finally made it to bed around ten. But by eleven, she'd been wide awake again, her mind spinning with facts. She knew a lot more than she'd known that afternoon, thanks to her internet research. While there were many genetic disorders that could have shown up on her test, the majority of the most severe had been ruled out. She could have heard that one or both of her babies wouldn't make it through the first year of life. She hadn't heard that.

There was still a slight chance she could. And a greater chance that either or both of the babies could have a chromosome disorder that would retard their development in any number of ways. She'd have the test results on Monday.

Along with sexes for both children. It had been an option on the blood test, finding that out. She'd checked that box, figuring she'd have something to look forward to hearing when the doctor's office called her back.

Until then, she'd worry. As she clutched the teddy bear, she reminded herself that there was every chance the first test had been a false positive. She reminded herself of the normal ultrasound. And she told herself she'd love her babies, whatever the test showed.

The physician's assistant had told her that afternoon that one of the reasons they wanted to check further immediately was because one of her choices, depending on the results, would be to terminate the pregnancy.

She'd shaken her head even while the woman had still been speaking. And she shook it again as she sat alone in the nursery. She couldn't even consider termination.

Just completely wrong for her.

Laying her head back against the chair, she rocked gently, hugging the bear, looking at the glow of the night-light on the ceiling. Tears came, dripped slowly down her cheeks. And they dried there.

Her mind slipped back in time to a similar night a month after Tucker had died. She'd been in his nursery, sitting in the glider rocker she'd used every single night of his life except the last one. Holding a stuffed penguin Julia, her coworker, had given him. Braden, who'd woken up and found her missing from their bed, had come looking for her. He'd tried to coax her back to bed.

When she wouldn't leave the nursery he'd started in again about calling someone to take everything away. He'd said she was making a shrine out of the nursery and that it was unhealthy. That she had to get a grip on herself.

She'd sat right there in that chair, clutching Tucker's penguin, and screamed at the top of her lungs, telling him he better not dare take away one thing of Tucker's. "Haven't you already taken enough?" she'd screamed, referring to the fact that Braden had taken away her chance to spend Tucker's last moments with him.

She'd never been so angry.

Now, sitting there in the new nursery, thinking back, she could feel the anger all over again.

She felt it anew as she considered his probable reaction to her current situation.

He hadn't been responsible for Tucker's death. Hadn't been in any way responsible for what had happened. Yet, she'd blamed him.

She hadn't been able to blame her son. And his death certainly hadn't been the nanny's fault. Mallory had blamed herself, of course. Not only for leaving, but for her body maybe not quite developing the portion of Tucker's brain that was in charge of breathing regulation.

But mostly, she'd blamed Braden. Because he'd taken her away. Because he hadn't allowed her to experience the pain that was eating her up inside.

He'd wanted her to be like him. To be able to move on. But she'd hardly been able to move at all.

Braden hadn't understood that, which had made her angrier.

She'd blamed him for an act of God.

The truth was clear now and, wide awake, she sat up straight, glancing around the room like there were people there, aware of what she'd done.

She saw her relationship with Braden as if in movie form. A movie of emotions. The way she'd slowly pulled away from him, starting when she'd found out she was pregnant. The relief and the exhilaration of knowing that she'd finally have a biological connection on earth. That she belonged to someone.

She saw, too, that maybe, just maybe, she'd never thought she and Braden would be married forever. People changed. Lives changed. And those you loved moved on.

Her mother had tried to keep her, till her life required differently. Her foster mother had been there, until she'd moved to Florida and found a new family. She was fine with both of those circumstances, didn't blame either woman.

Nor did she feel sorry for herself.

Now she realized that all along she'd expected Braden to do the same. To move on at some point, when their worlds no longer coincided.

So when Tucker came along, maybe she'd pushed Braden on his way.

Oh, not completely, and certainly not consciously. She'd never in a million years have done that. But the self-honesty which she'd had to learn to access to recover from Tucker's death told her that she couldn't keep ignoring the fact. She'd cut Braden out of her and Tucker's lives far more than she'd realized. She'd been living a future without him, while he'd been right there with them.

And when Tucker died, and Braden hadn't been able to handle her grief, she'd just kept right on pushing him away with her anger.

He'd been wrong. And so had she.

She'd spewed ugly words at him for things that weren't his fault. And yet, she'd been unable to let him go.

Because she'd still been in love with him.

Some things hadn't changed. Maybe some never would.

But some had to.

She had to quit needing Braden for things he couldn't possibly give her.

That's why she'd opted to have a child alone.

It was the only way that was going to work for them.

And so she sat alone in the night. She fought debilitating fear. She prayed. And, eventually, she went back to bed.

Braden had a great weekend. With everything falling into place he was able to play a round of golf, at which he had the chance to speak with the owner of several apartment complexes who was interested in having Braden Property Management take them on. Mallory would be glad to know that his L.A. presence was already being noticed.

She worried about such things.

He knew better.

But he was glad to know that she cared. The same way he was glad to know that he was going to be formally acknowledged as the biological father of her twins.

Throughout the weekend he thought of it often, at random times, and each time the thought gave him a lift.

He and Anna had a nice dinner-and-concert date on Saturday night, but things took a turn on Sunday. He got a call telling him a condominium complex that was a client of his in San Diego had sprung an underground leak, and more than a thousand people were without water.

The city was claiming the issue was the responsibility of the complex. Insurance said it was the city's issue.

First thing Monday morning it became Braden Property Management's issue. He had an agent in charge of the account working on it and reporting to him.

But the owner of the complex, Alex Mason, also owned five other properties in the San Diego area, all of which Braden's company managed. He thought it best to be on hand. Just in case.

He called Mallory to let her know he'd be in town, and when she didn't pick up, he tried the daycare number.

Julia answered.

"She's not here this morning," Mallory's second-in-command said. "She figured it was best if she waits at home, just in case. She doesn't want to alarm the children."

"Wait at home?" He was confused. Wait for what? And he'd tried her at home. She hadn't answered.

"For the call."

"What call?"

A quick intake of breath came over the line. "I assumed she'd told you. She usually tells you everything."

About The Bouncing Ball, sure. Just like he ran most of his big business decisions by her. But...

"Told me what?"

"You need to talk to her, Braden. If she didn't tell you...it's not my place... I'm not getting in the middle of it."

He could hear children's voices in the background, as though Julia was out in a playroom.

"No, that's good," he said. "It's just...well, I tried her cell and she didn't answer. Should I be concerned?"

"Try her again. Maybe she was on the phone."

Hanging up, he tried Mal's cell again. She picked up on the second ring.

"Hey, just calling to let you know I'm in town," he said. "I drove down early this morning." He told her about the water leak. She knew the account well. It had been his first big one. They'd celebrated the signing of that deal with a weekend in Cabo.

She asked a couple of questions about the situation, wanting to know why the city thought they weren't responsible for their own plumbing, if anyone knew yet what had caused the leak. And then she said, "Okay, well, keep me posted," in a tone of voice that sounded like she was ready to hang up.

"I don't see your car in the parking lot," he said, not wanting to hang Julia out to dry. The woman hadn't meant to clue him in to anything Mallory hadn't wanted him to know.

"I'm working from home this morning. Going over the finances."

That was it. Nothing more. She did like to do her financial rundowns at home, so she could be certain she wouldn't be interrupted. But usually she did them in the evenings. He'd never known her to miss work for it.

"You feel okay?"

"Yep."

"Any morning sickness?"

"Nope."

He tried to remember back when she was carrying Tucker and to figure out what could possibly be going on with this pregnancy that would "alarm the kids."

Nothing. He had nothing.

He didn't like it.

"You want to meet for a quick lunch?" he asked her.

"Can I get back to you on that? I'm expecting a call and I need to be able to talk freely when it comes in."

"Sure, okay. And everything's good with you?"

"I'm fine, Bray. Just preoccupied this morning. Lunch sounds nice. I'll let you know if something changes and I can't make it."

They agreed on a place and time and he hung up.

He was disgruntled for the rest of the morning.

Half an hour before she was due to meet Braden for lunch, Mallory was dressed, choosing a calf-length, loose, T-shirt tank dress she'd found at a flea market over the weekend. She was ready to go, but she still hadn't heard from the doctor's office.

She had looked at The Bouncing Ball's books. She just hadn't followed any one thought process long enough to do them any good. Finally acknowledging her lack of concentration, she'd taken a hot bath with a reality show playing in the background. Then she'd done her hair and makeup while listening to old sitcoms.

What she hadn't heard was the ringing of the phone. And she had to leave soon.

She really wanted to see Braden. At some point soon she was going to have to tell him some of the things she'd realized about herself. And she owed him an apology. But not that day.

Right then, all she wanted was to see his lazy smile, watch him consume his lunch like it was his last meal and hear about the Mason account.

She wanted things to be good between them, for the friendship that had seen them through the past three years to survive.

Five minutes before she needed to leave, she called the doctor's office, explaining her predicament.

"The results didn't come in this morning," the woman who answered the phone told her. "We generally don't get the afternoon delivery until after two, so you're safe. Enjoy your lunch."

Tearing up she thanked the woman. Then, taking a deep breath, she told herself to get a grip and hurried out the door.

Braden headed out for lunch ten minutes earlier than he might have if he hadn't spent the morning being visited by various scenarios of what could possibly be wrong with Mallory.

She'd said she was fine, but she hadn't said anything about the babies.

Surely, if something had happened to them, she wouldn't be fine.

No matter what it was, there'd be a way to handle it. There always was.

Still, he'd feel better knowing what it was he might be helping her handle.

If she'd needed his help, she'd have called.

And so it went. All morning long. Anytime he had a break in between calls.

Which, thankfully, hadn't been often.

He knew the second he saw her being seated at the table that something was up. She had a small furrow between her brows and her lips were tight. Until she saw him approaching. Then she smiled.

The light in her eyes gave him a lift.

"Bad morning?" he asked as he took his seat across from her at a little table for two by a column in the middle of the well-known sandwich shop.

She shook her head, but he didn't believe her.

She'd stayed home to go over the books. Was her problem financial? Had something happened with the business that she wasn't telling him about?

But how would a phone call regarding her financial situation upset the kids?

Maybe the problem was with one of the parents from her daycare?

A flashback to the year before reminded him of the couple who'd come into the daycare, claiming that one of Mallory's kids was the abducted son of a woman from Mission Viejo. She'd called Braden immediately and they'd met with the couple to discuss the situation.

Mallory had been noticeably upset by the whole thing, and seeing that could upset the kids.

So, yeah, maybe it was something with a parent.

She ordered tea from the waitress who approached. He did the same.

"I'm assuming, since you're here, your call came in?" Her business was her business, he reminded himself. She could share with him or not at her discretion. But not knowing what was going on wasn't sitting well with him.

Mallory shook her head. "I had confirmation that it will be sometime after two," she told him and looked at her menu.

She wasn't going to tell him.

So he let it go. He looked at his own menu, though suddenly he didn't give a damn what he ate.

"Mallory?"

She glanced over at him.

"Please, tell me what's going on. What's this call you're expecting?"

Her frown was full-scale, her hair jumbling around her shoulders as she shrugged and shook her head at the same time.

"Julia told me you stayed home to get it because it could upset the kids. She thought I knew what it was about. And she clammed up the second she realized I didn't."

"Oh." She watched him, seeming to consider something.

"Don't blame her. She's got your back completely."

"I know that. I'm sure she'll tell me about your call as soon as we next speak."

He was sure of it, too, which had been part of the reason he'd said what he had. But only partly. He mostly wanted her to tell him what was going on.

How did a guy fix something if he had no idea what to fix?

"It's nothing," she said now. "Nothing that you can do anything about."

He didn't know that. Not until he knew what it was.

"You know you don't have to take on every single one of my problems, Bray." Her smile was calm, almost serene.

That didn't set well with him, either.

"I know you can make it just fine on your own. I'm not trying to imply otherwise, even to myself. Or to think that I'm the save-the-day guy. I know full well I'm not. It's just…"

He needed her to understand. "I think about you," he told her. "I'd like to know that you're okay and—"

"I'm okay," she interrupted and he held up a hand.

"And to know that if something's bothering you, enough so that you stay home from work, and I'm right here and know something's going on, that— Oh for God's sake, Mal, please tell me what's going on."

She grinned, but it lasted only a second.

"I had a genetic defect positive come back on some blood work last week. The doctor isn't worried. It's not all that unheard of for this particular test to show false positives. I had a more in-depth test done on Thursday and I'm expecting the results today." She met his gaze the entire time she delivered the news.

And then she glanced at her menu as though there really was nothing big going on.

"You're telling me that the babies have something wrong with them?" And she hadn't called him immediately?

"Did you call Tamara?" he asked when she didn't answer.

"Yesterday," she said, turning the page of the menu. She was studying the thing like she couldn't make up her mind what she wanted.

He knew what she was going to order, so she must, too.

Reaching across the table he took her hand. She glanced over at him, a sheen in her gaze that was unmistakable.

Mallory wasn't as undisturbed as she seemed.

"You going to have the cranberry-and-turkey salad?" he asked.

She nodded.

He let go of her hand.

And they ate lunch.

Chapter Seventeen

The second he'd seen a hint of the emotion boiling up inside her, he'd shut down. Mallory recognized the response.

And so she did what their friendship required. She ate lunch. As much of it as she could get past the lump in her throat.

Her babies needed nourishment no matter what they were facing. Most particularly considering what they might be facing. They could have more than the normal challenges ahead of them.

Braden chatted about the Mason situation. The pipes in question became the responsibility of the owner when they were so many feet from the street. And an insurance policy, acquired by Mason before Braden Property Management was in the picture, required a rider to cover them. Braden had gotten a quote from a plumber to fix the problem. And he and Mason had decided to cover the cost.

They were also adding the underground plumbing rider to all of Mason's property policies.

She heard it all as she sat there, watching him. But she couldn't help the worry and fear from taking residence in her mind, as well.

On their way out to their cars, she finally explained the test to him. "It was a genetic disorder blood test. It looks for chromosomal abnormalities. That can be anything from a lack that often leads to death within the first year of life, or ones which could still provide a perfectly normal life expectancy. It could be trisomy 21, Down syndrome, which could be high functioning or not. There are others. A lot of them mean some level of developmental delay. If the babies are identical, it will most likely affect both of them. If they're fraternal, meaning they come from two eggs, it could go either way. The test seemed to indicate that it's not the most severe. And the doctor specifically stated that she wasn't particularly worried."

She smiled at him. "I've weathered worse, Bray. I'm going to be fine, no matter what we find out."

He didn't look convinced. He walked her to her car, waited while she let herself in and then shut the door behind her.

When he still stood there, she rolled the window down.

"Call me," he said. "When you hear, call me."

She nodded.

She'd have done so anyway.

He was her friend and she needed his support.

Braden was on his phone before he'd left the parking lot, arranging to stay in San Diego for the night. He'd had a dinner meeting that evening in L.A. that had to be rescheduled, and appointments in the morning, but he was able to fill his calendar in San Diego for the rest of the afternoon and set up a couple of video calls for the next morning.

He'd established a system that would allow him to work from either location, and it was serving him just fine.

He called Anna and let her know his business in San Diego was taking longer than he'd expected. She didn't ask if he'd be seeing his ex-wife while he was in town. He liked that about her. She didn't get all up in the drama of a situation.

He planned a sit-down with William, glad to have some time to spend with the man who kept his life running on time and on target.

In the meantime he was able to book a cancelled spot with the new physical trainer in the gym on the bottom floor of his building.

Up until his former trainer had been arrested—for having kidnapped his son—Braden had trained twice a week. He needed to get back with it.

The workout was good. He kicked it, hard, and came out sweating so much he stank. Showering off in his office suite, he changed back into his suit and looked at his phone. Three thirty and still no call from Mallory.

He'd had the cell on and with him in the gym. He'd even left it on the counter by the shower.

He couldn't plan his evening until he knew that Mallory wouldn't need him for anything. Not that there'd be much he could do. He wasn't a doctor. Or a miracle worker.

But he'd told her to call.

A knock sounded on his door.

"Come in," he barked, so not like him. He settled an apologetic smile on his face as the door swung inward.

Mallory stood there, a grin all over her face. She closed the door behind her.

"We're good," she said as she advanced. "Everything's fine."

Just when he was going to congratulate her he went weak for a second. He told himself it was because he'd pushed his muscles hard and probably needed a salty drink.

"They're fine?" he asked, standing in place so he didn't make an idiot of himself.

"Yep." She was right up to him, standing there, looking all expectant.

"What?"

"You want to know what we're having?"

What we're *having*, he repeated to himself, making note of the word choice.

"You know the sexes?"

"It was an option on the test," she told him.

"So?"

"Girls. We're having two girls. And they're pretty sure there's only one sac which means they're identical. They'll be able to tell that more clearly later, and it's still not for sure. They can do a DNA cheek swab after they're born to be absolutely certain."

Girls. Mallory was having two girls.

No boys who would need him.

It fit. It was right.

Pulling her to him, he held her tight.

Just so thankful that all was well.

She didn't mean to kiss him. There was no place in Mallory's plans for anything but the most platonic of friendships with Braden, but with her body pressed up against his, her breasts tingling from the contact with his chest, she didn't think about plans. She didn't think at all. Lifting up ever so slightly, she brought her lips closer to his. Watching them the space between his mouth and hers faded. The first touch was hello. The second... Mallory devoured the taste of Braden, the familiar touch of his tongue, the way his mouth said more to her in a kiss than it ever did with words.

She moaned, instantly needing more. Thinking about the quickest way to get her sweet spot free, about reaching for the zipper on his fly. Her entire being burned with that one touch of their lips. Bringing out the wild woman he found in her.

She didn't know who sprang back first, would like to think they'd both done so simultaneously.

"What was that?" she asked, out of breath, when he stood there looking almost pained.

"Yeah, I don't know," he tried for a chuckle.

Backing away, she moved toward the door. "I know you're busy." Half panting still, she was relieved one of them had stopped them before they'd made an irrevocable mistake. And was sad, too. "I just got a bit carried away there with the good news. Emotionally and all."

"Yeah," he said, standing right where she'd left him.

She was almost through the door when he called her back. "Mal?"

"Yeah?"

"I'm glad they're okay."

She nodded.

"And that they're girls."

She was, too. Boys would have been just as great, just as special. But Tucker was Tucker. For now, he was her boy. And she had two little girls coming who'd know his name from the very beginning. They'd grow up learning to love the big brother they'd never met.

They'd know their father, too.

From a distance.

With girls on the way, there was no way she could even think about more than friendship with Braden. If he thought handling Mallory's emotions was too much, she could just imagine what he'd be like with pubescent twin girls running around.

His frustration with emotional outbursts was one thing she'd protect her girls against. They were never going to be ashamed of who and what they were. Not as long as she was alive and in control.

And if she taught them right, they'd be fine even after she was gone.

Her lips were still tingling, her tongue still tasting Braden, long after she'd left his office. And that was something she'd have to get control over, too.

Immediately.

Praying it was just pregnancy hormones amping up her sex drive, she went to the daycare and put her mind to tasks that mattered.

Braden couldn't get her kiss off his mouth. He couldn't get the feel of her body out of his mind. He couldn't get rid of his hard-on long enough to think straight.

And he couldn't get enough of the salty drink to restore his electrolytes and get himself back on an even keel.

So he went to work. It's what he knew. What he did.

He put Mallory, her babies, their health and especially her kiss out of his mind and focused on making money. Lots of it.

For another hour he sat in his office and made calls, setting up more appointments for the next day. The morning in San Diego, the afternoon in L.A.

He had dinner at a pub with William, discussed accounts, members of his staff and the raise he'd offered the younger man.

He was putting William in charge of the San Diego office in his absence. The announcement would be made at the next staff meeting, but he didn't expect anyone to be surprised. The man might sit out front—his choice—but he was brilliant when it came to real estate.

Over a second beer, he asked William if he'd be willing to spend time in L.A., as well. William said he'd spend it in Alaska if it meant making money at a company that still put integrity and people at the top of the list.

And then dinner was over. William had a date waiting for him at the bar, a gentleman who'd been at the last holiday party. A boat builder, Braden thought, if he was remembering correctly.

It was a little after eight and he had nowhere to be. Nowhere to go but home. He could stay and drink more, but then he'd have to call a cab and wake up in the morning with the hassle of needing to get back to his car.

Paying the tab, he left, pulled off his tie as he walked to his SUV. He thought a drive down by the pier might clear his head.

He drove through the Gaslamp District and Balboa Park. He'd been in San Diego so long, he'd forgotten how the city had first drawn him.

When he passed by an entrance to the zoo, he thought about Mallory and her daughters. In his mind he saw the three of them laughing as she held their little hands and taught them something important about the animals.

Monkeys, he thought.

Mallory liked the monkeys best.

He ended up at her house. Maybe he'd known all along that was where he was headed. Maybe he'd just been giving himself time to change his mind. To come to his senses.

Senses didn't seem to matter anymore.

Mallory had spent an entire weekend alone, in fear for her daughters' lives. Alone. Just as she'd been most of her life.

It was criminal.

He knocked on the door, saw her peek out the side window a minute or so later and then, turning on the porch light, she opened the door.

"Can I come in?"

"Of course."

She was frowning as she opened the door wider and stepped aside.

She'd changed from the T-shirt dress to a pair of cotton shorts and a tank top. She wasn't wearing a bra.

When she caught him staring at the lusciousness taunting him, she crossed her arms over her chest and left the room, returning less than thirty seconds later wearing a baggy T-shirt.

"I wasn't expecting company," she said, crinkling her bare toes into the carpet.

"Marry me."

Her hands dropped to her sides. She half fell backward into the chair behind her. "What?"

"Marry me."

That was it. He didn't have anything else.

"Braden? Are you okay? What's wrong?" Her mouth hung open.

"I'm fine."

"Have you been drinking?"

"I had a couple of beers. You know I don't drive past my limit."

She nodded.

He liked that she knew him.

He waited, silent, until she spoke.

"I can't marry you, Braden," she finally said.

"Why not?"

"We'd hate each other within a year."

"Maybe not."

"Trust me, we would."

"We don't hate each other now."

"We aren't married now."

"You want me."

She licked her lips and he got hard. "Yes, but it could just be pregnancy hormones. And even if it isn't, that doesn't take away the fact that we're too different, Bray. I drive you nuts. You hurt me."

"I haven't hurt you lately." He hoped to God that was true. If he had, she hadn't said so.

"I'm not married to you."

She would listen to logic. It was one of the things he'd always loved about her. No matter how upset she might be, she listened to logic.

"It's the only thing that makes sense, Mal. Look at us. Three years divorced and we're right back where we started. A new building is going up, same plans, same daycare, and—" he stared at her stomach "—you're having my daughters."

He sat down on the corner of the couch closest to

her. He leaned over and took both of her hands in his. "We can't get away from each other, Mal."

"We were no good together."

"We were at first."

"Because we didn't have any real challenges to face. Everything was going our way. It was all fun and games."

He thought back and had to concede that she was right.

"But," she said, "when times got tough, when hard stuff happened—"

"—we made mistakes," he said, cutting her off before she could get into all that. No point in rehashing what they both knew.

She pulled her hands away from his.

"It was more than that, Bray. I realized recently that I never expected our marriage to last forever."

The words felt like a stab to the gut.

"Not because I didn't love you, but because I did. Love doesn't hang around forever in my world. At least I didn't think it would."

Adrenaline pumped through him. The salty pub food he'd had for dinner must have replenished his electrolytes.

"So at least I've proven that wrong," he said. "Even a divorce didn't keep me away."

Her stare had his heart thumping hard. Was she really going to consider his proposal? Did he want her to?

"I'm sorry that I didn't share Tucker's life and my first pregnancy with you more," she said. It wasn't quite what he'd been expecting her to say.

"It's in the past, Mal. Like I said, we both made mistakes."

"After he died I was so angry and had no one to take it out on. That, I shared all over you," she said.

Again, he thought he'd heard enough of the past. "It's okay, Mal. It's over." He took her hand again. "It's time to move on, just like we both said. And it's clear that we need to do it together."

She took her hand away. Braden watched her, trying to assess how she felt, trying to get them back to logic.

"It's not over, Bray." Her eyes had a suspicious sheen to them. No. No tears. Not when there was nothing to cry about.

"It's not over at all," she continued. "This afternoon is a perfect example of it not being over,"

"That's what I'm talking about," he said, energized again. "We can't keep our hands off each other. You know as well as I do that sooner or later it's going to happen. We're going to end up in bed together again. We can't stay away from each other, Mal. It's time to quit fighting it. We've got kids on the way."

The more he talked, the more she shook her head.

"That's not what I meant, Bray. I wasn't talking about the kiss."

"Then what?"

"Before that, at the restaurant. You wanted to be all in with what was going on until you saw that I was starting to cry. Then you were done."

He began to perspire. "Who says I was done?"

"You asked to order lunch."

And he had spent the rest of the meal talking business. He got it. He should have been more...

What?

The words of the counselor who'd done nothing but frustrate him came back to him. He should have "sat with her in her tears."

Or some such rot.

What did that really mean? Hand her a tissue? Sit and watch her cry for hours? Who did that?

He'd tried to console her during their marriage. Several times. Like that night he'd found her in the nursery, holding Tucker's penguin, sobbing her heart out. The nursery haunted her. Reminded her every minute of every day what she'd lost. They'd needed to get her out of there. To see that there was still good left in life. That there was more than what she'd lost.

But when he'd said so, she'd raged at him.

Standing, Braden shoved his hands in his pants pockets and strode to the window. He looked at the darkness and felt a storm building within him.

He took a deep breath, and another, waiting for calm to descend once again. He'd learned long ago that giving in to drama only made you do or say things that you'd either have to apologize for or that you'd feel embarrassed about. Like the time his mother had been running her mouth about Mallory, trying to convince him that she'd deliberately belittled her and his sister because his mother was jealous of another woman coming before her and his sister in his life. He'd lost patience with her. He couldn't remember what he'd said, but he remembered her response. "But, Braden, family always comes first and we're your family." What he remembered most of all was his response to that. "Not anymore we aren't." He hadn't meant the words. Not even the second in which he'd uttered them. And the pain they'd caused his mother, the doubt that still lingered from time to time that he'd cut her out of his life if she displeased him...

When he was calm, he turned around.

"We're having twins, Mal. Two daughters." He

should be there, helping with the responsibility. There'd be so much of it. At first, when she was still recovering from childbirth and both babies needed to be fed and changed and held, there would be two of them and only one of her.

They had to be practical. The rest would work itself out.

"And that's part of the reason this won't work."

When she spoke those words, he moved closer to her. She'd lost him on that one.

"Girls, Bray. Puberty. Drama. Think of your sister, multiply that by two, factor in me, and where would you be?" She was so calm, sounded so logical.

And then it hit him.

"You don't trust me with your children?"

"Of course I do. I trust you with their lives. I know without a doubt that you'll always be there for them. Anytime they call, you'll come running, no matter what."

Damn straight, he thought.

"But I can't have you around all the time, Bray. Not if we don't have to. The drama would make you nuts. And if you were here and then left, think how much more that would hurt them."

He turned back to the window, breathing deeply.

"Bray?"

He spun around. "What? What do you want from me?" He was yelling. Loud enough to be heard on the next block. Or so it seemed to him.

"I'm sorry," he said immediately. "That was uncalled for."

And then he saw the look on her face. Wide-eyed, Mallory stared at him.

"Don't look at me like that. I wasn't going to hurt you. I'd never do that."

"I'm not scared. I'm shocked, Bray. I think that's the first time I've ever heard you raise your voice to me."

"Yes, and I apologize. It's just...can't you see how frustrating this is? We belong together. It makes sense. I know you love me, Mal. I know it. I could feel it in your kiss today. And other times, too. Yet you're sitting here telling me that we can't be together for reasons that don't make sense."

"That's because you can't feel the results of them."

No, he couldn't. He didn't get it. But he knew that marrying Mallory again was the right thing to do. He sat down.

"So tell me how it feels."

"Your inability to understand my emotions makes me feel like a freak. It got so bad that by the time you moved out I felt like I had to cry in the bathroom with the fan on even when I was the only one home."

He stared at her. What on earth was she talking about?

"I was ashamed, Bray. Every single time pain welled up, I'd choke it back down. I hated that it was there, like it made me weak. And when I was happy or excited, you'd humor me."

He didn't remember it that way.

"You could never join me in being excited about anything," she continued. "Like this afternoon, I told you the babies are okay and you just stood there. I was ready to climb to the roof and fly, or to laugh and dance. But I'd have been doing it alone. When I told you we were having girls, again you just stood there.

"I got nothing, Bray. And that's fine for me now.

With us being friends. But think what living with that would do to our baby girls. They'd grow up learning to curtail their excitement, their joy and their sorrow, too, because little girls have an inborn instinct to please their daddies. You might not mean to teach them that, but they'd take it all in on an instinctive level. Just as I did."

Okay. Wow. Braden didn't have any idea what to make of that.

He stood. "So, just to be clear, you're telling me that because I don't get giddy or have crying fits, I'm not the right man for this family?"

It wasn't really what she'd said. But it seemed pretty damned close.

"I'm telling you that we're just too different, Bray, in a way that neither one of us can help."

So she thought he wasn't meant to ever have kids? Because he'd "rob them of their joy"?

That was another phrase from the counselor who'd done no good.

"I get excited," he told her. He reminded her of the time he'd caught a twenty-pound bass on a camping trip they'd taken early on in their marriage.

"Of course you do. But when the chips are down, when something is really important, bone-deep important, you aren't there."

"Where am I?"

"I don't know," she said. "Believe me, I've tried to figure that one out. You just space, Bray. And that's not wrong or bad. It's what works for you. It just doesn't work for me."

Sit in the fire with her.

Go deep into the woods with her.

He recalled the therapist's advice.

Mallory was right.

But it just wasn't him.

Turning his back on the only life that made sense to him, Braden quietly let himself out.

Chapter Eighteen

Mallory felt awful. On what should have been one of the best days of her life she felt like total and complete crap.

The only consolation, if she could call it that, was that Braden wouldn't be feeling the pain she'd caused him nearly as acutely as she did.

It killed her to hurt him.

To deny him.

She wanted him so badly, that killed her, too.

She was crying before he'd shut the door behind him. Great wracking sobs. She didn't even try to stop them. She just let them flow.

Five days of worry, of sometimes debilitating fear, of loneliness poured out of her.

What a cruel twist of fate that the love of her life would be a man who wasn't right for her. A man she wasn't right for.

It was worse than starting life with a prostitute mother. Much worse. Her mother had loved her enough to get her out of that life.

And while she'd never had a family of her own, she'd had a foster mother who'd loved her. Who'd kept her, helped her get to college.

She was healthy. Had a successful business she loved. Friends.

And now she was having healthy, identical-twin girls.

Still, she cried.

Because she couldn't imagine her life without Braden in it.

Sometime later she got up, took another bath, turned on the television and climbed into bed.

She'd survive.

She always did.

She had babies to provide for. Children of her own who were going to need everything she had to give. Children who didn't deserve a ripped-apart family and a torn-up mother. Which was exactly what would happen if she and Braden married and divorced again.

She couldn't do that to them.

Or to Braden or to herself, either.

As much as she hated it, she knew she'd finally grown up.

Braden left San Diego that night. He didn't make it all the way back to L.A. Instead, he found a hotel half an hour from the city and sat in the bar, watching a rerun of a baseball game and drinking beer.

The next morning, he was at his desk by six, sending texts to change the morning meetings in San Diego, making those he could video meets, and threw himself into each and every one.

He worked hard the rest of the week and into the next. It was what he did. What he knew.

When a decent amount of time had passed—meaning, enough for him to be right with himself—he called Mallory.

It had been almost two weeks since he'd seen her.

"I'll be in town tomorrow," he said. He had a meeting Wednesday morning with his staff and then a full day of appointments. "How about a quick lunch?"

He was going to tell her about William taking over the San Diego office for him, check in with how she was doing and then head back to L.A. that evening.

He might or might not tell her that he was no longer seeing Anna.

He'd broken it off with the woman when he'd returned from San Diego. He hadn't seen much point in continuing to see her. Clearly he wasn't into her enough if he'd practically begged his ex-wife to marry him while he'd been dating Anna.

"I don't think lunch is a good idea, Bray."

Mallory's response floored him. Almost literally. He dropped into his desk chair.

"What? Why not?" They always met for a meal, anytime either of them asked. That was their thing.

"Because we're just going to keep wanting more."

"But we're good, Mal. We know how to make it work. Forget the proposal. We're good."

"I can't forget it. I think about it all the time. And the kiss and so much else. It just hurts too much."

Wait. Just. A. Minute.

"I don't get it. We're fine. We're great. We have

plans. And just because I suggest we get married, now all of sudden it's over? All of it?"

It couldn't be. They were friends.

She was having his daughters.

He was going to be a father. From a distance, yes, but still there.

"For now anyway," she said. "I'm so sorry, Bray." She sniffed. He could tell she was crying.

"I'll call you tomorrow, when I get there. Let's talk then," he said and rang off.

He needed time to think. To find the logic. He knew, once he found it, it would save them. Ten minutes after they'd hung up, Braden texted Mallory.

You're not selling The Bouncing Ball, are you? Or moving it?

Her response was almost immediate.

No.

Okay, so they still had time. It wasn't over. It was just on sabbatical.

And you still want the space here?

He was pushing.

Yes, and fine, let's do lunch tomorrow. I can see we need to talk about things.

Damn straight they did. They were a team. Friends. Connected. They were having a pair of daughters before the year was out.

There was no way they could call it quits.

* * *

She just had to make it through one lunch. One more lunch as Braden's friend and then she'd be through with that part of her life.

It wasn't going to be easy. She knew that going in. It wasn't going to go well. She knew that, too. But they had history. They'd been friends a long time. She was a tenant of his and would continue to be one, and they needed to be good with that.

She was having his daughters.

That would be the hardest part.

But they'd done this. They'd made this mess. It was up to them to figure a way out of it.

When he texted, suggesting that he have lunch sent up to his office, her first reaction was to say absolutely not. The last time they'd been there together they'd kissed.

But the more she thought about it, she figured his choice was a good one. They'd need privacy to get through this meeting, for her to say what she needed to say. Chances were she was going to cry and she preferred not to do that in public.

After this, their dealings with each other were going to be limited to business.

A critical part of her life was ending. She'd never be in love again—not like she was with Braden—but neither could she be part of a mentally and emotionally unhealthy relationship.

He wouldn't be able to stand it, either. Not in the long run.

Just as he hadn't before.

She might have told Braden to get out when their marriage ended on their last bad fight. But he'd been the one to do it. He'd packed his bag, left and never spent another night under the roof they'd shared.

He'd come back to help her get the place ready to sell. To pack up his things. To take down the nursery and donate everything in it except the few things she'd already packed away, mementos of the son they'd lost.

But he'd never come home again.

She didn't bother changing out of her work clothes— maternity jeans and an oversize T-shirt—or dressing up, either, for her lunch with Braden. At twelve exactly, the time they'd agreed upon, she smiled at William and headed down the hall to knock on Braden's door.

She'd barely made a sound before the door swung inward.

Two Styrofoam containers sat on the table by the window, along with two glasses of tea. He motioned to one seat for her and took the other.

"You look great," he told her, glancing up and down her body as she approached. "I can't believe how big you are already."

She might have taken offense if she didn't know what he was talking about. "I know," she said, grinning. She hadn't gained anyplace but her breasts and belly, but she felt huge.

And she was loving it. Pregnancy, for all its physical downsides, really agreed with her.

He'd ordered her a grilled chicken salad with French bread on the side. She ate before she lost her appetite.

"So, have you thought of names yet?" he asked, digging into his container of spaghetti.

"Of course," she told him, glad that he was letting them start out nice and easy. Like old times. He was setting a tone that would, hopefully, get them through what was to come. "I was doing that before I knew what I was having."

She'd done the same with Tucker. Had chosen half a dozen names and narrowed those down to two before she'd thought to ask Braden's opinion.

He'd liked both of her choices and had left the final say up to her.

"Try them on me," he said.

She glanced up at him. He looked well. Fit. Too hot for her own good. She averted her eyes to her chicken salad.

"I went through the standards, Kaylee and Kylie, that kind of thing. But I really like Eva and Mari." She pronounced the latter with an "aw" sound.

He nodded as he chewed.

"Or there's Kelly and Cassandra."

He met her gaze and nodded again.

She went through a few more choices, adding middle names, as they ate. It was all very civil and kind.

"What do you think?" she finally asked when she was out of names.

"I like Madison and Morgan."

They hadn't been among her choices. She just plain hadn't thought of them.

"Madison and Morgan. Yeah. Madison and Morgan. I like them, too," she said, and they both smiled.

With that grin on her face, Mallory was gorgeous, choosing his names for their babies. He'd known to just back away, work, give things time to cool down, and everything would be fine.

It always was.

You just had to not get sucked up in the drama.

Like he had when he'd proposed. He'd been all up

inside himself, reacting instead of thinking. And he'd almost mucked it all up.

"Oh!" Mallory lurched, fork suspended, eyes wide. And then stark fear crossed her face.

"What?" He stared, tried to assess her expression.

"I just…" She shook her head and put a hand to her stomach.

"Is it the babies? What's going on, Mal?"

Her features had softened. "I think I just felt one of them move," she said, looking like some kind of madonna.

She jerked again, straightened, seemed to wait a second and said, "There. It just happened again."

"Is it the first time?"

He hadn't been present when she'd first felt Tucker move, so he didn't know if this was how it happened or how she'd reacted then.

"Yes," she said. "It's much stronger than I remember, from before," she said, half smiling. It was like she was there and yet not. She was probably tuned in to the children inside of her.

"Usually it starts more like gas bubbles, but this…" Her hand on her stomach, she stopped midsentence.

"You're sure it's not something wrong?" The sensations seemed to be coming somewhat regularly, and not minutes apart.

"I wasn't sure at first," she said, grinning now. "But it's definitely baby movement. It's not cramping, and it's not down low. It doesn't hurt at all. It just feels… odd. Different than with Tucker."

"Maybe because there's two of them in there sharing the same amount of space you had for one." Now that he knew for certain there was no danger, he was out of his chair, down on one knee beside hers.

He put his hand under hers on her stomach. Feeling Tucker move inside her had been the single most memorable part of the entire pregnancy for him.

He'd been moved—not drama-filled emotion, but different, calmer. More.

He felt nothing under his hand. "Is it still happening?" he asked, loving the feel of her roundness against his palm.

"Yeah." Her voice sounded different.

"I can't feel it."

"It's stronger than gas bubbles, but it's not that strong."

And there he was, his hand on her stomach, clearly hard. In his dress pants the reaction was obvious. She was staring at it, too. He looked at her when she raised her face, ready to apologize, and her eyes pooled with tears.

He held her gaze, reading far more than he could decipher in her look. She looked away first, out the window beside them. Down twelve floors or out to the horizon, he didn't know.

He cleared the table and threw away the trash.

She was right behind him with the glasses, taking them over to the bar where his cleaning service would take care of them.

She was the only woman he wanted in his life. She was having his children. He wanted to feel them kick inside her.

It was right that he should. Right that she shouldn't have to handle two babies alone.

He had logical reasons for their union. Their physical attraction was clearly mutual—and as hot it had ever been. But it wasn't just the sex. He wanted to hold her afterward, too. And before. To have the right to just walk into her home any time day or night. And to know it was his home, too...

"I came up here to tell you that I can't be friends with you anymore, Bray."

He turned, grinning. Thank God. She knew it, too. Had seen that them being married, not friends, was the only way for them to be happy. Somehow, this time they'd make it work.

She was standing at the sink, not doing anything, just standing there, her back to him. He moved toward her, wishing he had a ring to offer her. She'd kept hers from before. Would she want the same one?

She continued to speak. "If you're willing and in agreement, I'd like to continue our business association with The Bouncing Ball and Braden Property Management. And I will stand by my agreement to put your name on Morgan and Madison's birth certificates."

Something odd in her voice stopped him from touching her. He stood back, listening, thinking that this was her attempt to meet him on his ground, with logic, not drama.

It wasn't necessary. He could deflect the drama. He just couldn't sit in it with her. And that was good for both of them. She'd obviously realized that his control was an asset, that no matter how out of control things might feel, she'd always have him to maintain order in the chaos. To think while others reacted. To keep them from careening down a hill without breaks and crashing into little pieces.

He stood there while she continued.

"I will want the legal custodial agreement, with you signing over to me any rights to the girls, done before they're born. It's the only way I can put your name on the birth certificates. And that's all. Whether or not I tell them about you will be a decision made sometime in the future, as occasions warrant. I can tell you only that I would let you know before I said anything to either one of them. This is it, Bray. This is all I can do."

What? That last bit. What?

He stood frozen. Hearing her. Unable to process the ramifications.

She was over-reacting. That was it. Because of the sex. She'd said it would get the best of them, but couldn't she see that was a good thing? It was part of what kept bringing them back to each other.

"Take some time, think about it," he said. Time would bring rationality. Fear and panic would fade.

She turned, looked him right in the eye. "I don't need any more time. I'm not running scared here, Braden. This is something I know. We can't stay away from each other anymore when we're together. These babies have looped a new cord around us and it's drawing us closer every time we're together."

Exactly! So why didn't she see the obvious solution?

"When we're together, I need you to keep your distance," she told him. "Because I can't stay away from you. When we're in the same room, it's like you're a magnet, and I feel myself being pulled ever closer to you."

He took a step toward her, then another, his eyes intent on hers, silently telling her she was fighting the inevitable.

Holding up her hand, Mallory moved toward the door. "No, Braden." Her tone was unequivocal and he stopped instantly. "No more. Because when it gets down to everyday living and I'm me and you're you, it's not going to work."

She cut off his rebuttal. "Think about it. What if my test had come back positive a second time and I was dealing with possibly losing one or both of the babies I'm carrying? Or what if a few minutes ago what I felt hadn't been one of them moving? I know the risks I've taken on. I know I might face horrible heartache if anything happens to these babies. I know that I'm going to spend many nights watching them breathe, afraid that if I stop, so will they. But I'm also prepared to deal with that. And to deal, I may have to curl up in a corner and cry or sit in a rocker and hug a penguin. I can't do that when you're around."

She lay a hand on the doorknob as she continued. "And you…you need a home without drama, Bray. You deserve that. I love you and I know that's what you need, and knowing that I can't give it to you just about kills me, but not as badly as it would if we remarried and then divorced again." She shook her head, as if clearing it of the image. "I can't lose you a second time. Not like that."

It was logical. Every word of it. There was no drama. Just how he liked it.

With a nod, Braden walked to his desk, sat down at his computer and stared at a screen he couldn't really see. He heard the door open.

And close.

He didn't look up.

Chapter Nineteen

A week passed with no word from Braden. And then two. Mallory worked. She attended her baby shower, wept over the bounty of gifts and love her coworkers and friends showered on her. She had lunch with Tamara twice.

Her friend was pregnant. Tamara had never struggled to conceive. But with four pregnancies, she'd never been able to carry a live baby to term. She was having a hard time keeping herself above water emotionally as she faced going into her second month, and with Mallory grieving over the loss of Braden, the two of them made a sorry pair.

And yet they made it through each day. Not just functioning, but living. Hoping. Loving. Flint was a rock for Tamara, but it was Diamond Rose who was going to save her friend. The little girl who'd been conceived and born in prison was enough to show anyone that life didn't always work out as expected but it did work out.

Diamond Rose was still in her first year of life and already she'd healed two hearts and created miracles in two lives.

Mallory thought about Flint and Tamara and little Diamond Rose a lot. She talked to Morgan and Madison about them. They were a testament that she and the twins would know happiness. That things didn't have to be like a storybook to be right. That even when families weren't mom, dad and kids, they were still family.

Still candidates to be recipients for miracles.

It was that thinking that got her through the weeks without Braden.

At work, she watched the parking lot every day for his SUV. Once or twice a week she saw it there. Those days were better than others.

And harder, too.

When her phone rang on one of those days—Thursday of the third week since she'd severed their relationship—and she saw his number, she debated whether she should answer. The ringing stopped before she'd come up with an answer and then she debated whether to call him back.

Her phone signaled a voice mail before either side of her won.

"Mallory, I have the legal papers you requested. May I drop them off to you? Please advise."

She texted him rather than call him back.

I'll come get them.

She didn't want him in her space.

He was behaving like a sot. Someone he was ashamed to know. He could have left the papers with

William. Could have had his attorney mail them to her or to her attorney.

Perversity drove him to use the papers as an excuse to see her.

She'd get exactly what she wanted. He owed her that. But he wanted things, too. To see her. To reassure himself that she was getting along just fine without him.

And to clear up one other point.

If he was going to be free, he wanted it known that he was completely free.

She showed up at his office ten minutes after he called her. He'd purposely timed his call for her usual lunch break so he wasn't all that surprised.

In jeans and an oversize Bouncing Ball polo shirt, with a purple cardigan to match, she walked her matching purple tennis shoes into his office as though she had no idea she'd just poleaxed him with a shaft of pain so sharp he had to take a second to catch his breath.

Her hair was down, curled around her shoulders and lightly made-up face. And that belly. Already it was as big as he remembered her ever getting with his son. Which made him think about the back pain she'd suffered that last month with Tucker. She'd leaned her stomach against his back at night, using him to help her hold the weight of their baby. It had been the only way she could get comfortable enough to sleep.

She still had more than two months to go. How in the hell was she ever going to rest?

Not his problem, he reminded himself.

"You look good." He kept his tone neutral. No reason they couldn't be civil. Their differences were not the fault of either one of them.

"So do you."

He'd noticed her looking at him. For a second there,

hope flared, but he took hold of that response immediately. There'd be no inane reactions here that he'd have to pay for, or regret, later.

"Read this over. If everything meets with your approval, sign it in front of a notary and get it back to me. I'll countersign, my attorney will file it, and you'll get a final copy." He stopped short of suggesting that she have her own attorney look at it. Opinions and advice were a friendship thing.

She took the manila envelope. "Thank you."

He let her get to the door and then said, "Mallory."

She turned around. Relief flooded him.

He quickly put a clamp on it.

"There are some things that wouldn't go in the legal agreement, but that I need to have clear between us."

"Okay."

"Our friendship, the relationship we built these past three years, is ending. With that, all support ends. I need to know that you aren't going to call for advice or just to check in, that there will be no favors asked, or granted, on either side."

She blanched. He wasn't certain he'd ever actually seen someone do that before. His gut lurched but he pushed ahead.

"If, as you say, this has to end for the health of both of us, I find that I need to be free from all sense of obligation where you're concerned. When I go into a new relationship, I owe you nothing. My full loyalty will be to her."

He'd thought it all through, considering the reasons why things hadn't worked out with Anna.

"Of course." Her voice broke.

"I'll have my contractor call you when he's ready for

your input for The Bouncing Ball 2, as he's doing with every other tenant."

"Thank you."

He nodded. "I'm finished. You can go."

She left and he got back to work.

She was free. Completely, totally free. There'd be no more guilt. No more trying to be something she was not, to fit a mold that would make Braden happy.

No more worrying about him.

No more being concerned for his happiness.

There was someone out there for him. Someone who'd be concerned. Someone who'd actually make him happy—in good times and bad.

The good times were easy. It was the bad that had been their fatal trip up.

She read the papers he'd had drawn up. They were, explicitly, what she'd requested. The day after she'd seen him, she took the packet to her attorney for review. When she gave the go-ahead, Mallory signed them in front of a notary, with her attorney's receptionist as a witness.

She dropped them in the mail and told her babies they were going out for a treat. But after a few licks of a vanilla ice cream cone, she threw the rest away and went home. In the nursery, she sat in the new rocker, holding a teddy bear. She thought about the past and about the future, telling herself that while she felt ripped apart at the seams now, the future would be better.

Great things lay ahead for her. For her children. And for Braden, too. They just had to get through the dark moments.

She cried herself to sleep that night and woke up with tears on her cheeks.

Like she had after Tucker died.

And just like then, she told herself she'd get through this.

She was the daughter of a prostitute and a product of the foster care system. Her life experiences had given her strength.

The universe, fate, God—whoever—had blessed her with the ability to nurture. And so she would. Her children and others.

She would fulfill her destiny. Live up to her potential.

She would know joy again.

Because she was a survivor, wasn't she?

But, oh God, did living have to hurt so badly?

Braden spent the night in San Diego, mostly to prove to himself that there was no reason why he shouldn't.

The next day was Saturday and because he had no meetings, he decided to take the coastal roads back up to L.A. rather than joining the masses on the freeway.

Life stretched like an open road in front of him and he was going to find out where it led. He drove leisurely, stopping to have coffee and a muffin at a little café set atop a cliff overlooking the ocean. Later he lunched at a burger joint across the street from where he got gas. He thought about what he wanted to do when Braden Property Management was up and running in L.A.

Traveling sounded somewhat appealing. He and Mallory had always talked about vacationing on a Greek island, going to Italy and Paris.

He thought about calling his mother, to let her know that he and Mallory were no longer friends, but she knew all she needed to know when they'd divorced three years ago.

She didn't know about the twins. And now, all things going as planned, she wouldn't.

Cruising in and out of small towns, he took his time, watching people on the street, knowing that they lived differently from him.

And from everyone else, too.

When he realized the ridiculousness of his thoughts, he turned up his music and blasted tunes from high school, singing along when he knew the words.

Catching an outside glimpse of how ridiculous he was behaving he turned the volume down.

Mallory used to drive with the music turned up. She'd pull into the driveway of his apartment complex and he'd know it before he saw her car because he could hear her pop rock songs blaring.

He couldn't remember the last time she'd done that. At least when he was around.

Driving down a winding road, getting closer to the city, he slowed, not quite ready to arrive at his destination. The road narrowed as it turned sharply. Another car was coming and he had to get over toward the shoulder. His side had one, but the other side was blocked in by a rocky hill.

He took another hairpin turn, hugging the shoulder, and then it happened. He hit something.

Pulling off, he stopped his SUV, shaking as he looked in the rearview mirror. Something lay on the side of the road behind him. An animal. He couldn't tell what it was or if it was breathing.

Oh, God.

Getting closer, he could see that he'd hit a dog, some kind of smaller shepherd. He'd had an Australian shepherd growing up. They'd had to put it down when he was fourteen and his sister was eleven. She and his mom had carried on so much that Braden had been forced to be the one who carried the dog into the vet's office. And who'd dug the hole in the backyard to bury him. He'd had to act like it was no big deal or the two of them would never have stopped crying.

The animal on the road was still breathing but unconscious.

Scooping it up, he ran back to his SUV, laid it on the passenger seat and put the vehicle in gear.

It wasn't until he was back on the road that he realized he had tears on his cheeks.

Chapter Twenty

On Monday, a week after she signed Braden's custodial papers, Mallory was digging in her purse for Chap-Stick and came upon his key.

She'd forgotten she had it. Now she had to get it back to him.

Leaving it on her kitchen counter, she figured she'd put it in an envelope and mail it back to him.

But what if it got lost in the mail?

And how stupid was it to mail a key to the address it opened?

She didn't know his hotel room number. Wasn't even sure which of the properties owned by the chain he was at. They had two relatively close together near his L.A. property.

She could leave the key with William. That seemed the best choice.

Yet, what would he think, her leaving Braden's key? Braden hated company gossip of any kind, which was why, until the past few months, they'd rarely seen each other at work.

That's when she had her brainstorm. She'd take it to his condo, leave it there, locking the door behind her. She wouldn't be able to latch the dead bolt, but she knew the security code so she could reset the alarm.

Liking the plan, she put the key back in her purse and went to work.

The dog was still hanging on. Every day Braden had been making the half-hour trip from his hotel in L.A. to the veterinarian who had him. Dr. Laura Winslow was wonderful with the dog and with Braden, too. She let him come and go as he pleased, visiting the dog after hours when that was the only time Braden could make it there.

The animal had suffered a broken leg, which would heal, and damage to his liver, which might not. Laura had had to take him into surgery twice. They were now in wait-and-see mode.

Braden was footing the bill, of course, and in the meantime had put up flyers and asked all over the area to find the dog's owner.

There didn't appear to be one.

The dog was only about a year old, according to Laura. He'd had no collar, no identifying chip. He hadn't been fixed.

He could have been a stray or, more likely, according to her, a pup someone had left behind when they'd moved. It happened more often than people realized, she told him over coffee one night.

He was sorry to hear that.

Mostly he just wanted Lucky to get better.

That's what they were calling him. Laura needed a

name for her records so the dog became Lucky Harris.
Braden hoped to God the creature was lucky.

Laura called him on Monday afternoon, eight days
after he'd brought Lucky into her clinic.

"Any luck finding Lucky's owner?" she asked.

He was getting ready to go into a meeting downstairs
in the conference room at his hotel. He'd arranged to
use it as a temporary meeting site when the occasion
arose. "Not yet," he said as he walked down the hall
toward the elevator.

"Have you thought about what you're going to do
with him if he recovers?"

He shrugged. He hadn't thought about it. "I keep
thinking his owner is going to turn up," he said. "Let's
get him better first."

He sure as hell couldn't keep a dog. He lived in a
hotel suite.

"I think we're there." Her words stopped him on the
thick carpet. "His liver is functioning at full capacity.
He's up, eating. In my professional opinion he's out of
the woods."

Holy hell. "You're serious?" The dog was going to
live?

Her affirmative made him grin.

Mallory left The Bouncing Ball the second the last
child was out the door on Monday. She'd been checking on and off all day. Braden's parking spot had been
vacant for more than a week—and still was. Just to
be sure, she called William, not to ask about Braden,
which would be breaking protocol, but to make up some
nonsense about needing the L.A. contractor's number,
which Braden had already given her. She told William

she couldn't get a hold of Braden, but not because she was no longer free to call him.

She and Braden hadn't set forth a rule to govern her business contact within Braden Property Management. Would it still be him, so that tongues didn't wag over the change, or would he pawn her off on William?

Either way, she'd abide by his choice.

"Yeah, he's in a meeting this afternoon," William said, his usual friendly self. "He's got more tenants than he can use for the L.A. facility and he's interviewing them all himself."

So he was in L.A. She had her confirmation.

William gave her the number she already had. She thanked him, rang off and turned her car in the direction of Braden's condo.

It took a second to find a spot in the visitor's parking section and another few seconds to wait for the elevator. Watching the security camera as she stood there, she felt like a criminal.

She was trespassing.

But she had to get rid of his key. She couldn't have any connection between them.

Ironically Madison chose that second to give her a kick, too close to her bladder for comfort. She'd named the lumps on either side of her. Madison was left. Morgan was right. For all she knew, they switched. And it wasn't like she'd know which one was which when they came out. But for now, the names worked.

Naming them had made her babies real.

She had two daughters.

She just hadn't been able to hold them in her arms yet.

Madison kicked again. And Mallory got the message.

The key she was dropping off was not the only connection between her and Braden Harris.

But it would be one less connection.

She took the elevator up and went straight to his door without a pause. It was like she had a demon at her back, pushing her to get inside his space.

It had only been a little over a week since she'd seen him. She'd gone a lot longer than that before, and she was now facing an entire lifetime without him.

Being in his condo meant nothing.

And yet it meant everything.

The second she unlocked the door she knew she'd made a mistake. The place carried a waft of his scent. Or so it seemed to her.

She remembered the last time she'd been there. She'd eaten lasagna off his plate. And she'd wanted so much more.

But that was back before she'd known for sure how messy it was going to get. How complicated.

How impossible.

Looking around, she started to tremble and then to cry.

Leaving his key on the kitchen counter, she quickly let herself out, locking the door behind her.

Lucky needed a place to sleep. And someone to watch over him, at least for another week or so. Braden couldn't possibly provide either. But he could pick the dog up from the veterinary hospital as instructed and watch over him for a night.

Which was why, Monday night, he found himself back on the road to San Diego with a dog curled up asleep in a kennel that was strapped into the seat next to him.

He couldn't take Lucky to the hotel, but he owned his condo, managed the property in which it resided and knew for certain that he allowed pets. Laura had given him some pads that she said Lucky was trained to go on, and instructed him to keep them by the door for Lucky to do his business for the first few days. Just until he acclimated to his independence a bit.

Braden had no intention of owning the dog for a few days. He'd keep him for one night and then he'd make some calls. Lucky was a great dog—a purebred, Laura thought. She'd have kept him herself if she hadn't already had two dogs at home.

People paid a lot of money for purebred shepherds. No doubt he'd be able to find someone who'd be happy to give him a loving home for free.

The condo felt off to him the second he unlocked the door. The dead bolt wasn't locked. Leaving Lucky's kennel just outside the door, he stepped inside to check the place out. Had he been robbed?

The security system was set, as he'd left it.

How had someone been inside without setting it off?

Two more steps in and he knew who'd been there. He could smell her perfume. She'd been using the same subtle spray every morning after her shower since before he'd ever met her.

Another couple of steps and his suspicion was confirmed. There, on the counter, was his key.

Mallory was getting ready to leave for work early Tuesday morning, telling herself and her daughters that it was the first day of the rest of their lives, when she heard a knock at the door. Who was there at six in the morning?

Frightened, she grabbed her cell phone, just as it started to ring.

Braden?

How could he possibly know she was in trouble?

"Bray?"

"Yeah, it's me outside. I should have called first. I'm sorry."

Rushing through the house in her stocking feet but otherwise dressed for work, she pulled open the front door. He'd sounded horrible.

He stood there with a kennel in his hand. She could see a dog inside. It didn't appear to be moving.

Braden's eyes were red-rimmed. His hair was a mess, his pants and dress shirt wrinkled.

Had he been up all night?

"Braden, what's going on?" She looked at the kennel again.

He didn't do dogs. Years ago she'd suggested they get one, thinking it would be a friend to Tucker growing up, but he'd categorically refused.

"I hit him," he said, holding up the kennel. "On the way back to L.A. last week, I ran over him with my car."

And he'd kept him in a kennel?

Opening the door wider, she let the man in. He was clearly not himself. She just had to figure out what she was dealing with so she'd know whom to call.

It briefly occurred to her that they'd just promised they wouldn't do this. They wouldn't call on each other in need or support each other.

But there was no way she was turning him away this morning.

He sat on her couch, putting the kennel with the unmoving animal at his feet.

"Have you been drinking? Are you sick?" She sat on the edge of the couch, a foot away from him. Should she call a doctor?

"No."

"You look awful, Bray."

"I've been up all night."

"I thought you said the accident was a week ago."

"It was," he said. "Nine days, actually."

The night after they'd last seen each other. She knew the number of days, too.

He looked at her. His chin trembled, his eyes welled. Tears didn't fall. At least his didn't.

Mallory's did.

"Bray?"

"It's not your emotion I can't handle, Mal. It's my own. I wasn't blocking you, I was blocking me. Seeing you upset would upset me, and so I blocked."

His shoulders were fallen, his features ashen.

"I'm a fraud," he said. "I lost my dad. And then Gonzo. I was only fourteen and I had to dig his grave. And my mom and sister… Mom could hardly cope after Dad left. And my sister, she blamed herself. I had to be strong."

Heart pounding, she sniffled. She put her hand on top of his and glanced at the kennel, too. They needed to call someone about the dog.

And maybe about Braden, too.

Had he really been living with a dead dog in a kennel for over a week?

Shouldn't it smell?

She squeezed his hand, more in love than she'd ever been. When they'd first been married she'd known that Braden had depths people couldn't see. She'd just *known*.

When had she forgotten that?

"I pushed you away," he told her. "I couldn't handle the pain of losing Tucker. Or the blame. I shut down on myself. And then you. I couldn't handle it. I'm weak and a fool, Mallory, and I'm so sorry."

"You are not weak. You're one of the strongest men I've ever known," she told him. "And you most definitely aren't a fool." She felt the truth of the words to her core. But still she worried.

Clearly Braden had had an extremely difficult eye-opening experience. But at what cost?

She hadn't ever meant to break him. Didn't want to break him.

"Bray, it's okay. I never should have made the ridiculous mandate that we can't be friends. Clearly we can't *not* be friends." She was crying softly but was able to instill all the certainty she felt in the words.

He shook his head.

"Where have you been all night?" He said he'd been up. Surely not driving around with the kennel.

"At home. At my condo."

"You've been here, in San Diego?"

"I had to have a place to take Lucky."

"Lucky." The dog, obviously. He'd named a dead dog?

"He got out of the hospital yesterday afternoon and needs around-the-clock care for the first couple of days. Knowing that he could die if I went to sleep, I didn't."

And the dog had died anyway?

She glanced down, afraid of what another loss on his shoulders had done to Braden's psyche.

And that was when she saw two big brown eyes peering up at her.

"Bray! He's not dead! Look!" She jumped up so fast it startled the animal, which moved suddenly and then whimpered.

"Of course he's not dead," Braden said, opening the

door immediately, reaching in first to pet the dog, talking soothingly, and then carefully lifting him out.

He had a cast on one of his back legs. And a bandage wrapped around his torso where the fur had obviously been shaved.

"I told you, I've been up all night caring for him," he reminded her. "Which left me far too much time with nothing to do but sit alone with myself." Holding the dog, he looked over at her and met her gaze fully. "I was scared to death he was going to die on me. Really scared. I couldn't leave him there, go to work, go anywhere. I had no one to call. It was all on me. And it struck me how you'd felt in the nursery that night I came in there and found you holding Tucker's penguin."

She was crying again, slow tears dripping down her cheeks.

"Helpless, that's how it feels," he said. "And sometimes there's not a damn thing you can do about it."

"Except sit with it until it passes. Trusting that it will pass."

"Sit with it," he said, his eyes opening wider. "Sit with it. That's right. Sometimes, loving someone means being able to sit in depths of despair with them."

She coughed, trying to hold back a sob, and failed.

"That finally makes sense to me," Braden said.

She didn't get the significance of the statement, but clearly it meant something to him.

"I'm so sorry, Mal." He pet the dog, but his gaze was on hers. "I let you down at the most devastating time in our lives."

"Shh." She put a finger to his lips. "I let you down, too," she said. "Even before that. If I hadn't, maybe you wouldn't have. Maybe you would've. But what matters is that for the four years since, we've been hanging on to each other. We've been trying. Together."

Even after they'd said they wouldn't be friends she hadn't been able to let go. Not with The Bouncing Ball. Not with his name on his daughters' birth certificates.

"It was your key on the counter that did it," he said. "You rescued me, Mal."

"It sounds like I deserted you alone on a night of sheer hell."

"Nothing that could even come close to comparing to my emotional absence after our son died. I can't promise that I won't check out again at some point, for a time, but I can promise that I will always come back to you, Mal. That I will sit with you, and our daughters, no matter what you're feeling. Please, Mal, say you'll marry me. Please." His eyes got moist and as uncomfortable as that might have made him, he didn't seem to fight it.

"Oh, God, Bray, I…" she started to cry, but was smiling, too. "You feel like a trip to Vegas this weekend? I thought… Anyway," she threw her arms around his neck, careful of her belly and the dog. "Yes, of course I'll marry you," she said, kissing him with all of the need inside her.

It was a few minutes before either of them could speak. Braden kissed her so hard they fell back against the couch. When she'd been ready to take things to the bedroom, he pulled back.

"And Lucky? You're okay with keeping him?" She couldn't believe it, but for a second there she'd actually forgotten about the dog.

"I wouldn't have it any other way," she said, petting the animal who was sitting there like he belonged to them. Looking at them like they belonged to him.

"I was thinking maybe I'd have William run the office in L.A. instead of San Diego."

She grinned through her tears. Leave it to Braden to have the logistics all worked out. God, how she loved the man.

"And that I'd like to take you up on your offer and drive over to Nevada today and get married. I'd say fly, but we've got Lucky."

"Driving is good," she said. He hadn't mentioned any appointments he might have that day, but as for herself, she'd call Julia and let her know she wouldn't be in.

Braden continued to sit there, petting the dog.

"Bray?"

"Hmm?"

"You can put the dog down and make love to me now."

He froze, then stared at her.

"It's just dawning on me how much it's going to kill me if I ever lose you again."

"It's not going to happen if I can help it, but even if it did someday, you'll survive, Bray. Because that's what love does. It gives you the strength to survive. No matter what."

She had to hand it to him. He had the wherewithal to set the dog gently on a blanket on the floor before he grabbed Mallory up, laid her down on the couch and proceeded to get emotional all over her.

And in her.

Because just like she'd told her daughters, as long as they existed, they were candidates to be recipients of a miracle.

They just had to be patient until it arrived.

* * * * *

MILLS & BOON

Coming next month

HONEYMOONING WITH HER
BRAZILIAN BOSS
Jessica Gilmore

It was time.

Deangelo pushed himself to his feet and held out a hand. 'Come along.'

Harriet clutched her glass. 'What do you mean?'

'You wanted to learn how to be a Brazilian? Right there,' he nodded at the dance floor. 'That's where you'll find out.'

She clutched the glass harder. 'I can't go out there!'

'Why not? If he can…' he nodded at a rotund tourist, furiously jiggling away, his face serious as he tried to remember the steps his partner was teaching him. 'You definitely can.'

'But…' he didn't wait for her to finish the sentence, removing the glass from her hand and drawing her to her feet.

'The thing to remember about samba,' he said. 'Is you have to find the rhythm. It's three steps to two beats, the middle step is the quick one. Once you have that, then add bounce, keep your knees soft. So it's back, feet together, forward…' they were on the dancefloor and Deangelo swept her into his arms, murmuring the steps to her. 'That's it, back, together, forward, knees bent, let your body roll through the steps, don't be afraid to roll your hips.'

Harriet was clearly nervous, clutching his hand as she shuffled through the steps, her eyes on her feet. 'Look at me,' he murmured. 'Feel the beat, let it guide you.'

The music was getting louder and louder, the beat stronger and more insistent, the dance floor busier and busier. Deangelo lost track of time, knowing nothing but the woman in his arms, the softness of her under his hands, the way his pulse was connected to the music, the light in her blue eyes as she moved, the sheen of perspiration on her forehead as the heat intensified. How had he thought running would be the same as dancing? The solitary sport against this communal celebration of music and passion? No wonder he'd only felt half alive the last twelve years, replacing joy with monotony, the thud of his feet on the pavement instead of the thud of his heart to the beat. It was necessary, that half life, but such a relief to let the walls tumble for one night, to let the young man who had loved and laughed and dreamed emerge from the cold, professional persona he was caged in. Tomorrow would be time enough to tame him again.

Continue reading
HONEYMOONING WITH HER
BRAZILIAN BOSS
Jessica Gilmore

Available next month
www.millsandboon.co.uk

COMING SOON!

We really hope you enjoyed reading this book. If you're looking for more romance, be sure to head to the shops when new books are available on

Thursday 21st March

To see which titles are coming soon, please visit

millsandboon.co.uk/nextmonth